# KING'S ACRE

Christine Marion Fraser began her life in the tenements of the Govan district of Glasgow just after the war. At the age of ten she contracted a rare muscular disease, and has been in a wheelchair ever since. She now lives with her husband in Argyllshire.

A keen reader and storyteller, Christine started writing at the age of five, and got the idea for *Rhanna*, her first novel, while on holiday in the Hebrides. She has gone on to write six more volumes: *Rhanna At War*, *Children of Rhanna*, *Return to Rhanna*, *Song of Rhanna*, *Storm over Rhanna* and *Stranger on Rhanna*. She has also written three volumes of autobiography: *Blue Above the Chimneys*, *Roses Round the Door* and *Green Are My Mountains*. *Noble Beginnings*, the first in an exciting new series set in an Argyllshire powdermill town, has just been published.

*King's Acre* is the second volume in the popular series which follows the fortunes of the Grant Family and is set in rural Aberdeenshire and in Glasgow.

### THE KING'S SERIES

King's Croft
King's Acre
King's Exile
King's Close
King's Farewell

*By the same author*

## Fiction

RHANNA
RHANNA AT WAR
CHILDREN OF RHANNA
RETURN TO RHANNA
SONG OF RHANNA
STORM OVER RHANNA
STRANGER ON RHANNA

KING'S CROFT
KING'S EXILE
KING'S CLOSE
KING'S FAREWELL

## Autobiography

BLUE ABOVE THE CHIMNEYS
ROSES ROUND THE DOOR
GREEN ARE MY MOUNTAINS

# CHRISTINE MARION FRASER

## *King's Acre*

The author wishes to thank the following people for
all the willing and professional help she received:

William Stewart, Procurator Fiscal, Dunoon.
A.S. (Sandy) Jessop, Procurator Fiscal, Aberdeen.
A.G. Lynn Q.P.M., Chief Constable, Grampian Police.
A.S. Olgivie, Deputy Governor, H.M. Prison, Aberdeen.
Capt. C. Harrison (Retd), The Gordon Highlanders.
Ian Stirling M.R.C.V.S., Dunoon.
Les Wilson and Duncan McLeod, Strathclyde Police.

This edition published by Grafton Books, 1999


Grafton Books is an Imprint of
HarperCollins*Publishers*
77–85 Fulham Palace Road,
Hammersmith, London W6 8JB

This paperback edition first published by HarperCollins*Publishers* 1994
1 3 5 7 9 8 6 4 2

Previously published in paperback by Fontana 1987
Reprinted six times

ISBN 0-26-167346-7

Set in Times

Printed in Great Britain by
Caledonian International Book Manufacturing Ltd, Glasgow

For Lorna Thomson
a true Scot,
kenspeckle,
well kent,
who kens me,
and kens Ken,
better than we ken ourselves.

Lums o Reekie Village

Cragbogie

Doctor

School

Carnallachie's

Boglehowe

Loch Bree

Manse

Kirkyard

Rothiedrum House

Mains o Rothiedrum

Kelpie Pool

Railway
to
Aberdeen

River Birkie

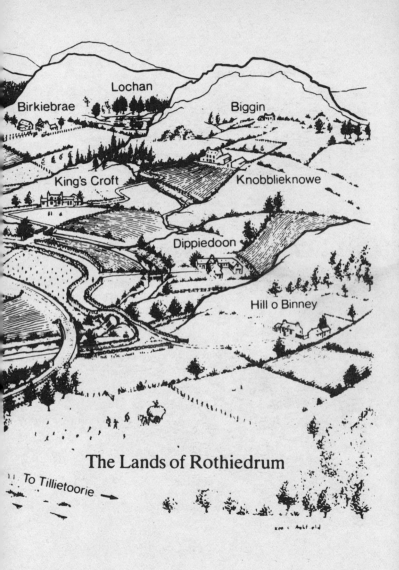

Birkiebrae

Lochan

Biggin

King's Croft

Knobblieknowe

Dippiedoon

Hill o Binney

# The Lands of Rothiedrum

To Tillietoorie →

# PART 1

# Winter, 1914/15

# CHAPTER ONE

For as long as she lived Evelyn was never to forget her first glimpse of the young soldier. His reflection in the bevelled glass of the little baker's shop in Cobbly Wynd was as insubstantial as the relentless dreams that had so often disturbed her sleep lately, yet his tall figure was too tangible for her to mistake it as a mere will-o'-the-wisp of her imagination.

It was a warm mellow day in late October; benign fingers of sunlight poked into dark places, clawing away sombre shadows, spreading gold over the grey granite of Aberdeen.

The pleasantly muted sounds of the city filtered up through the copper beeches that hid Cobbly Wynd from the world. It was one of Evelyn's favourite haunts. She loved its old world quaintness, the lacy patterns on the cobbles, the smells of fish, brine and tar winging up from the harbour, mingling with the mouthwatering aromas that drifted from the dim interior of Bert's Baker and Tea Shoppe.

The old men and women who occupied the benches under the trees seemed always to be there, smoking their clay pipes, talking in quiet voices about every subject under the sun, mutch caps and cloth bonnets bobbing back and forth. They gave a sense of peace to a landscape torn apart by war. Somehow Evelyn felt that as long as the wise old heads bobbed and nodded on the benches of Cobbly Wynd part of the old order would always remain the same even when all else might change.

This street held a lot of memories for her. It had been one of Johnny's favourite places too. In golden days of freedom and love she had walked these cobbles at his side and they had laughed together, the careless laughter of youth, sure of the future, of each other.

11

She had lost count of the times she had walked here with Johnny, and with golden-haired Florrie O'Neil who had been her friend from the remembered innocence of childhood. Now Florrie was dead and so too was Johnny. Both young and beautiful with all their lives in front of them – dead, dead as the tawny leaves of the beeches drifting like snow all around the shop doorways and closes of Cobbly Wynd. The heat of the sun embraced Evelyn and beat through the thick material of her coat. It made her feel uncomfortably hot and wish she had worn something lighter before leaving King's Croft that morning with her father and elder sister, Nellie.

No sooner had Fyvie clopped his way into the city than she knew she shouldn't have opted to come. The buzz of the streets and the noisy bustling of people irritated her beyond measure. Yet, in days gone by she had delighted in those trips into the city. There had been an excitement then, the very air had breathed of it. Even the unflappable Nellie had gathered some of it to her, till her gaunt cheeks became pink with anticipation and for once she was able to ignore the teasing, mischievous remarks cast at her by her fun-loving sister, Mary.

Mary was married now to Doctor Gregor McGregor but still she joined them on their trips into the city, bringing with her Donald, her infant son, who bounced and chuckled in his seat every time his mother's gay laugh rang out.

The day preceding such trips had entailed much careful planning for everyone concerned. In Evelyn's case, she enjoyed deciding what to wear, how much money she could afford to take. In the privacy of her little attic bedroom she counted the precious coppers she had saved out of her wages from Rothiedrum House. These were stored in an earthenware jar, which she kept safely hidden under a pile of underwear in the top drawer of her dresser. When the coppers were sitting in a neat little stack in front of her, she would stare at them for a long time before jotting down impossibly long lists of feminine wants: the ribbons and the jewellery and all the other bits and pieces considered too frivolous for a sixteen-year-old girl of the farmtouns.

In the evening her mother sat by the fire, writing down

things she needed from the Aberdeen shops. It was a very different list from Evelyn's, based mainly on calculations as to how much might be fetched from the sale of croft produce. More often than not certain small items would be omitted and only the bare essentials of the family jotted down and occasionally sighed over.

As she stared into the window of Bert's Baker Shoppe, Evelyn echoed her mother's sighs, not because she couldn't decide what she could and couldn't afford but because it seemed so long since she had looked forward to anything. The small things that had once filled her with a frivolous joy now had no meaning for her. Useless things they seemed, useless and silly.

Bowing her head, Evelyn pressed her hot brow against the cool window glass, so lost in thought she wasn't aware that she was no longer alone till she noticed the shadowy figure reflected in the glass. For a moment the presence of another human being failed to register in her mind. It might have been an extension of the ghosts that flitted in and out of her thoughts, an imagined form without substance.

'Something tells me you're not standing there sighing over Bert's baking – however tempting it might be.'

The voice was like rich velvet, with a nuance of laughter in the strong, Glaswegian accent. With a little gasp, she spun round and found herself looking up into eyes as dark and velvety as the voice. Smiling, he caught her shoulder and said softly, 'Hey, steady on, I didn't mean to startle you. I was just passing the time o' day, that's all.'

The rough material of his jacket briefly touched her cheek as he drew his arm away. His nearness confused her; the reality of his tall, commanding presence enveloped her, intruding into the bleak daydreams that had so recently consumed her.

'Ach – it's all right.' She drew away from him slightly, annoyed because she had stammered and sounded so cold.

His eyes appraised her steadily. The sunlight was on her wonderful hair, turning it the same shade as the newly fallen beech leaves at their feet; her luminous green eyes were big in the sweet pallor of her face, and her fragile

13

figure trembled slightly but grew still under the warmth of his glance.

'You've got freckles on your nose.' His voice was soft, intimate almost.

Self-consciously, she put her hand up to her face. 'I know, I always get them in the sun, they'll go when winter comes.'

'Pity.' The smile that was in his eyes reached his mouth, a wide, sensual mouth which curved up a little at the corners. He nodded towards the baker's shop. 'Don't think I'm trying to pick you up or anything, but would you care to come in and have a cuppy with me? I have some time to spare before I have to go back to the Depot.'

'No.' She drew further away so that she was pressed up against the window. 'I said I would meet my father and sisters in Union Street at twelve. I must be late – I – I forgot all about the time.'

His eyes went up to the clock above the shop door. 'It's only eleven-twenty, you have plenty o' time. You look as if you could be doing with someone to blether to and I'm a very good listener. You seem – lonely somehow.'

He was smiling directly into her eyes and she found that she was unable to tear her own away. A strange warm sweetness was sweeping through her veins, and her heart beat swiftly in her breast. Evelyn couldn't even begin to understand why a complete stranger should have this effect on her. He was just another soldier, one of the many who came into town from the barracks on Castle Hill where the Gordon Highlanders had their regimental Depot – a faint tremor went through her as she realized how few unmaimed young kilties were about that day. So many would never come back from the battles that had been on everyone's lips for the last few months. Mons, the bloody massacre at Le Cateau . . . She found herself wondering why he hadn't gone, and in the next instant was ridiculously glad that he was still here, whole and laughing beside her.

'Ay, I'd like a cuppy . . .' The words were out before she could stop them. Without further preliminary he put a hand under her elbow and guided her into the shop, as if afraid she might change her mind and escape.

The interior was dim and fragrant. From her place behind a mound of steaming new loaves on the counter, Bert's wife Meg raised a plump hand of greeting to Evelyn, while Bert himself screwed up one eye in a wink as the young soldier ushered her towards a small table set in the corner.

Evelyn melted unobtrusively into her seat, the flush on her cheeks heightening when a young girl came to take the order. She was fresh-faced and winsome, full of coy smiles and flirtatious glances aimed at the handsome young Gordon. He responded to her easily, his brown eyes coolly assessing her pretty face with more than a hint of pleasure. He obviously enjoyed flirting. The realization came quickly to Evelyn, and she was surprised to find herself resenting the girl's presence. She drew herself up. How stupid of her. She didn't know him and already she was annoyed at him for daring to look with enjoyment at someone else.

Covertly, she studied him as he and the girl discussed the order. He was quite handsome – no, more than that, he was beautiful – a beauty of youth and vigour blending with such charismatic good looks that she knew he must draw women to him like a magnet. His eyes were warm brown pools, fringed with the thickest lashes she had ever seen in a man; his brown hair was curly, little strands of it falling over a high forehead; his nose was straight and perfect, his skin smoothly tanned. His body verged on thinness but the rough material of his khaki jacket sat well on his broad shoulders – and that mouth of his, how many women had it kissed into submission . . ?

Abruptly, Evelyn pulled her eyes away from him, shocked by her own thoughts, not looking at him again till tea and hot buttered pancakes were brought to the table. She didn't remember drinking her tea, and nervously crumbled a pancake on her plate without tasting a morsel.

'That's no way to treat Bert's best baking,' he reproved her teasingly.

'I'm – I'm no' very hungry,' she said in an agony of shyness.

15

'No, you're not, are you? And here was me thinking that a wee lass like you would eat everything in sight. How old, I wonder? Fifteen? Sixteen?'

'I'll be seventeen next May.' She had thrown up her head at his question, and something of her old sparkle showed in the glinting green of her eyes.

'Sixteen,' he said gently. 'Too young for such despair. It was the first thing I noticed about you – your shoulders were heavy with it – and it's there in your eyes, lurking like a dark shadow, dulling the life of you.'

'Havers,' she managed to say lightly. 'Only the old are supposed to utter such wisdom – to have such powers of observation.'

He sighed heavily and threw her a crooked grin. Taking out a packet of Woodbine he offered it to her, and when she shook her head he took out one for himself and placed the thin white tube between his lips, looking at her all the time with quizzical eyes. Leaning forward, he whispered, 'Don't tell anyone but I'm really an old man of ninety disguised to look like a nineteen-year-old soldier. I forged my birthdate to get into the army.'

She giggled and he stared at her seriously. 'You're very bonny when you laugh like that. Am I seeing the real you? The girl you used to be before shadows darkened your life.'

'Ay, maybe you are at that.'

'Tell me about it. We may never meet again. I'm off soon – Burns comes to mind: "Farewell to the Highlands, farewell to the North, the birth place of valour, the country of worth—"'

'"Wherever I wander, wherever I rove, the hills of the Highlands for ever I love,"' she finished the verse for him. Unable to help herself, the slow tears welled in her eyes. She saw the bright valour of his youth shining through his moment of pensiveness. He was so whole and real and young – soon to be swallowed up in the trenches, the mud of the battlefields, along with all the others . . .

Somehow her hand was in his. It felt good and warm and strong. She looked directly into his eyes, found herself drowning in depths of compassion. She didn't know him,

16

yet felt as if he had been in her life all along, a vague shadowy dream, always just out of reach, waiting there on the edge of all things, intangible, unreal, beautiful. The strength of his young manhood seemed to flow through his hand into her.

For a moment they became one, one beating, trembling heart crying out for comfort, for understanding, for something yet to be born.

He was terribly, essentially alive, this young soldier, a stranger yet already more important to her than the sadness of her own life. She sensed the power and the passion of him, the depths of emotions she would never know. After this day they would go their separate ways, he to war, she back to a countryside empty of young men, back to the memories of a happiness she had known so briefly with her darling Johnny Burns. The realization made her feel unbearably sad. She stared at him with the haunted eyes of a young girl whose life had been so crushed by sorrow that it seemed as if laughter had always been a stranger to her small, pale face.

He saw the sadness in her eyes and wondered at the secrets which lay behind it. 'Little girl.' His voice hushed in her ears. 'Talk to me – tell me what ails you.'

He held tight to her hand, watching her face across the small table that separated them. The little corner in Bert's Tea Shoppe had become an oasis to Evelyn, a haven hidden from the rest of the world, inhabited only by her and by a stranger who had come to her out of the leafy shadows of that golden October day.

'I loved somebody – I lost him.' Her voice came out at last, the words jerky, unnatural, from another self who had disobeyed her will to speak of its own volition. It was easy after that, easy to pour it all out, to tell him about Florrie and how she had died from tuberculosis less than a year ago aged just sixteen – and then Johnny, not yet twenty, losing his life by drowning in a mill pond only two months ago. 'He was fighting with another boy when it happened.' She paused, remembering the thunder, the lightning, the rain lashing, Johnny jumping into the pond to save Gillan

Forbes of Rothiedrum House, smashing his head on the paddles of the mill wheel.

'Fighting over you?'

She came back to earth to look at him, aghast. 'Ay, they were.' She spoke in a horrified whisper. 'And I canna get over the feeling that I was to blame for Johnny dying. I see his face all the time – his eyes looking at me – before – before he went under.'

His fingers tightened over hers. She held onto him, a lifeline in the midst of her pain.

'You're young to have known such sorrow.'

She forced a laugh. 'I feel a million years old – yet only last year I felt I wasn't grown up enough to love Johnny. But I did and now – it's all gone.'

'You'll get over it, your youth will help you there. Och, I'm no' saying you'll forget Johnny but in time the pain will lessen, you'll begin to remember the happy times you and he shared.'

After that the talk turned to other things. She learned that he had been born and bred in Glasgow where he had become an apprentice cabinet-maker before joining the army in 1912.

A smile crooked the corner of his mouth. 'I'm a sergeant now. I've been doing my instructor at Castle Hill, teaching new recruits how to fight. It meant my own posting had to be delayed. Thank hell I'm going at last.'

'Hell?'

He grinned. 'Ay, it would be too sacrilegious to thank heaven for something as evil as war. The wars of the human race are spawned by greedy madmen who don't mind reducing mankind in order to gain more power. Give them some feeble excuse – like the assassination of the Austrian Archduke Franz Ferdinand – and all the old festering grievances between one country and another come spewing out like pricked boils. Forget the Hapsburg archduke, who the hell remembers him anyway? He was just the felled tree who toppled over and set the rest in motion, one against the other.'

He sounded so fiercely bitter that she stared at him,

seeing the glinting anger in his brown eyes. He shook his head. 'Sorry, I can't help it. My brother was killed at Le Cateau. The young bugger was only sixteen. My mother's hair turned white almost overnight. He was the clever one of the family. She had plans for his life – so' – he smiled, shaking off his gloomy mood – 'I'm going over there to sort Jerry out.'

'When do you go?'

'Almost right away, day after tomorrow in fact.'

She bit her lip. 'I'll pray for you.'

He didn't laugh. Instead he reached out a gentle finger to touch her cheek. 'I believe you will at that. It's nice to know you would do that for a stranger.' He stood up, pulling her to her feet. 'I hate to say I have to go but – I have to go. I've enjoyed this whilie with you – I'll remember it.'

'Me too.' He was standing so close she could easily have touched his lips with hers. Awareness leapt between them. The colour flooded her pale cheeks and abruptly she moved outside, leaving him to pay the fluttering-eyed girl.

Evelyn stood in the sunshine. The cobbled street was still the same: warm, drowsing. The old men and women still smoked their pipes, talked, laughed, occasionally screeched at some shared joke. The sad leaves of autumn were drifting from the beeches. One floated towards Evelyn and fell at her feet. Picking it up, she studied it. It was the colour of a ripe conker: rich, red, utterly beautiful in its dying glory. A small bubble of joy rose in her breast. Lifting her face, she breathed deeply of the tangy scents of damp woods. The world seemed a brighter place than it had been a short time ago. The clock was at twelve-ten. She had known the young soldier for less than an hour, yet already she felt as if her life had changed in some monumental way. A group of soldiers came towards her. They wolf-whistled at her, and in a moment of abandonment she returned the cheeky compliment. They roared with laughter and walked away down Cobbly Wynd.

'I turn my back for five minutes and find you seducing all the young men in sight.' He had come out of the tearoom to stand beside her.

19

'Ach you!' she laughed but grew silent at the look in his eyes. 'I'll be going then,' she said, not making a move.

He nodded. 'Ay, me too.'

Suddenly he reached for her hand and held it tightly, his eyes watching her face. She winced as something hard bit into her flesh. With a laughing gesture he removed the gold signet ring from his finger and slipped it quickly over one of hers.

'Oh, but I couldn't—' she began.

He laughed, his teeth white in the smooth tan of his face. 'Ach, of course you could. I won't need it where I'm going. Let's call it a memento of our meeting, a kind of good luck symbol. When we meet again, you can give it back.'

She knew they were just words. She would never see him again but something made her keep up the pretence. 'All right then. I'll keep it safe for you. Next to my heart if it pleases you.'

'It's the sort o' thing lovers would do.' He was laughing at her, impudent mockery in his voice.

She reddened, but catching the mischief in his glance she laughed too. Then the sound died in her throat. Nellie was coming up the brae, determined and grim-looking, her hands clamped to the hem of her prim skirt to stop it blowing up in the wind. Evelyn pulled her hand away from his grasp as if she had been burned, instinctively curling her fingers into a fist in an effort to hide the ring from view.

'So, this is where you are!' Nellie puffed up, the flush from her exertions staining her gaunt cheeks, her glance taking in the young man and then darting away to rest critically on Evelyn's flustered face. 'We've been waiting ages for you in Union Street. You know Aunt Mattie doesna like to be kept back when she has a meal waiting. Come you down this minute, my girl.'

She flounced away and Evelyn followed, humiliated beyond words, inwardly fuming at being treated like a child at a time when she had wanted to appear womanly. She felt his eyes on her. Turning her head, she threw him a quick half-smile to which he responded with a sweeping bow, right there in Cobbly Wynd outside the window of Bert's Tea Shoppe.

A giggle escaped her, making Nellie look round quickly

20

and say, 'How could you, Evie? The minute you get the chance you're off gallivanting wi' strange young men. I've lived wi' you all my life, yet there are times I just dinna understand you at all.'

'You've lived with a child all your life. I'm a woman now.'

Nellie's nostrils flared. 'A woman, eh! And that gives you the right to behave like a brazen wee whittrock—'

'Oh, Nellie!' Evelyn spoke sharply. 'We only had a cup of tea together and a blether. I never even found out his name. I'll never see him again – he's going away to fight – he's only a young soldier.'

Softness stole over Nellie's features. She glanced at her young sister's angry face. 'And he made you laugh, Evie, I saw the pair o' you as I came up the brae. He made you laugh and that's no bad thing. I havena seen you laughing since Johnny died.'

Evelyn was half-running to keep up with the other's long stride. 'Ay, he made me laugh and it felt very good. I'll remember him for that. You dinna have to tell anyone about it, it was only a small thing – and I've hurt no one.'

Only a small thing! Yet she would never forget him. Plunging her hand into her pocket she let his ring slide from her finger into it and she was smiling when she greeted her father and Mary in Union Street.

Jamie looked at her keenly. 'I thought you would be in the shops buying yon ribbons and things.'

'I felt like a walk, Father, so I went up Cobbly Wynd.'

Mary was climbing into the trap. 'Come on,' she urged impatiently. 'I'm starving. I can almost smell Aunt Mattie's lentil broth from here.' She made room for Evelyn at her side. 'Are you no' a bittie hungry yourself, Evie?'

Nellie was about to say something to the contrary but a look at Evelyn's face stilled her tongue. A pink glow diffused the girl's cheeks, and she welcomed it as she would a spring rose opening to the sun. It had been a long time since any sort of colour had touched that small, pale face and Nellie threw her sister a little smile of understanding as she took a hold of Fyvie's reins and urged him forward.

21

# CHAPTER TWO

Big Mattie, as she was known to most, lived in old Aberdeen or the Aulton as it was usually called. It was a quaint, peaceful little settlement with a cloistral air about it and a strong atmosphere of the past. Big Mattie's cottage was situated in College Bounds, a charming street in the old Scots style, broken by closes and little secluded lanes running along to neat cottages with green fields beyond. The College stood on a green sward a little way back from the street, a quiet bustle of comings and goings and students with books under their arms standing about, talking. The houses of working people rubbed shoulders with the manses of professors, the simple charm of one not detracting from the dignity of the other.

Evelyn had always loved the sequestered peace of the Aulton. A favourite walk of hers and Johnny's had been to take the road along the Chanonry, past the Cathedral to Don Street and the Brig of Balgownie, under which the golden-brown water of the Don tumbled its way to the sea.

Aunt Mattie, as she had always been to the Grant girls although she was no relation, was at the door of her cottage to greet them. Evelyn thought she had a face like an enormous red apple, with eyes like shiny black buttons and thick, curly dark hair which fell about her merry face in attractive disarray. She was a huge monument of a woman with massive arms and a big, soft bosom, a bit like a fluffy feather pillow, well shaken. Her voice was rich, fat and deep. She was wont to burst into loud and infectious song at any time of the day, no matter where or when.

As Fyvie drew up he was immediately surrounded by the children of the street to be patted and fussed over, while Jamie fetched the oat-filled nosebag from the trap. The sheltie gave a little whinny of pleasure, and was soon contentedly snuffling into his dinner despite the grubby hands that fondled his ears.

Aunt Mattie's face was wreathed in warm smiles as she drew the visitors inside. In bygone days she and Jamie had travelled country lanes with the gypsies and she still treated him like the Gypsy King he had once been, much to the amusement of all his daughters with the exception of Nellie, who didn't entirely approve of some of her father's friends. But she had a soft spot for Aunt Mattie and admired the way she kept the house in College Bounds so neat and tidy.

'Come away ben, King Jamie,' Mattie invited hospitably, her voice full of affectionate deference for the man who had been such a figurehead in her life. Always she addressed him as 'King Jamie', a title that had no bearing on his middle name of King but to his standing in her eyes.

The room in which they arranged themselves smelled of polish and soup. Brasses winked on the red tiles of the hearth, an enormous black cat snoozed contentedly on a sheepskin rug by the fire, dozens of faded sepia photographs jostled one another on the mantelpiece, and a brown and white cowhide was thrown over the torn back of a lumpy horsehair sofa which sat under the geranium-filled windowledge.

In a recess behind the door stood an enormous brass bedstead. In it reposed an ancient woman of ninety-five known as Grandmother. She was lying on top of a faded patchwork quilt, the top half of her wizened frame dressed in a black cape and bonnet after the style of Queen Victoria, the bottom half encased in red flannel pantaloons and thick, pink woolly bedsocks. Once she had been the Matriarch of the travelling people; now, too old and frail to move from her bed, she was looked after by Mattie who had given up her nomadic existence two years ago to devote herself to the old lady's welfare.

Grandmother might easily have been blood kin to both Mattie and Jamie. The ties of the travelling people were close, but whether she was related or not didn't matter to Mattie. Enough that Grandmother needed her. 'So long as there's breath in me, the old lady will no' end her days in some faceless institution,' she vowed.

'King Jamie – girls – ye're late!' Grandmother's imperious tones were scolding as she acknowledged their intrusion into her domain – for it was just that. Mattie berated, threatened, wheedled, but in the end it was Grandmother who made the rules and saw to it that they were carried out.

Stretching out a shrivelled hand covered with skin like yellowed parchment, she patted the bed and bade Evelyn sit beside her that she might hear all the news of King's Croft. 'How is yer mither? Yer sister Murn? And you, lassie, how are you? Still pale and thin I see.'

Obediently Evelyn sat down on the bed. 'They're all fine, Grandmother, and so am I. Mam will be along to see you next time and Murn will look in when she can.'

The old lady cackled. 'Murn! I'm no' grand enough for the likes o' her. She thinks because she's a teacher o' infants she knows everything but I could teach her a few things she would never hae learned in any university. Grace now, she's different. I like fine when she slips in to see me when she has time off frae the hospital. She looks that braw in her uniform, blue goes wi' that bonny hair of hers. Too pale though – like you – Mary's the only country-lookin' lass among the lot o' ye. Mind, Grace has her hands full wi' the nursing. It's no' for the like o' her. She has the look o' a real lady to her and should be livin' like one. It's worse for her wi' the war. She tells me they're takin' in wounded soldiers because the military hospitals canna cope wi' them all.' She sighed, her bony chest heaving under its layer of black silk as she rambled on about the war, the loss of young men from the land, her mind carrying her back to the Boer and Crimean wars.

Taking up a silver-backed brush, Evelyn began to work with the long silvery locks streaming from under the black hat.

Jamie was seated at the fire, puffing at his Stonehaven pipe, while Nellie and Mary were bustling about, helping Aunt Mattie bring steaming bowls of broth to the table. Without warning, Mattie burst into a loud and stirring rendering of 'The Holy City'.

Grandmother pretended to frown as enthusiastic 'Jer-oo-salems' and 'Whose Annas' rent the air, but under her breath she was humming the tune and joined in with Mattie as a particularly infectious 'Whose Anna in the high-EST' brought the song to its booming finale.

'Well, it makes a change from grace,' giggled Mary.

'Ay, we must try it at home,' supplemented Nellie, who had found herself unable to resist joining in the last rousing strains. 'We could get Mam to try it in that nice soprano she has.'

'Or even when she's going out to milk the kie in the morning.'

Nellie smiled sourly. 'I dinna think they would appreciate it, nor would anyone else at that ungodly hour.'

Evelyn tucked a white linen traycloth under Grandmother's hairy chin and helped her spoon soup into her mouth. The frail hands were too palsied now for even this simple task, but the old lady's fierce independence was such that she clamped her birdlike fingers over Evelyn's firm young hand as the spoon went rhythmically from bowl to mouth. Other than Mattie and Grace, Evelyn was the only living soul whose help she graciously condescended to accept. Despite her age, her appetite was as healthy as a horse. The broth disappeared in no time and Evelyn patted the old hand and stood up.

'I'll get my own now, Grandmother.'

'Ay, and see you sup it all, lassie. Your bones could be doin' wi' a bittie meat happed round them.' Her faded blue eyes peered kindly into the young girl's face as she added softly, 'Yer wee hert is sore for your Johnny, eh lass?'

'Ay, Grandmother, it is, but all the better for seeing you today. You're an old rascal but under it all your own heart's as romantic as my own.'

The infant Donald, having finished his soup, was toddling about the room, disturbing the cat who glared at him with one malevolent eye before burying his nose deeper into his tail.

'See the bairn up here,' commanded Grandmother. 'I like bairns aboot me. Mattie, take my teeth and syne them under the tap. He can hae a wee play wi' them. It will keep him quiet for a whilie.'

Mary opened her mouth to protest but it was too late. Mattie had rinsed the teeth and was scooping Donald into one plump oxter to dump him on the bed and hand them to him. With a gurgle of delight he grabbed the teeth and stuck them in his mouth, whereupon he treated everyone to a grotesque grin.

A disgusted 'Hmph' from Nellie turned into a snort of laughter, while Mary and Evelyn clutched one another and collapsed in a heap over the table. Jamie took advantage of the diversion to dunk bread in his soup, something he only did in the privacy of his own home and even then under Nellie's ever critical eye.

The door opened and a young man walked in, one of the students boarded by Mattie for a small fee. In return she heaped as much food on 'her lads' as they could eat, together with a bounty of motherly love and companionship. Since the country had seen the start of war, more and more of the College students had melted away. Hugh Saunders was Mattie's third boarder in less than three months, a bespectacled lad with angry red spots on his as yet hairless chin and nervous eyes that darted at once to Grandmother's bed as if she was the Big Bad Wolf in person, all dressed up for the kill.

But Mattie enveloped him in a spate of fond greeting and directed him to the sink to wash his hands and then to the table to sup his broth.

Mattie's table was a sumptuous one. Weekdays she worked at the slaughterhouse, puffing home at dinnertime to see to Grandmother's needs before steaming out again to put in another few hours of sweated labour. She stank excessively of slaughterhouse smells which she scrubbed out of herself each evening in the doubtful privacy of the tiny scullery off the kitchen. But if her job had its drawbacks it also had its rewards. The sheepskin and the cowhide were just a few of the perks, parcels of choice meats were another. A vast steak and kidney pie was brought to the table. Aunt Mattie picked up a knife and

26

sent it plunging without ceremony through flaky golden crust into savoury steaming depths.

Grandmother sniffed the air and without ado snatched her teeth back from Donald who immediately started to howl.

'Wheesht, lad, wheesht!' barked the old lady. The little boy immediately stopped crying to stare at her in awe, before slithering head first down the quilt to the floor and into his mother's arms.

'I'll have to adopt your methods, Grannie,' laughed Mary, burying her rosy face in the chubby layers of her son's neck.

'Ach, yer too soft for that,' snorted the old lady. 'All you young mothers are the same nowadays. A good skelpit leatherin' never did a bairn any harm. When I was on the road I used to keep an eye on dozens o' bairns as well as my own five and the whole jing bang o' them did everything I told them.'

'Ay, and fine Mattie and myself know it,' put in Jamie, his eyes shining with reminiscence. 'We were among those bairns and I can still feel the sting o' your hands through the seat o' my breeks.'

'Ay, and yer none the worse o' it the day,' Grandmother said sternly. 'Of course,' her eyes twinkled, 'I aye carried a sweetie or twa in my pooch in case I should run out o' steam, but I never did – and you know I found some o' these sweeties in my old frock no' so long ago, all melted and stuck to the lining. It just goes to prove there is no need for bribery if ye have a guid firm tongue in yer head—'

She paused to take her washed teeth from Hugh, who was holding them at arm's length as if afraid they were about to bite him at any moment.

'Ye see that,' she turned a triumphant face to the table. 'The loon washes my teeth wi'out being asked, and though the very sight o' me scares the shat out o' him he does these wee things for me because he respects my authority – is that no' right, son?'

'Please, Grandmother.' Hugh spoke as if he was addressing a much feared and respected headmaster. 'It wasna that – though ay, I do respect you a lot. It was just – well – whiles the wee boy was playin' wi' them I noticed he was sitting on them and, if you'll pardon me for being as frank as yourself, I think he had just shat his hippen at the time – it's runnin' down his leg now.'

All eyes turned to Donald's sturdy legs. 'The lad's right enough,' spluttered Jamie. 'The bairn's got the skitters by the look o' things.'

'Father,' reproved Nellie, rising out of her chair to go dancing round the room fanning the air with a newspaper, while Mary rushed her offspring through to the scullery.

A high-pitched cackling screech rose from the bed. Grandmother was lying back on her pillows, black hat askew, her toothless mouth a pink cavern in her seamed face, her skinny ribcage heaving, wrinkled fists beating the bedclothes as she gave full vent to an ecstasy of raucous mirth. Every so often she paused to stare at Nellie dancing round the room, at Jamie's suspended fork, at Hugh watching her in silent awe, his pimpled jaw hanging at half-mast, his spidery arms still folded respectfully behind his back, and then she was off again, pink heels pummelling little valleys in the quilt, fleshless stomach quivering under the red flannel pantaloons.

Evelyn wiped the tears of laughter from her eyes and looked at her father, glad to see him laughing in a way he hadn't done since Johnny's death. Since he had left Birkiebrae to come and work at King's Croft, the boy had been like a son to him. Jamie had lost his own sons in infancy. His five daughters were a continuing solace and joy to him but the rigours of working a north-east croft demanded the strength of men. An orra loon (youngest member of a farmtoun crew) was about the only hired help he had ever been able to afford, and the years of toil had taken the heart and the strength out of Jamie King Grant. Johnny's coming had eased so many burdens. The spring had returned to Jamie's step, he ceased to turn to the solace of the bottle and became more like the gypsy Jamie of old, black eyes clear and eager for life, shoulders back and straight with the returning of a faith in the harsh landscape that had been his hope and joy and finally his heartache and sorrow.

Now Johnny was dead, and so it seemed in the last weeks was Jamie. The deep dark eyes that Evelyn so loved were dull and hopeless once more, the shoulders stooped in a familiar weariness that was there all the time now. And he was drinking again, secretly and furtively as if he was ashamed of his own weaknesses. That hurt Evelyn more than anything. He had always taken his drams openly, and in so doing had allayed any doubts his family might harbour about his excesses. All the men of the farmtouns drank and no one blamed them for doucing the raw cold of the earth from their bones.

Evelyn wanted to tell him it was all right, she understood, but when she found the empty bottle hidden in the little shed he called his 'shoppe' she knew that it was too late to say anything. If she told him she was aware of his drinking he would know she had been to the shed, and would see her interference as a violation of the only privacy he had ever had in a house full of women.

He felt her watching him and he smiled at her, one lid coming down in a quick, conspiratorial wink. She smiled back, a little catch in her throat at the knowing that he trusted and confided in her so much. An affinity had always existed between them. She was the seventh of his children, the one most like him in temperament and nature. He told her she reminded him of himself as a child, the gypsy Jamie whose freedom of spirit found its echo in her. His hair, once black as night, was almost white now, yet his infectious laugh, his twinkling eye were still those of a young man, and she couldn't think of him as ever being old.

She was glad now that she had come to Aberdeen that day. So much had happened in one brief morning: first the meeting with the young Gordon and now Grandmother, dabbing at her eyes with a corner of the quilt, fully in command of herself once more as she took her teeth from Hugh's sweating palms and popped them into her mouth, then demanded help with her dinner which Evelyn went willingly to give.

The combined bells of the Cathedral and the College were chiming out the hour of two as the visitors were preparing to leave. A cursory ringing of the front-door bell heralded the arrival of a big, burly dark-haired man who came confidently into the room.

Relatives and friends were always popping into the cottage in College Bounds, but the latest arrival was greeted in rather an abrupt fashion by both Mattie and Grandmother. His bulk seemed to fill the room, blotting the light from the window. Nellie paused in the act of fastening her coat. Something about the man tugged at her, not recognition but something that was at the edge of memory, pushed down never to surface – except in the hideous, distorted, dark worlds of sweating nightmares.

She looked again at the man. He was watching her. A black phantom whose thick-set body loomed over her, above her – the blood froze in her veins . . . She was ten years old – alone in King's Croft except for her father and his friend drinking downstairs in the kitchen. In the dread shadows of night a man beast came to her, his weight crushing her down on the bed, his hot breath stifling the screams that rose in her throat. Horror after horror engulfed her along with the pain that ripped her virgin flesh apart and made her scream out for her father while the beast of the night grunted and moaned and writhed against her skinny frame, tearing her, inflicting upon her an unbelievable torture of mind, body, and soul. And her father never came. All through the night watch she lay whimpering and calling for him, for never once in all her childhood had he ever let her down. She had waited in terror, as afraid of the smothering shadows that crept all around her as she had been of the crouching man beast, but her father's familiar figure had not intruded into that endless night.

He was in the kitchen, in a senseless stupor, too drunk to hear, see, or feel anything until he flitted upstairs with the grey ghosts of morning and found her wide-eyed and petrified, lying on her bloodied sheets.

From that day she had never clapped eyes on the vile

creature who had so violated her innocence – until now, this moment of seeing him in flesh and blood that was no less evil to her than the cruel phantoms of her dreams.

Father! Father! You never came! The voice beat uselessly inside her head. It was an old accusation, one that seemed to have been there from the beginning of time. She had never forgiven him. She loved him, she wanted to forgive, but always the old, bitter, admonishment rang in her head, making her distrust all men, her father more than any for having betrayed her trust.

He too was staring at the new arrival, and she knew that his thoughts were carrying him back to that long-ago night of shame and degradation which had always haunted him. If only Nellie knew how he hated himself for having failed her, but she wouldn't discuss the matter, couldn't allow the subject to come up without all her old hatred and mistrust boiling to the surface. His heart turned over as he caught sight of her tortured face. Stark fear was in her eyes. She stood in a room full of people yet she was as terrified of Jake as she had been on that dark and godforsaken night of her childhood.

The man was looking round the gathering, rubbing his hands together affably, black eyes narrowing as they came to rest on Jamie. 'My old friend, are ye pretending ye dinna ken me? Surely ye havena forgotten the jokes and laughs we shared?' He stuck a thick grimy palm in front of Jamie's face but Jamie didn't take it. Instead he got up without a word and went to get his coat from the stand in the lobby.

'What are ye doin' here, Whisky Jake?' Grandmother had been napping when the door bell sounded and she was irritated by the interruption. But there was something else. An unease in her manner, a soft spark of fear in her eyes as Jake moved to the bed.

Sitting down he took her old hands in his huge grasp. 'Grannie, Grannie,' he chided, 'are ye no' pleased to see your old Jake then? I'm putting my roots down in Aberdeen for the winter, got myself a good job at the Stoneywood paperworks so I'll be able to visit my favourite old Grannie as much as I like.'

Grandmother snorted, unimpressed by Jake and his honeyed tongue. 'More like comin' tae see what ye can get oot o' me. You were aye a rogue and I'm no' too far gone to see ye havena changed for the better. Mattie and me dinna want ye here interfering wi' our lives so you stay away if ye ken whit's good for ye.' Jake laughed and, bouncing off the bed, began to prowl round the room, raising his voice to Jamie in the lobby. 'My, you've bonny daughters, Jamie lad, too bad we let the years slip away and me missin' my chance o' seeing them growing up.'

He ruffled Mary's bouncy black curls, paused to look at Evelyn and say, 'Ay, Jamie might be a wee man but he sure spawned some beauties. You must only hae been a glint in his een last time I was over at King's Croft.'

He turned slowly to Nellie, Nellie of the prim frocks and fair soft hair, framing a too severe face, an oddly mature face for a young woman, with high cheekbones and hollow cheeks verging on gauntness. But one forgot all else when looking at the arresting beauty of her amber-green eyes and the full, sweet softness of a mouth that was disturbingly sensual.

Whisky Jake put his heavy face next to hers, his cruel mouth twisting as he said mockingly, 'And you're Nellie, of course. You've grown a bittie since last I clapped eyes on you – ay—' His voice became oily. 'You're a severe-lookin' wee madam right enough but I happen to know there's more to ye than meets the eye – eh, Nellie lass?'

Nellie felt the room spinning. Her heart was racing so madly she found it difficult to get breath – she was suffocating, suffocating against that dark, hairy, sweating face . . .

'Leave her!' Jamie was there, warning the other man off, not laying hands on him but a dangerous glint in his black eyes giving a hint of the anger that seethed below the surface.

'Ach, Jamie.' Whisky Jake threw himself into a chair and lit his pipe. 'Dinna tak' on so. I was only makin' friends wi' yer lassies.' He studied the older man, noting the whitening hair, the waxen skin beginning to tighten over the

32

cheekbones, the sinewy frame bent and shoulders grown stiff from continual wettings in rain-soaked fields, the austerity of expression that came to men of the farmtouns while still in their prime and made them look older than their years.

'Dyod, ye've aged, man,' Jake remarked with brutal directness. 'Ye were just a stripling when I last saw ye. Ye've grown old, Jamie, old. It isna worth it, in the end the land will take ye and hap itself about ye, laughing at a mere mortal mannie for thinkin' he could reap a livin' out o' dung and sweat. Leave the croft, Jamie, move to Aberdeen and get a house. You could go back to your old trade as shoemaker or I could put in a word for ye at the factory. The wages are no' bad at all and ye could gie the lassies things they never knew existed.'

'You very effectively did that to one o' my girls and as a result you maimed her mind for life and made her curse me.' Jamie spoke thickly, his knuckles clenched to white. In a flurry of choking rage he forgot himself, forgot to keep a rein on his words. Nellie, face and neck stained crimson, was telling him to shush, the others were staring at him in puzzlement.

Nellie put a shaking hand on his arm. With an obvious effort he restrained himself and bade his daughters go out and wait in the trap.

They settled themselves silently, even Mary looking serious for once, like Evelyn sneaking cautious glances at Nellie who sat with her back ramrod stiff, lips folded into a tight, secretive line, eyes staring straight ahead.

'What did that man do to you, Nell?' Mary asked the question softly, her dark eyes full of a new sympathy for the sister whose spinsterish ways had so often incited her to teasing comment.

A fresh upsurge of blood stained Nellie's fair skin. The others couldn't tell if it was brought about by anger or shame for when she spoke her voice was tightly controlled, as if she was keeping her emotions on a tight rein. 'It is none o' your business, Mary. Just leave me be for I will no' say another word and that's final.'

33

'Nell,' Mary laid a gently persuasive hand on her sister's arm. 'We're your sisters. Surely you can confide in us. I've always felt there was something about you I never rightly understood. There's another Nell hiding under all those snide words and angry flouncings. Tell us, Nell, and maybe we'll be able to understand you better.'

'Ach, havers, Mary! You aye did talk nonsense!' Furiously she shook her sister's hand off, her bony fingers going to the reins, one black-booted foot tapping impatiently on the floorboards as if she couldn't wait to be off.

Mary looked at Evelyn and lifted her shoulders in a defeated shrug. Whatever lay at the back of Nellie's mind would never be divulged by her – that was a certainty.

Jamie had grabbed Jake's arm and pulled him into the lobby away from the curious looks of Grandmother and Aunt Mattie. 'See here, man,' he began warningly. 'I never thought to have the misfortune of laying eyes on you again but I should have known better. The bad penny aye turns up sooner or later.' He looked directly into Jake's sardonic eyes. 'Just keep out o' my road, that's all I ask – and if ever you lay one finger on any o' my lassies, I'll kill ye – and that's a promise.'

A half-smile touched Jake's lips as he surveyed the other man. Jamie's hands weren't quite steady; it was a tremor that reached up to his head so that it too shook slightly on the seamed brown column of his neck.

'Ye're an old man, Jamie,' Jake spoke mockingly. 'And frae the look o' ye I'd say ye're in need o' a good stiff dram – or maybe a bottle might be more in your line. I've heard things aboot ye, King Jamie, and from all accounts ye're no' the same man who less than twenty years ago could drink the night away and get up at five to sort the beasts.'

Jamie's fists knotted into sinewy balls. 'Leave them be,' he repeated softly, 'or I'll kill ye.'

Turning on his heel he went out of the room, Jake's softly mocking laugh following him as he went. As he was getting into the trap, Aunt Mattie came bustling out to push a soft, fat paper package into his hands. 'A wee thing for the pot. Wheest now, I have plenty.' Her apple-red face grew solemn and she seemed about to say something more, but thinking better of it she stepped back, her lusty cries of farewell following them all the way down College Bounds.

Maggie turned a hot face from the fire as they came through the door. 'Well, did you have a good day?' she inquired. 'Did you get the things I asked for?'

Jamie put the shopping bag on the table and smiled at her. 'Ay, we did that, lass, and a wee bittie extra besides. Mattie sent over some meat. We'll have roast for the Sunday pot thanks to her.'

'Ach, she's a good soul.' Maggie turned to her youngest daughter whose brightness of face hadn't escaped her notice. 'You've enjoyed yourself today, Evie. You have a wee rose plunk in the middle o' each cheek and yet this morning you were as white as the driven snow.'

'Aunt Mattie and Grandmother were a tonic, Mam. You'll have to come along and visit them next time.'

They regaled her with some of the goings on at the house in College Bounds. No one mentioned Whisky Jake though Maggie looked once or twice at Nellie sitting withdrawn and quiet at the fire. She hadn't even taken off her coat, but sat huddled into it as if she was cold despite the warmth of the room. Maggie turned a questioning eye on her husband but he avoided her gaze and went rather hurriedly with the bucket out to the fuel shed.

Wee Col came toddling in. He had been playing in the barn and his golden-red hair was full of jagged pieces of straw. The little boy had been born mentally retarded, and at almost six had the physical and mental capabilities of a two-year-old. At first everyone had been bemused by the small, quiet stranger and afraid too of what the gossips in the community would have to say about Maggie's failure to give her man a healthy son. For there was pride in the heart of Margaret Innes Grant, it showed in the way she walked, in the sparkle of her grey-green eyes and in the refined arrogance of her handsome face. She was the bastard daughter of a nobleman, one Lord Lindsay Ogilvie who was the uncle of Lady Marjorie Forbes of Rothiedrum

House and great-uncle to Gillan, the Forbes' only son and heir.

No one, not even Jamie, knew that his wife was related to the Forbes of Rothiedrum, and if she had her way it was a secret that would remain with her till her dying day.

But certain things were inherent in her. They manifested themselves in various ways and were an irritant to some of her neighbours who had, when Col was born, experienced a wicked satisfaction in the knowing that even superior-looking mortals like Maggie were by no means perfect. She hadn't wanted the boy in the beginning, his very existence reminded her of her shortcomings, but gradually, with the passing years, she came to love the flawed child. He was an adorable little creature who doled out love to his family without restraint. It was a bottomless font, springing freely from the happy, blithe heart of him, but if he had a favourite person in his untroubled life it was Nellie. She had loved him and cared for him from the start and it was to her that he now turned, holding out his arms and saying, 'Nella,' in a way that suggested the short time she had been away from him seemed more like a year.

'Ay, come on to me, my bonny wee mannie.' She snuggled him onto her knees to cuddle and kiss him and pick straw from his hair with which she tickled the back of his neck.

His laughter was as infectious as a summer cold, his big, dreamy blue eyes bright as he threw back his head and gave vent to warm, deep, fat, belly-shaking chuckles.

Evelyn smiled as she stepped over the cobbles to fetch butter from the milk shed, forgetting all about Whisky Jake in the warmth and security of King's Croft which happed about her like a soft warm blanket.

# CHAPTER THREE

Evelyn couldn't sleep that night, but tossed and turned while the disembodied faces of Nellie and Jake imposed themselves on her mind. All her former peace of mind left her, and try as she might she couldn't stop herself thinking about Nellie's reaction to the unpleasant visitor nor forget her father's strange words. The house was quiet. A breeze rustled the trees at the north gable, dry leaves spattered against the windowpane, a dog barked from some distant haugh. Then another sound intruded into the night – a footfall from the room across the landing, so hushed it was part of the heartbeat of the house. But Evelyn knew that behind her door Nellie paced, and she thought, Poor Nellie, if only I could go to you, talk to you, but you'll let no one into that proud, lonely heart o' yours . . .

Another face came to her, one that blotted out the rest. Sitting up she threw her shawl about her shoulders, lit the candle, and slipped her hand under her pillow to withdraw the diary she always kept there. It was the latest in a set of five, all handbound and decorated with little paintings of birds and flowers.

She had started to keep diaries from a very early age. Each one covered a span of perhaps two years and contained all the little incidents that had been of importance in her life. The first four were hidden away under a pile of old clothes and books at the bottom of the old kist in the corner.

The latest diary seemed to her to belong to Johnny. The pages, written in her still-childish hand, were full of him, things he had said, done, those precious times they had shared together. Since his death she spoke to him through her writing. In the still quiet hours of night it made her feel close to him, as if he was alive and well beside her.

Grasping her pencil she bent over the pages, her

37

crouched shadow a black companion on the wall by her
bed.

*October, 1914. Johnny, I met someone today. He came to
me like a ghost in the window of Bert's Tea Shoppe. You
probably know all this anyway but we had tea together. He
was a nice-looking man with laughter lines at the corners of
his brown eyes and dark, waving hair that seems to be two
colours, as if it was touched all the time by sunlight. I can
hear his voice inside my head. I think of it like that treacle
Mam used to spice with honey and nutmeg – the kind you
loved to spread thick on your piece.*
*I don't even know his name but to myself I think of him as
The Ghost Soldier. Don't be mad at me, Johnny. I've been
so lonely since you went and it was nice to have someone to
talk to. I told him about you, how I loved you, how you
died—*

Her eyes misted and the page blurred. Taking a deep
shuddering breath she went on:

*You're not a ghost to me, Johnny, in my mind you're real
and whole – just as he is. I don't know why I call him The
Ghost Soldier. There can be nothing ghostlike about a
young man who leaves for France on Monday. Darling
Johnny, if you were alive how long would you have stayed
with me before joining up? A lot of the boys we know have
enlisted. The battle of Ypres began on October 21st. The
Ghost Soldier told me. Billy Anderson and Dirty Wullie
were on the first casualty lists. The Ghost Soldier is with the
3rd Battalion Gordon Highlanders special reserve. He's
been in the army for two years and is a sergeant. Dear God,
preserve him and all the thousands like him. I shall never see
him again unless—*

Unless! Raising her head, she stared into the darkness
outwith the candle glow. Unless she was to go to the station
on Monday and watch him going away . . .
Her heart beat fast at the thought and she lay back on her

pillows, her fingers sliding away from the fresh entry in her diary. Mrs Chalmers, the efficient housekeeper of Rothiedrum House, would never give her time off – unless she had some very good excuse to make.

'Toothache!' The housekeeper spoke as if such a complaint had just been invented and in Evelyn's case it had been. She reddened under the older woman's inquisitive stare and with her fingers crossed at her back sent up a silent prayer for forgiveness of the white lie she had just uttered.

Martha the cook, bustling with pans at the fire, paused to wipe her hands on her apron and sigh. She was inclined to sigh a lot these days, for she missed the hustle and bustle of Rothiedrum in its heyday before the start of the war, even though she had often grumbled at Lady Marjorie's habit of suddenly announcing that there would be unexpected guests for dinner and expecting her to cope at a minute's notice. Martha had been rather peeved to be among those members of staff excluded from going to the London house, yet in many ways she was glad that Belle had gone in her place for she hated the noise of the city, and it had only been the matter of status that had annoyed her so. To use Martha's expression, Rothiedrum was at 'half steam' these days with the master and mistress in London and more than half of the younger servants either gone away to fight or gone to serve in some nursing unit or other.

Only the older ones, like Galbraith the butler, McTavish the head groom and a sprinkling of gardeners and house staff, were left to carry on and 'quite enjoyin' the peace' to quote McTavish who had been at Evander Forbes' beck and call 'wi' never a meenit to decently blaw his nose'.

He was quite happy grooming and exercising the horses with the help of old Coulter, whose services had been called upon when the young stable hands had gone to take the King's shilling. Both old men also shared a furtive enjoyment in tinkering with the engine of the big touring Lanchester. Meldrum the chauffeur had been loath to leave both it and the gleaming Benz behind, but Evander had lost his taste for the German-made car and despite his

39

wife's rather insincere protestations that they should save petrol in wartime, had opted to take the Rolls down to the city.

'Look to the potatoes, Greta,' Martha ordered and Greta, a small, thin girl with seedy eyes as Martha described them, glowered at Evelyn and made unnecessary noises with the utensils in the sink. Her place in the kitchen was a degree higher than Evelyn's, whose task it should have been to peel the vegetables. Martha studied Evelyn's flushed face. She had a soft spot for the girl and had been specially kind to her of late. 'Poor lass,' she murmured solicitously. 'You look as if you havena had a wink all night. Toothache is the de'il's own curse though it is naught but a memory to me.' Unconsciously she clicked her false teeth which in turn made Mrs Chalmers clench her own strong teeth tightly together. 'I hae the very dab,' Martha continued. 'Oil of cloves. My mither swore by it and I aye keep a wee bottlie handy for emergencies.'

'No, Martha, please don't bother,' Evelyn said in an agony of impatience. She wondered if she should just tell the truth but immediately decided against it. Mrs Chalmers would certainly not stand for the kind of romantic notion she had in mind. 'I – think I really ought to see a dentist – it might be an abscess.'

'Ach, let the lass go,' urged Martha. 'Greta and me will manage between us for a whilie – and less o' yer glowers, Greta girl. I ken fine you're sulking behind my back. Getting too big for your boots these days.'

Greta went to work furiously. Martha's word was law below stairs and her tongue could be razor sharp if she was out of temper.

'Right then, Evelyn,' nodded Mrs Chalmers. 'I'll get Coulter to drive you into Aberdeen. You'll get there and back all the quicker. I happen to know he coaxed Meldrum to show him how to drive a motorcar so you'll be quite safe with him.'

Greta paused in the act of peeling a large potato, and Martha stared at the housekeeper as if she had just taken leave of her senses. Mrs Chalmers had always taken the initiative but this was a downright liberty.

Evelyn's face had gone pale. 'But – I'll get the train from Lums o'Reekie,' she faltered, her thoughts running wild.

'Never fear, Evelyn,' said Mrs Chalmers stiffly. 'I will of course inform Mr Forbes of my action when he returns.'

'Petrol?' Evelyn said desperately.

The housekeeper smiled sourly. 'Meldrum began hoarding the stuff like a miser when he knew the war was coming. You mustn't worry, dear, this is an emergency after all.'

She *knows*, Evelyn thought, and she's enjoying it. The housekeeper's attitude had been distant towards her ever since she had come to work in Rothiedrum's kitchens. Normally it was Mrs Chalmers who interviewed prospective staff but Evelyn, ignorant of the class structure which existed among servants, had gone straight to the top. Via Gillan she had obtained an interview with Evander Ramsay Forbes himself and although nothing was said, the housekeeper had indicated her displeasure in various subtle ways.

Evelyn straightened. Removing her cap she tossed back her newly freed locks and said politely, 'That is very thoughtful of you, Mrs Chalmers. I'll be bidding you good day and will get back as soon as I can.'

Coulter was delighted to have an excuse to take the Lanchester for an airing. All his days he had worked with horses and though the innovation of the motorcar had met with his disapproval, curiosity about them had always titillated his senses and he had been secretly delighted when Meldrum departed, leaving the way clear for himself and McTavish to explore the mysteries of an automobile engine.

'Dirty, smelly brutes they are,' he greeted Evelyn as she came up to the quietly purring machine. 'They'll never tak' the place o' horses in my book. The reek that comes frae them would kill a good horse. At least when you feed a horse you get good dung out the other end – no' like these damt things wi' nothing but fumes comin' frae the back end.'

41

Evelyn smiled as she settled herself in the comfortable rear seat. Coulter had always been one of her favourite people. One of the best storytellers in the district, he had enriched her childhood with his tales of witches and warlocks and even now she wasn't past the entrancement she had always felt at the sound of his resonant voice weaving one magical tale after another at winter firesides.

She watched the countryside slipping by and, despite herself, began to enjoy the novelty of riding in the sleek car. Coulter was muttering to himself in the front, she could see the movement of his lips among the snow-white whiskers that covered his chin and upper lip. But there was pride in his squared shoulders whenever they passed a wayside croft or cottage, and a solemn-faced child or pipe-smoking old man followed their progress with guarded deference. 'Which dentist mannie are ye goin' to see?' Coulter asked as they neared Aberdeen. Taking a deep breath she told him that the toothache had been a lie. 'I had to get away, Coulter, there's someone I have to see off at the station.' The old man sucked in his breath and chuckled. 'Dinna worry, lass. You can trust old Coulter. I'll no' let on to auld Chamberpot. The station it is, and if you'll no' be tellin' on me I'll just tak' the chance to nip along to the harbour to see an auld cronie o' mine.'

'It's a deal.' Evelyn laughed, relaxing for the first time since leaving Rothiedrum House.

The station was crowded, busier than Evelyn had ever seen it. Royal proclamations and war posters were every-where. Behind his fiercely pointing finger (an accusing finger some said) Kitchener's face stared out, as familiar to everyone as the sheets on their own beds. No less eye-catching was Mr Frank Brangwyn's poster, depicting a somewhat aggressive soldier appealing to his countrymen to arm.

Underneath all the war paraphernalia, seated on benches, were groups of itinerant fishwives in their colourful dresses and shawls, talking nineteen to the dozen while keeping an eye on their bulging creels ranged alongside the wall. Evelyn made her way into the crowd.

Children, many of them wearing the little cardboard Glengarry caps brought out by a well-known jam company, were marching up and down brandishing toy swords, while the younger ones were cooried in their mothers' arms, tearful or joyful as the mood of the moment took them. Brothers, fathers, sweethearts were going off to war, and whole families had turned out to see them off.

The train was in the station, its engine being uncoupled, the fresh one shunting into place at the end of the long crocodile of coaches. At another platform, wounded men on stretchers were being carried from ambulance coaches. A few were walking, looking to be in the daze of sleep as they were led by Red Cross nurses into waiting ambulances. Silently Evelyn watched, her heart quiet and still within her at the realization that these haunted men with their grey faces and bloody wounds were the same boys who had only recently blithely and willingly left their couthy homelands in the rush to join up.

Amidst the sombre procession of wounded was Evelyn's sister, Grace. She stood out like a serene flower, her chestnut hair shining under her cap, her sweet face attentive and sympathetic as she talked to the men.

Evelyn shouted her name eagerly. It seemed so long since Grace had been home to King's Croft, a long time since her empty bed in the attic room had been occupied. She called out the name again but her voice was lost in all the noisy bustle.

A company of Gordon Highlanders was approaching, kilts swinging as they strode along. Everyone moved back to make way for them. A cheer rose as the poignant sound of the pipes skirled aloft. Hankies were out. One woman standing near Evelyn dabbed at her eyes and whispered to her husband, 'There he is, John, there's our Iain. By Dyod, is he no' a sight for sore eyes?'

Evelyn craned her neck, her heart beating strangely as she wondered in a rush of dismay if she might not recognize the man she had come to see. But no, she knew she wouldn't forget those eyes, that smile. The notes of the pipes died away, the company stood easy, smiling expectantly as friends and relations rushed forward to claim their own . . . And suddenly she saw him. No ghost, that tall young man, so handsome in his uniform her heart seemed to stop beating for a moment before rushing madly on.

He was climbing onto the train to lean from a window and gaze rather pensively into the crowd. Her breath caught. Surely he wasn't going off with no one there to bid him goodbye? She was about to rush forward, to go to him and wish him luck. She saw his face light up, and for one wild moment she imagined the look was for her. But a young girl had run forward to take his hands, to cling to them and laugh up at him as they exchanged greetings.

Evelyn bit her lip and moved back, overcome suddenly by her own temerity. Nellie would have called it brazenness and put forth her opinion of this episode in no mean manner.

Hot tears stung Evelyn's eyes. She tried to melt into the crowd, wanted desperately to recapture the anonymity that had been hers a short while ago. But she was too near the front. People were jostling, pushing her forward, intent on last-minute kisses and handshakes.

She looked round, eyes raking the throng, seeking a way of escape. But a part of her was drawn as if by a magnet to the window where he stood. The girl had gone. He was alone again. She saw him as that even though the faces of other soldiers were all around and behind him, meaningless blobs every one except for *his*. He was looking in her direction – her heart sped into her throat. He couldn't see her – and if he did, would he remember?

The deep pools of his eyes captured her own. Several yards separated them yet she had the sensation of drowning, of falling down, down to unknown depths of sweetness. There was a look on his face she couldn't fathom, a still, brooding look that made her feel uneasy. She tried to picture the scene from his eyes; the milling crowds, the laughing children, the nurses, the wounded men – the white face of a young girl framed in a mass of tumbled red hair. Was he perhaps wondering where he had

44

seen her before? Or was he lost in a moment of reverie, thinking about the unknown fate that awaited him over the sea, wondering if he might come back – like one of *them*?

She stood with her hands clasped in front of her, her eyes wide and luminous in the stillness of her face, feeling a unity with him for which she had no explanation.

Whistles blew, the engine released a great snort of steam which billowed upwards and outwards. The crowd swayed forward once more, taking her with it. An odd silence descended, a little lull as if time and tide were standing still for one breathless second. The air was heavy with unspoken thoughts, unshed tears, as an invisible bond caught and held everyone together as they gathered strength for the final show of bravado.

Evelyn felt herself caught up. Unconsciously, she straightened her shoulders as her gaze travelled along the rows of faces at the carriage windows. They were only boys, lads whose features belonged yet to children, too smooth some for the razor, the majority of them eager, shining, so caught up in the war fever that all apprehension seemed forgotten in the patriotic excitement of the moment.

Her eyes were too bright as the train began its slow shunt out of the station. Line after line of youthful faces sailed past her vision. The Glengarries were off, a blur of wildly waving colour. The crowd began to sing, 'Will Ye No' Come Back Again'. The evocative refrain was swiftly taken up, grew and swelled in intensity. Evelyn's lips moved, forming the words. The head and shoulders of the Ghost Soldier came nearer. 'Will Ye No' Come Back Again'. The words rang inside her head, keeping time to the rhythm of her heart, the clickety-clack of the wheels.

She could easily have put out her hand to caress for a moment the texture of his hair . . . Their eyes met, held, then he was whisked away from her, his Glengarry suspended in midair.

'I don't know your name!' The resonance of his deep voice filled her ears, cancelled out every other sound. 'I

45

don't know your name!' It was almost an angry protest now, the tones of the voice harsh and loud. Faintly, his final words came back to her, 'Goodbye, Bright Eyes!'

'Good luck!' she called out as loudly as she could. She lifted her hand but he was gone and she stood watching till the last carriage disappeared round a curve in the track. None of it might have been but for the smoke billowing back, the echoes of the pistons, the words of the song faltering on the lips of the families left behind. Bright Eyes! Would he think of her like that – if he thought about her at all? Like some moist-eyed puppy waiting for a pat of recognition from its master. A smile touched her mouth. He hadn't meant it that way. It was nice, something to think about when she had nothing better on her mind. Her fingers went up to her neck. The hard, gold band of his ring lay under the collar of her frock, out of sight of Nellie's eagle eyes. She had threaded it through with blue ribbon, wondering at the time what had prompted her to do so. He had called it a memento of their meeting and so she decided it would be, all that was left of the brief time they had shared together.

'Evie! Nellie's right about you, since you've grown up you've taken to daydreaming in the unlikeliest places.'

She spun round to see Grace smiling at her. 'Grace! I saw you earlier but I thought you had gone.'

'I came along to help with the men. I'm off duty for a couple of hours. Were you saying goodbye to someone special?'

'Only someone I met in the passing. Oh, Grace, it's grand to see you, it seems so long since you were home.'

'Ach, it's no' that long. Come on, we'll go somewhere and talk for a whilie. Would you like to go in for a cuppy?'

'Ay, I'd love to. But some place I can watch out for my car coming back.'

Grace laughed. 'Your *car*?'

'Coulter brought me in the laird's Lanchester. Very posh.' She linked her arm through her sister's. 'It's really good to see you. Every night I look at your empty bed and wish you were there to talk to.'

Grace sighed. 'Despite what I've just said it seems ages to me as well, Evie. The hospital is so busy now with some o' the wards given over to the wounded.'

'I wish I could train to be a nurse. Florrie once told me she thought I would make a good one.'

'You're too young, Evie, besides, Mam and Father need you at home.'

'They've got Nellie,' Evelyn said a little sulkily.

'Ay, but Father aye needed you and just now he needs you more than ever. I thought you liked working at Rothiedrum.'

'Ach, I do, but it's no' exactly in the heart o' things, is it? And with old Chamberpot forever on my tail it can also be very restricting. I had to tell her a lie to get this whilie off. I said I had toothache and the besom never believed a word o' it. She ordered old Coulter to bring me here in the motor thinking maybe he would keep an eye on me, when all the time the old de'il is just as bad as me.'

'You're a conniving pair o'rascals and have been from the start.' Grace squeezed her sister's arm affectionately as they found a windowseat in a little tearoom near the station.

Over tea and cakes they talked animatedly, Grace's face lighting up as Evelyn divulged all the gossip of home, laughter rising in her throat as she listened to a vivid account of the visit to the house in College Bounds; how Grandmother had cackled at wee Donald's antics, how Aunt Mattie had made the rafters ring with her 'Jer-oo-salems' and her 'Whose Annas'. Evelyn omitted mention of Whisky Jake, somehow not wanting that cruel-mouthed man to intrude into this precious time with Grace.

Reaching across the table Grace took her hands. 'It's so good to hear you talk about Mam and Father – about home. I miss it but more to the point it's good to see you laughing again. It's been a stranger to your bonny wee face for too long now. Nellie writes to me. In her own queer way she's been worried about you.'

'Nellie—Nellie's got a good heart under all that barking she does. I – if she was happier in herself she might keep a more civil tongue in her head. If only she could find a man she liked well enough to marry, we might all get a bittie peace.'

'She has found a man, Evie.' Grace's voice was soft. 'She's in love wi' Kenneth Cameron Mor.'

'Kenneth Mor – but—' Evelyn faltered to a disbelieving halt and put her cup down carefully on its saucer. 'I know Murn has always loved him – but – Nellie—'

Grace nodded. 'Ay, he's a married man and so in love wi' his wife he'd never dream o' setting eyes on another woman. But Nellie loves him and has done for quite a long while. She'd die if she thought anyone knew but I've noticed wee things about my sister, how quiet she is when Kenneth Mor's around, how she avoids going up to Knobblieknowe yet once she was never away from the place. Ay, she's found her man, Evie, and will die wanting him for she loves Jeannie wi' all her heart and would never do anything that might hurt her.'

'Poor Nellie.' Evelyn sounded stunned. A silence fell between her and Grace. When at last she looked up, her sister's gentle dark eyes were upon her.

'You're shocked, Evie, but you're old enough now to understand. In its proper place love can be a blithe and bonny thing but when it has to be locked away, the hurt o' it can be almost beyond endurance.'

Evelyn looked at her quickly. Grace nodded. 'Ay, me too, maybe that's how I understand Nellie so well. A surgeon at the hospital—' A wry smile touched her lovely face. 'It had to be that, eh? I used to smile at all those remarks about doctors and nurses and now I've fallen into the trap. Gordon Chisholm isn't a handsome man in the usual sense but he's gentle and considerate and so dedicated to his job he hasna the time nor the inclination to notice a foolish young sister who drops charts and thermometers when she accompanies him on his rounds.'

Evelyn's senses were reeling. So many revelations in such a short a time were too much for her to absorb. She wondered why she hadn't guessed at Nellie's feelings for Kenneth Mor and almost immediately knew the answer.

She had been too wrapped up in herself, too immersed in growing up and discovering her own loves, her own heartaches. Grace's vision of others had always been clearer. She had always been the unselfish one of the sisters, a girl with quiet insight and a love for all living things. She remembered the very young Grace, tending the sick and wounded animals who had found their way into the little menagerie she kept in the bedroom. She had been happy in those far-off innocent days, and Evelyn had always believed that when love came to her it would come sweetly and gracefully, not like some bruised and hurtful wound to be kept hidden from the world.

Grace leaned forward and placed a cool slender hand against Evelyn's cheek. 'Don't be sad for me, Evie. I'm far too busy most o' the time to worry about it – it's just – there's always the night and the sleep you need but somehow canna get.'

Always the night! Evelyn retreated into her own thoughts. The night with its silent shadows and eerie ways of impressing itself into your heart so that you felt the long darkness of it would never allow daylight to dawn over your world again.

'How is Martin Gregory?' Grace changed the subject. The question sounded forced, almost as if it was a duty.

'He asks after you all the time.' Evelyn spoke carefully, glad that she hadn't rushed out with the information that Martin Gregory haunted King's Croft these days, Grace's name never far from his lips. He taught in the local school at Rothiedrum and had been besotted with Grace since she was sixteen. He was now in his forties, Grace in her early twenties, and was more in love with her than ever though Grace had never allowed the relationship to become serious.

'Poor Martin.' Grace shook her head. 'He writes to me all the time but I never seem to find time to answer and never know what to talk about when I do. Evie, I'm a besom I know but I'm going to ask you no' to mention meeting me today. It would be awkward for you anyway with all the conniving you and Coulter concocted between you. Mam would only start asking when I'm coming home and so would Martin. I dinna get much time off but you write and tell me when next you'll be back at the Aulton. Bring Mam and Father and I'll see you all there. It's a good whilie since I visited Grandmother and it will be lovely to see the family again.'

Evelyn understood. She didn't want to spend her time away from Aberdeen and the man who held her heart captive, also—

'I dinna want to face Martin just now.' Grace's words were a continuation of Evelyn's thoughts. 'Not yet. I'll have to sooner or later but I need a whilie to get myself sorted out, Evie.'

Evelyn saw the Lanchester gliding to a halt outside the station. She stood up with a smile dimpling her cheeks. 'My chauffeur has arrived and has made me wait for him long enough. I shall speak to him about this.' She leaned forward and lowered her voice. 'I have a suspicion that the creature goes drinking when he ought to be working – servants! One has such difficulty with loyalty these days.'

Grace burst out laughing. 'You speak very well for someone who is supposed to have just come from the dentist. I have the very dab for your sort o' ailment.'   Rummaging in her nurse's bag, she withdrew a chunk of cotton wool. 'Stuff some o' this into your face and you might just pull the wool over Chamberpot's eyes – so to speak.'

Evelyn took the wad of cotton and turned away while she inserted some into her cheek. When Grace saw her they both shrieked with laughter, causing one or two heads to turn and people to smile for they were an attractive pair, these two sisters, with their shining eyes and happy young voices.

'No need to overdo it,' hissed Grace. 'You look as if you've a fatal dose of one-sided mumps. Go to the housekeeper looking like that and she'll either send you home or call out the doctor.'

'My dear, you are incorrigible,' Evelyn imparted haughtily. At the door she turned and winked at Grace, then walked regally over the road to the waiting car.

Coulter gaped at her. 'That's some gumboil you hae there,

50

lass. Tak' some oot till it looks like a wee plook inside yer face. Chamberpot's no' daft ye know.'

'Ach, it was only a joke, Coulter – though I hope Mrs Chalmers doesna see it as such.' Settling herself in the back she leaned forward to say imperiously, 'Drive on, my man, and dinna spare the horses.'

'Cheeky wee whittrock,' grinned the old man, as a laughing Evelyn waved to Grace who was standing watching from the opposite pavement.

'That's yer sister Grace, is it no'?' observed Coulter.

'Ay, it is, and dinna you go saying you've seen her, mind.'

'As far as I'm concerned I've seen nothing but the inside o' this motorcar for the last hour or twa.'

'She looks lovely in her uniform, doesn't she?' Evelyn asked proudly.

'A bonny lass,' agreed the old man. 'I mind her when she was just a wee thing, all een and hair and long, skinny legs like wee porridge spurtles. I worked at Cotterhill's place then and she used tae come along tae sell her eggs, then away she would go home wi' a wee injured bird or a hedgehog in her empty basket. She aye seemed tae find something to nurse. Carnallachie says she's no' made for the nursin' but the auld bugger has bools for een. Anybody can see she was born tae it – what else would she do?'

'Ay, what else?' echoed Evelyn, as Coulter let in the clutch and the car slid forward. She looked back at her sister standing on the pavement, a slender young woman in her nurse's uniform, the pale sunlight lighting her chestnut hair to a deep bronze. Hers was a gentle beauty, of the soul as well as the body. It surrounded her like a shining mantle and the thought came to Evelyn that she wouldn't for long go unnoticed by Doctor Gordon Chisholm. Suddenly she felt very sorry for Martin Gregory. He had waited so long for Grace, had waited patiently for her to grow up and begin to notice him as a man more than a good friend. He had Grace's affection but he would never have her heart – that belonged to someone else, and Evelyn's sympathies were very much for Martin Gregory even while she wanted

51

Grace to find her happiness with the man she loved, rather than someone for whom she had never felt more than a warm and caring compassion.

Evelyn sat back, her gaze contemplative as she watched the countryside slipping past. The Lanchester purred its way along, dipping down into misty haughs overshadowed by blue hills, breasting steep braes to run along by moors that were purple and gold in the mellow afternoon sunlight. Far, far on distant plains the buzzard soared and the stags ran with the hinds, only the white flashes of their rumps signalling their presence amongst the bracken. Evelyn allowed her thoughts to wander. She saw again a pensive face at a carriage window, the flash of a Glengarry held aloft, heard the shouted protest 'I don't know your name!' fresh and clear in her mind.

Her fingers crept to her neck to caress the hard, reassuring contours of his ring. 'Bright Eyes,' she said aloud, and smiled when Coulter grunted and threw back, 'And the same tae you – wi' knobs on.'

# CHAPTER FOUR

The November air was sharp and clean, hoarfrost crackled under Evelyn's feet as she made her way along the turnpike to Lums o'Reekie lying peacefully in the hollow, the smoke from its chimneys drifting lazily over the parks and haughs of Rothiedrum to settle in surrounding woods where it lay blue and still, softening the stark outlines of winter tracery.

The rooks were squabbling noisily in the frosted fields, poking and scratching among the furrows, a few of them flapping upwards every so often to soar as gracefully as buzzards in the cold blue sky.

Evelyn strode briskly along, swinging her basket, a feeling of quiet elation filling her as freezing air flooded her lungs. Stopping for a moment, she leaned her elbows on the parapet of the bridge to watch the Birkie burbling tranquilly over the stones. Life had felt good to her in the last few weeks, and deep inside herself she knew that the feeling had grown since her meeting with the young soldier in Cobbly Wynd. In the eyes of the world she remained a sober and quiet young lass mourning for Johnny Burns, but another part of her refused to be still, it gnawed at her and tormented her with its eagerness for living, made her rise from her bed each morning to take great, greedy gulping breaths of life. She was half-ashamed of this passionate, hungry thing that throbbed inside her, but no matter how hard she tried it wouldn't be repressed, and like a separate entity grew bigger all the time. She had no more tears left for Johnny – for Florrie – now there remained a hard, raw ache in a corner of her heart that was for them alone. Her gaze travelled upwards to Birkiebrae, aloof and distant in its shroud of mist away up there on the edge of the hillside. Johnny came to her, striding tall and fair down the track to meet her, his smile kindling fire in his blue eyes. She stared towards Cragbogie where Florrie had run in childhood, and she conjured a vision of a golden-haired girl running down to meet her and walk with her along the road to school, laughter ringing, echoing up and beyond the fields to the silent hills standing blue and aloof against the sky.

A mist blurred her vision, merged with the ghostly wraiths on the hilltops into which Johnny and Florrie seemed to vanish.

'I'll always love you both,' she whispered. 'But I canna help this thing that is life inside o'me. The world around me is so bonny, it calls me away from the dead, from the past.'

She shivered a little as she stood there, her curtain of red hair falling over her face as she stared down at the river, hating the thoughts that could take her from joy to despair. All through her life she had been haunted by a strange perception of things past, of those yet to be. Ever since she was a young child she had experienced an affinity with the spirit world. Old Hinney had told her she had the second sight and no matter how unwelcome it might be, it would always be there to annoy, frighten, and intrigue her . . .

'Evie!'

The Loon, otherwise Pooty Drummond, came shuffling along, his big, clairty feet scrunching into the grass at the roadside, a drip dangling at the end of his cold-reddened nose which he wiped unceremoniously away with the back of a frayed, fingerless woollen glove.

'I'll get ye up the road, Evie,' he said, grabbing her arm and marching her along at a pace that made her laugh and tell him to ease up.

'I canna,' he stated belligerently. 'Ma sent me to fetch a twist o'Bogy Roll and said if I wasna back inside an hour she'd skite me round the lugs – she would too,' he added darkly, and went on to regale Evelyn with some of his mother's exploits, which he told so colourfully and explicitly that they were often listened to avidly by the good folk of Rothiedrum who maintained he was neither as daft nor slow-witted as he made out.

'The old besom is worse on me this whilie,' he confided gloomily to Evelyn. 'She has a man, ye know, Evie. The pair o'them hit the bottle together and come out the inn, singin' and hoochin' along the road. They both smoke like lums and there they sit in the kitchen, her makin' a noise like a cat on the tiles and him playin' a wee moothie that keeps me off my sleep at night.'

'A man!' echoed Evelyn, staring at The Loon's disgruntled face in disbelief. 'I ken fine your mother enjoys a wee drink to herself and likes a puff at her clay pipe – but a man!'

Pooty dug his fingers into his thick yellow thatch and screwed up his face. 'Ay, a man, yon wee dwarf cratur who comes roon the doors sellin' sugar mice and bootlaces.'

'Ach, Pooty, you mean Muckle Willie. But everyone takes Willie in for a meal and a night in the barn. I had no idea he was in the area. I love when he comes wi' his ribbons and threads, and I have a whole collection o' his wooden dolls sitting on my dresser. There's no harm in Muckle Willie and you'd better no' go spreading rumours about him and your mother. You know what folks hereabouts are like!'

'He's stayin' wi' Ma, I tell ye,' persisted The Loon. 'I saw them wi' my very own een, Ma snuggled in the blankets and the dwarf's feet stickin' out the bottom o' them – he had holes in his socks too,' he ended in aggrieved triumph.

'But Muckle Willie's a tiny wee man. How could his feet stick out the bottom o' the bed? Was it no' your mother's feet you saw?'

'Ay, hers were there too, plunk on one side o' the bed, his at the other – at the bottom.'

Evelyn took his hand and made him hurry along, for in his earnestness he was inclined to pause every so often to stress a point.

The usual small group was outside the post office, scanning the casualty lists in the newspapers. Occasionally a sigh would ripple through the men and women as some well-kent name came to light. As Evelyn drew nearer a spindly figure detatched itself from the throng to hurry over and apprehend Evelyn, while sending The Loon smartly about his business with a few sharp words.

Kirsty Keith was a small, scraggy scrap of a woman, whose benign face belied a shrewish nature and an abrasive tongue. Evelyn scanned her lined face in some apprehension for one never knew what to expect from Kirsty.

'It's Alan,' she said without preliminary. 'He's talking o' joining up, Evie. You're the only person in these parts that he would ever confide in. Would you hae a word wi' him?' She twisted red, stringy fingers together nervously and surveyed Evelyn with pleading in her eyes. For once Evelyn felt sympathy for the scrawny mistress of Dippiedoon. All too often her vindictive tongue had stung Evelyn to sharp retort but no one could deny how long and hard she had laboured after her family especially Alan who, with his sensitive nature and artistic talents, was the apple of her eye. Both Kirsty and her husband Angus had made stupendous sacrifices to send Alan to art college, and Evelyn could well picture the blow his news must have given the family.

'Ay, I'll talk to him,' Evelyn said slowly. 'But I canna promise anything. Alan might be quiet but he has a mind o' his own and might resent my interference.'

She winced under the older woman's vice-like grip on her arm. 'I knew I could rely on you, Evie, and Alan never resented you – in fact, I often wish he would turn to me the way he aye turned to you when he needed somebody to talk to.' Her face crumpled. 'I wouldna hae asked – only – Alan's too good to waste in yon piggery across the sea.' Her lips twisted. 'I blame that mannie, Kitchener! Egging our lads on, telling them it's their duty to go and fight. Well, the rest can do as they please, it's no' for my son, his duty is here wi' folk who have worked their fingers to the bone to gie him his chance. We'll no' stand in his light, and by Dyod! neither will that bloody wee fart o' a Kaiser! Hmph! To think I once supported royalty! If they can produce dirt like that then I wouldna be seen dead wi' a Union Jack in my hand!'

Crimson-faced she scuttled away, leaving Evelyn to gaze after her speechlessly. Kirsty had indeed taken her son's patriotism badly. A regular churchgoer and a denouncer of all forms of blasphemy she had never been heard to swear, and one or two people stared after her while George the Forge, to the accompaniment of much mirthful encouragement, executed as perfect an imitation of her scuttling walk as his rotund figure would allow.

'Our Kirsty has indeed got a bee in her breeks,' greeted Bunty Lovie, the postmistress, as Evelyn came through the door. 'As if her lad was the only one to take the King's shilling.'

'Och well, I for one don't blame her,' said Evelyn. 'She's worked hard to see Alan through to college and it must be terrible for her to feel it's all been for nothing.'

Bunty sighed heavily, her round, cheery face growing sad as she rhymed off the names of several local lads whose names were on the recent casualty lists. 'But here,' she brightened. 'Were you after hearing about Dottie Drummond and Muckle Willie? My, my, the cratur must indeed be hard up for a man to take yon wee sowel into her bed – and you would think,' she lowered her voice, keeping one bird-bright eye on the people outside the window, 'wi' him being so wee he wouldna be much use to a woman though mind—' the flesh of her plump arms spread over the counter as she leaned towards Evelyn and further confided '– I mind o'hearin' that wee men are big made – you know?'

Evelyn put her hands to her mouth and erupted into gales of laughter. When Bunty Lovie got carried away it mattered not if her audience was nine or ninety, and Evelyn put her own arms next to those of the postmistress and gave herself up to the indulgence of a good chinwag, reflecting as she did so that Pootie was certainly adept at setting the wires of Highland Telegraph humming.

When finally she turned to go, Bunty called after her, 'Mary says to tell you to look in on your way home. She wasna her usual cheery self this morning. I doubt maybe the war has got to her too.'

The grey, douce exterior of the doctor's house belied the cheerily untidy interior. Mary had never been one to make

57

a fuss over what she considered to be unimportant details, a fact which had annoyed Nellie greatly during Mary's years at home. No matter what Mary had been doing Nellie was at her back to tidy up after her, and in the blithe years of her freedom she had left such scenes of havoc in the bedroom that Nellie had been forever clearing away stockings and petticoats while Mary went sailing out to meet some young man, looking like a duchess.

Rowanlea Cottage reflected her cheery personality. Slovenly, Nellie called it, but Evelyn liked the atmosphere of informal disarray and always felt at ease in the comfortably furnished parlour, with its winged armchairs and bookcases and fine oil lamps whose brass pillars gleamed richly in the fire's light. Mary used her parlour as often as she used her kitchen, breaking years of tradition imposed upon her in a crofting household where the best room might never be used from one Sunday to the next, except if visitors arrived unexpectedly.

But Mary broke with all that when she married Gregor and set out to make the parlour less of a showpiece and more of a place to relax in at any time of the day. The room was never exactly tidy. Donald's toys were scattered about on the floor, newspapers stuffed under cushions lent them extra height, and a round, beautifully polished red mahogany table by the window held the family bible together with numerous magazines and an assortment of books. Yet, despite her easy-going nature there was something of the lady in Mary. She never rose in the morning till the maid brought her tea in bed and laid out fresh clothes for her by the fire in the kitchen, so that all she had to do was rush downstairs to slip into the warmed garments. 'I've had enough o' freezing attic rooms and damp clothes to last me a lifetime,' she told Evelyn with a laugh, and when Nellie pointed out that she had once bathed her naked body in cold water from the ewer Mary gave her sister one of her infuriatingly angelic smiles, and informed her she had only undergone such torture in order to shock and disgust Nellie into sharp rebuke.

Her clothes were the very best that could be bought out

of a country doctor's income and Evelyn often reflected that, given a different set of circumstances, Mary might rise a little above her station, for she was wont to put on subtle airs and graces whenever the minister's dowdy wife or some of her husband's friends called in to see her.

In the few years she had been Doctor McGregor's wife, she had cultivated several acquaintances among the merchant brethren of Aberdeen which included country gentlemen and their wives. Gregor indulged her whims but went quietly about his own affairs without getting involved in her schemes, a fact which had at first annoyed her but which she now accepted with the good grace of her buoyant nature.

Evelyn went straight into the kitchen, gathering up Donald on the way and cuddling her face into his soft hair. She saw at once that her sister was looking unusually gloomy and with an inward sigh wondered if Bunty's predictions had been correct.

'Evie, I'm glad you've come. Sit you down and I'll make a cuppy.' Suddenly she halted in the middle of the room, her bonny face with its big dark eyes and flawless complexion taking on an expression of tragedy. 'I'm sorry, Evie, I have to tell you first. It's Greg! He's been talking so much about the war lately, impressing upon me how badly doctors are needed at the front. He thinks he has to soft soap me, prepare me for things he thinks I might no' be able to face when all the time I wish he would just come right out with it. It's getting on my nerves, and I wanted to ask you if you think I should tell him I know he wants to do his bit for the war effort.' It was an expression much in vogue at the time, but coming from Mary it sounded unnatural and Evelyn knew she had been listening to the chatter of her fine friends. Evelyn went to put on the kettle and to butter the hot scones the maid had left on the hob. 'Mary,' she said firmly, 'you dinna have to pretend with me. You want Greg to go, don't you? Underneath that tragic look I can see the patriotism shining. I know for a fact that these friends o' yours are blethering their heads off about what their sons and husbands are doing in France. You can just see your-

59

self, one o' the war wives, crying over your knitted squares and your woollen socks while you talk your head off about your brave Greg.'

Mary had the grace to blush. 'I never could fool you, could I, Evie? You're such a wee fart o' a lass to have such powers o' insight. But you're right enough and I feel a real bitch for even thinking o' wanting my darling Greg to join the rest. I ought to try and stop him thinking the way he does. He's doing a valuable service for his own country and if I persuaded him enough I know he would stay for my sake. It's different for the likes o' Kathy Sutherland. Her son was in the Cavalry before war broke out and it's natural he should be in at the start – but she boasts that much about him and Mamie Marcroft-Robertson with a hyphen goes on about her husband being a captain and how brilliantly he leads his men in the battlefield.'

Evelyn tucked a bib in at Donald's neck and sat him on the rug with milk and a buttered scone. 'You need never fear that Greg will be handed a white feather, Mary. He has more guts in him than all the King's men put together. I dinna think I like the sound o' your friends very much and Mam goes red in the face at the idea of a daughter o' hers getting high-falutin' ideas—'

'Did I hear my name?' Gregor came in, dumping his bag on the table and stooping to kiss Donald's upturned face.

'Ay, Greg, you did.' Evelyn poured another cup of tea and pushed him affectionately into a chair. She loved everything about her brother-in-law. He was kind, courteous and considerate, devoted to his family. To his patients he gave selflessly of himself, struggling out in all weathers and at any time of the day or night with only scant complaint. If he had a fault it was his indulgence of his wife, whom he openly adored. He had been up most of the previous night at a difficult confinement and Evelyn noticed that his strong shoulders were drooped from weariness, yet even so he smiled at them all and demanded to know what all the talk was about.

'Och, it's nothing, dear,' began Mary but Evelyn broke in, saying sharply, 'Mary knows you want to help in the war, Greg. She's stronger than you think about such matters. Isn't that so, Mary?'

Greg looked from one sister's face to the other. 'Have you two been arguing?' he asked in some surprise. 'If it had been you and Nell, Mary, I would understand it but you and Evie—?'

With a little embarrassed laugh, Mary went to stand behind him and massage his shoulders. 'Dinna fash, darling,' she soothed, stooping to plant a kiss on top of his curly head. 'I only told Evie I wouldna stand in your way if you really want to help in the war.'

Crimson-faced, Evelyn got up to slip her arms into her coat and grab her basket. 'Mam will be needing these,' she said shortly and paused only to ruffle Donald's hair before making her way hurriedly outside.

She was grateful for the clean sharp air which bathed her hot cheeks and made her feel less flustered. She took deep breaths as she walked along the turnpike, and reaching the track that led to King's Croft she stopped for a moment to watch the smoke curling lazily from the chimney.

How could Mary be so selfish? she thought, her departing anger leaving her cold and miserable. It was all so stupid and so senseless. Her sister loved Greg yet she was quite prepared to stand back and let him go off without a struggle. She wondered what she would do in a like situation and thought that if she had someone like Greg, she would fight furiously to keep him by her. But would that be the wise thing to do? Men were proud creatures, proud and a bit pigheaded, and her experiences of them were still very limited – would she ever know what really went on in their minds?

Without warning Johnny and The Ghost Soldier shot into her mind. One was dead – the other . . ? She put a cold hand to her mouth. God help him! He might be dead too! The casualty lists from Ypres alone seemed neverending – and she didn't even know his name. Perhaps it was just as well. At least she would never know if he was alive or dead and in the next instant she realized that was the worst kind of agony of all.

Johnny was still on her mind alongside the kilted, virtually unknown soldier yet she saw him as plainly as she saw Johnny.

You would have gone too, Johnny, she thought bleakly. They're all going, all the young men . . .

When she got indoors Maggie said quietly, 'What ails you, lass? You look upset.' In her anguish she told her mother everything, ending, 'Mary's always been a bittie frivolous, Mam, but to want the man she loves to risk himself in war – I canna understand it.'

'Whoever understood people's reactions to war, Evie?' Maggie said harshly. 'Mary canna be blamed. She's like a lot o' young women these days. They see only the honour and the glory and the bravery attached to fighting. Only those at the front know the hellish truth o' it and some o' them will never talk about it. At least Greg will no' be at the fighting if he goes.'

'No, his will be a different fight,' said Evelyn bitterly. 'A fight with torn flesh and bones and the struggle to keep life in broken bodies – and most o' them just boys.'

Maggie looked keenly at her youngest daughter. 'You're only a young lass – yet you feel so much of others' pain, as if you knew what it was all about.'

Evelyn shivered. 'I seem to see it, Mam – and to feel the pain and fear myself. I dinna want to feel like this.'

'You have something in you that is beyond comprehension, Evie.' Maggie stroked the shining head tenderly. 'You have the second sight.'

Evelyn sat down heavily in the inglenook. 'How did you know that?' she whispered.

'Hinney told me but she was only confirming what I already knew. You're a seventh child, Evie, and your father's gypsy blood runs rich in your veins. Your paternal grandfather was a well-known seer. It's a gift given only to a few, yet I would never have wished it on you.'

'It won't make me unhappy all the time, will it, Mam?' Evelyn's voice was low and tremulous. 'I want to be happy, I was today till Kirsty then Mary started on about the war.'

'Has that Kirsty been talking to you?' Maggie said

grimly. 'She was down here the other day ranting on about Alan and how she had sacrificed herself for him. I wouldna be surprised if the loon only wants to sign up to get out o' her way so dinna you go getting yourself involved in any o' the Keiths' affairs.'

Col toddled over to climb on Evelyn's lap and curl a strand of her hair under his nose.

'Look at him, Mam,' smiled Evelyn. 'He's the only really happy one among us. Even The Loon, for all he's a saftie, has his ups and downs like the rest o' us.' With a giggle she regaled her mother with the latest exploits of the Drummond family and in minutes the kitchen erupted with laughter, even Col throwing back his fair little head and echoing the mirth of the others. 'Mucky Villie,' he formed his tongue with difficulty round the name. 'Mucky Villie – mucky feet.'

'We'd better watch what we're saying,' said Maggie, wiping her eyes with a corner of her apron. 'Muckle Willie might be wee but he's got a king-sized temper when he's riled and wouldna like all these rumours going about concerning his feet.' She put her hand over Evelyn's. 'You have your father's mischief in you, lassie, and as long as you have that you'll get through your life wi' a smile. When first I knew your father he was never done playing wee tricks and laughing that happy laugh o' his. He maybe doesna do it so much now but the de'il is still there in his eyes just waiting to pounce.'

It wasn't tears of laughter that she wiped away now, and Evelyn looked tenderly at the top of her mother's bowed head and wished she had known both her parents when they were young and carefree and bonny.

Alan showed only slight surprise when Evelyn broached the subject of his intended enlistment. 'I knew my mother would get somebody to try and talk what she calls sense into me.' His sensitive mouth twisted wryly, 'but I didna think it would be you, Evie, you're a bittie young to come preaching to the converted.'

'She knows we've always been good friends, Alan, and

she's near daft wi' worry about you. She always had such plans for you. What about college?'

Seizing her hand he led her down to the river, to a spot where in summers past he and she with Florrie and Johnny had sat on the warm banks, boots and stockings cast aside while they steeped their feet in the cool green water and talked about all the things they were going to do when they grew up. The river was freezing now, the banks rimed with frost, tiny flakes of snow starting to fall from a leaden sky. The north-east winter was closing in and Alan's hand was cold in hers.

'It will wait for me,' he told her, his voice soft, his gaze turned contemplatively towards the foaming tumble of the river. There was a fragility in the long, clever fingers curled over hers, a delicacy in his slight frame that seemed to her to be more pronounced than she had ever remembered. Yet there was a strength in him that was not of muscle and sinew but of heart and spirit and a steadfast resolution that shone out of his grey eyes. 'I have to do this, Evie, no' because everyone else is doing it but for me – for my peace o' mind.'

'Peace of mind!' The exclamation was torn from her. 'How can war bring you peace of mind?'

'It will help me to forget Florrie,' he replied simply. 'I feel shattered inside. I must go somewhere far away from here, a place where I'll have no time to remember – how it was. There's nothing noble in it. I'm thinking o' myself, being selfish if you like. I forget what it feels like to be young and whole – I'm empty inside. Perhaps you more than anybody know how I feel.'

She stared at the cold green water slipping past, and knew Kirsty Keith should never have asked her help in trying to dissuade her son from going to war. 'Where will you enlist?' She held on to his hand and squeezed it tight.

'Castle Hill, where else? And I've already joined up. The Gordons were always such a smart regiment and bonny fighters into the bargain. I learned to play the pipes when I was young and if I'm good enough I might get to play the men into battle.'

His eyes were shining and she could see that he already imagined himself in the battlefield, marching out of the trenches playing tunes of glory. 'Ay, they are that,' she agreed absently, her hand going unconsciously to the band of gold lying inside her blouse, a smile at her lips as she thought about a young soldier raising his Glengarry to her from a speeding train.

'I'm just waiting to be called up for my medical.' Alan was speaking again and she nodded, a part of her hoping that he might not have the physical stamina required of him. But thin though he was, he was wiry and had never had a serious illness in the whole of his young life. Unless the medics found some other reason to exempt him, he would undoubtedly be declared fit enough to fight.

Without warning he pulled her to him and kissed her on the lips, an affectionate kiss but one which nevertheless took her breath away with surprise. Briefly, she felt the taut strength of his young body against hers before he pulled away to smile at her.

'I feel lucky now, Evie, I know I'll pass my medical with the taste o' your bonny lips on mine.'

His breath mingled with hers in the frosty air. Reaching out he took a strand of her hair and let it run through his fingers. 'Florrie's was like the cornfields in summer. I remember how it used to glint like gold in the sun. Yours is like autumn, holding to it all the rich red glories of the birks and braes at summer's end.'

His voice was husky with poignancy. She bit her lip and dashed a hand over her eyes. 'You're an artist, Alan, not a poet, but maybe the two go hand in hand.'

He stepped back from her, a glint of laughter dispelling his sombre mood. 'No, it's just my daft way o' asking you for a lock o' your hair – to carry wi' me over yonder, a bittie o' something to remind me of my homelands.'

'You shall have it when next I see you,' she promised, letting go of his hand. She stood watching him striding away over the fields to Dippiedoon lying in its mist-hazed hollow, his shoulders well back, a whistle at his lips as he scrambled down a dip in the fields and was lost to sight . . .

and in her mind's eye she imagined the burning fields of France filled with the sad corpses of young men like Alan who had once walked tall and proud in the shining valour of their youth.

'Hallo, Princess.'

With a gasp of complete surprise Evelyn spun round, almost dropping the heavy vase of magnificent bronze chrysanthemums which she held clasped in both hands.

'Gillie!' she cried. 'What on earth are you doing here?'

'I live here – remember?' He was smiling at her, his dark, handsome face lit with the pleasure he felt at having so obviously caught her unawares. Seizing the vase of flowers he placed it on a nearby ledge, and putting his hand under her elbow he guided her to a little padded seat set into a deep alcove in the corridor.

'Gillie,' she protested, but feebly. 'Chamberpot – I mean Mrs Chalmers sent me to put these in the drawing room. There isn't so much work below stairs now and she likes to keep us busy – also she is a great believer in keeping the place as fresh as it was when the family were all here.'

'Never mind Chamberpot—' He grinned. 'A very wicked title but with a ring to it that appeals to my corrupt sense of humour.' They both giggled and then he leaned forward, and taking her in his arms kissed her tenderly on the lips. 'It's so good to see you again, Evie, really good. You'll never know how much I miss you when I'm away. It seems so long since that last time yet it's only a couple of months really.'

They were both silent, remembering the sadness of their last time together. Neither of them had said so but both had felt the raw, terrible guilt of having been somehow to blame for Johnny's death and a great constraint had arisen between them. It was over now, though. They were close enough both spiritually and mentally to sense one another's feelings to a large extent, and a great burden seemed to slip from their shoulders as they sat together in the alcove.

'I canna bide long with you, Gillie,' she whispered, leaning out to peep either way along the corridor. 'Tell me

66

why you're here and how long you can stay?'

'Only a short time, I'm afraid,' he said ruefully. 'And I'm here to see you and to explain what's been happening since last I saw you. It's all talk about war at the London house just now and has been for ages. Father is very involved in his various business projects. He owns several shops which weren't doing well before the war but which are now booming. He's also into military supplies as well as his agricultural interests and his biggest baby is the munitions factory. It's all grist to the mill as far as he's concerned and he was never backward about his love for moneymaking. We've had some blazing rows lately. Mainly because I wanted to leave school and train for war—'

'Gillie!' she said, her face blanching. Putting a finger to her lips he took her hands.

'Listen to me, Evie. I have left. I only had a term or two to go anyway. I didn't go back after the summer holidays but applied instead for a place in an Officers Training Unit. Both Father and Mother almost had apoplexy when I told them I wasn't going back to school, and Father lost a lot of sleep trying to talk me into a managerial position in one of his factories. I stuck to my guns as it were and they both grew resigned to my side of the argument. I'm going off to camp next week – that's why I came back to Rothiedrum, to let you know, and to ask – if you would write to me while I'm there. I'm going to feel strange for a while, though my stint with the Officers Training Cadets at school might make me feel less of a greenhorn.'

She had withdrawn from him. He looked at her bowed head. A weak November sun was slanting in from one of the long corridor windows, setting its beams on the rich tresses of her wonderful tawny-red hair. She sat huddled in her corner, not looking up, so silent in her deep reverie that his heart twisted with the love he had felt for her all the years they had known one another.

'Evie – Princess,' he murmured huskily. 'I'm sorry if my news has – hurt you. If you were mine, I would never want to be anywhere else but at your side but you're not mine and never will be – I know that now though I'll never be resigned to it, nor will I ever stop hoping that one day you might – love me back.'

She looked up then, a glitter of tears in her green eyes.' 'You were always more than just a good friend to me, Gillie. If you weren't, I really wouldna care one way or the other about your plans. But I do care and I'm angry at you, at you and Alan and all the rest who are throwing up their dreams and their careers in their rush to follow in one another's footsteps. But my anger won't keep you, I know that well enough by now.'

'Your love would.' His brown eyes were dark with the intensity of his feelings, and she wound her fingers round his and touched them with her lips. 'I'll write, Gillie. It won't be grand talk, mind. Just things about my family and the croft and what's going on in Rothiedrum.'

'That's all I want, all I ever wanted. I love this place – everything that was ever precious to me belongs here.'

Gathering her into his arms he held her tightly, and she clung to him, a lost, tremulous sadness in her for all the dear and familiar people who seemed to be slipping out of her life.

# CHAPTER FIVE

Kenneth Cameron Mor came striding into King's Croft kitchen, brushing snow from his kilt, shaking flakes of it from his red head and magnificent silken beard in the manner of a dog running wet from the sea. He was a superb figure of a man, well over six feet in his socks with a strong though finely boned face which glowed with his love of life. His eyes were the cool blue of a Highland loch but became filled with a dangerous fire if he was riled in any way. His fine, high-bridged nose had a wee bit of a twist to it as befitted his surname, which was 'Camshron' in Gaelic and meant crooked nose.

His great voice came booming out of his mighty lungs as he called, 'Are you in, Maggie lass? I've brought Tandy to see you.'

Maggie came through from the scullery in time to witness the arrival of Tandy the Shepherd close on Kenneth Mor's heels, bringing in with him a blast of freezing air and a skelter of snowflakes from the windy funnel of the close. She had barely time to rush to the door and close it before she was seized in a bear-like hug and waltzed round the kitchen.

'Tandy McQueen!' she gasped. 'You get dafter each time you come back to these airts. Let go of me this minute.'

'Ach, it's just pleased I am to see you,' Tandy grinned, letting her go with a playful smack on the bottom which brought green sparks to her eyes even while she couldn't refrain from laughing at his audacity. Tandy and Kenneth both hailed from the Western Highlands and the two were so alike in looks and temperament that they might have been brothers. Tandy was as tall if not taller than Kenneth, with unruly rusty fair hair, huge ox-like shoulders and a marvellous physique and bearing. His unusual tawny-yellow eyes could be as sleepy as a cat's or as wild as

69

a tiger's, and when he and Kenneth had had a few drams they would march about the hills together, playing the pipes and skirling with untamed merriment which induced great excitement among the children and young maidens of Rothiedrum, the latter of whom did everything in their power to get Tandy to notice them. But popular as he was among the womenfolk, he remained as free as the wind, an itinerant creature who roamed the highways and byways with his flock and his dogs. Whenever he came to Rothiedrum he lived in a bothy known as Shepherd's Biggin, which stood cooried into the lee of the hill up yonder on Kenneth Mor's land.

The two gigantic figures made King's Croft kitchen shrink in proportion, and Maggie shooed them to seats by the fire after first making Tandy remove his snow-caked boots. 'It's time you had a woman to look to you,' she scolded, winking at Kenneth Mor who had removed his footwear in the porch. 'A good wife would train you and tame you in two shakes o' a lamb's tail – though mind—' she cast a speculative eye over him – 'I doubt there's a woman in the land who could completely break that wild streak you have in you. A good sheepdog would be easier to train than yourself.'

'Och, Maggie, stop nagging,' he laughed. 'It's Christmas soon, but I'll no' bide for it if you dinna tell me your heart pines for me when I'm out o' your sight.'

Maggie snorted and went to hang the kettle on the swee, talking as she did so to Kenneth about Jeannie, who was ill in bed with a bad dose of flu. She could see that it was worrying him as he was a lot quieter than usual.

Evelyn and Nellie came in from a walk with Col accompanied by Murn, whom they had met trudging along the snowbound turnpike from the station. All of them had frost-stung cheeks but at sight of Kenneth the glow in Murn's deepened to crimson, for she had loved him from the start and did everything in her power to get him to notice her, even though the passing years had proved to her how fruitless it was.

Everyone gathered round the fire to drink tea

companionably with the visitors, although Nellie became so discomfited by Murn's efforts to please Kenneth that she couldn't stop herself throwing a few dark looks at her sister which Murn ignored easily through long years of practice. Even so, it was an amiable enough gathering, but when a tired and damp Jamie came in from settling the horses in the stable, the drams were brought out and something cold and cheerless clutched at the heart of Margaret Innes Grant. Jamie was pretending, pretending to ignore the whisky in his glass. She saw the tension in him, the slight trembling of his hand when he eventually downed his whisky in one gulp, before refilling the glass almost to the brim.

A small, imperceptible strain seized hold of the Grant girls. Murn moved restlessly in her seat and laughed too loudly at Tandy's words of nonsense, Evelyn grew still and quiet and kept her face averted from her father. Only Nellie displayed an outward show of disapproval. Lips clamped tightly together, she got up from her seat and on a flimsy pretext went through to the scullery, there to stand with clenched fists and the sigh of her father's name on her lips.

There Kenneth Mor surprised her, coming in at her back as silently as a cat in his stockinged soles, his voice when he spoke as soft as the snow that drifted down outside. For he could be tender and gentle when he liked, this big laughing Highlander, with a nuance in his tongue that lilted along like music. 'Nell, Nell, you mustna judge your father so harshly.'

The stealth of his entry, the quietly reproachful murmur coming at her so unexpectedly, set her pulses racing, and she could no more stem the tide of colour that flooded her face than she could the quickening of her unsteady breath. Placing her hands on the cold marble shelf in front of her, she leaned forward, steadying herself, playing for time by forcing herself to breathe evenly and deeply, all the while praying that he would never guess what his nearness did to her. Throwing back her head she said in a gruff whisper, 'Kenneth, Kenneth, you're the one doing the judging. I canna bear to watch him slowly killing himself – for that's what he's doing – as sure as my name is Nell Christina Grant.'

'Nell.' He came nearer, placed a gentle big hand on her arm. 'He'll get over this. I've known Jamie for a long time and maybe because I dinna live with him I see him clearer than you and your family. Johnny was the son he never had, he needed the lad in his life and now he's lost him. It will take him longer than it will Evie to get over that loss. She's young and resilient with all her life afore her while he has lost the strength he had in Johnny and must feel there's nothing much left to look forward to. But that will pass, Nell, you must have faith in your father. He's no' a big man but the heart o' an ox beats inside o' him. That and his spirit will bring him up out of this. But he needs to feel the love of those around him, and he has it in all – but you, Nell lass.'

His touch had sent shivers along the length of her spine. She shut her eyes, as if by so doing she could shut out her terrible awareness of him. 'I'm no' the loving kind, Kenneth, even you should know that by now. I – I've never had it in me to love, to need.'

'That's blethers and we both know it.' His voice was just a breath away, she could feel the warmth of it hushing over her neck. 'You have a heart all right, Nell, it's warm and beating in the breast of you and growing so big with all the love you bottle up in it that one o' these days it's going to burst like a dam and come flooding out. I hope when that day comes your father will be the first to taste its sweetness.'

'Go away, Kenneth,' she thrust at him angrily. 'I dinna need you dinning your nonsense into my lugs.'

'I'll go, Nell.' His own voice held a trace of anger now. 'But no' before you say you'll come up and see Jeannie. You used never to be away from Knobblieknowe and Jeannie often wonders to me what's gone wrong between you. She loved you as a sister and she's lonely for you, Nell. She's such a wee thing and the only strong thing about her is her love for those around her. The farming life o' the north-east was never for her. She's a lass o' the west winds and I often wonder if I did right bringing her here.'

She spun round suddenly, her beautiful amber-green eyes

bright with unshed tears. 'Tell her I'll be up – I've had a lot to do here since Evie went to work to Rothiedrum and wee Col needs me so much – but, oh, I'm sorry, I should never have neglected Jeannie.'

She rushed past him, through to the hallway and up the stairs to her cold attic bedroom. The banging of the door seemed to reverberate through the house. Kenneth Mor shrugged his great shoulders and then went to seek the less complicated companionship of the men at the kitchen fire.

The snowclad plains of Rothiedrum stretched as far as the eye could see, broken only by little woods and the snaking march of twisted black hedges and grey dykes. Evelyn climbed with Col and Nellie up the track to Knobblieknowe which stood silhouetted gauntly against the sky, with the barn mill a little way off and the cornyard on a knoll where the wind could get at the ricks. The bracing air brought a sparkle to Evelyn's face and she took deep breaths as she trudged upwards, all the while repressing terrible urges to gather handfuls of snow and hurl them at Nellie. If it had been Mary or Grace she wouldn't have thought twice about it, but she could not recall a time when Nellie had allowed abandonment to overrule sober restraint and she dared not take any liberties now, with Nellie plodding silently along, keeping to the middle of the track, coat hem held slightly aloft to keep it dry, looking as if that and the placing of her trim, black-booted feet on the least slippery ground were the things uppermost in her mind. But Evelyn knew better. She saw the tension in the clenched jaw, the apprehension in the amber eyes.

That same look had been there two days ago after Kenneth Mor's visit, and she was too offhand when she had said to Evelyn, 'You're due an afternoon off soon, Evie. Will you spend it wi' me up yonder at Knobblieknowe? I'd like fine to see Jeannie and Col is always asking to go up and visit Cal.'

Evelyn had opened her mouth to argue that Nellie had never before needed to make an issue out of visiting Knobblieknowe, but then she remembered the things

Grace had confided and she had looked at Nellie and seen the embarrassment lying deep in her eyes. 'Ay, Nellie, I'd like that fine,' she had nodded. 'It's a good while since I saw Jeannie and the baby must be growing big and bonny by now.'

She was glad that she had said she would come. It was so good to be out in the open air after being cooped up in the heat of Rothiedrum's kitchens. As she scrunched over the bridge, listening to the muted purling of the burn, noting the great expanse of white lying under the sombre grey sky, a euphoria gripped her being. The war seemed very far away up here among the hills where only the clouds warred with each other and the buck hares, wearing winter coats of purest white, boxed at one another playfully behind the gorse bushes.

Seizing Col's hand she swung it high, and bending down to his upturned face she said laughingly, 'Did you know that the witches o' Knobblieknowe bide here, Col? In amongst the bushes under the bridge? That's why Kenneth Mor planted the rowan trees there, to keep the old witches at bay, but even so they sometimes come dancing out and away they go leaping, over the corries on the hill, their skinny wee black legs fairly birling along while they scraich and skirl at one another in high-pitched grousy old voices.'

Col's dreamy blue eyes shone. 'Witches,' he grinned, and nodded as if he understood every word. He and Evelyn often played the 'witches game', and he loved every magic word she used to describe the fairies and witches of the north-east lowlands. Often, he would repeat the most favoured words under his breath, nodding and smiling as he did so, for there was no fear in his world, only a shining trust in those around him.

'Evie!' Nellie rebuked sharply. 'You'll frighten the bairn wi' all that silly nonsense. You've listened far too much to that old de'il Coulter and now you're every bit as bad as he is.'

For answer, Evelyn swung Col's hand higher. 'Swing him, Nellie. He loved it when me and Johnny used to do it. Up to the sky he used to shout – didn't you, Col?'

'Up sky,' the little boy nodded eagerly, and gave an impatient tug at Nellie's sleeve. As always she responded to his request, and she and Evelyn swung him between them till the laughter bubbled out of his throat and his golden-red hair blew back in the wind. He was small and light for his age and for the rest of the way they swung him so that he leapt and slithered along. By the time they reached Knobblieknowe they were all pink-faced and laughing, and though the hem of Nellie's coat was soaked she either didn't notice or didn't care.

Calum Alasdair Cameron, otherwise known as Cal, came running over the yard to meet them, a handsome sturdy boy with eyes and hair almost the same colour as Col's. The boys had been born within days of one another and for a time had been known as the December Twins, but only a few called them that now. Cal had the same strong physique as his father, the same hearty booming laugh. Both shared like characteristics of strength coupled with a sweetness of nature. From the beginning Kenneth's son had loved and protected Col, and it was oddly touching to see how patiently Cal explained things to the other, how he rejoiced at all of Col's small achievements and how his loyalties had never waned even after he had entered the bigger world of school. He told Col about things he had learned, drew pictures for him, guided his hand over big coloured letters of the alphabet, and though Col never appeared to absorb much of it, it was enough for Cal to hear the infectious joy in the voice of his small, flawed friend and to see the trust shining out of the big dreamy eyes.

They greeted each other rapturously and went off to the barn to see some new kittens, leaving Nellie and Evelyn to make their way into the house.

Knobblieknowe's kitchen was a place of friendly warmth and savoury smells and Nellie gazed around with silent appreciation.

Katie Menzies, the kitchen maid, was there with Isla Nell, a beautiful doll of a child with her mother's enormous brown eyes and glossy black curls clustered round a heart-shaped face. At sight of the visitors the dimples deepened in her satin-textured cheeks and her pearly teeth flashed, though she promptly turned away shyly and stuck her thumb into her mouth.

Katie, a cheery-looking girl with big buxom breasts and thighs, clicked her tongue and banged a rolling pin vigorously over a round of dough on the table. 'She's been fretful wi' her mither laid up and me too busy to pay her much attention. She's a good wee soul, but Dyod! she gets under my feet all day long and wants to follow me everywhere – even to the wee hoose and would sit in there wi' me if I'd let her.' She ran a floury hand over her brow and banged the rolling pin with even more emphasis on the table. 'It's too much. I'm no' paid to be a nursemaid and that Cal is supposed to be off school wi' the cold, yet he's up fleein' around, no' too ill to shift muckle plates o' food and steal the scones the meenit my back is turned.'

Nellie ignored the complaining monologue and went to pluck Isla off the rug and into her arms. The little girl surveyed her shyly. 'Nellie.' She spoke the name gladly, savouring the sound of it on her tongue.

'Ay, Nellie's here.' She kissed the small warm face. 'And Nellie needs a good skelpit leathering for staying away all this time. We'll go up and see your mother together, but you must be quieter than a wee mouse for she's no' too well the now.'

Evelyn followed them, marvelling as she always did at the change which came over her sister when she was dealing with children. They had the capacity to pluck everything that was loving and good from the depths of her soul. With them she smiled and sang, and underwent a metamorphosis from a shrewish, hard-tongued woman to a soft-spoken, feminine girl with love shining from her face.

Katie had left her battered dough to watch them ascending the stairs, only the tip of her nose and her eyes peeping round the door post. She and Evelyn had gone to school together and Evelyn retained cherished memories of Katie's roguish and highly exaggerated accounts of her exploits with boys of all ages, including one episode in which sedate, earnest Martin Gregory had supposedly kept her in after school with the sole purpose of seducing her behind the blackboard. Impishly, Evelyn stuck out her tongue at Katie and stifled her giggles as the gesture was promptly returned. Evelyn hesitated, torn between a desire to spend some time in Katie's lighthearted company and the wish to see Jeannie. An uneasiness had seized her the minute she left the kitchen to go upstairs. She felt as if something was tugging at her, an inner self that rebelled against facing more sickness . . . it was as if she was re-enacting her time with Florrie . . . and she wasn't ready to face all that again. But she shrugged off her feeling of depression and went up slowly in Nellie's wake.

Jeannie looked small and frail in the big feather bed, a girl yet at twenty-four, black hair streaming about her slight shoulders, the darkness of her eyes emphasized by the pallor of her thin, tired face. Two spots of hectic colour burned high on each cheekbone and neither Evelyn nor Nellie needed a doctor to tell them that Kenneth Mor's wife was very ill.

At sight of Nellie, her eyes lit and she struggled to sit up. 'Nell! Och, Nell, you've come! At last you've come,' she cried gladly.

Guilt flooded Nellie's being. She had allowed her own selfish feelings to come between her and the only woman friend she had ever loved or needed. The terrible shame of that almost tore her in two as she went to the bed and took Jeannie's burning hands in hers.

'I'm sorry, Jeannie. I – well – I've been busy but I should have made time for you,' she faltered lamely. 'But I'm here now and you'll no' get rid o' me in a hurry. I'll see to you, Jeannie, and I'll take Isla home wi' me and come every day to visit you and Cal.'

Jeannie lay back, spent with the effort of sitting up. Her breath was short and rapid, weak tears filled her eyes at Nellie's words.

'There's no need for you to come up every day, Nell,' she whispered. 'But I would be awful grateful if you would take the babby. She's been lost this whilie back and will be fine wi' you. Both my bairns love and trust you and I'll get

77

better the quicker knowing the wee one is in good hands. Auld Hinney sprachled up a few times to see me but she couldna bring the trap through the snow, and it's a fair trek at her age.'

'Wheesht, Jeannie, wheesht,' soothed Nellie, 'you mustna worry any more.'

Evelyn had retired to a seat at the fire to read the letter she had received that morning from Gillan.

*'This is rather different from the school Training Cadets,' he wrote, 'and I thought that was hard work. I fall into bed at night, too tired even to dream of you, Princess, but I manage to slip you into the odd spare moments in my day so that I've been labelled here as a bit of a dark horse. I'm determined to get into the Gordons if I can. Father knows it's a combat regiment and I know he will start trying to pull a few strings. He has influential friends in the Government and in the military and will do his damnedest to get me a staff job. But I'm having none of it. The days of coddling little Gillie are over. I'm my own man now and have become every bit as stubborn as yourself!! I can say that in a letter without fear of you warming my ears for me.*

*This is on the Q.T. but I think some changes are in the offing for Rothiedrum House. Mother is bursting with all sorts of plans at the moment and has never been happier. I can't say more except to tell you not to worry. Father likes you and will see to it that your position at Rothiedrum will remain secure.*

*Take care and goodnight, Princess. Yours as always, Gillie.*
*xxx*

Evelyn folded the letter and put it back in her pocket, a smile hovering at her lips. She loved those letters from Gillie. He was so forthright about everything, so much his own man now, so different from the shy, hesitant Gillie of old. She wondered what he meant about plans for Rothiedrum but had no time to ponder the matter.

'Evie, go down and make us a cuppy,' Nellie ordered imperiously. 'I'll bide here wi' Jeannie and the bairn.'

On the way downstairs Evelyn almost collided with Gregor making his way up. His boots and trouser bottoms were snow-caked for it was impossible to get a vehicle of any sort up Knobblieknowe's track, but he was only slightly out of breath and looked fresh and vigorous. Evelyn found herself thinking how deprived the parish would be if he took himself off to France. Mary, perhaps sensing her youngest sister's feelings on the matter, hadn't broached the subject again and Evelyn wondered if he himself had reached any sort of decision.

He read her thoughts. 'Ay, Evie, I'm going, but no' for a while yet. First I have to find out if the army will take me then I have to find a good, retired doctor, fit enough and willing enough to take my place for as long as need be – so don't look so worried, lassie.'

'Someone has to,' she said briefly, inwardly cursing Mary and her lax attitude to such a momentous issue. 'If you were my husband I wouldna let you go so easily.'

He grinned at her. 'You're angry at your sister. Don't be. Mary is Mary and nothing will change her and I thank God for that. She's maybe gotten a wee bittie above herself this whilie back but a spell with a crotchety, demanding old G.P. will soon cure her of that. For she'll have to see to him, you know. Cook for him and clean for him and do all the things she does for me.' He winked. 'And with none of the little rewards that a loving husband would give. I don't intend to get myself maimed or killed, Evie, and before I'm halfway through Mary will be writing me letters begging me to come home.'

'You're no' going away just for that, surely?'

He laughed. 'Hell, no, lassie! Mary and I love one another and always have. Absence could never make our hearts any fonder than they are now. In a way I'm glad she's no' the clinging, weepy sort o' woman. You see, Evie, I really want to go and do my bit as Mary calls it. She knows it and won't try to stop me. That's love, Evie, to let your man have his way once in a while.'

She smiled at him. 'You're a bonny talker, Gregor McGregor, you've convinced me. I'll bring you a cuppy

79

when you're ready. Go on up, Nellie's there with Jeannie and the baby.'

'Nellie.' He gave a mock groan and drew a finger across his throat, emitting a strangulated sound which made her giggle as she went on down into the kitchen, where she found Katie with her feet up at the fire drinking tea. She was in a companionable mood and only too eager to talk to Evelyn on the subject of former romantic conquests.

'But they're thin on the ground now, Evie,' she said, staring morosely at a tea leaf floating in her cup. 'Look, there's one! Short and fairish but well built wi' good muscles. I used to believe the teacups. I mind once I had three assorted tea leaves swimmin' in my cup and sure enough, the whole jing bang o' them came to me one by one frae the chaumer. One was a first horseman, no less, a chancy chiel too but no match for the ploughman who came next, and *him* no match for the orra loon at that time. Barely seventeen he was, but Dyod! built like an ox wi' all the equipment to go wi' it—' She sighed heavily and scooped the tea leaf from her cup to flick it into the fire. 'The war's taken them all, Evie, all over the airts there's cauld beds and caulder bums – and in this weather too,' she ended indignantly.

Evelyn's eyes flashed as she refilled the teapot and put it to warm on the hob. 'You could always try wishful thinking, Katie, you seem very good at that.'

'Cheeky wee whittrock!' Katie was up, bosoms heaving as she gathered her skirts and chased Evelyn out into the snow, where the pair of them dropped all reserve and enjoyed a good going snow fight, soon joined by Col and Cal and two of the younger sheepdogs.

Gregor frowned slightly as he held Jeannie's wrist between his fingers. Removing his stethoscope he stuffed it into his bag, but remained seated at the edge of the bed. 'Right, young lady,' he smiled at Jeannie, noting her over-bright eyes, the dew of sweat on her upper lip. 'You'll be fine if you stay in bed and keep warm. I'll get Katie to come up and make up the fire. It's cold in here and you mustn't allow yourself to become chilled. You have a bad dose of flu but with rest and care you'll be better in no time. I'll be back whenever I can manage.' He patted her hand and went to the door where Nellie was hovering with Isla in her arms. 'You needna worry about her, Greg,' she told her brother-in-law firmly, 'I'm taking the babby down to King's Croft but I'll be up here every day till Jeannie gets better.'

He glanced back into the room. Jeannie was lying with her eyes closed but she was restless and unsettled. 'She needs all the care she can get, Nell, Jeannie was never very strong and this is a bad flu. She's very fevered and her pulse is fast which is normal enough with a fever, but in her case there's an irregular beat to it which I don't like. It's good o' you to take the bairn, I know you have a busy life.'

She coloured under his keen scrutiny. 'It's the least I can do – I – well I've neglected her a bittie this good whilie back.' She frowned as sounds of merriment drifted up from outside. 'That Evie! I sent her to make tea and she's out there frolicking like a bairn.'

'She is a bairn.' Jeannie opened her eyes and inclined her head towards the window.

'If I had the energy I'd be out there wi' her. I used to love playing in the snow and still do when no one's looking.'

At that moment Evelyn came upstairs panting and rosy, a tea tray in her hands, Col and Cal at her heels. 'I waited till I thought you'd be finished up here,' she said with a quick look at Nellie, who snorted and put out her hand to restrain the boys who were all for barging into the bedroom. 'Downstairs the lot o' you and take your tea in the kitchen. I'll have mine up here wi' Greg and Jeannie.'

There came a sound like a tornado from below as Kenneth Mor burst in, never halting in his rush but coming straight upstairs, his damp kilt swinging about his knees, hair and beard glistening with melting snowflakes. Seeing the crowd on the landing he paused and laughed his big booming laugh, his sweeping glance taking in all the faces but coming to rest on Nellie's whose hands he took in a huge, heartfelt grasp. 'Nell, you've come then,' he said simply but with such gratitude she coloured again, the crimson rushing up over her neck to her face as she outlined her plans for Isla and Jeannie.

'Ach, Nell, you're a good friend,' he told her warmly, and turning to the doctor, 'and Greg, trekking up here in this weather. I came in to see how Jeannie was, but finding you all here I know she's in the best o' hands.'

'Kenneth.' Jeannie's voice came quiet and warm from the bed, a light shining in her eyes at sight of the big red-haired Highlander who was her husband. 'Stop your blethers and come and have a cuppy wi' me. I'm that thirsty I could drink the whole o' Loch Bree in one gulp yet never slake my thirst.' In two strides he was at her bedside, gathering her into his arms and pressing his lips to her hair. Nellie turned away quickly, but not quickly enough to hide her look of longing from Evelyn who was standing quiet and observant just inside the bedroom door.

For the next few days Nellie was never away from Knobblieknowe, while little Isla remained at King's Croft and played happily with Col and the animals on the rug by the kitchen fire. The Loon, having heard about the troubles at Knobblieknowe, chanced into King's Croft frequently on the pretext of asking after Jeannie, though Maggie knew fine he only came by to play with the children. He loved childish play and childish games did The Loon, and never missed a chance to be in the thick of them if he could. Maggie didn't mind his visits even though his big clairty feet left trails of slush on her clean kitchen floor. He was good with the children, giving them 'coaly backs' and 'donkey rides' till they were more exhausted than he, and eventually glad to sit quiet by the fire while The Loon told them stories in his bubbly soft voice. Coulter too was a regular visitor, and between them he and The Loon kept the children well amused with games and fairy tales.

Only Jamie seemed discontent and aimless at that time. He fretted morosely around the croft, his stubby pipe hanging from his mouth, one eye on the winter parks smothered under successive falls of heavy snow.

The weather had worsened that week with the wind

keening low over the plains, shrieking across the moors, soughing round the steadings and moaning like a banshee down the lums. Each day, more and more thick yellow-grey clouds piled over the hills, heavily pregnant with snow and hail which blattered off the rooftops and mercilessly pelted exposed flesh till the sting of it seemed sprung from some deep, raw wound.

In long-ago days Maggie had never minded the north-east winters. She had been born to them. They were as much a part of her existence as sleeping or breathing but now they incurred an unease in her, an echo of the restlessness the enforced winter idleness brought to the men of the farmtouns. Over the years it had become more pronounced in Jamie, for he was a man who revelled in hard work even though that often brought him more pain than pleasure with little financial reward to counter the hardship.

A cobbler by trade, he had continued after his marriage to make shoes for the rich folk of the area. It had supplemented his income, had helped to keep his family warm and fed, and when the north-east winters had closed in he had turned to his craft with willing vigour. But his strength had waned with the passing years along with his enthusiasm, and now his lasts and hammer lay dusty and forgotten in the little shed he had proudly christened his 'shoppe'. The only time he ever went there now was to tune and play his fiddle in sombre quietude and more often than not to seek guilty solace in the bottle.

Nellie was the only one of the Grant girls to lose patience openly with her father. The rest had far too much respect and love for him to hurt him with harsh words, but Nellie was frank to the point of brutality. The incident with Whisky Jake had brought all her old feelings of mistrust and bitterness flooding back, so that she was inclined to pick on her father for the least thing and to snap at him if he so much as put one foot wrong.

'What's gotten into you, girl?' Maggie asked one morning. 'You're worse than ever of late and I will not stand back and listen to you demeaning your father.'

'I dinna have to do that, Mother,' Nellie retorted with a meaningful look at Jamie sitting quiet and pale at the fire after a night of hard drinking. 'He's perfectly capable of demeaning himself. You have to respect yourself before other people can respect you.'

She flounced away outside to meet Tandy, who had courteously called to help her up the steep brae to Knobblieknowe. The farmhands had cleared the track of a fresh overnight snowfall but even so it was treacherous underfoot, and for once Nellie was glad to lean on the rocklike arm of the man who so often goaded her to fury with his teasing remarks regarding her unmarried state.

With a sigh Maggie watched them go before turning to Jamie with a kind of desperation in her glance. 'Have you nothing to do but sit at the fire dreaming?' she said more sharply than she meant. 'You used to make such bonny shoes,' she continued in a softer tone. 'If you started again it would while away the winter days. It's a pity to let a good thing go to waste.'

Slowly he arose, taking time to straighten as if his muscles needed to adjust to the effort, deliberately lingering by the fire to tap his pipe out on the bars of the grate. 'Maggie, Maggie,' he chided gently. 'There are no customers left – the folk from the big houses have dwindled away or have forgotten me altogether.'

'Ach, stop feeling sorry for yourself!' She was goaded to sharp reply. 'Souter Jock has got plenty to keep him going and so have his like the length and breadth o' the country. There's plenty keeping themselves busy since the start o' the war – and customers enough for everybody if you stop to think about it, Jamie,' she added meaningfully.

He took his relit pipe from his mouth, and looked at Maggie as if he were seeing her for the first time in years. She was a magnetic woman, this wife of his. Because of her, life revolved sweetly both in and out of the croft, and he knew then as he had always known that without her determined influence none of them might have survived the precarious existence of the crofting life. She was his supporting pillar, and a new awareness of her womanly strength crept over him. The darkness of his eyes deepened, and under the heavy Kitchener a half-smile crooked the corner of his mouth. Reaching out to the hook on the door, he took down his heavy tweed jacket and shrugged himself into it before going out on to the porch to don his boots. 'I'm away out to sort the beasts,' he said, as if somehow he had to escape the deep and enormous faith she had in him, which never seemed to waver despite the hardships her life with him had placed upon her. Turning on his heel he went abruptly outside. From the window she watched him walk heavily over the slushy cobbles, the spring in his step only a memory, yet something about the lift of his shoulders brought a small hope to her heart.

The children were squealing with mirth from the fireside, the baby Isla guiding Col's hands into a bag of flour which she had lifted from the table as soon as Maggie's back was turned.

'You wee besom!' Maggie rushed to rescue the precious flour, but it was too late – children and animals were already covered in white dust. At Maggie's hurried approach the dog rolled over on his back and beat his tail on the floor, sending clouds of flour into the air; the cat sneezed thrice before stalking disdainfully away, tail held stiffly erect; Col giggled; Isla showed her white teeth in a cherubic smile.

Maggie straightened, clutching the depleted bag to her breast. A familiar sound beat against her eardrums, familiar yet lost in the mists of memory, its rhythm recalling to mind times of half-sleep when that self-same sound had drummed against the black velvet of night. It was like her own heart beating, beating, insistent and real.

Going to the door she opened it and stood, listening. A smile touched her wide, attractive mouth. The dull ringing of metal striking metal filtered through the frosty air from the shoppe. It was a glad sound, the sound of a cobbler testing a long-disused hammer against a dusty, almost forgotten shoe last.

# CHAPTER SIX

Grace came home for Christmas, a sparkling, lovely Grace, face aglow with happiness and life, better looking than anyone had ever seen her. Evelyn didn't need to ask any questions to know that her sister's love for Doctor Gordon Chisholm was no longer a secret, hidden thing.

On the evening of her arrival she and Evelyn went to bed early, and once they were safely in their room Grace threw herself on her bed and cried, 'Oh, Evie, I'm so happy. I feel like – like running outside and dancing in the snow!'

'We'll do that tomorrow,' laughed Evelyn. 'First I want to hear all your news – and that includes your love life.'

'Right.' Grace got off the bed and, taking her sister's hands, did a joyous little dance with her round the room.

'Are you two trying to make holes in the floor?' Nellie popped her head round the door, a smile on her face for Grace, the sister who incurred the least of her wrath. Murn too came into the room, eager to share the aura of happiness that Grace always seemed to bring with her to King's Croft. They all loved the sweet, gentle girl who had always healed more than she had hurt, both mentally and physically.

The beds were divested of their blankets; each sister wrapped herself in one and then they arranged themselves cosily together on top of Grace's bed. They chattered for at least an hour, though no one mentioned affairs of the heart. Grace's love was too new for that, Nellie's too well hidden, Evelyn's too sore and uncertain. Only Murn wore her heart on her sleeve, but even she knew that her adoration of Kenneth Mor was a useless emotion and she seldom spoke of him now. But when at last they decided it was time for bed, Murn turned at the door and said softly to Grace, 'Of us all you're going to be the one with an uncomplicated love affair. The rest o' us dinna ken which way to turn in life – no' even Evie, young as she is.'

86

'She says daft things, doesn't she?' Evelyn said a trifle uncomfortably, after she had gone.

Grace looked thoughtful. 'Murn has always been a strange sort o' lass. She watches people a lot and takes in more than any o' us will ever know. I don't think she's ever been truly happy. She tries too hard to get things out o' life – and somehow she never gets any o' the things she really wants.'

'She'll never get Kenneth Mor, that's for sure.'

'No, nor will Nellie – yet, if things had been different he would have chosen her before Murn.'

'Nellie?' Evelyn questioned doubtfully.

'Ay, in many ways he and she are suited. He always got on well wi' her – long before she ever knew she was in love wi' him, and where Nellie's concerned that's quite an achievement.'

'Ach, forget about them just now.' Evelyn was rushing into her night things, not bothering to do up fiddly things like buttons in her haste to dive into Grace's bed which was nicely warm from its recent occupancy. 'It's you I want to hear about. You promised you would tell me everything.'

'I will.' A glint showed in Grace's dark eyes. 'If you tell me whose ring that is you're wearing round your neck.'

Evelyn's hand shot up to her neck almost guiltily but then she smiled. 'Who said Murn was the only one to notice things? Come on then, get into bed before your bit gets cold.'

They cooried under the blankets, snuggling against each other as they had done since they were tiny children, and in the deep silence of the night they whispered the innermost secrets of their hearts.

The sisters all went Christmas shopping in Aberdeen together, and in Bert's Tea Shoppe in Cobbly Wynd they met Doctor Gordon Chisholm. Evelyn felt strange going back to the place which for her contained such sweet memories of that brief meeting with the young soldier. It was such a familiar place, yet for her it would never be the same again. The old men and women were still there,

87

sitting on the bench opposite the tea shop smoking their clay pipes as they nodded and spat on the cobbles and huddled into their layers of winter clothing; the trees were bare now but couthy and well loved in their time-worn setting; the boots of working men still sent sparks flying from the worn cobbles; the cart wheels rumbled; the cold sharp smell of the North Sea pervaded the air. It was a public place for everybody to share, but to Evelyn it was a private little haven and she resented its invasion, even by members of her own family. But the feeling was short-lived. Bert winked at her as she went in and she winked back, putting a finger to her lips and smiling to herself at the idea of sharing a conspiracy with the bald-headed, cheerful little man.

Gordon Chisholm was as Grace had described him. Not good-looking in the usual sense, but attractive in his own way with keen grey eyes and a full, aesthetic mouth. His was a serious countenance and one might have expected a like personality until his dazzling smile flashed out, lighting his eyes with roguish good humour. In every sense he was a presence, the kind of man who attracted attention without seeking it. He wasn't so much tall as broad, a big bear of a creature who dwarfed even Nellie, the tallest of the Grant girls. His was a commanding personality yet he was gentle, considerate and every inch a gentleman.

He sat in their midst, drinking tea and eating hot buttered scones, and within five minutes had won the sisters over by making each one feel a special individual. He was well versed on a variety of subjects and spoke to the young women about the things that most interested them. He had that knack of drawing the best from people, so that even Nellie responded to him with a warmth that made Murn look at her in surprise.

'Of course, I have an advantage,' he smiled, taking Grace's hand and squeezing it gently. 'This lass is full of talk about her home and family. I feel I know King's Croft very well indeed and the folk who bide in it even better.'

'You must come and have a meal with us,' Nellie told him at the door. 'It will no' be anything fancy of course, but better to take us as we are without a lot o' fuss.'

'I couldn't agree with you more, Nellie, and I would love to come and meet the rest of the family. And don't think I'm in any way above myself. I was born in a kitchen in Edinburgh and am as proud of my beginnings as you are of yours.'

A shadow darkened the door and there was Whisky Jake, leering at Nellie, eyeing her from head to foot, licking his thick lips in a suggestive fashion before moving on without uttering a word. Nellie recoiled as if she had been struck, crimson stained her cheekbones, fear lay stark in her eyes, and Gordon put a steadying hand on her arm as he asked quietly, 'What ails you, Nellie? That man? Do you know him?'

'You could say that,' she whispered; then, with a toss of her head she was herself again, straight-backed, proud, her lowered eyes hiding their secrets from the world. Gordon looked at her for a moment as if hoping that she might say more, but she turned away and he didn't pursue the subject.

'I'm glad you and Grace got together at last,' Evelyn told him when she had him to herself for a moment. 'If you dinna mind me saying so you took your time about it.'

He smiled and ran a hand through his thick black mop, a habit of his and one which caused his hair to be in a constant state of disarray. It gave him away as being basically a shy man and this more than anything endeared him to Evelyn.

'You're the frank one of the family,' he told her with a twinkle. 'The truth of the matter is I had no idea that such a beautiful girl as your sister could possibly see anything in a sedate creature like myself. I simply couldn't pluck up the courage to ask her to go out with me and nearly fell over backwards when she accepted my eventual invitation.'

He put out one huge arm to draw Grace close to him. She looked delicate and insubstantial caught up in his embrace. He was obviously besotted by her, and had the look of a man still bemused by the fact that such a young and lovely creature could possibly return his feelings.

They parted in the best of spirits, Grace to make her way home with her sisters, Gordon Chisholm to take his reluctant leave and plod up the hill back to the hospital.

89

'You'll have to tell Martin Gregory about him,' Murn said as they stood watching the doctor's dark, retreating figure. 'You canna allow two men to entertain high hopes of you, Grace.'

Evelyn fancied a certain amount of jealous resentment in Murn's tones, and she was so annoyed at her sister for voicing such thoughts that she gave her a sharp little kick on the shin.

'Besom,' hissed Murn, but in such a subdued voice that Evelyn knew she was sorry for bringing a look of worry to Grace's hitherto happy face.

'I ken that fine, Murn,' she said in a small voice, 'and I will tell Martin, I promise I will.'

But she couldn't bring herself to take away Martin's happiness at having her back at Rothiedrum. Since her return he had haunted King's Croft, eyes alight that were usually sad and dull. There was something mournful about Martin Gregory. He had lost his wife in childbirth and had never gotten over that loss. Only Grace had the power to reach the hurt depths of him, only she seemed able to make him laugh and raise up his head in thankfulness for everything that her youth and sweetness promised. Yet she had never indicated that her attachment to him was anything more than just an honest friendship given with all the generosity of her compassionate heart. She had still been a child in school when he had lost his wife, a little girl sitting in his classroom watching him with her big black eyes as he filled her head with wisdom. She was still only twenty-two while he was well into his forties, though with her he seemed to throw off the maturity of his years and become youthful again.

And so Grace walked with him through the virginal countryside, talked with him by the winter hearth, listened to him with quiet attentiveness, allowed him to hold her hand and put his arm around her shoulders, because to rebuff him would have appeared petty and childish and would have hurt him more than her kindly heart could have borne.

And all the time he never attributed the change in her to anything other than well-being. She was sparkling, brimming over with the joy of living, her eyes and her face shone with happiness. He told her she was more lovely than he ever remembered and a voice inside her cried, 'Oh dear God! Does he think it's because of him? Don't look at me like that, Martin. I can never return your love. I'm sorry for you, you're my dear, dear friend but that is all you can ever be to me.'

Once she turned to him and said, 'Martin, I must talk to you, I must tell you of the things I feel—'

But he had placed a finger upon her lips and said, 'Shush, my dear, dear girl. We must talk, I know, but it can wait. There are things to be done first and then we will talk and talk and talk.'

She hadn't wanted to question his meaning. There was an intensity about him that frightened her and she had led him onto lighter subjects, away, far away from the dangers engendered by affairs of the heart.

'You havena told him yet – about Gordon Chisholm?' Evelyn said one night as they were getting ready for bed.

Grace turned away. 'No, I canna hurt him, Evie. He looks to me for a bit o' comfort in his life and I'm no' strong enough to rob him of that. Sometimes I wish I was more like Nellie or Murn. They say what they think and dinna mind who they hurt and while that may be kinder in the long run I never had it in me to be so direct.'

Evelyn picked up the brush and began to run it through Grace's bright chestnut hair, her eyes seeking and meeting the other's in the mirror. 'Nellie has invited Gordon here for a meal. What if Martin and he come face to face?'

'Then Martin will have to be told,' Grace said miserably. 'And I'll wish to God I might never have been born.'

But Gordon and Martin never met, Grace made sure of that. With three days to go to Christmas she suggested to Martin that he ought to go and visit his aged mother in Dundee, and so he went, wishing to the last that she would come with him but accepting with good grace her pleas of having too much to do within her own family circle.

'And that's that, Grace Margaret Grant,' she told herself guiltily as she waved him goodbye, and turned out of the station to meet Gordon and travel with him back to Rothiedrum.

He brought gifts for everyone, a marvellous big Santa Claus of a man, sweeping Col up in one arm and jogging him round a room which seemed suddenly filled with light and life and an atmosphere of such love it spread out to embrace everyone. For Doctor Gordon Chisholm was in love. It shone in his eyes, echoed in his deep happy laughter, oozed volumes over Grace at whom he looked at frequently over everyone's heads.

The meal was a happy family affair. Nellie had come down early from Knobblieknowe, worried about Jeannie but soon caught up in the aura of Gordon Chisholm's presence. Mary and Gregor had come over from Rowanlea and the two doctors immediately became the best of friends, retiring after dinner to chat quietly in a corner of the room.

'He's a fine man, Grace.' Jamie put his arm round his daughter's shoulders and drew her close. 'I doubt you'll no' find better.' He cleared his throat and went on quietly, 'It's your business, I know, but Martin deserves to be told how things stand between you and him. He's been a patient man all these years.'

Grace bit her lip. 'I know, Father, God how I know! But – there's nothing yet for me to tell. I'm only just getting to know Gordon, nothing's been said. It's far too early in the day.'

Jamie squeezed her shoulder. 'He loves you, lass, that's plain for all to see – he's a man wi' a light burning inside o' him, and it shines for you, lassie, just for you.'

Grace said nothing. Her love for Gordon Chisholm was too deep to express in mere words, but the devotion she felt for Martin Gregory had been a part of her life so long that she couldn't forsake him as if he had never been. She was torn in two, love for one man encompassing her heart, compassion for another searing into her gentle soul.

She looked at Gordon. He and Gregor were engrossed in quiet talk. Their faces were serious and she knew the subject of their conversation. What did all men talk about when they got together these days? War. War! War!

A snatch of words drifted to her ears. She was right; it was about war. Gordon looked up and caught her eye. His smile lit up his face. She didn't smile back. A cold little prickle of apprehension touched her spine and remained with her for the rest of the evening.

Kenneth Mor had cut a little fir tree and placed it in a corner of the kitchen for Cal and Katie to decorate with any little shiny pieces they could find.

Wee Col came up for tea on Christmas Eve and Kenneth carried Jeannie down to the kitchen fire despite her protests that she was fine able to walk. But she wasn't. She was far too weak. Her pale face turned towards the plains of Rothiedrum smothered in layers of sparkling white. The snowstorms had abated. The sky was a pure, cold blue merging into pale gold on the horizon. It was a beautiful Christmas. Everyone said so, not least Jeannie.

'It's so bonny, the nicest Christmas I've ever seen.' She clasped her thin hands to her mouth and coughed. Over her head Kenneth looked at Nellie and she saw fear in his eyes.

On Boxing Day, the entire Grant family travelled to the Aulton to visit Grandmother and Aunt Mattie. The old lady had dressed up for the occasion. Following strict instructions Mattie had encased the frail old body in rustling black silk, scuffed in places but hardly so one noticed, so dazzling was the general effect created by beads and bows and a wonderfully showy velvet black hat, decorated with enormous birds' wings dyed a shocking pink. Attached to the hat were long, streaming silk ribbons tied in a large bow under the old lady's wizened, whiskery chin. The whole ensemble was gaudily offset by a pair of bright pink pantaloons with fuzzy wool bedsocks to match, which looked for all the world like a pair of baby bootees so small were the feet that they enclosed.

'Maggie, Maggie!' she cried, greeting them all in a voice high-pitched with excitement. 'I had Mattie do me up special for Christmas. Say how awful I look right away and be done wi' it, and dinna forget to notice I wore my teeth so I can smile at you all quick before I put them back under my pillow.'

Maggie gathered the old lady to her bosom while Jamie winked at Mattie and remarked with a chuckle, 'I'm no' surprised you dinna have a Christmas tree. Grandmother would outshine any ornament in the land and still have enough glitter left to light the way to fairyland.'

It was a happy reunion, made happier still by the arrival of Gordon Chisholm. Grandmother hailed him with pleasure, and when she discovered he was a doctor she clung to him like a leech to a leg for the rest of his visit.

Without preliminary he sat on the bed beside her. They made an incongruous pair, he so big and vigorously healthy, she so dainty and little and old. She told him tales of her travelling days, bringing Aunt Mattie and Jamie into the colourful descriptions of her youth. The years rolled away and they became children again, with holes in their socks and gaps in their teeth.

Mattie bustled about, dispensing bowls of steaming broth and large, flat floury rolls filled with best mutton. She too had dressed for the occasion. Her great feather pillow of a breast was becomingly happed in a gypsy-style blouse, which was tucked into a large black skirt so generous in its proportions that little Donald took the opportunity to creep beneath its layers and pop his head out the front as if he was surveying an audience from a set of stage curtains.

'That lad has ambition,' observed Gordon Chisholm, in such a droll voice that Grandmother leaned back on her pillows and went off into one of her cackling outbursts of merriment which were so infectious that everyone joined in whether they had heard the joke or not.

But for Nellie and Jamie the day was spoiled by the arrival of Whisky Jake, who had consumed just enough drams to fire his natural belligerence.

'Well, well, fancy all this,' he commented as he came in the door. 'How did I ken all my favourite folk would be gathered here the day, eh? Come on now, Mattie, how about a festive kiss for old Jake and I'll hae one from my dear old Grannie as well.'

Both Mattie and Grandmother sourly evaded his attentions, and thus thwarted he turned them on Nellie, leering at her knowingly and dropping one heavy eyelid in a mocking wink. 'My, my.' He rubbed his hands vigorously together. 'What rare beauties you spawned, Jamie lad. If any o' you quines cares to join the queue I'd be only too happy to favour ye wi' a kiss. I was aye renowned for my affectionate nature – is that no' right, Nell lass?'

Maggie was staring at the new arrival as if unable to believe her eyes. She hadn't seen Whisky Jake for years. She had never liked nor trusted him but had put up with him for the sake of peace, though she had found it hard to ignore the lewd suggestions he had made to her out of Jamie's hearing.

She had thought him gone out of their lives forever and now here he was, large as life and twice as repugnant. He had always liked young girls and he was eyeing her daughters – particularly Nellie – in a way which made Maggie shudder and glance inquiringly at Jamie.

But he turned away from her questioning gaze – and so too did Nellie – and Maggie's suspicions were strengthened that father and daughter shared some dark secret which had somehow poisoned their relationship with one another. And it had been something momentous, perhaps the thing that lay at the root of Nellie's mistrust and dislike of men in general.

She began to wonder too why Jake and Jamie had so suddenly lost sight of one another all these years ago. She had been too relieved at the time to question it, but as soon as they got home that night she faced Jamie point blank with it.

He turned away from her and blew out the candle. 'Jake's a wandering man, Maggie. He could never settle in any one place for long and he couldna thole it when I married and put down roots. We outgrew one another, lass. He was never my sort anyway, a good laugh at the time but no one can build a friendship on laughter alone.'

Maggie lay in the darkness remembering the dark nervous flush staining her elder daughter's face when Whisky Jake had made his abrupt entry into the room. Maggie had lived the greater part of her life keeping the secret of her true identity hidden from the man who now lay, breathing gently and evenly, by her side. For the first time, she realized he had his secrets too and the knowledge of that filled her with a sense of terrible unease.

Gillan ran his fingers over the bound volume of Burns' poetry which Evelyn had bought for him in a second-hand bookshop in Aberdeen.

'Merry Christmas, Gillie,' she said, a trifle breathlessly. 'I know how you love Burns and pounced on this when I went into the bookshop with Grace.'

It was a night of cold stars and glistening white hills silhouetted against a black-velvet sky. He was on embarkation leave and had danced her onto the frost-sparkled terrace in front of Rothiedrum House. Behind the dark window drapes lights shone, people laughed, caught up in the revelry of the annual Christmas ball Rothiedrum had always thrown for its tenants. No one had expected one this year, but Lady Marjorie and Evander Ramsay Forbes had come up from London for the festive season, she full of sparkling plans and heady with the excitement of doing her bit for the war effort.

The questions that had been on everyone's lips were at last answered. Rothiedrum had opened its doors to convalescing officers; young men who, past the casualty stage, were seeking a place of quietude before going back to the front. Several were present that night, mingling with the farm folk and the villagers, fit enough to eat and drink well and dance with the prettiest girls. Some, with empty sleeves and over-bright eyes, would never go back. These were the lads who talked too loudly and drank too much and were wont to huddle in dark corners away from questions and sympathetic eyes.

Lady Marjorie had arrived well in advance of her husband to organize sleeping arrangements and to liaise with Mrs Chalmers on the servants' new duties. Some were relegated to entirely different positions from the ones with which they were familiar, but the younger female servants didn't mind and went willingly enough to attend the needs of young men who had so valiantly fought for their country.

But it was deemed that Evelyn's position would remain unchanged. Lady Marjorie looked at the young girl as if viewing her from a great height, and told her rather coldly that her place was still in the kitchen and would remain so for the duration.

Evander arrived a few days later, called her to his study, and in the course of chatting to her about this and that informed her that he was putting her in a position above stairs with a fairly substantial raise in her pay.

'Time you had a change, Evelyn,' he smiled, placing an intimate hand on her shoulder. Once, Evelyn would have cringed away from it, but she knew him too well for that now and was able to handle his flirtatious approaches. At first he had frightened her, but now she liked him and admired his frank honesty and unsnobbish attitude to his own privileged lifestyle. 'These lads need someone young and attractive to cheer them up,' he went on. 'It's a waste hiding you in the kitchens, so above stairs it is. I'll see Mrs Chalmers about getting you into a nice little housemaid's uniform. Something that fits well. I hate to see a good figure hidden under baggy clothes. You've got curves, show 'em off, give us all something to think about, eh, lass?'

Her eyes sparkled. 'No harm in thinking, sir – if that's all you do, you'll stay out o' trouble.'

His coarse laugh boomed out. 'Spirit! That's what I like. Little wonder Gillan lost his head over you. You're a lass after my own heart.'

Lady Marjorie went red in the face when she heard the news. 'How could you go behind my back like that,

Evander?' she cried, tears of rage dancing in her eyes. 'You've made a complete fool of me. How can I uphold the laws of this house when you sneak about repudiating everything I say? That girl must be laughing up her sleeve at me.'

He turned on her, a dangerous glint in his eye. 'Girl? Oh, you mean Evelyn Grant, Gillan's cousin. Should think you'd be pleased she and her kin haven't claimed their rights to half the estate by now. Surely you don't grudge an Ogilvie-Forbes a position above stairs, my dear.'

She stared at him wildly. 'You know that – but how—'

'Made it my business to find out. You brought it on yourself, Marjorie. Acted so damned unreasonably about the Grants after your uncle came here to get over the death of his wife. I wrote asking him why and he told me – it's that simple. So, he's Margaret Grant's father, she's your first cousin, which makes Gillan and Evelyn second cousins. They don't know that, of course, and aren't likely to now. But if I were you, Marjorie, my dear, I'd count my blessings for having a close-lipped relative like Maggie. If she wasn't such a damnably proud creature she would have blabbed the affair over the whole of Rothiedrum. As it is, she's so bloody angry at her father's treatment of her mother that she hates his guts and probably ours as well, and would die rather than lay claim to us.'

He rocked on his heels, his coat tails held aloft to allow the fire's heat to soak into him. 'So you be nice to Evelyn Grant. I'll hear about it if you start coming the lofty aristocrat with her. She's a spirited lass, mind, Oggie's blood flows proud in her veins and like him her heart rules her head. If she had been a little schemer she could easily have won Gillan. As it was she went for that lad, Johnny Burns, poor as a kirk mouse but she saw only the romance in him – as old Oggie saw it in a little maidservant all these years ago, randy old sod.' He grinned delightedly.

'Oh, Evander.' She threw out a theatrical hand. 'I believe you're enjoying this. You've always taken pleasure in watching me suffer. I sometimes think you have no feelings left for me at all.'

'Nonsense, Marjorie,' he smiled at her affectionately. 'You're a pampered, scheming little vixen but I knew that when I married you. I loved you then for all your faults and still do, and it's for your own good that I make you toe the line now and then.'

She threw herself at him and sobbed out her tensions on his ox-like shoulder. He responded by enclosing her in a lusty embrace even while he smiled over her head, as if enjoying the power he had always exerted over her.

Gillan was delighted when he heard about his father's manipulation of Evelyn's position at Rothiedrum, and though he never knew the reasons behind any of it he accepted the deal as part of his father's fair and honest nature and was more drawn to him than he had ever been.

And now he stood close to Evelyn on the terrace, savouring this time of being alone with her. She was the only member of the Grant family present. Maggie had never attended any of the functions thrown for Rothiedrum's tenants and her husband and daughters, respecting her decision, had always followed her example, though with regret on Jamie's part for he had always got on well with Evander Forbes. It was different for Evelyn, now. She worked for the laird and saw no reason why she shouldn't enjoy his hospitality.

Gillan looked pale in the white light reflected by the snow and very handsome and proud in the uniform of the Gordon Highlanders. His appeal for a commission in the regiment had proved successful and having passed out of the Officer's Training Camp as a second lieutenant, he was now at Castle Hill in Aberdeen awaiting his posting.

Something tugged at Evelyn's heart as she beheld the dear, familiar face of him. He had been part of her life for so long and very soon he would be going out of it – yet not completely, she told herself quickly. He would write to her and she would write back – as she would to Alan Keith who was also on embarkation leave, and who now mingled with the others inside the big house, too thin in his uniform, his beautiful boy's face taut with staunch resolution despite his mother's tight-lipped disapproval and her over-loud comments about the futility of war.

She watched Gillan as, slowly, he opened the book. On the flyleaf she had inscribed: *To my dear, dear Gillie, my love and friendship always*.

The subdued light from the windows filtered over the page and he touched the words lightly. 'Your friendship.' His voice was very low. 'I should be grateful for that anyway – and I'll treasure this always.'

Tentatively, he reached out to stroke her hair. She had tied it back with a blue ribbon so that the rich, shining tresses flowed down her back. '"My love is like a red, red rose just newly spring in June".' The words fell, soft as teardrops in the blanketed silence of the dreaming countryside. He laughed shakily. 'What a man was Burns, eh, Princess? To put into words everything I'm feeling now.'

Tears rose in her throat. Through a watery veil she saw him, so tall and dark and beautiful against the lawns of virgin white – soon to go away across the divide of the ocean – away, away . . .

'Gillie,' she murmured huskily and moved into his arms to hold him tightly and savour the warmth of his body. 'You'll always be special to me – the most wonderful friend anyone ever had.'

He didn't answer. Instead he took from his pocket a small box, and opened it to reveal a tiny pear-shaped pearldrop snuggled against black velvet. 'A falling tear.' He was smiling now, a smile which didn't reach his eyes. 'Think of it as one of mine, suspended in time till love comes and wipes it away.'

He clasped its fine chain round her neck, and stood back to admire it lying against the taut whiteness of her throat. 'Merry Christmas, my lovely, lovely Princess. I can't kiss you goodnight. I couldn't trust myself to do that in the rational, undemanding manner of a good friend. I'm leaving here tomorrow. I've been invited to spend a few days with people in Edinburgh. Don't worry about Alan, I'll keep an eye on him as much as I can. Drink a toast to me at New Year – I'll be thinking of you then – and beyond.'

He walked away from her, across the slanting oblongs of orange light splashed over the snow, and was soon lost amongst the shadows of the house.

She felt bereft of everything she had ever known and loved. The little pearldrop was cold and hard under her fingers but soon made warm by the tears that trickled down and ran over it.

# CHAPTER SEVEN

It was warm in the bedroom. Katie had piled the fire high with logs and peat. Flames licked the ragged edges of the turf, then went racing and dancing over the rough fibres so that myriads of orange sparks went crackling up the lum. The weather had closed in again and now, in the second day of the New Year, the snow whirled in a blinding fury, great wind-driven gusts of it blotting out the hills and bringing early dusk to the wild afternoon. Huge feathery flakes spat against the windowpanes and slithered down to meet the little drifts piled on the windowledge. Occasionally, a blast of wind sent a flurry of flakes down the chimney, to land on the hot logs and vie with their cheery, resinous hissing.

Nellie sat on a rocking chair by the hearth, her nimble fingers sending the wool flying round her knitting needles while the firelight gleamed on her fair hair and brought an attractive flush to her finely moulded cheekbones. Corrie, an old retired sheepdog tired of Katie's clumsy feet on his tail, had crept upstairs to take full advantage of the bedroom fire and he lay stretched out blissfully beside Nellie, his muzzle resting heavily on her feet.

On the face of it it was a contented and peaceful scene, but Nellie's rawboned body was as alert as a cat's, her eyes darting continually to Jeannie tossing and turning on the bed, her small face burning with fever, her pale mouth cracked and dry. Her flu had developed into acute bronchitis and the doctor, Katie, Nellie, Kenneth Mor and even Tandy had sat with her in their turn, while she coughed feebly and had to be restrained from getting up out of bed in an effort to cool her fevered body. Gregor had ordered that a kettle be kept steaming at the edge of the fire day and night, and that she take steam inhalations every hour or so.

The severe weather had forced both Tandy and Kenneth

to stay in or around the farm, though Tandy made frequent, difficult trips out to the edge of the fields to check anxiously that none of his sheep were buried in the drifts.

On one such trip he came back with a huge icicle which he had broken off the byre roof. Cal laughed and grabbed at it with the intention of putting in it to his mouth to suck the delicious coldness, but his father snatched it away from him and stared at it as if he had made a new discovery. 'The very thing! Greg said we must get your mother's temperature down. Put on your boots and go out and gather all you can, son. We'll keep them in a bucket by the door. Greg will tell us how best to use them. I'm going out to meet him, he said he would be here about now.'

Wrapping his plaid around his shoulders he went out into the whirling snowstorm, a huge red-haired giant, bending his magnificent body into the wind, his heart sore and sick in the breast of him with worry for the wife whom he adored with all the passion of his fierce and loving soul. The wind blasted him, whirled his kilt about his legs, seared his skin to raw pain and plastered his long, silken beard against the sark which lay open at his neck despite the bitter cold.

When he met Gregor labouring up the track towards him, both men looked like snow creatures moving painfully in the savage white landscape.

'Greg! Greg! God, man, ye must be frozen!' He put out his arm to the doctor, who all but fell into its powerful embrace and for the rest of the way was thankful to lean on its reassuring support.

In the kitchen Gregor collapsed into a chair while Tandy stood over him with the whisky bottle and made him swallow two good drams.

'Thanks, man, I needed that.' The doctor drew his hand over his sopping forehead. 'It's as fierce as I've seen it out there. I doubt even a dog could survive that bitter wind for more than a few hours.'

Childlike in his anxiety, Kenneth showed the doctor the bucket of ice.

'You have brains in that fiery head of yours,' said Gregor nodding. 'Get some towels. We'll wrap them round the stuff, and Cal – keep it coming, son, for it will melt in no time in the heat.'

Nellie was more relieved than she could have thought possible at sight of the doctor coming through the door, but she said not a word, busying herself instead with helping him place the ice packs round Jeannie's burning body.

'Only a minute or two at a time,' warned Gregor, 'we must get that temperature down but don't want her chilled in the process.'

'Will you stay for a while, Greg?' Kenneth asked tensely.

The doctor passed a weary hand over his eyes. 'As long as I can, but I doubt the whole of Rothiedrum is coming down with the flu. I have several calls to make and won't see my bed this side o' the clock. If only Hinney was here. She would have stayed as long as need be, but at the moment she can hardly make it out her own door, never mind up here.'

'I'll sit wi' her, Gregor.' Nellie avoided the stark gratitude in Kenneth Mor's eyes. 'Mother is good wi' the babby but she'll no' go to her bed for anyone but me, so I'll have to be back down for at least nine.'

'We'll manage fine between us. When Nell goes I'll bide wi' Jeannie through the night.' Kenneth was stroking Jeannie's hair as he spoke, talking to her in a voice so gentle it sent shivers along Nellie's spine and reminded her of the day he had rescued her from the lustful and brutal attack on her body by Peter Lamont, one-time grieve of the Mains. That day would always stand out clear and terrible in her mind, for it was the day she had acknowledged the love that was in her for the master of Knobblieknowe. He had spoken to her then as he was speaking to Jeannie now, and Nellie's heart ached at the remembrance of his arms about her for the first and last time.

Abruptly she turned away from the betraying glow of the lamplight. 'I'll go down and help Katie wi' the tea,' she murmured and hurried softly out of the room.

By teatime Jeannie was resting easier. She had managed to swallow some thin soup before drifting into an exhausted sleep. Gently, Nellie pulled the blankets around the small shoulders before going downstairs to join the others. The kitchen was warm and welcoming, its cosiness emphasized by the wind keening at the windows and rattling the door in its frame. Draughts moved the curtains, melting snow slithered in from the porch and found its way onto the newspapers placed against the crack under the door, but try as it might, the savage night couldn't rob the room of its warmth. Katie had built up a good fire. The flames leapt up the black mouth of the lum, their glow bathed the kitchen in a warm, tawny light which shone on the old fender brasses and brought life to the sepia photos arrayed on sideboard and mantelpiece. On top of an ancient piano set in a corner of the room was a picture of Jeannie and Kenneth on their wedding day, smiling yet secretive in their love for one another. It was flanked by family photographs. There was one of Kenneth's parents standing at the door of their croft, another of Jeannie's mother and father and two young brothers stacking peats on the moors.

It wasn't usual to see a piano in a farmhouse kitchen. If a family owned one it was kept in the parlour, the dusty keys only ever touched to celebrate weddings or christenings. But Kenneth Mor had never been one to live by rules. He had bought the instrument at an auction and had installed it in the warmest room in the house so that Jeannie could play it in comfort. Music was as natural to her as breathing, and in the evenings she would sit down to play, her head thrown back, her black hair cascading about her shoulders as the tunes ran free as hill burns from her fingers.

With the coming of the Camerons to Knobblieknowe it had become a place filled with music, and if Kenneth and Tandy weren't striding about on the braes with their pipes they were inside playing them or just sitting back at the fire, their drams warming on the hearth while Jeannie entertained them with her playing.

Evelyn had always loved Knobblieknowe for that and she and Jeannie often played little duets on the piano, inciting Kenneth Mor to sing in his wonderful deep bass voice which Jeannie said he had stolen from a fairy well way over yonder in the land of Tir nan Og which was Gaelic for Land of the Ever Young.

Something caught at Nellie's throat, a yearning for all those happy times she had missed by staying away from Knobblieknowe. How long? A year – almost a year – she looked up and caught Kenneth watching her, and in confusion she went to help Katie ladle broth into bowls. Good soup it looked too, thick with vegetables and pieces of mutton. The enticing fragrance of it filled Nellie's nostrils, reminding her that she had eaten very little of her dinner, yet when she came to sit down she found that she wasn't hungry. Her throat was so dry she could barely swallow and her heart jumped every time Kenneth spoke to her or tried to bring her into the conversation.

Fool! she told herself, miserably. Behaving like a silly schoolgirl over a man to whom her existence mattered little. And if she went on like this the tongues would start wagging. Poor old Nellie! Growing queerer and more old-maidish with every passing year . . .

'Nell, you're no' coming down with flu as well I hope.' Gregor was surveying her anxiously. 'You look a bit drawn. I could give you something while I'm here—'

'No! No, Greg.' She hastened to compose herself. 'I'm fine, just the heat from the fire making me drowsy.'

Katie stifled a huge yawn. 'Me too, I'm early to bed once I've seen to these—' She eyed the dirty pile of dishes with distaste and glowered at Nellie who had risen to clear the plates saying, 'Better get these done quickly, then, while I see to Cal's bedtime.'

'But Nellie,' the little boy protested, 'it's early yet and I have an awful lot to do before bed. Mr Gregory says—'

The doctor scraped back his chair, smiling. 'And I have an awful lot to do before I get home to my bed.' He turned to Kenneth. 'Jeannie should sleep the night through but if she wakens, see she keeps warm and give her plenty to drink.'

'I'll be right by her side, Greg.' Kenneth held the doctor's coat while he shrugged himself into it. 'Jeannie only has to sneeze and I'm there holding the hanky.'

Tandy too had risen and was waiting at the door with a storm lantern, his shaggy beard snuggled into the woollen layers of his plaid which was swaddled warmly and securely round his huge body. 'I'll see you down the road, Greg. I wouldna send a dog out there on its own this night. I'll never make it back up to the biggin so I'll bide down there wi' Jamie and Maggie. They'll find a corner for me in the chaumer.' Playfully, he slapped Katie's bottom as she flounced by with a pan of water. 'You behave yourself, young Katie, till I get back.'

She threw him a sidelong, flirtatious glance. 'You could bide here the night, Tandy. It will be a whilie before the snow clears enough for you to make it over yonder to the biggin. I'm sure there are plenty of wee corners at Knobblieknowe you could sleep in.'

Tandy grinned. 'Ay, you in your small corner and me in yours, eh, you sly whittrock? Na, na, I'll be safer at King's Croft – at least—' he looked deliberately at Nellie '—that's if the Grant lassies can bear to keep their hands off me.'

Nellie stuck her nose disdainfully in the air, and to the accompaniment of Tandy's loud laughter and the snarl of the wind the two men departed into the night.

Katie giggled as she rattled dishes in the scullery. 'Thon Tandy's an awful man,' she called through. 'I doubt you'd better lock your door the night, Nell—' she broke off and came into the kitchen drying her hands. 'He's coming back, I can hear his clairty big feet scrunching the snow.'

Tandy opened the door a crack and poked his head through. Although he had only been gone a few minutes his hair and beard, even his sandy eyebrows, were snow-plastered, and there was genuine concern in his voice when he said, 'You'd best come down wi' us, Nell lass, for you'll need a helping hand going down the brae. I skited on my own erse just now even though me and Greg were holding each other up.'

Kenneth Mor strode into the lamplight. 'Dinna worry Tandy,' he urged. I'll see Nell down – or else she can bide here the night. I'd never hae let her struggle down there on her own. What kind o' a man do you take me for! Go you back to the doctor before he freezes to death out there.'

Tandy withdrew, closing the door on the wind which had swooped in to rob the kitchen of much of its heat.

A flutter of panic had seized Nellie at Tandy's words. The very idea of spending a night under the same roof as Kenneth was almost too much for her to bear, but worse was the idea of him holding her upright on the snowbound track . . . Dropping Cal's nightgown onto the rug she said in a strange, breathless voice' 'Tandy's right, I'd better get my coat. If I hurry I can catch up wi' them.'

She half-ran to the door to tear her coat down from its hook, and was pushing her arms into it when she was seized roughly by the elbow and spun round to look into Kenneth Mor's face.

'What on earth's got into you, Nell?' he demanded harshly. A glitter of anger shone in his blue eyes, his very beard seemed to bristle with indignation as he went on, 'I said I would see you home and I damned well mean what I say – and if you think I'm no' as good a man as Tandy then you'll bide here till morning. By God! Maggie and Jamie between them conceived a thrawn besom in you but surely there's sense lurking somewhere in that stubborn wee head o' yours.'

Nellie's shoulders sagged, signalling her defeat. 'It's no' that, Kenneth – it's – the babby,' she finished lamely, her voice husky with repressed emotion.

'Dinna worry about the babby.' He was watching her, a strange look on his face. 'I'll get you down there in one piece and if the weather gets too bad then the babby will be fine wi' Maggie.'

Katie was watching furtively from the scullery doorway as Nellie removed her coat, hung it heavily on the hook before turning her attention back to Cal, who put his arms round her neck and whispered a request for a bedtime story into her ear. She cuddled him, her love for Jeannie's son overriding her feelings of unease.

'All right, if you wash and get into your goonie in less time than it takes a cat to lick its whiskers,' she promised.

The little boy gave a soft chuckle and went happily to her bidding.

Katie darted about, seeing to all the night chores before huddling herself into outdoor garments to take the bothy men their supper of brose and bannocks. Normally they came to the kitchen at day's end, but with Jeannie so ill Kenneth had asked that she shouldn't be disturbed. So Katie went out, grumbling under her breath, while Kenneth went upstairs to see to the fire.

Nellie snuggled Cal on her knee. It was suddenly peaceful in the room, and warm despite the draughts that sneaked in..

'Dinna bother reading to me, Nellie,' Cal decided, blinking and sleepy as a big soft cat on her knee. 'We'll hae a blether instead.'

She let him talk, her mouth pressed to his warm, bright hair, smiling as he went on about school, about Mr Gregory whom he liked and respected.

'He's in love wi' your Grace,' he confided. 'Did you ken that, Nellie?'

'Wheesht,' she scolded, 'you're too young to know about love.'

'No I'm not,' he said indignantly. 'I love a whole lot o' people. Mother and Father, Fiona McNab though she's only five and a girl – and wee Col, I love him – and I love you, Nellie.'

She laughed and nuzzled his hair. 'And I love you even when you're being thrawn like your father—'

'Ach, you love him too, Nellie.' The little boy leaned trustingly back against her and, reaching up, wound a strand of her hair round his fingers, unaware that his words had sent shivers of apprehension down her spine which remained long after his next words robbed the statement of its intensity. 'Everyone loves Father – and Tandy too. I'll be like them when I'm older. I'll play the pipes and wear the kilt all the time and I'll grow a big beard like theirs. I dinna like some folk, though – like that Jenny Burns. She has wee sly eyes and punches the wee ones on the back when Mr Gregory isna looking. She—'

The door flew open and the wind blew Katie into the room. After just a few minutes in the teasing, boisterous company of the bothy men she was her usual sparkling self again, and breathlessly demanded to know the whereabouts of 'the maister' as she had a message to impart from the stockman. She intercepted Kenneth at the foot of the stairs and Nellie heard her telling him that one of the cows was calving, but not to worry as Tom McDougal would see to it. After that she went off to bed in the attic room at the top of the house, while Nellie took Cal upstairs to tuck him in and kiss him goodnight.

She stood for a few moments outside his door, loath to go downstairs. Kenneth was down there and the last thing she wanted was to be alone with him.

'Liar, Nellie Grant!' she told herself fiercely. It was the one thing she longed for above all else, all she thought about when she lay sleepless in her lonely bed at night.

She shuddered. It was wicked! Wicked and weak. And she of all the women in Rothiedrum had thought herself to be so strong when it came to men. She should have gone with Tandy and Greg, shouldn't have allowed herself to get into such an awkward situation – she shook herself. How selfish of her to think only of herself. Jeannie needed her.

It was cold on the landing, and going quickly to the door opposite the stairs she opened it. The room was shadowed and steamily warm. A draught moved the curtains at the window but a good fire kept the bitter night at bay.

'Jeannie, are you awake?' she whispered.

'Ay, I canna sleep. I'm hot, Nell, so hot.'

'I'll give you a nice cool wash before I go.' She busied herself, filling a basin from the steaming kettle on the embers, cooling it from the bucket of melted ice at the side of the hearth.

'Make it really cold, Nell,' Jeannie urged and Nellie cooled the water as much as she dared before sponging Jeannie down. Helping her into a fresh nightdress she put the basin away and then sat on the edge of the bed to brush the young woman's glossy black hair.

'You're bonny, Jeannie, so bonny.' Nellie's voice was

110

tender as she moved the brush rhythmically over the rippling waves. 'It's so nice to be with you – to talk to you like this. I've missed coming up here, you're the only young woman hereabouts I ever took to. I'm no' one for fancy words but I'm proud to be your friend. I'll never forget how you gave the wee one my name. It made me a bittie proud o' myself somehow.'

Jeannie tried to speak, but was seized with such a violent fit of coughing that Nellie rushed for the cough mixture left by Gregor. Jeannie was spent, too exhausted to talk. Beads of perspiration stood out on her brow and Nellie went to open the window and bring in a jug of ice pieces which Kenneth had thoughtfully left there. She gave Jeannie a piece of ice to suck, and gently bathed her fevered brow with a cloth wrung out in melted ice water.

'Nell.' Jeannie's grip on her arm was suddenly strong, her eyes black with intensity as she went on, 'Nell, this might sound daft – but – if anything happens to me will you look after Kenneth and the bairns?'

Nellie drew back, disbelief stark in her eyes. 'Nothing is going to happen to you, Jeannie! You've just got a bad dose o' flu, that's all. You'll get better in no time.'

Jeannie moved her head restlessly on the pillow. 'Och, I know, Nell, but please, please listen to me. Kenneth has made such a good job o' this place. He loves it here – he loves the people. I do too, but betimes I canna stop myself thinking o' the west. I see the hills o' home, the bonny lochs and the ocean studded with wee islands – and I feel the wind, soft and gentle on my face . . .'

Her voice went on. Nellie sat perfectly still and quiet. A strange, palpable feeling invaded the shadowed silence of the room; as of tides, and winds that hushed and beat against lonely, white Atlantic shores before soughing on over sleeping blue hills and into purpled glens. Shiver after shiver touched Nellie's spine as Jeannie's murmured descriptions of her homelands fell like gentle waves upon her ears.

'I long for it, Nell,' she ended with a sigh. 'It was a kinder land than this but after Kenneth and me were wed he heard

111

o' this place, and was so eager to make a success o' it I just allowed myself to get carried along with him.' A smile touched her pale lips. 'He's like a lad in his enthusiams – as much of a bairn as Cal or Isla Nell – I can never let him see I'm no' strong enough to take it—'

'But you must, Jeannie!' cried Nellie. 'He worships the ground you walk on and would never wittingly do anything to make you suffer.'

'No, Nell.' Jeannie was breathless with the effort of talking. 'He's put too much into Knobblieknowe for me to ever spoil it for him. And dinna you go telling him anything I've said. It's between you and me and aye will be, but I still want you to promise you'll look to him and my babies if I'm no' around to see to them myself.'

'Ay, Jeannie, I promise.' Nellie spoke miserably, frightened by the words she had just uttered. She became brisk in an effort to rid herself of the gloomy mood. 'Rest for you, my girl. Come morning you'll see everything in a different light and will feel ashamed o' yourself for making me utter such nonsense. I'll be back up to see you then and we'll laugh about the daftness o' this night.'

She busied herself about the room, clearing things away, refilling the kettle from the jug and setting it at the edge of the fire where it was soon sending little spurts of steam into the room.

When she turned back to the bed, Jeannie was asleep. Gently, she pulled the blankets around the slender figure and stooped to place a kiss on the smooth brow. 'God keep you, my dear, dear friend,' she whispered. Straightening, she stood for a long moment staring down at Jeannie's face, so sweet and childlike in its repose. Then she turned abruptly and tiptoed away downstairs.

Kenneth Mor came stamping in from the yard as she entered the kitchen. 'I was over in the byre wi' Tom,' he explained, going to the fire and holding his hands to the blaze. 'It's Beinne Uisge Mor's first and it looks as if it will be a long night.'

He always called his cows after the hills and lochs

112

surrounding his old home in the west. Great long Gaelic
names they were too, and the folk from round about teased
him unmercifully by shortening them to more pro-
nounceable forms, to which Kenneth ably retaliated by
changing the names of their own beasts into Gaelic and
insisting that they answered better to the true tongue.

Nellie, for all she was flustered by his almost overwhelming presence, smiled sourly at his words. 'A long
night for a cow wi' a title as long as my arm. Sit you down
and I'll make you a cuppy.'

But he went to get her coat, which he held thoughtfully to
the fire as he said, 'No, Nell, we'd best get you home. It's
getting worse out there by the minute, unless—' he threw
her a sidelong, challenging glance '—you've changed your
mind and have decided to stay after all.'

She hesitated, one half of her longing to remain at
Knobblieknowe with Jeannie and Cal and – why deny it to
herself – with him, the other half warning her against the
sweet joy of sharing a few short hours with him in the
wonderful, warm intimacy of that cosy kitchen.

'No, I'll go home.' Almost rudely, she snatched her coat
from him and shrugged herself into it. 'Jeannie's sleeping
and should be all right if she isna disturbed.'

'She won't be,' he said rather shortly. 'I'll bide down here
in the chair by the fire –' he glanced at her again '– as I have
done for the last week or so.'

She looked at the chair indicated, big and comfortable
and so companionably close to the one opposite . . .

'Wouldn't it be handier to bide in the one by the fire in
your own room?' she suggested dryly.

He grinned, his blue eyes glinting in the firelight. 'I tried
that for a night or two but I snore when I sleep upright. It
disturbed Jeannie so I moved down here. But dinna worry,
I only catnap and go up every hour or so to see to the fire
and to her if she needs anything.'

He wound his plaid round his shoulders, and picking up
the storm lantern from the sill crooked his arm at her. 'I'm
ready if you are.'

At any other time she would have wished away every

step of that treacherous journey down the slippery brae to King's Croft but, huddled close to him, feeling the heat of his body beating into her, she wanted the precious interlude to last forever. Snow spicules stung their faces, the icy wind forbade speech of any kind, the little circle of light from his lantern danced along in front of them and seemed the only light in the world up there on the edge of the hillside. It was the only light she needed or wanted just then.

The night enshrouded them, cold, dark, oddly mysterious, filled as it was with looming black shapes that seemed to leap out at them from nowhere. The silence was eerie with only the snowflakes whispering over them. She needed no excuse to huddle close in to him. His arm was around her waist, rock-like, reassuring, steadying her when once she tripped and half-fell. She felt his heartbeat against her breast, the soft brush of his beard on her face – the yellow glow cast by the lantern mesmerized her, seemed to lead her on and on into an eternity of warmth and closeness and a wonderful, breathless completeness – then other lights intruded, the lights of King's Croft, and the world imposed itself on her strangely beautiful, timeless dream.

Kenneth Mor led her to the door, briefly held her hands. 'You'll be fine now, Nell, I'd best get back to Jeannie.' His lips brushed her face, frozen, yet searing into her flesh like brand burns. 'Thanks for all you've done, Nell. You're good, truly good. I know you canna stand the sight o' me, you've made that clear enough, but I'm grateful anyway for your kindness to my Jeannie.'

And he was gone, swallowed up in the night and the cold which suddenly happed itself around her, though that wasn't what made her shiver. His words rang in her head. He imagined she disliked him! Oh God, she thought, let him always think that. It will make my love for him easier to bear—

Yet she couldn't stand the idea of him thinking her a cold, unfeeling woman when all the time the blood leapt warm and passionate in her breast, and she had to stand for a few moments in the cold in order to compose herself into an appearance of normality before she faced her family.

Jamie leapt up at her entry, his dark face relieved at the sight of her. 'Come you to the fire, lass, you must be frozen,' he said kindly, taking her hands and drawing her to the hearth where Tandy removed his stockinged feet to make room.

Tears sprang to her eyes at the concern in her father's voice. His hands felt frail in hers. Strange that, she thought, his hands have always been strong, strong and – yes – loving. She looked at him, seemed to see him properly for the first time in years. He was growing old and she had hardly even noticed the changes in him. His springing curly hair was more grey than black, his kindly face seamed and thin. Suddenly, she wished with all her heart that she could reach out and take him in her arms – but she didn't know how! She had pushed all her loving emotions down till they were so deeply buried she was hardly aware that they existed – until times like these, when she was confronted with the reality of her own father's waning youth and the love that shone from his brown eyes like twin lamps burning in the darkest of nights. She bit her lip. 'I'm fine, Father, Kenneth walked me home. Jeannie was sleeping when we left and seems better than she has been.'

Almost shyly she met her father's steady gaze, and was the first to turn away.

Evelyn came into the room. 'I put the babby to bed, Nellie, she went for me.'

Nellie had forgotten all about the baby and she looked dazedly at her young sister's triumphant face. 'That's good, Evie, it's well past her bedtime.'

Maggie poured tea, hot and strong. 'Drink this, lassie, it will warm you in no time.' She smiled mischievously. 'I put a wee drop o' the hard stuff in it and dinna bother to protest for I'll no' listen.' She took Nellie's hands and chaffed them, saying as she did so, 'You're no' cold at all, Nellie, your hands are near as warm as my own.'

Murn looked up from her book. 'Ay, even your face looks warm, Nellie, I doubt Kenneth happed his plaid round you on the way down.'

She smiled, rather knowingly, Nellie thought. Her lips

tightened. 'Take your feet off the stool, Murn, and let me into the fire. Wi' all that imagination you have you shouldn't be reading books – you should be writing them!'

Kenneth Mor came round the corner of the steadings, and was apprehended by Tom McDougal who was standing outside the byre peering through the glare of the lantern he was holding aloft. 'Ye'll come in and hae a peek at the beast, Kenneth,' he said, greeting him thankfully. 'She's havin' a bad time and I doubt we'll hae to use the ropes on her later.'

Kenneth hesitated, looking towards the house standing grey and battered by the blizzard. 'I'll just go and see if Jeannie's all right,' he said, and plodded away.

Jeannie was still asleep, flushed and warm but settled and quiet. Silently he attended to the fire, topped up the kettle, tiptoed to the bed to kiss his wife gently on the brow before going softly downstairs and back into the bitter night.

The byre was warm and steamy. Beinne Uisge Mor moved restlessly in her stall, her eyes rolling uneasily in her big, bovine face while she expressed her distress with soft little bellows.

Kenneth examined her and then went to sit beside Tom on a bale of hay. 'We'll have to wait a whilie before we use the ropes. It's going to be a long night, Tom. You go on to your bed and I'll call you nearer the time.'

Tom pushed bogy roll into his pipe with a stubby thumb. 'I'll bide here wi' you,' he grunted. 'It's warmer here than in the chaumer.'

Kenneth was exhausted from nights of broken sleep. He sat back and allowed his body to relax, his thoughts to wander. Come the spring he would take Jeannie and the bairns home for a break. She had been talking a lot of home recently, a wistfulness in her voice that had not escaped him. A tender smile touched his mouth. He thought, I'll take you home, my darling Jeannie, and you'll flourish like a rose in the warm winds o' the Atlantic.

Tom put his pipe between his teeth and settled his

shoulders against the stall, enjoying the quiet companionship of 'the maister' who, in a restive mood, was smiling to himself at some pleasant private thought.

Jeannie woke with a parched throat and drank a glass of water at the bedside. But it was stale and lukewarm. She wanted something cold – like that ice Cal had brought in from the byre roof. The room was suffocatingly warm. She felt as if a heavy weight was pressing on her chest and no matter how hard she panted she couldn't seem to get enough air into her lungs.

She lay for a while, wishing Kenneth would come up but not daring to shout for him in case she awoke the household.

After what seemed an eternity of waiting she struggled to sit up and gazed longingly towards the window where Nellie had placed the jug of ice. She put her legs out of bed. They almost gave way beneath her, but holding onto pieces of furniture she made it to the window, only to find that she wasn't strong enough to open the swollen sash. Sweat poured from her, she sagged where she stood, every fibre in her crying out for water – for air. Her shepherd's tartan shawl was thrown over the back of a chair. With difficulty she placed it round her shoulders and somehow reached the door. At the top of the stairs she swayed dizzily, a wry smile hovering at her mouth. How often, she wondered, had she run down those stairs without thought or effort? Now she felt as if she was standing on top of a mountain looking down, down. She descended on her bottom, one painful step at a time, sweat soaking her nightdress, making her shiver even while she burned. At the foot, she put her head on her knees and gasped for air. When she looked up there was a mist in front of her eyes. 'Kenneth.' She tried to shout his name but only a feeble whisper came out. How long she sat there she didn't know, but finally she got shakily to her feet and half-ran into the kitchen, her husband's name on her lips. It was empty – empty and as stuffily warm as the bedroom had been. Panic seized her. Where was he? Had something happened to him? Nellie had said something about him seeing her down the brae to King's Croft.

117

Sobbing a little with weakness she struggled to the door, opened it and gasped as the bullying wind whipped her and robbed her of the small amount of air in her lungs. Snow flurries blew over her and caressed her face, melted on her dry lips. She spread her arms as if to welcome a long-awaited friend. It was beautiful. Cold, so cold. She strained her eyes into the darkness, and through the driving snow she saw a tiny sphere of warm light. The byre. Kenneth was in the byre and growing from the byre roof were those delicious icicles Cal had brought earlier that day.

She took a few tottering steps outside. The world spun. The wind took her and hurled her cruelly down into the smothering white blanket. Icy hands seemed to embrace her and hold her in a grip from which she was too exhausted to escape. Her dark eyes stared into the night; then the white blinds came down and she could see nothing, nothing – behind her the door swung back and forth for a few seconds before a blast seized it and jammed it almost shut. Its creaking ceased, gusts of air filtered round it and set the sodden newspapers flapping feebly on the flags. But that was all. The house dreamed on, dour and grey and silent up there on the edge of the hillside, its shoulders hunched under the weight of the snow quilt spread over its bulk.

In the early hours of the morning Kenneth found her where she had fallen. The wind had abated, the clouds had rolled back to reveal a cold black sky spiked with stars. At first he could see nothing in the drifts that had piled around the doorway, then he saw a lacy black pattern spread out on the snow. At first nothing registered, nothing penetrated the disbelieving horror that momentarily numbed his senses.

'Jeannie!' He spoke her name like a protest, his lips unwillingly forming the word. Dropping on his knees beside her he took her in his arms and cradled her. She was icy cold and unyielding, not the warm, soft Jeannie that he knew and loved.

Her night-black hair flowed over his hands. It had been his pride. He had never allowed her to cut it. It was part of her, part of the childlike sweetness of his bonny Jeannie. It was cold now, cold and wet and lifeless. Tendrils of it clung to his hands and made him shiver. He knelt there, rocking her in his arms. Away to the east a thin grey haze diffused the darkness. Night moved on regardless. Morning was far away, barely a promise on the cold, bleak horizon.

# PART 2

Spring/Summer, 1915

# CHAPTER EIGHT

A shaft of warm sunshine lay over the flags of the kitchen floor. Nellie paused at the step with the broom in her hands and looked up towards Knobblieknowe, gaunt and aloof against the blue of the sky. How different it appeared now that winter was past and the new green of spring was furring the hillside. Yet nothing had really changed since that dreadful time of sorrow and heartache. Kenneth was no longer the man everyone knew and loved.

No one could really believe it: big, laughing, thundering Kenneth, all the life gone out of him since the death of his beloved Jeannie. Nellie had gone to the Western Highlands for the funeral. She could still see him standing there, so tall and still beside the grave, everything that had been the life of him as dead and cold as the body of his young wife upon whose coffin the first sprinklings of earth were spattered.

The burial had had to be delayed for two days because of the unyielding hardness of the ground. It was unusual that, everyone said. There in the west the earth stayed soft, but then it had been an unusually cruel winter all over.

She had met Jeannie's mother, a bonny little woman with Jeannie's dark eyes and hair, but only the menfolk came to the funeral. Jeannie's father was a fine-featured, kindly-looking man, her two young brothers tall and dark and thin and like twins, so near they were in years. The snow had been falling again, shrouding them all in a misty white blur, smatterings of it drifting down into the grave to spread a thin white coverlet over the shiny new wood of the coffin. The tiny cemetery stood on a knoll overlooking the sea, a grey sea that day but Nellie remembered thinking how it would look come the spring – blue and

123

beautiful, so well loved by a young woman who had once gazed upon it with bright, shining eyes – and she had come home, home to her west winds and her beloved glens . . . But dear God! did it really have to be like this?

Nellie had been cold standing there, the only woman amongst a gathering of black-coated men.

It was the right and proper thing for men to come to gravesides while the womenfolk waited in shuttered parlours with hankies to their eyes, consoling one another till the menfolk came back to the funeral repast.

But for once Nellie had flouted tradition. The only true friend she had ever known was gone from her and she had to be there to make that last, heartbreaking farewell. When it was over she walked away to catch her train back to the north-east. She had been invited to stay, of course, but it was enough to have been there without having to face all the eating and drinking that followed a Highland funeral. Tandy had played the pipes at the close of the ceremony. Their haunting sound had followed her out of the kirkyard. She hadn't looked back. Her last glimpse had been of Kenneth Mor, stunned and silent, his great shoulders bowed, his red head sunk onto his chest in his lonely, terrible sorrow.

Her promise to Jeannie haunted her night and day for she had only been able to fulfil part of it. She had told Kenneth that she would keep little Isla Nell at King's Croft for as long as need be. Jeannie's mother had offered to take her. Kenneth had hesitated before shaking his head and saying, 'Thank you kindly, Peggy, but you have enough to see to here—' His voice had broken. 'It's maybe selfish o' me but I would miss my wee lass sorely – she's part o' Jeannie, you see and I – well, I just canna bear to let go of her.'

And so Isla Nell came to stay at King's Croft, a happy little creature who kept everyone on their toes and whenever possible went with Evelyn or Murn and sometimes Mary up to Knobblieknowe to visit her father. But Nellie couldn't bring herself to go, and the feeling of treachery lay in her heart like a leaden weight. And he never came down to King's Croft nor to any of the crofts and farms round about. Folk went up to Knobblieknowe to visit him, all the kindly neighbours and friends who had loved and admired both him and Jeannie from the start. They went with a determined spring in their step but came away chastened and bewildered, for Kenneth Mor had withdrawn into himself and no one, it seemed, could get through to him.

Only Tandy stayed up there with 'the maister'. It was Tandy's habit to resume his wanderings after the New Year, but this time he stayed on all through that sad, bitter winter. Yet the pipes which had once wakened Rothiedrum with their wildness and gladness never once came skirling down the braes. The very hills upon which Knobblieknowe stood were hushed and dour in their silent dreamings. In days gone by the two big Highlanders had often gone wild with the drink, but somehow Nellie knew Kenneth wouldn't find his comfort in a bottle. He and Tandy would be together all right; they would work together and talk quietly together and in the evenings they would sit down with a dram or two to warm them, nothing more. Wee Cal would be lost and bewildered in their company, feeling he ought to behave like a little man and all the while the child in him crying out for a warm place to shed his lonely tears. A pain like a knife twisted in Nellie's heart at such thoughts, and she of the dry eyes and proud spirit would bury her face in her pillow and cry as she had never cried all the days of her life.

And now it was spring. The peesies were tumbling in the blue haze of the sky. All over the plains of Rothiedrum the farm folk were harrowing, ploughing, and seeding the ground. The smell of earth and dung pervaded the air and the yellow was on the broom, its sweet scent thick as pure nectar in every hollow and haugh.

Jamie was out in the yard, humming under his breath as he wielded the dandy brush over Queenie's broad back. From first light he had been grooming her, and now she was polished and gleaming, the blond hair of her mane and feet washed and combed till it would have sat with pride on the

125

shoulders of a young girl. Jamie was younger and fitter-looking than of late. His sinewy body was taut and lean, his eyes brighter. The coming of spring always did that to him. Normally he would be away at this time of day to 'look over his acres' as he called it. The wakening of the earth was a time of quiet reflection for him, as he assessed his bit of ground and very probably his own life as well, but this morning the stallion was coming to King's Croft to couple with Queenie, Jamie having scrimped to pay the staig fee as a good foal could fetch anything up to a hundred pounds in wartime.

Nellie hated the upheaval that the coming of the great wild-eyed beast brought to the croft. She was also afraid of the hot-bellied creature, and took great care to keep herself well out of the way whenever it made its appearance. But today her attention was diverted. Today was Friday. Both Murn and Evelyn had the day off work and were at home, the latter getting herself ready for a lone trip into Aberdeen as everyone else was too taken up with spring cleaning and croft work with Maggie away at Lums o'Reekie visiting friends.

Murn could easily have volunteered to go with Evelyn and help with the purchase of supplies at the market but she had other matters on her mind, none of them connected with the croft.

Breakfast was no sooner over with than she announced her intention of taking Isla Nell up to visit her father. 'I'll take Col as well,' she said expansively when she and Nellie were in the scullery washing the dishes. 'He'll enjoy seeing Cal though it's not for that reason I'm going. I'm fed up with seeing Kenneth Mor so lonely and neglected-looking and I'm going to ask him if I can live up there as his housekeeper—' she slid her sister a sidelong, assessing glance. 'He needs a woman about the place and I don't mean that Katie. I mean a real woman who can look after him the way a rich-blooded man needs to be looked after.'

Nellie couldn't immediately answer, so flabbergasted was she. 'A housekeeper!' she eventually got out. 'But what about your teaching? Your job at Tillietoorie—'

Murn tossed her head, an almost feverish flush of excitement on her face as she replied disdainfully, 'My job. Do you really think teaching class after class of snotty-nosed infants is my only aim in life? No, no, Nellie. I've made do with it because I had to, but things have changed and I'm not going to miss out on my opportunities any longer. You know how I feel about Kenneth Mor—' She laughed, a short bitter laugh that changed her from an innocent-looking girl into a shrewish, calculating woman. 'The whole world must know how I feel about him. I've been patient. God, how patient I've been! I've sat in the background, a flower on the wall, always hoping that Kenneth would notice me but he never did. When I was a very young girl I once told him that one day he would notice me, well, that day has come, Nellie – and I feel, I feel wonderful.'

'You brazen hussy.' Nellie's voice was low and tremulous. 'Jeannie is hardly cold in her grave and you have the audacity to set your sights on her man. How – how could you, Murn? My own sister!'

For answer Murn untied her apron to toss it flippantly on the draining board. 'I could because if I don't somebody else will get there first. Kenneth is a fine, handsome big man, Nellie, and if you haven't noticed that then you must be blind as well as daft.'

And she was gone, up the stairs and into her room, there to don her best clothes, colour her face with rouge and lipstick before coming back down, breathless and determined, Isla Nell clinging to one hand, Col to the other.

Nellie watched them go, her whole being diffused with a seething rage and a terrible, grudging understanding for the sister whose love and devotion for Kenneth Mor had remained through thick and thin.

She never knew what really transpired that morning between her sister and Kenneth Mor. All morning she hovered by the door, finding all sorts of excuses for being there, her eyes straying frequently to the hill track while her arms ached from beating mats, washing windows and sweeping floors. An hour and a half after Murn's departure her vigilance was rewarded. A small black speck was descending the brae, walking slowly, defeat in every line of it. A few minutes later Murn came over the cobbles, her sad young face pale with hurt.

'I left the wee ones up there,' she explained briefly. 'You or Evie can collect them later.'

She made to brush past, but Nellie's detaining hand was on her arm and she paused unwillingly. 'He doesn't want me, Nellie. He sent me away as if I was a daft wee schoolbairn – I feel so humiliated I could die!'

She had carefully modulated her voice over the years till the north-east 'twang' that had sounded so right and good in the sweet tones was almost erased. Of all the Grant girls Murn was the one who had tried hardest to achieve burning ambition in life and had somehow only succeeded in making herself an unhappy, unnatural young woman. She and Nellie had never got on. 'There's something about you,' Murn had once said, 'something that I never understood nor ever will.'

'And there's something about you,' Nellie had retaliated ably, 'which minds me o' thon folk who go on the stage and act their way through life. If you go on as you're doing, you will end up a poor cratur you yourself will never know.'

Murn had responded with some cutting remarks about Nellie's own ability to smother herself beneath a shell of suspicion and mistrust, but now the two sisters faced one another, all emnity suspended in a shared moment of sympathy.

'You were wrong to barge in on him the way you said you were going to.' Nellie chose her words carefully. 'He's – he's a bruised man now, Murn, and I suppose he really does just want to be left alone to nurse his wounds. He loved Jeannie, wi' all his heart he loved her and I doubt there's another woman in the land who could ever take her place. You should have let him be, Murn, it's far too early yet for him to be rational about anything and certainly no' able to cope wi' the kind o' feelings he kens fine you have aye had for him.'

'I know that now.' Murn twisted her fingers, her voice

128

bleak. 'And I've shamed myself in his sight and ruined any chance I might ever have had with him. I'm a fool – a stupid, immature fool! You've said that often enough of me but I never thought I'd see the day I would admit you to be right.'

She rushed away upstairs and her door banged. The kitchen seemed all at once silent and peaceful. Nellie hesitated, wondering if she should go up and try to comfort the sister who had always irritated her most. She had never regarded Murn with much affection, yet there was a first time for everything and she was getting to a stage in her life where she had to reach out to those around her and let them see that she wasn't the cold, unloving woman they all imagined her to be. But she had no time to make a move. From the track there was a great scraiching and skirling, and a few seconds later five figures came fleeing over the cobbles with Maggie, Betsy O'Neil and Hinney in the lead, the latter's mutch cap sitting squintily over one large ear, her greying carroty hair sprouting untidily over the other as she puffed after the agile Maggie, her spindly black-booted feet fairly pounding the stoor from the yard as she hammered along. Despite the encumbrance of loose flopping breasts and a big stomach, the otherwise skinny Betsy was literally abreast of Maggie and the pair of them skited into the kitchen, followed closely by Hinney. At their back came Jessie Blair of the Mains, treble chins wobbling, great breasts heaving under her voluminous smock, fire-mottled legs chafing against each other as she ran so that they made an odd, rhythmic rubbing sound like dry linen sheets scuffing together. Behind her came The Loon, spiky yellow hair sticking up wildly, his big clairty feet fairly flying along so that bits of dried dung flew up from his heels as if from the hooves of a carthorse.

'Dyod! What on earth . . .' Nellie rushed to the door, her broom clutched in her hands, her eyes popping almost out of her head. 'Mind my clean floor!' she yelled as the first pair thundered towards her, almost knocking her over in their rush to get indoors. Jessie's fleering skirts released a terrible hotchpotch of odours as she pelted past Nellie;

The Loon's great tackity boots cracked against her shin making her curse as she had never cursed before. Mud, dung and dust littered the gleaming flags. Nellie put both hands to her head as if to tear out her hair, in the process pulling out some of the restraining pins so that tendrils of it fell free and fair about her red, contorted face.

'The door!' Maggie panted. 'Shut the door!'

Hinney was spreadeagled on an upright kitchen chair, too winded to speak as she fanned herself with a copy of *The Press and Journal*. Jessie was also speechless and just lay where she had landed in the inglenook, fanning herself with old Tab's tail, the first thing that had come to hand. He had slunk up there when Nellie wasn't looking and now his eyes rolled back in abject submission to human wiles, although, as Jessie's aromas filtered to his nostrils, his whiskers twitched and he arose, getting down from the seat with all the dignity an old sheepdog can muster in rheumy limbs. His tail between his legs, he slunk from the room, shame and disgrace in every stiff muscle, taking all the blame for Jessie's smells fairly and squarely on his old shoulders.

The Loon turned hastily to shut the door, but before he could do so the mat went from under him on the slippery floor and down he went, the segs on his heels throwing up sparks and a fresh smattering of mud onto the tiles.

'Mother!' Nellie expostulated. 'Would you mind telling me just what—' She stopped short. A great commotion came from outside. The dogs were barking madly and running up and down in great excitement with their tails tucked between their legs, while the hens clucked and screamed and ran helter-skelter up the yard in a flurry of feathers. Even the sparrows flew off the barn roof and made for the safety of the trees, where they twittered to one another in nervous discord. The stallion, or *staig* as he was known in these parts, had arrived at King's Croft, sweeping all before him on his journey along the turnpike and up the track. His name was Endeavour, an apt title for a beast by whose efforts around a hundred mares a season were impregnated, with rarely a failure amongst them. Endeavour was a polished, gleaming brown, as aware of his pedigree as he was of his power, a magnificent, wild-eyed creature whose dancing hooves struck sparks from the cobbles and rang out their own particular rhythm. His great head was arched to the stallion bar, but every so often he lifted it and tossed his forelock away from his rolling eyes, champing his bit and sending flecks of foam flying over his rippling shoulders. He was a ton weight of splendid bone, sinew, and hot flanks and looked too much of a handful for the little man who walked beside him holding him on a short rein. But Lang Will Studdie, as he was quaintly known, was, in proportion to his size, possessed with as much bone and sinew as his charge. He was a familiar figure in the north-east landscape and for twenty of his forty years had 'travelled the staig'.

Early on in his career he had earned himself his nickname for, if gossip was to be believed, his prowess with the servant lasses was legendary, his reputation every bit as coarse as the horses he handled. But apparently oblivious to the strings of bairns he was reputed to have left in his wake, Lang Will Studdie went on his lonesome way, 'a teenie wee man wi' guid room in his trousers for mischief', his big brown mouser almost obliterating his weatherbeaten face, his tackity-booted feet striking out purposefully along the highways and byways.

A droll man was Lang Will Studdie, so straight-faced when cracking a joke or telling a funny story that he could be a mile up the stoorie road before folk realized his words had been meant to be laughed at.

A contingent of dogs and small boys followed behind him as he led Endeavour into King's Croft yard. The stallion's nostrils flared and he tossed his mane as Queenie's scent filtered to him from among numerous farmyard smells. The mare strained at her tethers at sight of the great beast coming towards her, and while Jamie hurried to greet Lang Will Studdie, Nellie rushed to shut the kitchen door with an almighty bang which rattled the window sashes.

'Mind you,' commented Hinney with a twinkle as she

took off her boots to rub her feet, 'I dinna think the beast will get its girth through that wee space.'

'Och well now, I'm no' so sure o' that,' Betsy grinned with a sly glance at Jessie, 'it's amazing the things that manage to squeeze themselves through these doorways.'

'Ay, amazing,' snorted Jessie, pulling in her stomach and eyeing Betsy's balefully. 'And if you're hinting at me, Betsy O'Neil, I can tell you mine is honest to goodness fat and no' a blubber o' slack muscles brought on by carryin' too many bairns. I only had my Laurence, bless him, but when I did I carried him well and no' somewhere down about my ankles so that the very cobbles themselves might bash the brains out o' him.'

'Ach, Laurence Bless Him Blair didna need the brains knocked out o' him for he had none in his skull to start with,' Betsy retorted, her eyes gleaming as Jessie rose indignantly to the taunt, though her flow of insults was stemmed abruptly and rudely by Nellie whose eyes were glued to the window, watching the progress of Endeavour.

'Stop your bickering,' she chided them acidly, her clean floor forgotten in all the upheaval. 'When all's said and done an elephant could try to squeeze through that door if it had a mind and I for one am taking no chances. These staigs are vicious craturs and I aye keep out o' their way – though I doubt I would ever go stampeding through folk's houses just because one happened to be at my back,' she ended meaningfully.

'I saw one once, over by Clintock,' volunteered The Loon who was recovering from his tumble by taking his ease in a chair which Nellie had recently polished. She had made him remove his filthy boots and his dusty jacket, but even so threw him glances of outrage as he went on, 'It smelled a pan o' brose cooling on the kitchen table and tried to squeeze itself in through the door to get at it. There it was, its great erse stuck neither in nor out, the groom pulling at the outside end and the mistress o' the house poking it wi' a broom at the other . . .'

'Ach, Pooty,' Nellie scolded him scathingly. 'That mother o' yours fills your head wi' far too much nonsense. I doubt she got that one from the men at the inn when she was fu' to the een wi' the drink,' she concluded in rank disapproval of Dottie Drummond, the only woman of the parish to frequent the village inn, much to the chagrin of the good wives of Rothiedrum and the secret envy of a few.

The Loon's face crumpled. 'It's true I'm tellin' ye! I saw it wi' my very own een, and if you think I'm lying what way for why did ye shut the door?'

Maggie stood up and removed her hat. 'No matter which way, the beast fairly put the wind up us when we met it on the turnpike. When it saw us it began cavorting and snorting and we just took hands and flew along. Now that we're here, we'll all have a good strong cuppy to revive us.'

'Are ye comin' tae help us, Nell?' Lang Will Studdie was peering in at the window – and just inches away was the stallion's great foam-flecked face. The groom's features were perfectly composed and serious, and only Maggie and Hinney saw the twinkle in his eyes. After the first horrified glimpse, Nellie saw nothing. She dropped the tea canister she was holding and went shrieking away ben the house to the safety of the parlour.

Lang Will Studdie winked at Jamie. 'Well, man, it looks as if we'll just hae to see to the coupling ourselves. Go you for the mare and I'll take Endeavour roond the corner.'

'Roond the corner' was a place at the blind side of the steadings away from curious eyes, for despite his droll teasing the groom would have had a fit if he thought a female of any sort had witnessed a coupling. Such things were for the eyes of men only and in his efforts to keep the affair as private as possible the little man took a stout stick and chased away the small boys – though there was no real need. The fearsome whinnyings and snortings that rent the air as the coupling took place saw to it very effectively that the blind end of the steadings remained free of unwelcome onlookers.

'You can come ben now, Nellie,' Betsy called. 'When the staig next passes the window he will have no strength left to even lick a fly from his withers.'

'No,' Nellie called back emphatically. 'I'll bide in here till the beast has left the croft. It's no' flies *it's* after.'

The Loon poured his tea into his saucer and drank from it noisily. 'I was just thinkin',' he mused, in a voice much louder than normal. 'It's a pity Evie's no' here the day.'

Hovering uncertainly in the lobby, Nellie pricked up her sharp ears. 'What do you mean – Evie?' Her indignant voice floated in. 'Evie never took anything to do wi' a coupling.'

'Oh ay she did,' goaded The Loon gleefully. 'She and me watched it often enough – ay, and Johnny and Florrie too when they were alive.'

'Never – oh, how could she?' Nellie's strangulated protest came loud and clear.

'Easy – oh ay, easy enough. We just got in the straw shed and peeked through a wee knot in the planks. It was good too. Folks think the staigs do all the work but Lang Will Studdie does most o' it, ay. He has a good steady hand on him for seeing the staig into the right place.'

'Pooty Drummond! You're a liar and a disgusting one at that!' Nellie cried in horrified disbelief.

The Loon lay back in his chair, clutched his stomach and gave way to one of his wheezing fits of laughter which Betsy had once likened to the sounds made by a wind-tormented cow.

The womenfolk looked at The Loon. His big horny toes were sticking up out of his holey socks, his unkempt yellow head was thrown back, his mouth stretched wide as he gave full throttle to his huge enjoyment. Bit by bit he was sliding off his polished perch to land eventually on top of one of the cats, which screamed mightily and scampered away to nurse its injured pride.

'My, my, the poor cratur,' Jessie nodded sadly, her chins wobbling in unison.

Maggie looked at Hinney, Hinney at Betsy and with one accord they threw up their hands and joined The Loon in his noisy, infectious mirth.

# CHAPTER NINE

It was spring in the Aulton. Along by the Brig of Balgownie the Don burbled its tranquil way down to the sea, and fat green buds were ready for popping into full leaf on the trees where branches hung over garden walls, gently tapping the heads of tall people who chanced to walk beneath them. Outside the Town House a few old men stood close together in desultory conversation while children played happily in cottage gardens, their peals of laughter echoing the chiming of the Cathedral and College bells.

Evelyn experienced a wonderful sense of euphoria as she rode in the cart down towards College Bounds. The blossoms were pink and white bowers on the apple trees, the birds were flirting and singing from every hedgerow, and Evelyn looked at it all and felt as if her life was just beginning that bonny blue day. She felt as if she had awakened from a long dark dream and was seeing everything for the first time. She gave Fyvie his rein and allowed him to canter, and just then she passed Gordon Chisholm and her sister Grace walking arm in arm along the Chanonry. She shouted but they didn't hear, and brought Fyvie to a halt outside the sedate, eighteenth-century Town House which had once housed provosts and baillies but which now incorporated a police station and a reading room.

She apprehended Grace and Gordon as they were turning the corner. The latter's great bear of a hug smothered Evelyn, while Grace's warm greetings rang in her ears. But when Evelyn surfaced from Gordon's embrace to look at her sister, she saw that her eyes were too bright in her lovely face, masking the terrible mixture of emotions that must have been in her heart.

For Gordon was going away to work in a field hospital in France. Gregor had recently gone, leaving behind him

Doctor Sandy McDuff, a grizzled, bewhiskered old gentleman who was already driving Mary to despair with his
eccentricities and carnaptious nature.

McDuff the Guff, the folk of Rothiedrum had soon
christened him for a variety of reasons. 'He canna tell the
difference between a plook and a boil,' bemoaned Betsy
painfully, after experiencing McDuff's none too tender
administration on her affected parts. 'There he took and
lanced the wee pimples on my bum, like a bloody great
chieftain going into battle wi' his claymore. Before I could
blink I was nearly drawn and quartered, and when I said it
was only a few plooks I had come about he just grinned that
lecherous grin o' his and told me I had the finest crop o'
boils he had ever clapped eyes on!'

Only four weeks had passed since Gregor's going, yet
already everyone was speaking his name with fond reverence and wishing for his speedy return. But it would be a
long time before Gregor returned to the rural peace of
Rothiedrum. In March of that year the British offensive to
capture the Aubers Ridge had seen heavy losses at the
Neuve Chapelle salient, and these days it seemed there was
always a crowd outside Bunty Lovie's scanning the casualty
lists, Kirsty Keith to the fore, her face pale and strained,
her bony hands working nervously as she confided to
Evelyn, 'If he's even taken prisoner it will no' be so bad – at
least he'll be alive, Evie, he'll be alive.'

'Greg will no' be back for a whilie, Evie,' Mary said
bleakly, her eyes big in her bonny face as she stood with her
sister outside the post office. It was as if the gravity of war
had touched her for the first time and Evelyn tossed her red
head and said tightly, 'No, Mary, he wasna going over there
just for a holiday you know.'

Mary's tragic face smote her heart, and regretting her
hasty words she hurried her sister back to Rowanlea, there
to sit her in the kitchen and ply her with whisky-laced tea
while McDuff the Guff stomped round the room, waving
his coat tails gently up and down and clicking his teeth
together, an action which became intensified when he was
agitated in any way, and as that was a frequent occurrence,

they seemed to be forever clacking furiously inside his head. Jessie Blair put everyone's opinion in a nutshell when she commented, 'The sound o' his wallies chapping one another fair sets my own on edge. If he'd just take the damt things out and gnash his gums it wouldna be so bad, but no! Squelch, click, grate, all day long. 'Tis no wonder his poor wife died a raving lunatic in the asylum.'

The doctor's habits irritated Mary beyond measure, and once she had been moved to ask the reasons for the waving of the scuffed and shiny coat tails.

'It keeps my vitals cool, Mary, lass, keeps them cool,' he had explained graciously, with a wicked twinkle of humour which was not appreciated by the irate young woman. 'Besides,' he had continued, with a thoughtful twirling of his waxed grey moustache, 'it also helps disperse the wind – at my age you get to be full of it – very embarrassing, my dear, ay, but needs must, lass, needs must.'

Despite all that, Evelyn liked old McDuff. Irascible and irritating he certainly was, but he could also be interesting and amusing and she suspected he exaggerated many of his eccentricities for Mary's benefit. Secretly, Evelyn hugged herself with delight at the outrage he instilled in her sister and though she didn't ever say so, she felt that Mary had met an able match for her own little quirks and contrariness of nature and she certainly appreciated now all that Gregor had ever meant to her.

It was different with Grace. She didn't need Gordon's absence to make her heart grow any fonder than it was already. With all her heart she loved him, and had been devastated when first he told her of his intentions to help the wounded in France. To Evelyn she had poured out her fears, but now she appeared calm and cool and ready, if not willing, to wave her beloved Gordon goodbye. These were his last few hours with her. She touched him with her hands, her eyes, yet she did not cling to him or speak to him with undue sentiment. She was bracing herself for the loneliness that was ahead of her and Gordon, sensing this, held her very close and tenderly. They asked Evelyn where she was going, and when she told them she had been shopping for the weekly supplies but was now on her way to Grandmother's, Gordon took her arm and said, 'Then we'll all go. Grace and I were just on our way there. I would never hear the end of it if I didn't say my farewells to that grand old lady.'

He paused, his head went up. Evelyn's hand went to Fyvie's reins to draw him in closer to the pavement. Life and light was in the air that day in the Aulton, but now it intensified and grew. The children stopped in their play, a spark of interest gleamed in the eyes of the old men, and one and all gazed towards the Chanonry where the College gentlemen were making their leisurely way home to lunch. Round the front of the Town House came the procession of the urban cows, udders swinging gently, tails flicking away the flies which converged on them from the surrounding fields and gardens.

In among the huddle of houses the town dairies thrived, the dairymen bringing in cattle feed from the farms round about. Twice a day in spring and summer the town cows were driven to open ground beyond Cluny's Point, and nothing did the Chanonry gentlemen desire less than their sedate, homeward footsteps coinciding with the dung-splattered ones of the inquisitive urban cows. For the beasts took a positive delight in tormenting the peaceful gentlemen of the Chanonry. One could see Satan himself dancing devilishly about in those deceptively gentle bovine orbs.

Fooling about, butting the air, feigning panic and complete surprise, they lifted their tails and sprayed the Chanonry with dung and torrents of urine. Hot steam arose, the gentlemen pirouetted around the molten puddles, waving their newspapers and sticks ineffectually in the air and making haste on their way, with the cows in placid but devilish pursuit.

Grace, Gordon and Evelyn watched the show with bated breath. Then, as one irate gentleman hurried past, brandishing his umbrella and muttering, 'Disgraceful! Disgraceful!' they all fell one upon the other, forgetting to be restrained and dignified in a public place.

'Those cows *know*!' gurgled Gordon. 'They damned well know they're doing wrong and they revel in it.'

Evelyn clutched Grace, her red head touching her sister's chestnut locks. She felt outrageously happy, a great warmth pulsed in her heart. There was something else – something more than this day of spring, of people, of laughter . . .

'So I'm not the only one to recognize the marvellous sense of humour these cows possess.'

The words fell on her ears, cool as raindrops, rich as the purpled shadows of night-darkened haughs. She raised her head and looked into her sister's eyes and in their dark depths she saw recognition, for to Grace and Grace alone had she confided her dreams together with a word picture of the man who had waved to her from a speeding train, so long ago that it seemed to belong to another time and place.

Slowly she turned and there he was, standing against the sun, his hair the same shade as newly turned earth yet brushed with red and gold so that it wasn't of two colours as she remembered but like spring and summer and autumn all rolled into one.

'You remember me, don't you – or am I asking too much?' He was laughing, that faint trace of mockery in his voice, his eyes. She said nothing, she couldn't. He introduced himself. David – David Alexander Grainger. At last, a name for that face – that boy's face she felt she knew so well, yet didn't know at all. He was older, thinner, with hollows in his cheeks that hadn't been in her memories of him.

'You're Evie's friend.' Grace's hand went out to take his. 'I've heard a lot about you. I'm Grace, her sister, and this is Doctor Gordon Chisholm.'

'Well, *I* haven't heard of you.' Gordon was smiling his big warm smile. 'But sisters are like that, keep all their little secrets to themselves.'

'We're going along to visit our grandmother,' Evelyn spoke breathlessly, too aware of him, of her own rapidly beating heart. 'At least we call her that but she isn't really. She and Aunt Mattie, who isn't really our aunt, are great friends of ours through my father.'

She was speaking too rapidly, and in utter confusion she

139

grabbed hold of Fyvie and began leading him along College Bounds, Grace and Gordon following, the new arrival falling into step beside her.

'So, you're Evie,' he smiled 'The guessing of your name has been a great comfort to me these last months. When I had time to think I endowed you with all sorts of titles but in the end I always came back to – Bright Eyes.'

Her head went up. She didn't let him see how pleased she was that he had actually thought about her all through that long cold winter. 'I'm Evelyn McKenzie Grant in actual fact and—' she turned the full radiance of her smile on him '—it's so nice to meet you again, David, to know that you're real and no' the ghost I was beginning to think you must be. I christened you The Ghost Soldier – it seems so daft now that you're here beside me in the flesh.'

'I'm real enough, Evie – and I hope I might get the chance to prove it to you.' His hands began to tremble suddenly, and he fumbled quickly in his pocket to withdraw a packet of Woodbine. 'I took a bit of a bashing at Neuve Chapelle,' he explained quietly. 'Oh, nothing too serious, a stomach wound, it shook me up more than anything. I was laid up for a while at a Red Cross hospital in France before I was shipped back here to recuperate. As soon as I can I'll be going to Glasgow to see my parents but meanwhile—' His dark gaze rested on her. 'I could be doing with a lovely young redhead to cheer me up, help me to fill in my time.'

They had arrived at Grandmother's house. Big Mattie was at the gate, beating a rug to a dusty pulp on the spars. Her huge arms rose and fell, rose and fell, her great feather pillow of a bosom bounced majestically inside the loose confines of her pinafore, her apple-bright cheeks were shiny with the sweat of her labours and about them tumbled rich fat sausages of night-black hair. At sight of the visitors her dark eyes lit up, and in between coughing and spluttering on lungfuls of dust she hailed everyone with delight and bade them indoors where the kettle was 'singin' its heart out on the hob just waiting to be made into tea.'

Evelyn smiled at David. 'You could start by visiting

Grandmother. She looks like the big bad wolf in disguise but I promise she won't eat you.'

His hand touched hers. It was warm and firm. 'All right, if you come for a walk with me afterwards. I'd face a thousand wolfish grandmothers if I knew you were waiting for me at the end o' it.'

Grandmother greeted Grace and Gordon rapturously but she was highly suspicious of David Alexander Grainger, barking out questions at him, peering at him critically over her specs. Hugh, the young student lodger, was just finishing his dinner. Hearing the tone of Grandmother's voice he sidled off his chair, and was about to slink through to his room when the old lady's shrill bark stayed him.

Come back here this meenit, lad,' she ordered querulously. 'You will take and wash my teeth in the sink before ye go and bury your nose in these books o' yours. You ken I trust ye to do that for me, don't you, son?'

'Ay, Grandmother,' agreed Hugh meekly, standing by the bed with his hands folded behind his back as if he was on the headmaster's mat. 'It's just, well, seeing you have visitors I thought you winna want me butting in.'

'Butting in? Ach, ye're dafter than I thought. You're as good as family, son, and no' all my visitors are kent by me. You can see yourself there is a stranger among them.'

Mattie scowled darkly at the old warrior, while Evelyn squirmed and wondered what David was thinking. He was at the window smoking another cigarette, and Evelyn marched over to the bed and hissed, 'Grandmother, what ails you? Davie is my friend and you're behaving like an ill-mannered old dragon.'

The old lady's face softened. She took Evelyn's hand and made her sit down close by her. 'I want tae see what he's made of, Evie. He's a fine-lookin' laddie and I ken fine he's had a hard time over yonder but a brave soldier doesna necessarily make a good husband.'

Evelyn was flabbergasted. Crimson washed over her face, flooding into the very roots of her hair. 'Husband! Grannie, be quiet! I only found out his name a few minutes ago. I dinna ken him at all yet.'

141

The silvered head nodded wisely. 'Ay, that's just it,' she murmured. 'You dinna ken a thing aboot him and already you are that sore in love wi' him ye canna tell if ye are right comin' or goin'. You've been hurt too much already in your wee life and I winna want ye tae suffer like that again.'

'We all have to suffer in one way or another,' Evelyn said softly. 'If we didn't, we wouldn't recognize the happy times when they come.'

Grandmother looked at Grace and Gordon, so engrossed in each other they were hardly aware of anyone else in the room. The old lady sighed. 'Ay, ye're right, my wee one. That bonny doctor and your sister are good examples o' that. Is it no' awful, Evie? She has just found him only to lose him in a wee while. And the pair o' them that sore in love it makes my auld heart beat funny just to watch them.'

'She won't lose him, Grannie. He isna going to fight, just to help people who are.'

'Ay, you're maybe right at that – people like that young lad over there wi' the thin quiet face and the eyes o' him showing the awful things he must have seen. What did ye call him again?'

'His name's Davie – well, David really, but I like Davie best.'

At that moment the peace of the house was broken. Loud and tuneless singing came from the lobby, and next minute a drunken Jake came staggering into the kitchen, eyes wild, face red and sweating.

'Have ye the kettle on, Mattie?' he demanded. 'I've come tae hae a cup o' tea wi' my favourite old Grannie.'

Mattie's lip curled in uncharacteristic loathing. 'You're drunk, Jake, get out o' here this minute and dinna dare come back in that state ever. Can ye no' see we have guests and canna be doin' wi' the likes o' you under our feet?'

'Guests is it, eh? No' just plain old visitors but guests no less.' Brutally, he dug his thick fingers into the soft flesh of Mattie's arm before tottering drunkenly round to survey the room. 'Oh ay,' his fleshy lips stretched into a leer, 'I see what ye mean, Mattie, and among them Jamie's youngest quine, only a bit lass, yet by Dyod! enough to make any man go weak at the knees . . .' He made a lunge towards the bed. Before Evelyn could move he was on her, pawing her, slavering over her face with his soggy wet mouth . . . The next moment he was lifted up by the scruff of the neck and marched without ceremony towards the door.

'Out.' David's voice was firm and cold. 'You heard what the lady said. She doesna want you here so off you go and leave these good folk in peace.'

Jake looked as if he would like to kill the young soldier standing so squarely and coolly in front of him, but something in the steady brown eyes stayed the swing of his big meaty fists and he contented himself by saying thickly and contemptuously, 'Lady you say? The bloody war must have knocked you stupid if you think our Mattie's a lady. Now that one—' his oily gaze slid lecherously in Evelyn's direction – '*that* might be called a lady if it wasna for the glint in those bonny green een o' hers. You must ken it too or you wouldna have sprung so eagerly to defend what ye might be hoping to get for yourself. I'll reckon wi' her again or my name's no' Jake McPhee . . .' The words strangled in his throat as he was seized once more by the scruff of his grubby collars and bundled from the lobby straight into the street.

David came back breathing a little heavily, visibly shaken by the effort of removing the bull-like Jake from the premises.

'Come over here, laddie,' Grandmother beckoned with a rheumy finger. David straightened, and composing himself went to stand in front of the old lady. He said a few words to her in traveller's cant.

She gasped, Mattie stared. 'Where did ye learn that, son?' asked the old woman in downright astonishment.

A smile quirked David's pale lips. 'From an uncle of mine. I was only a boy at the time and only picked up a few words but those I never forgot.'

Grandmother was impressed. 'An uncle you say? Sit ye down by me, boy, and tell me all about him. He would be living in Glasgow, for you yourself are a Glaswegian and no mistake. If ye tell me his name I might know who he was. *Mattie – .'* She raised her voice. 'Go you ben the house and bring through that bottle o' whisky from the cupboard. This laddie looks as if he could be doin' wi' something stronger than tea.'

Evelyn watched as David smiled. He was in and he knew it.

The drams were passed around. Half an hour later a flushed and garrulous Grandmother was lying back on her pillows humming a bothy ballad while Mattie sang in the scullery at the top of her voice.

'Onward Christian so-o-o-o-ldiers marching as to-o war . . .' A pause as the words were forgotten then a triumphant, 'See his ba-angers go.'

'It's banners, ye daft wumman,' screeched Grandmother, while everyone else listened with bated breath as Mattie swung into another song, 'John Brown's body lies a-hummin' in his grave but his soul goes ma-a-rching on.'

With a whoop of delight, Gordon was on his feet and running into the scullery. He and Mattie emerged, she now singing her favourite 'Jer-oos-alem', not one note of it faltering as the doctor danced her round the room and added his own deep bass to her infectious 'Whose Annas'. When it came to the finale everyone joined in, even David, whose eyes were sparkling and whose face had lost its seriousness as '— In the high-est, whose-anna for-eeever more' hit the roof.

When it was time to leave, Gordon drew Evelyn aside. 'You'll look after my Grace, won't you, Evie? She's the most precious thing that's ever happened to me—' He drew in his breath. 'I hate myself for leaving her but I would hate myself even more if I didn't go. I was never much good at anything in my life except mending broken bodies. It's the one thing I do reasonably well and I feel I have to do this small service for my country.'

Evelyn put her arms round him and kissed him on the beard. 'You're a very modest man, Gordon Chisholm. Dinna worry about Grace. She's prepared herself for your going and I'll try and see her as often as I can.'

He patted her shoulder and turned to take Grace into his

embrace. Evelyn watched them walking away, then went slowly to meet David who was waiting for her by the gate.

Without a word he helped her climb into the cart. Taking Fyvie's reins, he turned his nose up towards the Brig of Balgownie. In the green fields beside the river they unhitched the little sheltie to allow him to graze the sweet grasses, then hand in hand they walked down to the river. The water tumbled clean and sweet over the stones; blackbirds sang from snowy hawthorn bowers, and the moss was soft beneath their feet. The scents of spring surged on the breezes; the tang of the sea lent a clean sharp fragrance to the air.

'Thanks for rescuing me from Whisky Jake.' She spoke quietly, unwilling to break the silence.

'Who is he anyway? He looks a bad lot.'

'I dinna ken really. Father knew him from long ago. Both Mattie and Grandmother seem afraid of him. There's — there's also something odd between him and my elder sister, Nellie. She's more than afraid o' him, yet she won't talk to any o' us about him.'

'You watch him.' David was looking at her strangely. 'He's no' the sort to let go in a hurry and he's got his eye on you, Evie.'

They fell silent after that. She didn't know how long they walked without speaking. It could have been minutes or hours: she neither knew nor cared. From time to time, she stole a glance at him. He had changed in some momentous way. Dark shadows lay deep in his eyes, haggard lines were deeply etchcd at his mouth. In just a few months the boy had grown into a man — yet he was only nineteen, the same age as Johnny when he had died. Johnny had still been a boy then, uncertain about so many things.

Davie's hand was strong over hers — yet, she shivered, every so often a faint tremor ran through him into her. She wondered what he was really like. She knew so little about him — but why, then, did she feel as if she had known him all her life? — as if he had been in it all along, waiting — just waiting for the hour, the day, the moments — like these.

Abruptly he stopped, and pulled her close to him. His

145

hands were on her hair, stroking it, letting the silken strands run through his fingers. He bent his head and kissed her throat. 'It's really you,' he said at last. 'I hoped but never really believed I would ever see you again.' He was staring at her, wonder in the deep pools of his eyes. 'I never let go of that last picture of you – standing at the station amongst the crowd. It was your hair I noticed first, such a bright beacon of flame in all the drabness. I thought you had come to see someone else away; never, never did I think it could be me. Then you waved and it was too late – the train went on and on away from you and I thought I had lost you – until today.'

'And I thought – that girl who came to say goodbye to you—'

He pulled her closer. 'The sister of one of my mates. She's a good lass, always makes a point of seeing the loners off.'

She made no protest as he gathered her into his arms and sought her mouth. Again and again they kissed, breathlessly, hungrily. His mouth was warm, vibrant and demanding. Passion rose in her, frightening her with its intensity. She never wanted to let go of him. His fingers strayed across her breasts. She arched her neck and cried out, 'Davie, oh, Davie.'

Afraid of her own terrible need for him, she pulled herself out of his arms, shaking her head in disbelief. This couldn't be. She couldn't allow it to happen. Once she had dreamed of such a love, a powerful passion that would sweep her off her feet and make her lose all reason. But that had been the foolish dream of a child. Love for Johnny had been a quiet, beautiful emotion. She had loved Johnny, with all her heart she had loved him, and now this – this searing raw desire which laid bare her soul and made every one of her senses vulnerable to attack . . .

'I – I must go home now.' With shaking fingers she straightened her clothes and made to turn away from him. But his hand was on her arm, cool, firm, determined.

'Evie, you can't run away from this. It didn't begin here today by the riverbank. It began months ago when first I saw your lovely face in the window of Bert's Tea Shoppe. You can't deny it or you would be lying. You didn't forget me, Evie, you remembered. Your sister Grace told me so today and you must have remembered pretty well to have described me so thoroughly that she knew who I was as soon as she set eyes on me.'

'Ach, dinna flatter yourself,' she cried, more angry with herself than with him. 'You're just passing your time wi' me as you must have passed it wi' hundreds of others. Here . . .' Her hand went up to her neck to pull off the blue ribbon with his ring at the end of it. 'This is yours, take it back for I dinna want it any more.'

He looked at it dangling in front of him and smiled, the same mischievous smile she had seen on his face during their meeting in Bert's Tea Shoppe. 'Our good luck symbol – and you wore it near your heart as you said you would. I want you to keep it, Evie—' Fiercely he pulled her to him once again and crushed her mouth against his '—it might bring us more luck, and who knows – someday you may need my ring to fool the world.'

Warmth enveloped her again, her legs felt like jelly. He released her and she turned on him. 'Just what did you mean by that? Fool the world?'

He shook his head. 'I don't know, I don't know why I said it. I'm a bittie tired, and saying things that mean nothing.' His fingers clamped round her wrist. 'I know one thing though, I must see you again. Tell me when and where.'

'I have an afternoon off next week,' she murmured weakly. 'I'll meet you at Bert's shop in Cobbly Wynd at two o'clock.'

'As long away as that? Make it sooner. You must get time off in the evenings – what is it you do anyway?'

She told him, ending, 'Unless I'm needed for something special I get away around teatime – though I have my chores to do after that or I would never hear the end o' it from my sister Nellie.'

'Right, I'll get the train up to Rothiedrum tomorrow evening. I'll be at the station around seven.'

'Seven! Oh, but I'd never—'

'Seven,' he repeated obstinately.

'You're very sure o' yourself,' she told him, frowning a little.

He smiled, the warm, beautiful smile she had cherished in her dreams of him though when he said, 'I'm sure of you, Evie,' she glared at him and turned away once more. Over her shoulder she threw back, 'Was it true what you told Grandmother? About having an uncle who was a gypsy?'

'Ay, the title uncle being in the same context as aunt for your Mattie.' There was laughter in his voice. 'I loved that old man and haunted his house when I was a boy. He told me such bonny stories about his travelling days. In many ways he was like your old werewolf back there, all bark and no bite. There's something about these travelling folk that's utterly fascinating.'

'I know,' she said, still suddenly.

'There's a bit o' the gypsy in you, isn't there, Evie? I felt it the moment I saw you.'

'Ay, more than a bit – I'll tell you about my family some time.'

'I'll look forward to that. But, for now, goodbye – Bright Eyes.'

She ran from him then, retracing the path they had trod together, her feet flying over the sun-dappled earth, the breath catching in her throat, her heart singing in her breast in a way she had never thought it could again, after young Johnny Burns had been laid to his final rest in the old kirkyard beside the peaceful waters of Loch Bree.

Her father met her in the yard as she came out of the stable, and taking her arm, he led her over to his shoppe. 'I have something to show you, Evie. Come away inside.' His voice was filled with quiet elation and her heart beat a little quicker as she stepped over the worn pavings and into the dim recesses of the small shed. She had never been back in there since that last heartbreaking time when she had found his empty whisky bottles hidden in a jumble of rubbish behind the work bench, and she held her breath

148

now, as if expecting those selfsame bottles to leap out at her from nowhere to mock her prying eyes.

It took some little time for her eyes to grow accustomed to the dimness after the brightness of the day.

'Come in, Princess, come in.' Jamie pulled her further in. His eyes were on her face, eagerly, expectantly, as if he didn't want to miss one moment of the expression of surprise he so obviously wanted to see there.

She gazed around blankly, seeing only the cobwebs and the dust, biting her lip a trifle desperately as her eyes raked the gloom.

'Evie, Evie lass.' His voice was filled with an anxiety that was tinged with despair.

'Father,' she said half-heartedly, and was about to ask him why he had brought her here when she saw the reason, and after the first disbelieving glimpse she wondered why her sight had remained shuttered for so long. Hanging from the rafters, piled on dusty shelves, were rows and rows of boots. The air reeked with the delicious pungent scent of new leather and she breathed it in as if she could never get enough of it, all the time berating herself for being so senseless as to have missed it in the first place.

She ran all over the little room, touching the boots, running her fingers over them with reverence. They were serviceable and sturdy, yet each one was stamped with Jamie's special touch. They were a labour of love from the fingers of a highly skilled craftsman.

'They're for our lads, Evie,' he explained, watching her. 'Your mother gave me the idea o' it and somehow it just grew from there.'

'But the leather, Father, where did you get it all?'

'Ach, I scrounged bits o' scrap from Souter Jock and the rest I just bought from saving the shillings I used to spend on drink—' He lowered his head, shame sitting heavily on the stoop of his shoulders. 'I'm no' that much use to anybody these days, Princess, but making boots is second nature to me and it was the least I could do to help in wartime.'

She threw back her head and put her clenched fist to her

mouth. 'Father, don't – don't ever say that again! Where's the pride I always knew in James King Grant? You're no' some bit carthorse wi' its shoulders low to the ground. You're my father and the best there is, and I'm proud o' you for what you've done here – but no more proud than I was before!' Going to him, she put her arms round him and kissed the top of his head. 'I love you, Father, never forget it. I always have and I always will.'

'I know that, lassie, I know,' he said huskily. 'You've been the comfort o' my life, but whatever you say I've failed you – I've failed you all. I'm no' the strong man you thought I was when you were a wee bit bairn. You're grown now, Evie, and you can see my weaknesses and many's the time I've hated myself for it.'

'Ach, havers,' she scolded with a watery smile. 'We're all weak in some way and you're no worse than any o' us, so stop blethering on like an old woman and come over to the house for your tea before Mam skelps us both round the lugs.'

He laughed. 'You're getting to be worse than your sister Nell.' He stayed her at the threshold of his shoppe. 'It's been good talking to you, Evie. I dinna get much o' a chance o' that nowadays, you're aye that busy elsewhere. You used to creep away to be by yourself so that you could write those stories o' yours. What happened to all your dreams, Princess? Have you given them up?'

'No, they gave me up. I was a bairn when I had all those grand notions in my head about writing and books. All I have to say now goes into my diaries. I still keep those and suppose I always will, though they'll never be any value to anyone but myself.'

'But you're happy, lass? Happier than you were. I can feel it in you and it's there in those bonny eyes o' yours for all the world to see.'

'For you to see, Father. Of all the people in my world you were aye the one who could read me best – I'm the book I might never write and I'm that faint wi' hunger I'm beginning to sound like The Loon when he gets carried away with himself.'

150

It was late. The house slept. Evelyn lay on her back, gazing at the shadowy ceiling, listening to the rain pittering off the slates, a soft rain that fell from the low clouds which had gathered after dusk. Clasped to her breast was the little corn dolly that Johnny had given her on her fifteenth birthday, and lying open at her side was her diary. In it she had just written:

*It is spring, 1915, and I am afraid. Today The Ghost Soldier came back into my life, no ghost but warm living flesh and blood. I was with Grace and Gordon in the Aulton when I met him again and we all went to visit Grandmother and Aunt Mattie in College Bounds. Grandmother was an old devil to Davie – his full title is David Alexander Grainger – but I like Davie best. He soon won her over – as I think he could any woman be she young or old. Whisky Jake came into the house drunk and began to pester me. In minutes he was back outside again, thrown there by Davie himself. Grandmother was impressed, even more so when Davie spoke to her in cant. She got a bit drunk and talked a lot while Mattie sang at the top of her voice in the scullery and danced with Gordon. He's going to work in a field clearing hospital in France and my darling Grace looked lonely already.*

*Later Davie and I walked by the Don. The hawthorn was on the branch and the birds going wild in their courting. If I could be like them, flirting so blithely and so briefly – but nothing could be so beautifully simple for human beings. For me it is just beginning and I'm afraid because I don't know where or how it will end. His kisses are still warm on my lips and through it all I think of Johnny. I can't write directly to him like I used to. That is the worst part of it – it's as if I'm growing away from his memory yet I know that's not true. He's as real to me as he ever was. It might be guilt that makes me feel like this even though I know I can't go on living in the past. Oh, but it was safer that way, I could control my thoughts and feelings. Florrie and Gillie were right*

151

*about me. They both warned me that my heart would always rule my head. If I could smother it down in my breast and make it behave, I would be all right, but only Nellie can do that – or can she? Since Jeannie died the heart of Nellie has become more dominant. It's there, in her eyes, and in her tears when she comes up to her room at night and cries for Kenneth Mor.*

*Father took me into his shoppe when I came back from Aberdeen. He has made boots, lots and lots of lovely boots for the soldiers and some of the old sparkle was back in him again, though he seems to think that he has failed us all in some way. I know one thing, he has never failed me. He has always been there when I needed him and I hope one day I'll marry a man just like him – except for the drink. I could never cope with a man who drinks too much. I admire Mam for the way she has stood by Father through thick and thin. She is strong, is my Mam. Come to think of it, Davie is a bit like what Father must have been like as a young man. The same deep brown eyes, the same dark, curly hair. But there is something in Davie that was never in Father. Grandmother tried to warn me about it but she didn't have to. From the first I knew he had a selfish streak in him. He's the sort who'll go after what he wants and get it, yet – for all that I still –*

'For all that I still love him – I'm in love with him.' In her mind she spoke the words she hadn't been able to bring herself to write down in black and white in her diary. Turning over, she drifted into sleep, the corn dolly clasped to her breast. Johnny would have smiled his slow smile and told her she was clutching at straws.

# CHAPTER TEN

She was late getting out of the house the following evening. Nellie had been more exacting than usual, finding so many things for her young sister to do that she was eventually driven to cry out in exasperation, 'Nellie, I'm going out and I'm no' going to do another thing so you needna bother trying to think up anything else!'

'Going out, eh?' Nellie retorted witheringly. 'Ay, just as I thought. You've been putting on scent and are wearing your bonniest blouse under your peeny. You'll be meeting a lad no doubt, for where else would you be going at this time wi' only half your chores done? You take care, my lass. You're a mite young yet to be roaming the countryside after dark.'

They were in the milk house, which was situated well enough away from the house for their upraised voices not to be heard. It wasn't often that Evelyn tackled her elder sister, knowing from long experience that she almost always came off worst in any argument with her, but she had waited patiently all day for the arrival of evening and Nellie's words had just told her that she was being kept back deliberately, simply because it had been noticed that she had put a little scent behind her ears. Just who did Nellie think she was, anyway? Her keeper?

Almost feverishly, she turned on Nellie and said defiantly, 'It isn't dark! It's spring in case you havena noticed and the days are getting longer.'

The older girl flushed at the other's unusually sharp tone. 'It will be dark by the time you get back from your wanderings. It's easy to see you have Father's gypsy blood in you, the way you cavort round the countryside wi' that hair o' yours hanging down your back and yourself half-naked into the bargain! And dinna you use that tone to me, my girl. You've been like a hen on a hot girdle ever since you got back home yesterday and I for one will no' stand for it. What on earth ails you, I'd like to know!'

Evelyn's eyes sparkled with rage. 'The same thing that ails you – only I'm no' like you, Nellie. I canna squash my feelings down and live in a world where there is no place for love. It's all around you, beating and real, but you've aye been too blind and too stubborn to see or feel any o' it!'

She had said too much and took a pace backwards as Nellie advanced, bony hand raised to strike her. Evelyn had felt the sting of those sharp knuckles many times in the past and knew she wasn't beyond feeling them again, for in Nellie's eyes she was still very much a child to be tamed into submission when the occasion arose.

'Just what do you mean by that?' Nellie's voice was low and controlled though a dangerous glint shone in the amber green of her eyes.

'I – I mean—' Evelyn faltered, then, bracing herself, went on in a rush, 'I mean it's high time you faced up to facts, Nellie Grant. You're in love wi' Kenneth Mor and you're behaving like a right old she-cat because you won't own up to it even to yourself! He's up there, all alone since Jeannie died and you never go near him, never speak his name, never go to him wi' a word o' comfort on your lips! If that's the kind o' love you have for him then it's maybe just as well you never go near him, for you're no' capable o' showing affection to any living cratur and – and if I was you, I'd rather be dead than go on living wi' a stone for a heart!'

Nellie's face had blanched, she was shaking from head to foot, even her mouth trembled, and Evelyn at once regretted her outburst because she didn't know if the trembling was of anger or of pain.

'Who told you these things, Evelyn Grant?' Nellie questioned through numb lips. 'Tell me this minute or I'll skelp the life out o' your impertinent wee body.'

'I – I just know.' Evelyn turned tail and ran, away from the croft and out onto the road, never slowing till she reached the station, breathless, flushed and shaken. It was well after seven o'clock and she thought at first he hadn't waited. The little station was very quiet. It was a well-kept place and had won quite a few prizes for its neat appearance. The waiting rooms and the stationmaster's house had been newly painted, the flowerbeds were a riot of spring flowers, even the name board had been newly washed. Outside the booking office a fat black cat was sitting in the sun contentedly washing its whiskers.

David appeared from the booking office at the same time as Saft Sam, the booking clerk, who hailed Evelyn warmly and threw her a knowing wink. She knew that by tomorrow afternoon the whole of Lums o'Reekie would know that she had been meeting a young soldier at the station for, like many folk of these parts who had been bestowed with nicknames, Sam was the complete opposite of his, sharp as a harvest sickle with a tongue to match, and a knack of being able to size up a situation at the drop of a hat.

'A fine night for it, Evie lass,' he commented wickedly, hooking his thumbs into his lapels and rocking on his heels as he surveyed the flowerbeds with satisfaction.

Evelyn had no time to reply. David hurried up to her, seized her arm and led her away, a frown on his handsome features as he said tightly, 'I couldn't have been more thoroughly cross-examined just now if I'd been in a court of law, and it wouldn't have happened if you'd been here on time.'

'Och, don't *you* start!' she threw at him sharply. 'I've had enough o' that sort o' thing from my sister Nellie! I told you seven was too early but you wouldn't listen. Let go of my arm this minute and I'll just go back home. I'm sick o' folk telling me what I should and shouldn't be doing.'

'Oh no, you don't, he said grimly, hurrying her away from the station towards the fields. 'We only have a short time together and we're damned well going to make the most o' it! I have to catch a train back to Aberdeen, remember, so we have two hours in which to be alone.'

'I dinna think I want to be alone wi' you,' she cried,

almost in tears, dismayed by the turn that events had taken.'

'Yes you do. You've wanted it from the first minute you set eyes on me, so stop being awkward and just do as you're told.'

She gasped at his audacity. Hot tears pricked her lids, she put up her free hand to push back the hair which had come loose from its ribbon on her flight away from the house. She felt hot, untidy and panic-stricken. This young man with the set jaw and the cool anger in his eyes wasn't the same one she had sat with in Bert's little teashop. Something had happened to him. The war had changed him. He was like an overstrung violin, so tense, jumpy and irritable he gave a violent start when a cow mooed loudly from behind a nearby hedge.

Compassion took the place of anger in her heart. Those beautiful eyes of his had witnessed horrors she couldn't even begin to visualize. Only those directly involved in the fighting knew, and they would only ever tell some of it. They were men and they had to be stoic and brave and tight-lipped about their experiences. Perhaps that was the only way they could handle the hellish reality – not to talk about it, never to bring it out into the open. The young officers who came to Rothiedrum seemed almost jocular about war. They laughed and made gruesome, cynical jokes about some of the terrible wounds they had suffered. There was also a recklessness in them as if they were implying, 'What the hell! Live now and to hell with the consequences, for tomorrow we might be dead.' Those at breaking point cried quite easily and openly, beyond caring what anyone thought. Others maimed and scarred for life cringed away from sympathy as if it was some terrible disease. She had learned early on never to show pity but to keep everything on an everyday level, to give practical help by just talking, laughing, writing letters, though often she couldn't keep a lump from her throat when some armless young man directed her to put down: *Dear Mother and Father, don't worry about me, I'm nearly back to normal . . .*

David's hand was on her arm, helping her over a stile. She stole a glance at him. He looked so good and proud in his uniform, so essentially alive as he strode through the sweet green grasses of the end rigs, his gaze fixed directly ahead – those long, thick lashes of his curling so attractively over his eyes. She wondered what he was thinking and wished he would speak, say something, anything that would let her know his thoughts were with her and not in some place far away and unknown to her . . .

The rain caught them unawares, pelting down from clouds that had gathered unnoticed by them over the surrounding hills. He grabbed her hand and they ran, but in minutes they were soaked and searching round for shelter. At the top of a rise, they stood looking down at a farm lying below, the barn mill standing some little distance off. Without a word they flew down to it, opened the door and rushed inside, stopping for a few minutes to regain their breath. Evelyn shivered in her thin clothes and wished she had brought a jacket. He saw her trembling and said succinctly, 'Come on,' and led her towards the corn loft stairs. It was very dim and quiet up there in the loft, the floor was carpeted with chaff, straw, and piles of old sacks. He was staring at her, as if seeing her for the first time that evening. The rain had moulded her blouse to her breasts, the nipples stood out sharp and clear. 'Evelyn,' he breathed and his hand came out to caress the tender swellings.

She shivered again and drew back. She felt trapped and told herself she should never have consented to this evening meeting. From the start it had gone wrong, and now this – this dangerous close intimacy with a man who was very nearly a stranger to her, and old Dan McCrae ensconced by his fire with a hot toddy at this time of day, his dogs locked in the straw shed so that they wouldn't disturb him with their barking – no one would come along here to the old barn mill at this hour.

'Take off your clothes and dry yourself with these.' He picked up a couple of sacks and threw them at her, then without further ado he stripped off his own clothing and

157

began rubbing at his wet skin with the rough sacks. She stood rooted to the spot staring at him, the sacks clutched to her breasts, her eyes big and round in her rain-washed face.

'Go on,' he urged, not looking at her, 'you'll catch pneumonia in those wet things.'

Scuttling behind a large hay bale, she peeped over the top and simply couldn't refrain from a smothered giggle at the sight of him dancing about in his birthday suit, his glengarry still firmly on his head, cursing at the feel of the rough sacking material against his skin.

Her teeth were beginning to chatter, and in a burst of decision she stripped off her sodden blouse and skirt, placing them carefully over a nearby rafter before beginning to rub herself down with bunches of straw and anything else that came to hand. She emerged, wrapped in one of the ungainly sacks at the same time as he came towards her happed in similar rig.

They looked at each another and with one accord erupted into gales of laughter.

'Och, Evie, I'm sorry.' His voice was soft and velvety. 'This is a fine way to start off a promising friendship. You're cold, sit down here beside me and I'll warm you with my body.'

His lack of embarrassment, his mastery of the situation failed to strike her, she was too preoccupied with the shivers his words had sent running down her spine. He was being his most charming, the tone of his voice was laden with a warm, sensual nuance that brought back to her how much she had longed for this evening so that she could be alone with him. But she held herself back, knowing that if once he was to touch her she would no longer be her own mistress. He gave her no time for reflection. Reaching out, he pulled her down beside him onto a pile of straw which he had covered over with sacks. She was too confused to wonder when he had fashioned this cosy little nest into which their bodies nestled comfortably. She tried to resist him but it was a feeble effort. She wanted him to kiss her – more than she had ever wanted anything in her life before. There was no shyness about him, no sign of hesitancy. He was all at once masterful and possessive, and so completely in control of every one of her senses that she was beyond denying him anything. His mouth moved over her throat, lingering on the delicate bones of her shoulders before coming up to play with her ears. Her spine tingled, her entire being quivered with anticipation. But he took his time with her, stroking her hair, kissing her neck, almost as if he was testing to see how long he could hold her passion suspended. When he came finally to her mouth he merely pecked at it, swift little kisses that took her breath away with delight.

'Davie, I love you,' she whispered, lost now, wanting him to crush her till it hurt.

He gave a little laugh, tinged with a wicked mockery. 'I know,' was all he said before he stopped playing with her. With a swift movement he tore the rough sacking material from both their bodies and stared at her. Her slender body was white in the dimness, her young breasts taut and thrusting up towards him, inviting him to take all that he would of their sweet beauty. Lightly, he ran his fingers over her belly and up over her hard nipples, his fingertips whispering over her skin. She began to tremble. Deep inside herself a voice told her that she was lying in the arms of an expert lover, someone who had trod this dissolute path many times before, but she was beyond caring. He was here with her now and that was all that mattered and he had brought her body to a peak of such desire with just a few teasing caresses that she couldn't even begin to visualize what it would be like once he really let himself go.

'Evie,' he murmured, 'you're so lovely and so virginal I know I should be gentle with you, even while I also think – that I won't be able to stop myself from – hurting you.'

His mouth came down on hers, rough, hard, seeking. She met his passion with her own, as a wildness rose in her that was completely without her control. The world spun, whirled away. His tongue played with hers and she reacted as if some inner self was commanding her responses. Her inexperience flew off on vanquished wings and she never even realized that it had gone. Her body burned under his touch, an excruciating heat pulsed in every clamouring cell. His skin was satin smooth beneath her exploring fingers but the muscles beneath were hard as steel. She held onto him, little gasps of pleasure coming swiftly into her throat, her brow moist with perspiration.

He had long ago lost control of himself. His breath was rough and uneven, his lips brutal and unrelenting over hers, his body a tensely coiled spring of heated passion.

'Davie,' she whispered pleadingly, 'I can't bear it – please – please don't make me wait . . .'

He thrust himself into her with a savagery that thrilled her entire being. Her fever climbed, higher and higher, she gave a little cry and bit into her fingers. Then came the warmth, spreading through her like a fiercely burning flame, a warmth that grew and intensified till she felt she couldn't bear the wonderful sweet ecstasy of it. He called out her name in agony, his mouth still and helpless against hers, his hands entwined in her hair. Together they trembled, then gradually became still. For long minutes they lay locked together, spent and peaceful, then he rolled away from her and got up to pad over to his jacket and extract a packet of cigarettes from the pocket. Coming back to her he lit one and lay back to smoke it, one arm behind his head, his long legs relaxed next to hers. But there was a tremor in his hand that he couldn't quite control, the same tremor she had noticed yesterday as they walked together in the Aulton. Yesterday! It seemed a lifetime away. She felt as if she had known him forever, yet she had still so much to find out about him. She would, in time she would. She lay back beside him, a fulfilment in her that made her feel weak . . .

'I was wrong about you.' His voice broke the silence, a trace of anger in its tone that made her turn swiftly to stare at him inquiringly. 'I'm not the first, am I? You're so young, you seem in many ways a child yet, but you have experience for such a little lass, eh, Evelyn McKenzie Grant?'

Instinctively, she covered her nakedness with one of the sacks, and drawing up her knees she turned away from him. 'Please,' she whispered. 'Don't cheapen what we've just had. It – it was a wonderful experience and I dinna want it ruined.'

His fingers bit into her flesh as he pulled her round to face him. 'You're no virgin, are you, Evie? And you just sixteen years old! God, where did you learn to love like that?'

'I'll be seventeen next month,' she countered childishly, tears making her husky. 'And I didn't learn it anywhere. It just happened, you made it happen. I – I suppose it's a natural thing between a man and a woman.'

'A woman,' he threw back scornfully. 'Oh ay, I will no' deny you responded to me like a woman but you're just a babe in arms yet, and you haven't answered my question – who was it, Evie?'

The unreasoning beast of jealousy stared out of his eyes and she turned her own away from that most frightening of emotions.

'It was Johnny, if you must know.' She spoke in a low voice, unwilling to bring the dear memory of her childhood sweetheart into that scene of recent passion. 'I told you about Johnny Burns. We knew one another for most of our lives and in the end we were to be married. I only let him make love to me the once and that was long before you ever came on the scene!' she finished, angry at him for prying into her heart's innermost secrets.

He blew smoke into the air and asked casually, 'How long?'

'Stop it!' She turned on him furiously. 'It's none o' your business and you have no right to ask me about such things.'

His fingers tightened once more on her arm. 'It is my business and I have a right,' he said insistently. 'You're mine now, Evie, and I want to know everything about you.'

'I don't belong to anybody – least of all you!' she retaliated, the green of her eyes darkening with rage.

'You've only just arrived in my life and have a damned cheek to poke your nose into things that dinna concern you.'

'How long, Evie? If you don't tell me this minute I'll take you over my knee and skelp your backside for you.'

'You wouldna dare!' she gasped. 'No' even my very own father has ever done that!'

'There's a first time for everything and I can assure you I'm perfectly capable of taking that initiative – so just you behave yourself and tell me what I want to know.'

She knew that he wasn't bluffing. In all her life, she had never come across anyone quite like him and she was fascinated, uneasy, and angry all at once.

'It was away back – the beginning of last September . . .'

'As long ago as that?' he laughed sarcastically. 'My, my, you certainly stayed in mourning for a good few weeks . . .'

Her hand came down on his face, as hard as she could make it. His jaw tensed and his hand streaked out to crush the soft flesh of her arm painfully. His eyes raked her face, the anger in them softening as he saw the terrible shame and sadness in her expression.

'Evie, oh, my darling little girl.' He stubbed out his cigarette, and drawing her down to him, kissed her on the lips, a tender kiss filled with remorse.

'Why?' she whispered, shaking her head. 'Why are you so cruel? From the very start o' this evening you've been angry wi' me – and I dinna ken why.'

'Evie.' He held her close, stroking her hair back from her flushed face. 'I thought you weren't coming. I was almost mad with disappointment in that station waiting room, listening to that old geezer prattling on and you never turning up. Ever since meeting you I've been haunted by you. I thought I would never see you again, and then yesterday there you were, your bonny red hair shining in the sun. It seemed too good to be true and I couldn't wait for tonight to see you again – and you were late. I was a complete and utter pig – and I don't care how

162

many men you've loved in your life just as long as you say you love me now.'

He put his arms round her and held her so close she could hardly breathe – but her heart was singing as she said into his hair, 'I've known three men in my life and I've loved them all. My father was the first, Johnny the second. We were maybe too young to know what love was. We couldna really handle our feelings but it was a gentle, kind and good love that we had for one another and I'll never forget him. The third is you, Davie. I never thought another man would come into my life so soon after Johnny, but you did and I feel I've known you for a very long time – also I feel as if I've loved you forever. I could never have let you make love to me if you were just another man. Whatever you may think, I'm just no' that sort o' girl.'

'I ken fine you aren't, I just said all those rotten things to hear you say the things you've just said.'

He looked suddenly very weary, and as they lay close together she stroked his hair soothingly and murmured her words of love into his ears. After a few minutes, she could tell by his breathing that he was asleep. A tenderness such as she had never known before seized her as she studied him in his repose. His face was very close to hers and she was able to take in every feature: the straight nose, the curling lashes, those new mature lines at the sides of his mouth, the deep cleft in his strong chin into which the tip of her little finger fitted perfectly. His lean, lithe body looked perfectly strong and healthy, but her gaze was drawn again and again to his stomach where a crisscross of scars showed where he had been wounded. Gently, she put her lips to them before covering him as best she could with the little material there was to be had.

He trembled slightly, and she held him close and wondered what he was seeing in his dreams – or his nightmares. He had obviously suffered much, not just physically but mentally and emotionally as well. That would account for his irritability and his anger but she was aware that these things were also inherent in him, the war had only served to bring out the darker side of his nature. He wouldn't be the easiest of men to put up with, but she loved him and knew that whatever he said or did to her in the future she would always forgive him – he had captured her heart and some deep inner sense told her she would never be quite the same again . . .

David was half aware of Evelyn beside him yet, strangely, he was not there with her. He was drifting off into some endless night where the sun would never shine again. Somewhere in the darkness there was a skirling of sound which gradually emerged as 'Blue Bonnets Over the Border'. And then he saw them away off to his right, a group of grey, ghostlike figures wearing the uniform of the Gordons, hunched forward into the acrid mist of dawn, piping the battalion out of the trenches. Someone beside him was kissing a lock of red hair, holding it against his breast like a bloody crucifix – and he was praying. Red hair – he wished he could steal it, it might bring good luck. But there was none of that here in this hell. Fires lit up the northern horizon like a giant torch, bolts of flame erupted from the German lines, distant machine guns sounded like blatters of hail hitting off a tin roof. Waves of men were running towards the German wire only to melt away, and the pipes had stopped playing – it was his turn. He ran forward with the rest. Blood was spurting, flesh tearing apart like butter. He knew he was going to die. Men were falling all around him. Something hit him and he dropped like a stone, writhing in agony – his guts were on fire – someone must have grabbed a flaming torch and was pushing the living fire into the raw flesh of his belly . . . Someone was screaming beside him, screaming out a name – 'Florrie!' Who the hell was Florrie?

Out beyond the jungle of barbed wire, a man was shrieking. The ragged waves of agonized sound beat and pulsed into his swimming senses. Let him die, he thought as the sickening screams went on and on . . .

'Christ! Let him die!' he called out in torture, and woke up lathered in sweat.

'Davie, I'm here, it's all right, my darling, it's all right.'

He blinked once or twice and stared at her. 'Sorry, I was dreaming.' He sounded shaky. She put her arms around him and held him close. 'Davie, you shouldn't have come out here tonight. You need rest.'

'Havers, I need you.' He snuggled against her, glad of her nearness, her warmth.

'We'll have to go, Davie,' she said unwillingly. 'You've to catch a train, remember.'

Taking his watch from his jacket pocket, he glanced at it. 'Damn, it's quarter to nine. We've been here almost two hours. Come on, we'll have to hurry.'

She rushed behind the hay bale to struggle into her damp clothes and in minutes they were flying over the fields, his hand in hers, his long stride forcing her to run to keep up with him. In the distance they could see the lights of the station through the gathering dusk – and just pulling out of it was the little dark green locomotive with its caterpillar of coaches snaking along behind.

He slowed to a halt and stood staring after the train, a soft curse on his lips. 'Damn! What do I do now? Walk? It's a fair trek into Aberdeen and I somehow don't feel up to it at the moment.'

'Come on.' She took hold of his hand again. 'Saft Sam might lend us his horse and cart – and if no', Ian Gilmore will let you have the use of a bike.'

But a better solution presented itself as soon as they reached the station. Coulter was there, helping the station staff unload the laird's Rolls from a motorcar wagon and Evelyn's eyes shone.

'I've just remembered. The Forbes are coming back here for the summer and the motor has been sent on ahead. It arrived yesterday and Coulter mentioned something about coming along to collect it this evening. If I talk nice to him he might just give us a run into the city.'

'A Rolls no less.' David sounded disapproving. 'What does it run on – water?'

'Meldrum the chauffeur scented war coming and began hoarding petrol like a miser. There's a Lanchester, and a Benz as well though it's about to be sold. Evander Forbes really prefers horses to anything but all the horses except two have been given to the army, so Evander likes his Rolls to hand just in case, though he'll either have to drive it himself or make do wi' Coulter or McTavish. Meldrum has gone off to be a driver with the army.'

She went off to draw Coulter aside, and after a few pleasantries mentioned casually that David had just missed the train, and if he couldn't get the loan of a bike or a cart would be forced to walk to Aberdeen.

The old man's eyes gleamed. 'Is that so, is that so?' he nodded, pulling contemplatively at his long white beard. 'And are you no' the sly whittrock wheedling roond me the way you're doing? Bike or cart, my big toe. It's a run in that motorcar you're after and to tell the truth—' his wheezy laugh tickled her ear '— I've just been racking my brains as to how I might get a good chance o' her myself. Go you and wait wi' your soldier laddie outside the station and I'll be along for you in a wee whilie. I dinna want these gowks knowing what I'm up to, so be ready to hop in quick the minute you see me coming.'

Fifteen minutes later the big sleek car came purring along, and into the back seat jumped Evelyn and David. 'There's no need for you to come,' he protested, but mildly, his arm already out to bring her to him.

She was content to lie against him with her head nestled on his shoulder as the miles slipped silently away. All too soon they were in Aberdeen and Coulter was bringing the car to rest at the foot of Castle Hill.

David kissed the top of her head. 'Tomorrow?'

'No, Davie, let's make it a proper day. Next Wednesday at two o'clock in Cobbly Wynd.'

'Have it your way.' He sounded sulky but the face he turned back to her was relaxed, and his lips when they briefly sought hers full of warmth.

'I dinna ken ye had a soldier laddie,' Coulter probed gently when they were once more driving in open country.

In the darkness she smiled. 'Until this evening neither did I,' she said briefly.

'He'll be on leave then?' Coulter's questions were losing

some of their subtlety. 'He doesna seem hurt in any way though of course there's no telling wi' some o' these lads.' She allowed him to go on in a like vein for a few moments longer before relenting and telling him all she knew about David Alexander Grainger. She was longing to tell someone. If only Grace was close to hand. They had always confided so much to one another, and now that they were grown into women they confided even more. She would have to see Grace somehow. Not just to tell her about Davie, but to try to help her over these first lonely days without Gordon. It was very difficult. She got so little time off from Rothiedrum House – and now there was Davie, a jealous, possessive Davie who wouldn't be pleased if he had to share her with others . . .

Coulter was a good listener. He made not one word of interruption all the time she was talking.

'Ye're in love wi' him, lass?' He nodded wisely. 'Ye might think I'm just an auld blether wi' nought in my head but fairy stories, but I ken more aboot love than you might credit, oh ay. When I was just a wee bittie older than you are now, I loved a lass that sorely I near died wi' the hurt o' it when I found she was seeing another. Look you, come and sit by me in the front here and I'll tell ye aboot my Rosie. I keep thinkin' there's a witch wifie in the back every time I squint in the mirror and see your green eyes keekin' at me.'

He stopped the car and she settled herself beside him to listen to his soft, liquid voice talking quietly about a young love who had betrayed him so badly he 'hadna set one een on another lass for nigh on six months.'

'Is that all?' Evelyn asked, disappointed. 'I thought you were going to say for the rest o' your life!'

He chortled wickedly. 'Oh ay, but you see Rosie wasna the one, oh no, along came Sheena and after her a wee bit squirt o' a thing called Jessie. Now, she *was* the one, no' very bonny, mind, but the black eyes o' her so big you could lose yourself in their darkness, and lips on her so soft they were more enticing than the finest feather bed in all the land. We were to be wed, Jess and me, and then she went

167

and took diphtheria and died on me. From that day to this I never looked at another lass nor will I ever till the day I die.'

'Oh, Coulter.' In the darkness Evelyn's eyes filled with tears, and she squeezed the old man's horny knuckles which were gripped tightly on the steering wheel. 'I never kent you had loved so well.'

Coulter took one hand from the wheel, and from an inner pocket withdrew a large grubby square into which he blew his nose soundly. 'Ay, lassie, to you I'm just an auld man wi' a frosty pow and whiskers to match but I was young once, that I was.'

'It hurts, doesn't it, Coulter?' she said sadly. 'Love is supposed to be a happy thing but sometimes it hurts more than you can bear.'

They made an incongruous pair, the slender red-haired girl and the white-haired old man, but from the start they had been conspirators and purring along the quiet country roads in the shining Rolls, they were closer than they had ever been as they spoke of the loves they had had in their lives.

'I tell ye this, Evie, my bonny quine,' Coulter said huskily, 'I've watched ye grow and become bonnier and bonnier wi' the passing years. I saw how it was wi' you and young Johnny and my heart fair bled for ye when he passed on. Now there's another, and though I only was wi' him for a wee whilie I could tell he's a fine young man – but ca' canny wi' him just the same. He's no country lad but one who's tasted a good bit o' life already. Just you try to aye be one step ahead o' him and you'll be fine enough. And one more bit o' advice from an old man – keep your pride, lassie, whatever you do, hold on to that. Never run after him too hard, men like a bit o' a chase, I'm one so I should ken what I'm talkin' aboot, though dinna run *too* far – the way is strewn wi' winsome maidens, and if a man has to stop and catch his breath he's liable just to grab the nearest and make do wi' her.'

The motor slid to a halt at King's Croft road end. She scrambled out, then leaned back into the vehicle to kiss the tip of Coulter's generous nose. 'I'm grateful to you, Coulter, for everything. It's been grand sharing things wi' you – and if Chamberpot asks, just say you've been spending a passionate evening wi' a fiery redhead. She'll be that dumbfounded she'll no' say another word on the subject – just in case you take her into the pantry and seduce her as well!' His gusts of wheezy, delighted mirth followed her along the track to the croft. Now that she was so near home, she remembered Nellie and the row they had had. Fervently, she hoped that her sister would be in bed and asleep. If not, she would have to thole the dark glances, the indignant flouncings – worse, Nellie might follow her upstairs to her room and squeeze out of her some sort of apology for those things she had said. She tossed back her hair. Well, she wouldn't. This time she wasn't going to say she was sorry. She had only spoken the truth after all, and if Nellie didn't like it – well, it was just too bad. An owl hooted eerily as she came round the side of the steadings. Mischievously, she covered her mouth with her cupped hands and answered it. An answering hoot came back at her, then another, louder this time. Unable to resist she called again, to be rewarded with a fluttering from the byre roof and the next instant a huge, unblinking pair of eyes gazing down at her in wonderment from the chimney of her father's shoppe.

'Hoo – hoo!' she threw upwards then, smothering her giggles, she lifted her skirts and ran silently over the cobbles to the house . . . glad that she could still do such daft things even though she was nearly a woman of seventeen – and in love.

Everything was in darkness when she let herself indoors. The kitchen was silent and peaceful with only the faint glow of the smoored fire infiltrating the warm, thick shadows. Everyone was in bed and she was glad, for suddenly she wondered how she could have faced them all after . . .

A faint creaking from the ingle made her spin round. Her eyes raked the gloom. On tiptoe she went further into the room, and by the faint light she was able to make out a dim figure sitting in the inglenook.

'Ay, Evie, it's me.' Maggie's voice came softly. A taper stole a flame from the fire and the next instant the lamp flared into subdued life.

'Mother – you – you shouldn't have waited up.' Evelyn was annoyed to find herself faltering over the words.

'Oh, I should, Evie, I should,' Maggie said calmly. 'Sit you down opposite me so that I can see your face.'

In that instant the last thing Evelyn wanted was for her mother to look upon her face, for she imagined that everyone in the world must surely see those secrets she so desperately wanted to keep hidden. Hot blushes consumed her. In panic she knew these alone would give away her – her what? Her guilt? Was it such a crime to be in love – to have allowed a young soldier to make love to her? Before the thought came to an end she knew the answer. Of all Maggie's daughters she was, for her age, the most vulnerable where men were concerned. Not even winsome, earthy Mary, for all her flirting and teasing, had allowed herself to become seriously involved with any man till Gregor came along . . .

'I think I'll go up to bed, Mam, I'm tired and I have an early start in the morning.'

'You will come and sit by me, my girl, and none o' your nonsense.' Maggie was speaking in that firm voice Evelyn knew so well and none of them, not even Nellie, had ever dared disobey its command.

Like a child in school she flitted obediently over to the chair indicated, to sit on its edge and wait with folded hands for her mother to speak.

'You've been out courting then, Evie,' Maggie began conversationally, her quick eyes taking in her youngest daughter's chastened appearance in one fell swoop.

'Who told you, Mam?' Evelyn asked quietly enough though her clenched fists itched to get at the traitorous Nellie. Only she had guessed, only she would have . . .

'No one needed to tell me, Evie, but you've just confirmed what I already jaloused. You look as if you've had a fine time to yourself wi' your bonny best blouse all crumpled and your skirt looking as if it hasna seen a

170

washtub in weeks. I've seen the kitchen maids look like that after a romp in some barn wi' a fee'd man – but you're a daughter o' this house and as such you have certain obligations to withhold.'

Evelyn stared down at her hands. 'I've never shamed this house, Mam.'

'No, not yet, my girl, not yet, but the trouble wi' you, Evie, is that you've grown up too quickly and too soon—'

'You never thought that when you wanted me to marry Johnny.' Like a flash it came out, and biting her lip she retreated once more into a shell of passiveness.

'Maybe I did want Johnny for you a bit sooner than later,' said Maggie softly. 'He was devoted to you and in him I saw a lad who would make a good husband, one that would be true and faithful. I'm no' hounding you, lassie, I only want what's best for you. That was why I waited up for you tonight, to talk to you and try to give you the benefit of the things I know. Your father wasna for it at all, he feels that young folk should have their freedom just as he had when he was young – but it's different for a lad, they dinna have the same sort o' responsibilities as womenfolk.'

'You're trying to remind me of what happened to my grandmother, aren't you, Mam? I know all about that well enough, you dinned it into us all from an early age. I'm no' being impertinent. I just want you to know that I understand how difficult it must be having daughters, and I'll – I'll be careful.'

'No, Evie, you won't, you're too eager for life, your nature's too passionate ever to give caution a second thought. You're so like your father that way, a blithe, carefree spirit thirsty for love and romance. You've been restless this whilie back – and now I know why. Who is he and what is his name?'

Evelyn looked up, her eyes sparkling suddenly. 'He's David Alexander Grainger and he's with the Gordon Highlanders. You would like him, Mam, I know you would.'

'Ay, maybe.' Maggie's tones were dry. 'So – he's a

soldier,' she went on thoughtfully, 'and he's back on leave from the war.' She got up and went to take her daughter's head to her bosom, to lift the fiery strands of her hair and let them fall tenderly through her fingers. 'Such bonny hair. Mine was like that once – before care robbed it o' its youth and colour. Don't fall in love wi' this young man, Evie, his life isn't his own – it belongs to King and Country and you've had enough heartache to last you for a good long while to come.'

Evelyn raised a stricken face. 'I canna help myself, Mam, it happened without my permission.'

Maggie laughed. 'You aye did have a fancy way o' putting your feelings. Bring him to tea and we'll have a look at him, but right now get along up to your bed or you'll never hear the cock crowing.'

Evelyn went, willingly and gladly, relief making her feel weak. For one dreadful moment she had thought her mother was going to ask outright if she had lain with David Grainger, and she couldn't tell if she would have admitted to the truth or not. Never yet had she deliberately lied to either of her parents – only the little white lies that everyone succumbed to whether they liked it or no – never yet. But there was a first time for everything, as everyone around her was so fond of preaching.

In the privacy of her room she stripped and washed her body from head to foot in cold water from the ewer, holding her breath as the first agonizing douce met with her warm skin. Tingling all over, she hurried into her nightgown, and then sat in front of her dressing-table mirror to brush her hair till it fell to her waist in glossy tendrils. By the dim light of the candle her face was shadowed and enigmatic in the mirror, her eyes big as she stared at her reflection, trying to see if she looked any different since the last time she had viewed it.

'You're a bit red in the face,' she told herself and smiled, her hand going up to her neck to play with the gold signet ring. The little velvet box containing Gillie's necklace caught her eye, and seizing hold of it she opened it to gaze at the exquisite pearldrop. She had hardly worn it, there had been little opportunity to do so as yet. Tenderly, she pressed her lips to the cool drop. 'Dear Gillie,' she murmured, 'I wonder what you are doing at this minute, how you are faring.'

She hadn't heard from him for some time, though she wrote to both him and Alan whenever she had a moment to spare.

Exhaustion swamped her suddenly, and padding over to her bed she got in and drew the covers up to her neck, her eyes closing the second she lay back on her pillows. But she couldn't sleep, not until . . . Sluggishly, she reached under her pillow and withdrew her diary, hardly seeing what she was writing in it for the sleep which was overwhelming her. Her pencil scrawled a few words. She was asleep as soon as she put it down.

The diary lay open across her breast. In it she had written: *11.30 p.m. Saturday April 30th. Tonight I sinned – and enjoyed every minute . . .*

# CHAPTER ELEVEN

David came to tea at King's Croft not once but several
times, and each time he grew more relaxed in the company of the Grant family, more relaxed altogether whoever he was with, whatever he was doing. His face lost
some of its tension, grew fuller and smoother so that the
lines round his mouth began to fade and he was more like
the boy Evelyn had first met.

As his nervousness decreased so too did his irritability,
and without these things to contend with his natural charm
came to the fore, he began to smile more, to laugh at
himself. He enjoyed doing odd jobs around the croft, and
as soon as he had familiarized himself with the workings of
the place, he went off to the fields with Jamie to help in
the preparation of the ground for the root crops, or to the
moss to cut and stack the peats for the winter fires.

When Evelyn's seventeenth birthday came round in
May, he presented her with a beautifully fashioned jewel
box, so smoothly polished she could see her face in it.

'But how could you—' she began before she remembered he had been an apprentice cabinet-maker before joining the army.

'I enjoy working with wood,' he explained when he saw
her face. 'I don't get much chance o' it now but I whittled
away at this in my spare time.'

'You and Tandy ought to get together,' she told him.
'He makes lovely things from wood and I know fine he's
back in Rothiedrum. You would enjoy meeting him.'

So he made it his business to acquaint himself with
Tandy. They all went to Shepherd's Biggin away up there
on the hilly moors, and while Tandy and David sat happily
whittling wood and chatting, she made tea and little
scones on the roughly hewn fireplace, which were carried
outside to be enjoyed in the sunshine. She had never been

happier sitting there with her back to the warm stones of the biggin, gazing down over the plains and houghs of Rothiedrum, the peesies calling from their nests in the heather, the skylarks singing in the sky above, her hand warm and secure in Davie's grasp.

When they went further afield she never allowed herself to be alone with him in intimate places for, with both Coulter's and her mother's words of advice ringing in her head, she was determined to conduct herself with decorum – though that was no easy matter with David's body warm and hard against hers, his kisses passionate on her mouth.

'Evie,' he would implore, 'I only have a short time left. I'm growing fitter every day and must go back to the front soon. Please let me love you, I can't forget how it was that first night. I'm desperate to hold you in my arms again.'

The urgency of his body proved the truth of his words and it took every shred of her willpower not to succumb to his pleas, not to let him see that she desired him as much as he did her.

When the situation became unbearable, she would arrange for them to meet Grace and they would walk in the Aulton together, visiting Grandmother, scouring the market place where they bought bags of fruit which they ate strolling through the busy bustle of the harbour. Once or twice they came upon Whisky Jake, and though he eyed the girls mockingly he was in no mood to hang about with David there beside them, his eyes flashing a warning at the big, lumbering traveller.

David never seemed to mind these outings with Grace; in fact, he thoroughly enjoyed them and flirted with her mildly despite Evelyn's enraged glances.

'I ken fine you like Grace,' she told him. 'Everyone likes Grace but you have to go one better, you have to flirt with her as well. You're wasting your time, I might tell you. She loves Gordon Chisholm and is just counting the minutes till she sees him again.'

'Now who's jealous?' he teased. 'Of course I know my attentions mean nothing to Grace, but she's a beauty and I

175

never could resist a pretty face. Of all your sisters I like her best, though Mary comes a close second. Your brother-in-law is taking quite a risk leaving that one to her own devices, she's just ripe to fall for a bit flattery – unlike Nellie. You could pay her compliments till you're blue in the face but I doubt she would know what you're on about – though mind you, she's got something. She keeps it well hidden but it's there, just below the surface to – well, for want of a better expression, to set the heather on fire.'

Evelyn said nothing. There was something elusive about Nellie these days, something strange and sad, all mixed up with a tension that made her jumpy and snappish. To Evelyn's complete surprise she hadn't said one word about their argument, she wasn't even particularly vengeful in her attitude towards her young sister, and Evelyn experienced dreadful attacks of remorse as she began to attribute Nellie's new strangeness to the harsh truths that had been thrown at her. Several times Evelyn was on the verge of apologizing for her hasty words, but something always held her back. Why should she, after all? She had only told Nellie the truth. It was time someone did and if she wasn't big enough to take it then it might do her good to stew in her own juice for a while.

But there was something else, a quietness that had never been in Nellie, a withdrawn quality that was oddly disquieting. She was becoming more and more absent-minded with each passing day, and wasn't even paying much attention to the children which in itself was a point of worry.

Maggie and Jamie exchanged frequent meaningful glances, and when the latter remarked whimsically, 'I canna get used to a quiet Nell. The very walls are ringin' wi' her silences and even the animals are lookin' gey uneasy. I saw old Tab watchin' her yesterday, waitin' for the broom to chase him away from the fire, and when nothing happened he dropped his tail and slunk out the door to go along the road and be shouted at by Carnallachie.'

Maggie nodded and said, 'I ken fine what you mean,

Jamie, though it's the daftest way o' putting things that I've ever heard. I just hope the lass is no' sickening for something. She's lost a good bit o' her bonny colour and her eyes are dull.'

'Maybe she's sickening for love,' Jamie said thoughtfully, never dreaming just how near the truth his words were . . .

It was a perfect day in late May. The sun beat down warmly from a cloudless sky, and all along the track leading up to Knobblieknowe the scent of the broom hung heavy and sweet; newly hatched peewit chicks ran with their protective mothers, looking like tiny balls of fluff on legs; the burn purled musically under the bridge, little calm pools near the banks creating looking glasses for clumps of primroses growing profusely on the mossy damp earth.

Nellie climbed the brae, treading the same path she had last trod with Kenneth Mor on that fateful night of raging wind and snow, seeing nothing before her, her mind oddly numb now that she had at last taken the momentous decision to go and visit him, wondering vaguely as she went along if he would be indoors on such a day. His men were working in the fields but his red-haired figure was not among them and no matter how much she squinted her eyes into the sun in search of him she failed to see him anywhere. The numbness left her and panic seized her. Now that she was so close to Knobblieknowe, the last thing she wanted was to find him there. Far, far better if she could just leave a note in the kitchen saying that she had been. She would have fulfilled her obligations then, and half-hearted though that might be, she would at least have salved her conscience to some extent.

She plodded on, wishing now that she had worn something less flimsy than the high-necked green blouse and the long golden-brown cotton skirt which sat so attractively on her narrow-waisted body. She asked herself what had possessed her to buy things that were so out of keeping with her usual plain garb. She had been shopping with Grace at the time, and Grace had persuaded her to make the purchases as only she could.

But what would *he* think? Would he see her as some kind of temptress who had gone mad with her own desires? A small smile twisted her mouth at the ludicrousness of her own thoughts, but even so her throat was dry at her temerity in coming up here today, let alone arriving in a style so outwith her usual one.

Her courage nearly failed her as she approached the house, and for long moments she had to hold onto a fence post tightly to give her shaking legs time to steady themselves.

The basket she was carrying seemed suddenly very heavy, and shifting it to her other hand she straightened and went slowly forward, passing the steadings and the sun-splashed cobbles as she decided quickly not to go straight in at the kitchen entrance but to go round to the front of the house instead where she would have less chance of coming directly upon him. This part of the house faced the blue, sleeping hills on one side and looked down over the wide sweep of Rothiedrum on the other. It was still and very peaceful, with brown honeybees fumbling amongst the wild honeysuckle which grew by the gate and along under the house. In a little walled-off section of the garden the roses were in bud, with one or two deep red petals unfurled enough to give off a most heavenly perfume which mingled with the heady fragrance of the honeysuckle. She lifted her head and breathed deeply, letting the delightful scents wash over her. Of all the flowers she loved roses best, but had little chance of growing them in King's Croft garden where almost every inch of precious space was taken up with vegetables, and the rest given over to a drying green upon which two goats were tethered in summer who were forever breaking lose to go foraging in amongst the cabbages and carrots.

Opening the gate and reaching the door, she noticed that the paint on it was peeling and her heart turned over. Oh, Kenneth, she thought, has it come to this? You that put so much o' your strength and pride into this place.

She raised her hand to knock on the blistered door panel, but held her knuckles suspended without bringing them down. Never, never had she to knock on any door here to gain entry. Like everyone else, she had just to call out to proclaim her arrival before simply walking inside. How formal to start knocking now. He would think her too strained and unnatural for words, so without any more hesitation she opened the door and went into the cool little hallway, and from there along the passageway beside the stairs to the kitchen.

He was there all right, but he hadn't heard her entry. Alone by the empty grate, his red head in his hands, he seemed oblivious to everything. He was hunched up, desolate and hopeless-looking, his limbs so wearily loose she thought at first that he must be drunk. But when he raised his head to look at her with red-rimmed, disbelieving eyes, she knew at once that he was as stone cold sober as herself, that it was grief and exhaustion that weighed him down so heavily.

'Nell,' he said in an odd husky sort of voice very different from its old, vigorous timbre. 'Nell, you've come, at last you've come.'

He held out his hands to her. Her throat tight with anguish she went forward to take them, unable to speak, biting back the tears that misted her eyes.

'Nell.' He stood up, his great body towering over her. 'Your hands, they're like ice yet it's a hot sun that burns out there.'

'I know, I – och – to tell the truth, Kenneth, I was a wee bittie nervous coming here today, I dinna ken why – I suppose I'm still the same old Nellie being foolish again. I didn't think you might want to see me—'

'Not want to see you? Nell, Nell, of all the folk in Rothiedrum you're the one I needed most in those dark, terrible days after Jeannie died. I needed the strength o' you, lass, for my own was at a gey low ebb at the time. When time passed and you never came, I began to think you had only ever come here to see Jeannie.'

In confusion she pulled her hands away from him and

179

almost ran to the basket she had left beside the door. Seizing it and placing it on the table, she rummaged inside to withdraw scones, a steak pie, a variety of little cakes and butter shortbread.

'Mother sent these up,' she lied for she had baked every last crumb herself. 'I'll put them ben in the pantry and then—' Her eyes roved round the room which was dusty and neglected-looking. Katie had departed Knobblie-knowe some time ago to seek her fortunes elsewhere, leaving Kenneth to fend for himself for he hadn't bothered to hire another kitchen maid. 'I'm going to get started in here. That stoor on the floor looks as if it's been there since the year one and that . . .'

'Oh, no you don't,' he interposed, coming over to stand beside her. 'The dust can wait as it has done for weeks now. Look outside, the sun shines, the birds sing, and we're no' going to waste another minute indoors.'

'But, you – I found you indoors just now.'

'That was before you came, Nell. I couldna be bothered wi' work, I havena been bothered wi' anything this whilie back. Nell,' his voice was low, 'I've missed having you about the place, in some strange way I've wanted to see you and even have you shouting at me now and then. Those days were good, lass, Jeannie, me and the bairns, all together, you coming up the brae to see us—' His voice broke and she turned away from his pain, her own eyes swimming with the poignancy of his words.

'Nell.' His big hand came out to take hers. 'Will you walk wi' me? Keep me company for just a wee while.'

Blindly, she allowed him to lead her outside and together they climbed the heathery slopes, her long skirts swishing rhythmically through the tall moor grasses, his kilt swinging round his fine strong legs upon which a furring of fair hairs grew in ebullient confusion.

Up here the air was clean and fresh, the scent of it like good wine, light but heady. She breathed deeply of its fragrance. Her face grew warm and flushed as if she had been drinking, and she was drunk all right, drunk with a raw deep happiness, the like of which she had never known in all her years. She felt light-headed with the power of her emotions. 'Nell, Nell, you're the one I needed most.' His words ran in circles inside her head. He had thought of her, in all his dreadful despair he had given thought to her, and mingling with her happiness was a feeling of such humble gratitude to him it was all she could do not to cry out her love for him there and then.

They walked for a long time as the sun reached its zenith in the heavens, and all around them the breezes died down and the perfume of the fresh young heather shoots became so intense she felt that if she was to hold out her arms, she would gather it up and take it back down the hill with her.

Eventually he paused beside a meandering burn and stood gazing down at the panorama of glens, woods and fields spread out below, with the sea a silver streak glittering way off in the distance. Around them, the delicate little heath moths fluttered; the bees were daft with indecision as they went from whin flowers to buttercups, from bell heather to the bluebells growing by the myrtle-shaded banks of the burn.

'Look at it, Nell,' he breathed, his blue eyes sweeping over the rich green beauty of an Aberdeenshire spring. 'Jeannie loved this time of year. As the flowers bloomed, so too did she. Roses came to those white cheeks o' hers, the very blue o' the speedwell shone in her eyes – oh, Nell, I loved her so, tell me, how am I going to live my life without her?'

She pressed her fist to her mouth and threw back her head to stem the tears. 'I canna tell you that, Kenneth, but I'll do my best to help you in any way I can. Before Jeannie died, she made me promise that I would look after you and the bairns. At the time neither she nor I had any idea of what lay ahead, and I thought only to humour her when I made that promise. I've despised myself for failing to keep my word to the only true friend I ever had but all that's done with. If you'll let me, I'll do everything in my power to help you and the bairns – as Jeannie would have wanted it.'

'Is that your only reason? Because Jeannie asked it of you? Nell, don't you like me just a wee bit – for myself?'

The nearness of his virile power swamped her. She felt as if she was drowning, falling down into a bottomless well that was sucking all the breath from her body.

'Like you? Oh, Kenneth, I've loved you for so long now my life hasna been my own to command. That was why – I never came near, I—'

She faltered and grew still and quiet, utterly dismayed at herself for voicing such feelings to a man so recently widowed. Turning on her heel she ran blindly from him, her heart pounding so rapidly she thought she was going to fall down in a faint. With a few rapid strides he caught up with her, spinning her round to face him.

'Please, Kenneth, let me go!' she whispered. 'I never meant to tell you any o' these things. We need never speak of it again. I was a fool to say any o' it. Now – I, I don't think I can look to you and the bairns after all.'

She was very attractive standing there, the sun glinting on the tendrils of hair escaping the confining scarf, her face tanned and flushed.

'Nell, you're a very bonny young woman,' he told her, his eyes fixed on her face. 'I've always felt drawn to you, but never more – than now. There's a warmth in you – deep down and well hidden but very much alive.'

His hand sought hers and they moved together back up the brae, to a sun-drenched little hollow beside the burn.

For a long time he looked at her, then he gently removed the scarf from her hair, letting it flutter at their feet, one by one he took out the pins that held the locks captive. The heavy silken wash of golden hair cascaded down, right to her waist. It framed her face, transforming it, making her look beautiful. He took the gleaming strands in his hands and stared at them as if he had discovered gold. 'Nell, I had no idea you had such beautiful hair – you always kept it hidden and scraped back . . .'

She shivered at his touch and took a step away from him, the old familiar fear and mistrust of men rising into her throat to obliterate her reason. 'Please, Kenneth, you mustna touch me like that. It isn't right and I canna allow it . . .'

His head blotted out the sun, dark, so dark. She gave a small apprehensive whimper which died in her throat as his lips came over hers, gentle and warm.

'It's time, Nell, time you were loved – as you deserve to be.'

He stared deep into her eyes, mesmerizing her. She felt his hands at her throat, unclasping the cameo brooch that held the high neck of her blouse together. His mouth came down to caress the hollow of smooth flesh between her shoulder-blades. Nellie closed her eyes, her legs waxen under her while her own fingers unbuttoned the bodice of her blouse, trembling fingers that fumbled but became still as his own steadied them and helped her remove the light garment. His mouth was still on hers as they sank to the ground together. The last of her clothes came off under his guidance. She felt the sun beating over her naked body and in a final flurry of inherent modesty she grabbed at her skirt to cover her breasts.

'No, Nell.' Without using force of any kind he prised the garment from her fingers, revealing the totally unexpected perfection of her body. Like everyone else he had thought the eldest daughter of King's Croft to be a scrawny young woman with very little shape to her, had pictured her breasts to be flat and unwomanly beneath the drab, confining frocks. Instead she was ripe and voluptuously curved, her breasts smooth, full and firm, her waist neat, the hips of her well-rounded and shapely . . . he also saw that she had no idea of her own attraction. Her doubts were mirrored in her eyes, her shame and embarrassment evident in the crimson staining her neck and face.

'You're a beautiful woman, Nell,' he told her softly and lay down beside her to kiss away her fears. Wordlessly she clung to him, her senses swimming, the blue vault of the heavens blurring and whirling away as he brought her unawakened body alive – so sensuously, wonderfully alive. When he removed his own clothes she remembered suddenly that terrible time in the woods when the beastly Peter Lamont had tried to ravish her, but the wonder and beauty of Kenneth's powerful body next to her own chased the phantoms of the past out of her mind as if they had never existed.

She couldn't get enough of that hard, muscled body arched over her own, she wanted to hold him to her forever, to kiss his deep chest, his lips, that wonderful fiery beard that tickled her nipples and incited cravings in her that surprised, excited, frightened her all at the same time. She had never imagined it could be like this with a man – hadn't wanted to imagine it, not even with him. His mouth moved all over her body till her breasts were on fire and a deep, exquisite warmth flooded her belly. The abrasive hairs at the pit of his stomach felt rough between the smoothness of her legs, but she welcomed their touch and was ready to meet his passion with hers when at last he entered her body. He was gentle with her, held back his excitement, remembering all the time that this was Nell Grant, a woman who had never before given even a small part of herself to any man – but then something happened to him in that sun-drenched hollow with the larks trilling in ecstasy all around and above them, and the burn purling its tranquil music into their ears as it wound its way to the river far below – Nell's obvious rapture transferred itself to him.

She was moving beneath him, sensually, provokingly, tantalizing him with her breasts, her mouth, that wide, beautiful mouth which had so long remained chaste, denying its secret, wanton passion to the world. The very sight of her raw, turbulent ecstasy kindled his own natural fire and he forgot himself, abondoned his tenderness and met her passion with his own so that they were carried together to heights of such intoxicating pleasure they both cried out and clung to one another in their mutual, final agony.

Time passed, silently, peacefully; the sun washed over them, lulling them to sleep as they lay locked in each other's arms. When a cool little breeze wakened them they said nothing, but got dressed slowly sitting on the warm moss of the moor, and then they lay back down again and held one another, her head on his chest, hearing the deep, steady booming of his heart – that beautiful warm, generous heart that she loved so deeply and so well. Her limbs were heavy with contentment. All the upsetting emotions she had ever experienced in her life seemed to have departed, the anger, the fear, the discontent, the sense of bitterness that had beset her when she witnessed her sisters growing up one by one and following their natural instincts. They had all had men in their lives, even Murn, for all her frustrated yearnings after *this* man, had found a certain solace with several members of the opposite sex – and Evie, that bonny, vivacious little sister of hers for all she was still a child, had had boys at her heels almost from the time she could walk.

Kenneth stroked the hair from her warm face. 'Nell, are you angry?' he asked uncertainly.

She shook her head, not looking up. 'I should be – at us both – but most of all with myself for allowing it to happen, yet I feel nothing but a deep, quiet calm that fills every part o' me. Maybe later I'll feel angry at myself, but not now. I just want to lie here and enjoy my contentment.'

'To think there was a time when I thought you didn't even like me very much – and now—'

'Now you know I love you. I'm almost twenty-eight years old and never thought I would ever say that to any man, but today I have and nothing can change that or take it away.'

'Nell, I don't want you ever to be hurt again but you ken fine how it was wi' me and Jeannie. She's so near and dear to me but – time will pass and perhaps—'

Sitting up, she placed her fingers over his lips. 'Hush, there's no need to say it, to even try and explain your feelings. I know what you're trying to tell me – you loved Jeannie, you will always love her, Kenneth, and I'll never try to take that away from you. But you need a woman in

185

your life and I'm damned if I'm going to start being all Nellie-ish and tell you I canna ever see you again because of what happened. It's because it happened that I *am* going to see you and take care o' you and the bairns so you needna think you're going to get rid o' me so easily.'

He gave a shout of laughter. 'That's my Nell! Next thing I know you'll be telling me to wash behind my lugs and no' to dirty the floor wi' my boots.'

'Ay, you're right there. I hate to see great muddy boots all over my clean floors so I'm warning you now, Kenneth.'

Jumping up, he pulled her to her feet and kissed the tip of her nose. 'And I'm warning you, Nell Grant, that what happened today was just the beginning. You have a lot o' catching up to do and by Dyod! I'll make sure you do it right well. You're quite a woman, Nell, and I just hope I have the staying power to keep up wi' you.'

Giggling like children they walked away down the slope, his arm round her waist, her steps light and carefree on the wild flowers of the moor.

It was almost eleven when the knock came to Evelyn's door. She was in bed writing up her diary, but hastened to hide it in the lockable tin box she kept it in now that it contained so much of her intimate thoughts. The door opened and Nellie stood there. Evelyn gulped, wondering if the moment of reckoning had at last come, but Nellie's voice contained no anger when she whispered, 'Can I come in, Evie? I have something I want to say to you.'

She moved to the bed and sat down on its edge. 'I just wanted to say thank you but couldna get you alone earlier to tell you that.'

'To – thank me?' Evelyn murmured uncertainly.

'Ay, for making me see sense. At first I was that angry wi' you it was all I could do to keep my hands off you, but then I got to thinking it over and realized it wasna so much wrong as courageous of you. It's no' many would face up to me the way you did but then—' she smiled and Evelyn noticed the soft flush on her cheeks, making her altogether more attractive than usual '—you're Evie and you aye did speak out your mind.'

Evelyn wriggled uncomfortably, still uncertain of the reason for her sister's visit. 'Maybe I say too much at times. I'm sorry if I hurt you, Nellie.'

Nellie took her hands, a glow in her eyes as she went on, 'I'll aye be grateful to you, Evie, so dinna apologize. You see, at long last I've been to see Kenneth Mor – ay, it's true. It took a lot o' soul-searching before I found the courage but I went this afternoon – and everything's all right now.'

Evelyn could tell by the soft, secret expression in her sister's eyes that everything was more than just all right. She had seen anger in Nellie, sometimes a sadness, an uneasiness too since Whisky Jake's intrusion that day in the Aulton, but now it was all washed away. Nellie looked serene and happy in the candle glow – in fact, she had that same look on her that Evelyn had witnessed in her own reflection after the wonderful night of love with David. Something pretty amazing had happened to Nellie that day and Evelyn was so astounded by the revelation that she said not a word, but just lay staring at her sister's face. Nellie blushed under the scrutiny and Evelyn knew at once that her surmise was correct. It was earth-shattering, she could think of no other word to describe it to herself. Nellie of the spinsterish ways and aversion to men had at last succumbed to all those emotions she had bottled up inside herself for so long . . .

'I'm glad, Nellie, really glad,' she said warmly. 'You'll be going up to Knobblieknowe a lot more from now on?'

'Oh ay, I will that. Isla Nell doesna see nearly as much o' her father as she should and both Cal and Kenneth need a woman to see to them.'

'I think the same might be said for Martin Gregory,' said Evelyn, thoughtfully. 'He was here when I got home, asking after Grace, wondering when she's coming home. She hasna been back since Christmas yet there was a time when she managed even the odd weekend.'

'She canna face Martin,' Nellie said grimly. 'If Grace

187

has a fault it's that she canna bring herself to hurt anybody, no' even if it's for their own good. If only Martin would leave her alone. He's old enough to be her father and surely canna believe that something is going to come out o' his friendship wi' our Grace. For that's all it is to her but—'

'But no' to him,' nodded Evelyn. 'There's something about him I dinna like, Nellie, a kind o' wildness staring from his eyes. I have a feeling things wi' him and Grace are going to come to a head soon. I heard tell that he's been spending a lot o' his spare time painting up his house, being very furtive about it and no' letting anyone inside to see it, yet hinting that it's for a special occasion which everyone will know about soon enough. I used to like Martin but now he sends shivers up my spine just to look at him.'

Nellie sighed and stood up. 'The time has come for him, Evie. We go on wi' our lives, day by day, doing the same old things, then one day it all changes – and when that happens, our time has come to make the big decisions we couldna face up to before.'

'Like your decision to see Kenneth Mor?' asked Evelyn softly, her heart warming to this new, thoughtful Nellie.

'Ay, I suppose you could say that.' She gazed down at her young sister. 'Davie is going back to France soon, I hear.'

Evelyn nodded miserably. 'The day after tomorrow.'

Nellie stooped and put her arms round her sister. 'It's hard, babby, hard to say goodbye to someone you love as you love him.'

Her arms were strong yet warm, so warm. Evelyn held on tight to their reassurance, a memory coming to her of those same arms holding her close when she was just a tiny wee thing. Now they were both grown, they were both in love – at last Nellie understood what that meant and all at once she felt deeply comforted by the realization.

She and David walked, arms tightly clasped around each other, not speaking because there was too much they

188

couldn't express in mere words. She felt the heat of him, was very aware of the lean edge of his hip against her soft one. He looked fit and well, the David she had first noticed in the window of Bert's Tea Shoppe. Those last weeks of relaxation, of sunshine and fresh air, had erased the lines of mental and physical pain. His skin was tanned, his face rounded, his walk full of spring and bounce.

They were making for the barn mill down by Plookie Plains Farm. Although it was past seven in the evening the sky was wide and bright, the larks still singing above the fields. They had arranged that their last evening together would be spent in the same setting as the first. He had come down to Rothiedrum by train. Tonight she hadn't been late meeting him, having contrived to get away from the big house earlier than usual. Saft Sam hadn't had even two minutes in which to ask his prying questions, and she had almost felt sorry for him at being deprived of his favourite pastime.

She was wearing the same skirt and blouse that she had worn before, all the creases neatly pressed out, and when she had gone upstairs to dress Nellie hadn't said she was half-naked, but had commented instead on how nice she looked and had given her a quick, sympathetic peck on the cheek.

She wanted everything to be as it had been on *that* night, only it wasn't of course. Nothing ever stayed the same, no two situations were ever alike. For one thing he hadn't just arrived home on sick leave; very soon he was going away from her, back to that awful hell that made young men look old. For another there was no rain to make them seek the shelter of the barn mill, their footsteps there were entirely premeditated, for neither of them could deny any longer their naked yearnings.

It was quiet at Plookie Plains Farm. She knew old Dan McCrae all right. Come rain, hail or shine he locked his doors after tea to enjoy his hot toddies by the fire. The other farmers teased him about the habit, the norm being to relax by the fire with the drams when the day's work was done.

189

'Ach, I need to kittle myself up after a hard day,' was old Dan's excuse, and as to the locked doors, 'The meenister might come' was all he would say, smiling his wicked old grin into his steaming toddies.

The barn loft was brighter than it had been the last time, with sunbeams slanting on the cobwebs that hung from the rafters and bits of silvery stoor dancing in their rays. From a corner a half-wild she-cat, protective of its newborn litter, hissed and growled at them before retreating with flattened ears back to its young to wash and feed them.

'Just like a woman,' David grinned, standing back from her as if the last thing he wanted in the world was to touch her.

'Ay, and just like the old tom who covered her to keep out the way at her time o' need.'

'She would eat him,' he laughed.

'Well, she has to eat something,' she returned reasonably.

He shook his head appreciatively. 'You always have an answer, don't you? I think that's what I like most about you – your cheek, that and the fact that I've never seen you look more beautiful with the sunlight shining on your hair and bringing out the green sparks in your eyes.'

'There isn't much time,' she reminded him, her breath growing tight in her throat, her heart beginning its familiar tattoo in her breast.

With eyes fixed on one another they undressed, slowly at first, then as desire leapt between them, tearing off the last of their clothes. He came towards her and enclosed her warm, naked body with his, a great sigh breathing out of him, his mouth buried in the silkiness of her hair. 'Oh, Evie, you feel so good, I've longed for this, for you—' He kissed her mouth, her breasts, his excitement mounting rapidly. 'Last time,' he murmured, 'I was tired and ill. I'm well now, darling, and I promise you I won't fall asleep this time. I'll show you how much loving can be achieved in two hours.'

His voice was rough with his need for her, his eyes

dazed with longing. His hands moved over her body, came to the base of her spine, whispered up the full length of it all the time pressing her in closer to his taut, demanding hardness.

Oh, Dan McCrae, this is far far better than the hottest toddy you're ever likely to taste, she thought in a burst of humour, before giving herself up to the rapture of loving David Grainger with her heart, her soul, and her body.

He had told her he didn't want her to come to the station to say goodbye. Far better that their last memories of one another should be of this place that had come to have such a special meaning for them. To them it was no ordinary old barn mill but a place of romance, a haven which they felt was theirs alone. The weathered wood of the walls had absorbed their quiet murmurings of love, the very rafters had rung with the ecstatic cries of their lovemaking.

She sat where he had left her, very still and quiet, the fires of passion quenched, a cold emptiness curling inside her as she listened to his footsteps retreating down the loft ladder, going over the straw-littered floor, receding, fading, till finally there was silence, a silence that echoed still with his voice, his laugh. It grew in intensity till it became a hollow ringing in her ears and then there was real silence, the sort that was so thick and dark it could very nearly be felt.

Drawing her knees up to her chin, she clasped her arms around them and gazed unseeingly in front of her. The days and weeks stretched before her, empty, meaningless. Their promises to one another belonged to another time now. 'You know I'll write, Evie,' his voice hushed into her mind, 'and I'll get leave – don't look like that, as if this is farewell forever. How could I ever forget you, forget one single moment of this wonderful summer?'

Such dear, sweet pledges whispered in the aftermath of passion – already he didn't belong to her any more. The world had swallowed him up, he belonged to it now and might never be hers again. The eyes of strangers would look at him, their ears would hear those soft, velvety tones which had so recently and effortlessly charmed her into complete and utter submission . . .

The dogs were barking from the steadings of Plookie Plains Farm. Old Dan McCrae had abandoned his doubtful pleasures and was maybe off with his hammer to mend his paling wires, or out there in the fields with the fee'd men.

She examined her clothing. This time there were no creases, only a few bits of straw which were easily enough brushed off. Maggie wouldn't be able to find any fault there. She climbed down the loft ladder and made her slow way home, her eyes on the far distance where the little locomotive carrying David was bustling its important way to Aberdeen.

# CHAPTER TWELVE

Gillan and Alan arrived home on leave within days of one another, Alan arriving first, a more manly-looking Alan, his new maturity lending angular planes to his boy's face, his stubble of beard noticeably darker. The harsh months since leaving home had forced him to grow up a lot sooner than nature intended. Evelyn thought the changes suited him, but Kirsty threw up her hands in horror and made haste to fill him with her best cooking, all the while telling him, 'We must fill out that poor, sunken face you have on you.'

Unlike David, he was ready enough to tell Evelyn of some of his most frightening moments, and sensing his need to talk to someone outside of the family she listened quietly as they walked together through the perfumed summer evenings. He had been wounded but hastened to make light of it. 'It was only a scratch and never even needed a stitch so I was able to carry on soon after.' He smiled at her, colouring a little as he went on, 'Before I went into that fray I mind praying to God and kissing the lock o' hair you gave me. When I went down I heard myself calling out to Florrie, so between you, you brought me luck.'

She chewed her lip, shame in her for having once thought he mightn't be strong enough to pass his army medical. Alan was strong all right, strong in so many ways. Many men would have welcomed a Blighty to get them home for a while, but he had been glad to be fit enough to carry on. But even while she admired his courage she couldn't stop herself wondering if his enthusiasm for fighting was entirely natural.

At the beginning of the war all the young men had been fired with patriotism, but that had been before any of them knew the dreadful reality. Too many men had faded away, fatally wounded in the mud of the battlefields. The haggard faces of those who returned, embittered and disillusioned, told their own tale yet Alan looked, if not exactly in the full bloom of health, exhilarated, as if he couldn't wait to get back to a hell where normal thinking was very nearly annihilated, and death and misery were everyday affairs. He had never gotten over Florrie's death, but surely – he couldn't want that terrible final oblivion to relieve his broken heart? She took his hand. 'Forget about war for a while, Alan. If you thought you were lucky wi' a lock o' my hair in your hands you're about to be even luckier just touching me. I happen to know Nellie's just baked a batch o' your favourite treacle scones. If you come home wi' me this minute she'll take one look at that "poor sunken face" o' yours, and give you a plateful all to yourself.'

He laughed then, and seemed to return to the delights of his summer homeland. They took hands and ran through the warm meadows and down leafy lanes – as they had done as children in another time that wasn't years but worlds away.

The innocence was long gone, and with it the carefree freedom they had once taken for granted.

Evelyn enjoyed the less formal atmosphere that had presided at Rothiedrum House since it had become a refuge for convalescing officers. As more and more seriously injured young men came there to recuperate, it had become necessary to turn most of the house over to them. Though it could in no way be considered a hospital, some of the more badly maimed still needed a certain amount of nursing and so a small band of Red Cross nurses moved in, headed by a matron who was built like a tank and moved like one, scattering all and sundry who dared to get in her path. To quote Coulter, she was 'pidgin-chested and pig-headed', using her bosom like some sort of battering ram as she marched about, instilling fear into the breasts of three little VADs who had dared to offer their services to Rothiedrum.

Lady Marjorie did not take kindly to the new restrictions imposed upon her, but it was for the war effort after all and she did so enjoy thinking up all sorts of pleasant little amusements to keep the men happy.

Added to that particular spiritual and emotional fulfilment was the further spice of pitting her wits against Matron, whose strutting figure was a formidable force that few came up against willingly. But come against it Lady Marjorie did, and with such obvious relish that the two never encountered one another without a perceptible corset-induced bristling, coupled with an anticipatory tightening of the lips indicating that swords were about to be drawn at any moment. Matron was far too busy to collaborate in Lady Marjorie's morale-boosting little schemes, while Lady Marjorie was far too idle to pay heed to Matron and in the end, after much pulling of hair and gnashing of teeth on Matron's part, she got her way, her efforts doing much to enliven the men and disrupt Matron's routine.

Evelyn still carried out her duties above stairs, but Evander had asked that she devote part of each working day to the men. 'Talk to them, lass, that's what they need most and who better to confide in than a pretty girl? You know the sort of thing, write the odd letter or two for them, keep them on their toes and let them know they're still alive and needed. I would appreciate it too if you joined them in these little parties my wife spends her time dreaming up. Just the odd evening here and there – do us all the world of good to have you about the place.'

He had eyed her slender little figure at that point and dropped his lid in a flirtatious wink, and wasn't in the least put out when she had winked back and told him she would enjoy doing as he asked.

She had become quite a favourite with the young officers, many of whom confided to her their doubts and fears as they struggled to resign themselves to an existence without full physical capabilities. Their emotions were raw, uncertain. Some appeared to accept their situation though not without a certain cynical view of life, others gave vent to suppressed anger and frustration by behaving frivolously and often outrageously. No matter what, each individual response was a cry for help, a fact which Evelyn wasn't slow to recognize.

Her engagingly frank approach, her sense of humour, her down-to-earth manner, her grace and vivacious beauty, all combined to make her a much sought-after companion and she was never without a partner, be it for dancing, talking, or just walking in the gardens.

Her ladyship was quick to notice Evelyn's popularity, and in the beginning had looked down her haughty nose at the idea of a servant girl associating with the young officers, many of whom were titled. How could Evander encourage such a thing? He really did take too much upon himself, and had such poor grasp of the proper order of things. But gradually a certain admiration for the girl infiltrated her lofty façade. She watched Evelyn walking in the gardens with sightless men, some whose facial disfigurements were so severe they didn't recognize themselves when they finally plucked up the courage to view themselves in a mirror. Evelyn never once flinched, nor seemed anything other than interested or amused at the things they spoke about – into an ear just a bit too close to be in good taste, her ladyship sniffed to herself – but, of course, one had to make allowances, this was a crofter's daughter after all and as such could hardly be expected to understand about social refinements. Even so the girl had grace and charm, she had to admit. Not many could have danced holding on to a man's empty sleeve and still managed to make the whole procedure look effortless and dignified. And where had she learned to dance like that, anyway? Certainly not at those dreadful village affairs, or at those wild ale and meal celebrations held in dusty barns. But of course, the men themselves had taught her, all eager to hold on to that lithesome young body, to look into the sparkle of those amazing green eyes.

In a burst of benevolence which was not entirely lacking in ardent curiosity, Lady Marjorie invited Evelyn to partake of tea in the part of the house that had been made into a comfortable unit for the family's use.

Evelyn, with as much curiosity as Lady Marjorie herself, accepted the invitation, though, remembering her first social visit to Rothiedrum House when she had been the subject of much scrutiny regarding her suitability as Gillan's friend, she went with a certain amount of misgivings and not a little defensive air about her.

But Lady Marjorie welcomed her most charmingly and in a short time she found herself relaxing, blossoming even as the mistress of the house spoke pleasantly about general things. She went on to inquire after Evelyn's family, asked her about her writing ambitions, her plans for her life, in fact she went out of her way to make herself amiable and likeable to her guest, and for a time Evelyn glimpsed a warm and generous spirit hiding beneath all the snobbery, the airs and graces.

'You know, you're very good with the men, Evelyn.' She stirred her tea thoughtfully. 'Have you never considered taking up nursing? The hospitals are crying out for volunteers to nurse the wounded.'

'Oh ay, I've considered it.' (Never a 'ladyship' or a 'ma'am', Lady Marjorie noted. Were all the Grants so inherently proud that they considered it beneath them to address their betters properly? Or were they just plain ignorant?) 'But I'm needed at home as much as I'm needed here,' Evelyn went on. 'And, besides, I'm no' of the proper social standing to train as a VAD or anything like that. I need the money I get working to Rothiedrum, so I'm quite happy to remain as I am till something better turns up.'

Her ladyship flushed. Had the girl read her mind? And what cheek! Till something better turns up, indeed! If it wasn't for the fact that this child of the soil had so successfully sneaked her way into Evander's affections, she would most certainly have been shown the door long ago. Or would she? Heaven help her. She was dealing with blood kin here. It wasn't just a simple matter of favouritism. Evander would always be fair in his dealings with the girl.

Evelyn's eyes were on her – smiling? Or triumphant?

'You are quite a character, my dear,' Lady Marjorie said dryly. (These farming types often were.) 'And also disarmingly frank. What a pity we didn't get to know one another sooner. I never had anything against you personally, you know, but you must see that it is my duty to do what's best for my son.' (Back to that again – why had she said it? She hadn't meant to.) 'Gillan always had so much catching up to do,' she continued, flustered and annoyed at herself. 'He was never the best judge of his own character and seemed always to want to be in the wrong places—'

'With the wrong people,' Evelyn interposed softly. She put down her cup and stood up. 'You have worried yourself for nothing, Lady Marjorie. I love Gillie, I gave him friendship when he needed it most – and that was all it ever was between us, at least as far as I was concerned. Gillie would have married me if I had said yes, oh ay, it's time you knew the truth about how things were. I was tempted, mind, he's a fine lad and his money would have meant a life of ease for both me and my family. But I never loved him in that way, and for me there has to be equal love on both sides for a relationship to work. He'll tell you himself, my heart aye did rule my head and when I marry it will be for love, not position or wealth.

'He's still my very dear friend though and I'm telling you now, when he comes home I'll see him as often as I can if he wants it that way.'

'You – have received a letter?'

'Yes, I have. We write to one another regularly.'

'Oh, Evelyn.' Lady Marjorie's voice was low. 'Isn't it wonderful that he's coming home? I can hardly wait to see him. It's been so long – he had a very short leave at the beginning of March when he came over to London, but he was gone again almost before we knew he'd been.'

Evelyn stared at the woman's pink, excited face. In moments like these she looked just like any other mother in the land, waiting impatiently for her offspring's homecoming.

'We'll have a welcome home party of course,' Lady

Marjorie went on. 'Matron won't like it, naturally but—' She gave a sudden, gay little toss of her head. 'Damn Matron and what she thinks!'

'Lady Marjorie, that's hardly ladylike,' Evelyn dared to say in mock disapproval.

Her ladyship laughed. 'I felt like it, it must be your influence, Evelyn.'

It was Evelyn's turn to smile in wry appreciation at having the tables turned. She went to the door.

'I didn't think I would, but I've enjoyed speaking to you, Evelyn.' Lady Marjorie had composed herself, she was once more the elegant, self-possessed mistress of Rothiedrum.

'Ay, I thought you would,' returned Evelyn, softly. 'But if we are perfectly honest with each other we would admit to being as curious about one another as two cats in an alley. I aye thought of you as a bit o' a dragon, living way up there beyond the ken o' mortal men – but today I have found you to be human after all. You should smile and laugh more often, it suits you and makes you look years younger.'

Her ladyship's mouth fell open. Really! The girl positively flirted with chance. She couldn't have this – this familiarity, not to mention insubordination. She must get Evander to fire her at once – but, it was so difficult to get staff in these hard times . . . Lady Marjorie permitted herself a small, hard, long-suffering smile. 'You may go, Evelyn,' she said tightly. The door shut. She got up to rush to the mirror and smile at her reflection. The girl was right. She did look years younger – what a perceptive little beggar she was – coarse, but amusing. In fact, if things had been different she would have made a delightful companion – a great pity she couldn't allow herself to get to like the girl too much, she could have taught her such a lot about the finer things in life . . .

Evander Ramsay Forbes was coming upstairs just as Evelyn shut the sitting-room door.

'I was having tea with Lady Marjorie,' she explained before he could speak.

He grinned. 'Indeed? Wonders will never cease.'

'No.' Evelyn dimpled wickedly. 'And, of course – there's a first time for everything.' She ran lightly downstairs, triumphant that she had at last found an appropriate moment to quote the phrase which, hitherto, had always been the province of those around her.

Evander found his wife standing thoughtfully by the fireplace. 'I hear you have at last condescended to be social to your young cousin,' he greeted her in some amusement.

She ignored that. 'You know, Evander, she's quite a girl, that one. In different circumstances she might have been something of a socialite.'

'In different circumstances she might have been many things, my dear Marjorie, but a spoiled little debutante, never! She's got far too much fire and independence to have ever fitted into that sort of artificial scene. Mind you,' he continued, musingly, 'there have been one or two unforgettable rebels along the way. Lady Caroline Lamb, for instance—'

'Evander! Your tongue runs away with you. Now, if you had equated her with Lillie Langtry that would have been much more fitting . . .'

He went to the drinks table to pour himself a brandy, his mind on business matters as he sipped the contents of his glass.

'Evander – she, she called me a dragon and an alley-cat all in the same breath. She also told me if I smiled more it would make me look younger.'

Throwing back his head he roared with appreciative laughter, so enraptured by her words he didn't notice her answering smile – head tilted sideways so that she could capture the effect in the mirror above the mantelshelf.

'You haven't told me how pleased you are to see me alive and well,' Gillan teased Evelyn as they stood together in the drawing room sipping champagne and wincing a little as the talk and laughter around them grew in volume along with the gramophone someone had brought to 'liven things up, old boy.'

This party was different from the others. It was Gillan's 'welcome home' and his mother had thought to please him by inviting a number of young people for the weekend. Several of them had travelled from England and were determined to make the most of their stay. The girls were elegantly dressed, talked rapidly, frivolously and superficially in a bid to forget that it was wartime and times like these, once part and parcel of their lives, were to be enjoyed while the going was good. One or two worked with the Red Cross in London and talked loudly about the wonderful spirit of the troops departing for France, until the dark looks thrown at them by the officers reminded them that those returning might be far from whole in mind, body and spirit.

Women far outnumbered the men present yet even so there seemed an unwillingness among the young officers to integrate. Evelyn knew why. They simply couldn't be bothered with small talk, it was too pointless, boring and irrelevant. Also, they weren't yet ready to face a sympathetic, pitying society whose patriotic comments about giving all for King and Country were just too naive to swallow with good grace.

One girl, a vibrantly attractive creature with black hair and deep-set blue eyes, was divulging her opinions on a composer named Irving Berlin. 'You simply must listen to him, I've brought one of his records. Clear back the chairs and we'll dance.'

Evelyn turned to Gillan. 'If I could hear myself talk I would tell you how glad I am to see you but I knew you were alive and well, you told me so in your letters.' She grinned at him. 'It is good to see you, Gillie, and looking so handsome too despite everything.' She shook her head. 'I'm sorry, I canna be natural in this company – and just look at me.' She drew back from him and examined herself critically. She was wearing her white blouse and a matching skirt which she had coaxed Murn to make from a piece of material purchased in Aberdeen specially for Gillan's party. 'I thought this was bonny but compared to what the others are wearing it looks plain and homemade.'

He took her arm, his dark eyes roving appreciatively over

her slim body. 'You're the best-looking girl here and would be even if you were wearing two sacks tied together – let's get out of here, Princess, I want to talk to you – properly.'

The girl with the dark hair came dancing over to wind her arm possessively through his. 'Come on, Gillan,' she coaxed, 'you've been hiding yourself away in this corner all evening.' Her eyes flicked over Evelyn as if seeing her for the first time. 'Well, I can see your reasons for keeping to this cosy little corner. Introduce us, Gillan. Where are your manners?'

'Evelyn McKenzie Grant, Wilhemina Victoria Oxton, Wilhemina Victoria Oxton, Evelyn McKenzie Grant,' Gillan introduced them stiffly, adding as if as an afterthought, 'Lady Wilhemina Oxton.'

Evelyn had never heard him speak so formally and she was seized with a nervous desire to laugh, though she resisted the temptation. She wouldn't make a fool of herself, not in front of this lovely young woman who looked so enchanting and expensive in a cream silk dress with a long string of pearls cascading over her flawless throat.

'Gillan, what on earth's gotten into you?' chided the girl in some annoyance. She turned her blue, unblinking gaze once more upon Evelyn. 'Just call me Vicky, everyone does.'

'And I'm Evie—' Evelyn began.

'Princess Evie,' said Gillan, solemnly.

'Princess—?' The girl started to ask, then paused abruptly as she caught the laughing, conspiratorial glance that passed between the other two.

Someone had exchanged the Irving Berlin record for a frenzied Texas Tommy.

'Damn!' The girl spun round. 'Some people have no taste! Still—' she brightened '—it's fun. Let's join in, Gillan—' She turned back. Gillan, with Evelyn's hand in his, was threading his way through the girating bodies to the door. There, he was apprehended by his mother.

'Gillan, you aren't deserting your guests, surely?' she reproved him with a quick glance at Evelyn.

'Fresh air, Mother,' he said faintly. 'All this excitement has gone to my head.'

'You do look a little pale. Perhaps I should have made it

202

just a small family gathering.' She gave Evelyn a meaningful look. 'Don't keep him out there too long, Evelyn. Too much fresh air is as bad as too little.'

They darted outside, smothering their giggles. 'You were bad-mannered, Gillie,' Evelyn told him as they paused on the terrace to regain their breath, 'to leave that girl talking to thin air.'

'Never mind that. Do I detect a change in Mother's attitude to you? She sounded almost friendly just now.'

'Maybe she's just getting used to having me around. Gillie, that girl, Vicky, have you known her for long?'

'All my life. You're not jealous, surely?'

'Ach no, it's just she gave the impression of being very attached to you. I think she's in love wi' you.'

'Vicky's always in love with someone.' He led her towards the lawns and a little wooden summerhouse nestling among flowering shrubs. They sat in silence for some time, content just to be alone together. Then she told him about David, her enthusiasm catching in her throat, all her yearnings and feelings of loneliness tumbling out of her so rapidly she didn't pause once to see his reactions. When she at last stopped talking, he squeezed her hand. 'I'm glad you've found someone to please that romantic heart of yours – though it galls a bit to know that you weren't as lonely for me as I was for you.'

'Och, Gillie, you know I'll always miss you when you're away from me.' She pushed back a lock of his hair and studied his face in a beam of moonlight streaming over a silvery bank of cloud. 'How are you? Do you want to talk to me about what it was like? Some don't, in fact most of them won't.'

He moved restlessly. 'I'd rather forget it and enjoy my leave, if you don't mind. I'll just say this, I never imagined it could be – as it was.'

'Never mind, if you'll let me I'll help you. We'll have a bonny time while you're here. Alan Keith's home too, so we can make a threesome and enjoy ourselves.'

'Safety in numbers, eh?'

'Gillie! Dinna start all that again,' she warned. 'Or – or

203

I'll just leave you to the mercies o' all your posh friends in there – of course,' she added slyly '—maybe that's what you want. Lady What-do-you-call-Her looks a very determined sort o' girl and—'

He pulled her to her feet and held tight to her arms. 'How would you like me to carry you off bodily to the Kelpie Pool and dump you in?'

'No' tonight, we'll save that for a warm evening wi' maybe The Loon and Alan there to make sure you behave yourself.'

His fingers went to her neck. 'I see you're wearing the necklace I gave you.'

'For the first time. I dinna often get the chance to wear it, it's so bonny a thing I never want to lose it or wear it too much.' She stood on tiptoe and kissed his cheek. 'I must get home. If I'm out too late Mam waits up for me in the kitchen and asks all sorts o' funny questions.'

He sighed. 'I often wish I had your sort of life, Evie. You can always be yourself whereas I have to do things like go back in there and try and look charming and pleased to the guests Mother chose for me, when all the time I'd rather be out here with you or down in the kitchens eating Martha's buttery scones.'

She giggled. 'If you want to, you will, Gillie, and if you canna get past Matron then you can come along to King's Croft tomorrow and eat Nellie's buttery scones. She fills Alan so full of them he's beginning to look more like Jessie Blair's son than Kirsty's.'

'Will you let me walk you home?'

'Ach no, better not. You get back in there and do your duty before your mother comes out to make sure I'm no' seducing you.'

With a laugh she was off, running like a deer through the woods and over the fields to the short tunnel under the railway that took her to opposite King's Croft road end.

Nellie was coming down the track from Knobblieknowe and the two sisters went into the house together, Evie marvelling that such a thing could possibly be when always before Nellie was either in bed at this hour or in the kitchen seeing to the nightly chores. But Nellie's routine had undergone a complete turnabout. She still rose at five each morning to take her share of the croft work, but all her spare time was spent up at Knobblieknowe – though she was careful never to be seen going if Murn was about. That young lady was already showing suspicion at the radical change in both Nellie's appearance and her outlook, and without a word being spoken everyone saw to it that Murn was none the wiser for any of it. Both Maggie and Jamie were too delighted at the change in Nellie to take any risks that might jeopardize her new-found happiness, so everyone trod very carefully indeed where Murn was concerned. If the story of Nellie and Kenneth's developing friendship reached her ears, there was no telling what she would do. All these years she had waited, hoped, even demeaned herself in an effort to get Kenneth to notice her, and the irony of the latest development might prove to be the last straw.

An invisible, protective net had been thrown about Nellie's activities, and had thus far proved so effective that not even the most curious of neighbours had any inkling as to what was happening between the eldest daughter of King's Croft and the master of Kobblicknowc.

The sisters went upstairs together, threw one another an odd little conspiratorial smile before departing to their separate rooms. Evelyn went quickly and gladly into hers. Grace was home for a two-week summer break and Evelyn was delighted to have her favourite sister back, to confide in her, to hear her talk about Gordon who had had a hectic time in France but was soon coming back to Aberdeen on leave. But when she shut the door and turned, her experiences of the evening ready to tumble from her lips, the laughter died in her throat for Grace was lying back on her bed, pale, strained, and worried-looking.

'Oh, Evie, it's Martin,' she confessed when her sister sat down on the bed and took her hands. 'Ever since I came home he's been acting strange but tonight he was saying odd things as well. He spoke about having secrets, that the time was near for them to come out. He said I would be pleased when I discovered what he'd been doing, that it was all for me and soon I would never have to work or worry again. Dear God, Evie, what am I to do?' She ran her fingers abstractedly through her shining cap of chestnut hair, her huge eyes dark and haunted in the exquisite smoothness of her lovely face.

'Grace, you must tell him about Gordon. He has to know some time and it seems to me the time has come.'

'Oh, fine I ken that. I've tried to tell him, but every time I began to speak about my life in Aberdeen he brushed it aside, almost as if he didna want to hear. I – I never meant him to get to like me the way he does. I just felt sorry for him after he lost his wife. He was aye so lonely-looking I had to help him. I was so young, Evie, only sixteen, I never kent he would look seriously on a bairn like me. In all the time I've known Martin I never even let him kiss me, or encouraged him in any way – and now – it's come to this,' she faltered miserably.

'When do you have to see him again?'

'Tomorrow evening. He wants me to go to the schoolhouse. He's making quite a fuss about it, cooking a special dinner, he says, and opening a bottle o' champagne some friend gave him a whilie back. It's to be a celebration – only I dinna ken for what and I dinna want to—' She turned on her side to gaze out of the window. 'I wish I didna have to go, Evie, if I could maybe think o' something . . .'

'No, Grace.' Evelyn spoke firmly. 'Go and be done wi' it once and for all. Tell him about Gordon and finish it there. It might be cruel but it's the only thing to do now, and whether you like it or no' you'll have to do it.'

'I know – if only I had told him sooner. It might never have come to this – I just hope I havena left it – too late.'

Evelyn, Gillan, and Alan were standing on the bridge near Carnallachie's place, passing the time with Dottie Drummond, The Loon, and Carnallachie when Martin Gregory passed them in his trap on his way to collect

Grace. He was wearing his best Sunday suit, his dark hair had been brushed back and slicked down with cream, he looked ready to burst with exuberance as he lifted his whip in acknowledgement.

'He looks happy,' commented Alan, watching the trap rounding the bend at the Manse.

'Ach, he's just plain daft if ye ask me,' grunted Carnallachie, hurling a gobbet of spit to the ground. 'Behaving like an old woman this whilie back wi' all his wee furtive comings and goings. I ken fine he's been in Aberdeen buyin' bits o' furniture and paint but when anybody asks what he's up to he's no' for tellin' a thing.'

'And why should the laddie be daft just because he wants his house nice?' Dottie barked with asperity, puffing her clay pipe into Carnallachie's grizzled countenance.

'I wish we could get paint for ours,' said The Loon mournfully. 'The walls havena seen the lick o' a brush since Queen Victoria was put on her chamber.'

'Throne,' corrected Dottie acidly, the nicotine-stained little hairs on her upper lip fairly bristling with smug satisfaction at having the opportunity to let the others see she wasn't as 'saft' as everyone made out. 'Anyway, how can you ken the likes o' that? Ye werena even born then nor me myself if it comes to that.'

'They *look* as if they havena been touched since then,' persisted The Loon. 'You should get Muckle Willie to do them next time he comes roond.' The Loon gave his mother a sly look. 'It would help to pay for his keep.'

'Faith! You've a mucky mind on you, my lad,' Dottie hurled back at him. 'Forbye, I wouldna gie thon wee trollop good paint to waste!'

'Na, but you would gie him other things,' The Loon muttered darkly, but well under his breath so that she couldn't make out the insinuation.

Alan and Gillan were enjoying the exchange for nothing was more refreshing than the unconscious humour shared by The Loon and his mother, but Evelyn said nothing. The trap was coming back, in it the small, slender figure of Grace dwarfed by Martin's bulk beside her.

As they drew nearer Evelyn saw her sister's white face, the great, worried dark eyes. As they passed, she turned slightly and threw Evelyn a despairing look.

'Grace doesn't seem very happy.' Gillan's whisper tickled Evelyn's ear.

'No, Gillie, she isn't,' she agreed, and shivered despite the mildness of the summer evening.

# CHAPTER THIRTEEN

'Well, Grace, how do you like it?' Martin opened the door of the schoolhouse with a flourish and ushered Grace inside.

She stared around her, appalled and afraid, not so much at what she saw but at the realization of just how much time and effort the schoolteacher had put into the house. The once dingy walls gleamed with new paint and paper, much of the heavy old furniture had been removed, and in its place were pretty new chintz armchairs and sofas, tables and bookcases made with a fine wood, lightly stained. Colourful rugs were scattered over the new linoleum – and to complete the picture, vases of wild flowers reposed on the windowsills, piano, and mantelpiece. That last touch was so like Martin Gregory. He was a sensitive man, one who had always appreciated the freshness and beauty of the wild things of forest and field. She hardly dared look any further, but against her will her eyes were drawn to the walls which were oddly bare and desolate-looking. For a moment she asked herself why she should have expected anything else. The last time she was in this house she had been little more than a child, and like every other young person who had ever visited Martin Gregory she had shivered in an atmosphere that was heavily redolent of the past. In her schooldays children had spoken in whispers about 'the hoose wi' the ghaisties', and it had been true enough that everywhere you went in it eyes had followed you from old photos hanging everywhere, accusing eyes, limpid eyes, eyes so faded with age that the sockets were empty which made the effect all the more terrifying.

And now, almost nothing – only one or two insipid little prints of sailing boats, some framed group photographs of schoolchildren – and, unobtrusively to the left of the fireplace, a sepia-tinted photograph of Mary Ann, Martin's dead wife. Grace had looked sadly at that photograph on her last visit, seeing it through the romantic, tearful eyes of a child. She had been young that bonny woman, young in the picture, young when she died in childbirth, but in the naivety of her own youthful years Grace had soon forgotten those haunted eyes, that cloud of dark hair, the droop of that sensitive mouth, the look about the face as of one glimpsing, in the shutters of the camera, the premature drawing of the blinds on her own life . . .

Oh God, Grace thought, she could be me. Martin's in love with a ghost, all along he's looked at me – and seen Mary Ann . . .

He was at her back, courteously helping her off with her jacket, hanging it carefully on a peg in the hallway. 'You needn't say anything now, dearest,' he told her in his kindly, quiet voice. 'It can wait—'

'It's lovely, Martin, lovely—'

He put his hand under her elbow and guided her into the kitchen which had also been redecorated and refurnished so that it no more resembled a country schoolhouse kitchen than a stable hung with tapestries and lace.

The table was set cosily for two, white linen napkins lay neatly by the cutlery, a centrepiece of red roses made a vivid splash of colour against the freshly laundered, white tablecloth.

Martin pushed her gently into a chair by the fireplace and smiled down on her benevolently, the light from the window glancing off his glasses so that she couldn't see his eyes. 'A little celebration drink first, my bonny Grace. Later, if you feel cold, the fire is all set and just needs a match.'

Her senses were reeling; as if from a great distance she heard the cork popping from the bottle of champagne, the busy fizzing and bursting of the bubbles as he poured it into glasses.

He held his glass high. 'To us, my dearest Grace, and to all our beginnings.'

Her hands were icy cold, her fingers locked so tightly round her glass she felt it must shatter at any moment. With a great effort, holding onto it with both hands, she held the glass to her numb lips, unable to stop the trembling of her head, quite sure he must notice and at any moment smother her with his concern, perhaps even try to take her in his arms.

But he was in a disquietingly euphoric mood, more taken up with making certain that everything was to her liking, too busy straightening the cutlery, re-arranging a flower here and there. He had always been a slow, purposeful man, small details had rarely bothered him. He had been the studious type, clever, thoughtful, always surrounded by an aura of absent-mindedness. Now . . .

He bustled about, exclaimed that the table wasn't properly set and went ben the scullery to search for the missing accoutre.

Grace lay back in her chair, utterly exhausted though she had barely moved since her arrival. Outside the window the lush parklands stretched, wide, free, beckoning. Down in the little woods beyond the village the cuckoo was calling the last of his summer song; Cuck – cuckoo, cuck – cuckoo . . . She wanted to get up and run out into that golden freedom beyond the schoolhouse but she felt leaden, weighted down. In spite of the new furniture, the paint, the atmosphere inside the house was heavily oppressive, more so than it had ever been.

Oh, Gordon, she thought, if only you were here. Cuck – cuckoo, cuck – cuckoo . . . She put her hands over her ears. There was a sense of madness here, it was all around her, cloying, closing her in . . .

Martin was back, she glimpsed his eyes behind the glasses, staring, feverish. 'Everything is ready now, Grace. Sit you in at the table and I'll serve the meal. Nothing fancy mind, I've been too long on my own to know much about the small niceties. I always have my meals on a tray by the fire, but I remembered – about setting tables, Mary Ann was in service before she wed me and knew how to do things properly. I watched – when we had visitors she brought out all the best china, cutlery. Oh ay, a woman's touch, a home needs a woman's touch.'

He gave a strange high-pitched laugh that sent shivers up Grace's spine. He was pulling out a chair, standing by, waiting. She arose, legs trembling, wondering – should she make some excuse about feeling ill, get him to take her home?

'Come, Grace, darling, I've spent all day preparing for this. Sit down, sit down, dear child. There now, that's a girl.'

He was speaking to her as if she was a small child. She could hardly bear to look at him, to see that selfless, mad love shining from his eyes.

The meal couldn't have been more perfect if it had been cooked by the best chef in the land. Thin soup in which floated tiny squares of toasted bread, thick steaks sizzling on the outside but sweet, tender and juicy inside, fresh mixed fruit, diced and topped with clotted cream, served in fragile, paper-thin dishes. It was unnatural, unreal, no table in these parts had ever held such fare. He must have spent days, weeks perhaps, dreaming it all up, delving into cookery books. She didn't taste any of it, and only through a supreme effort was able to swallow some of it down. He ate and drank well and with obvious relish, high with excitement, a faint flush on his cheekbones, his napkin held frequently to his mouth to dab away gravy, wine, fruit juice.

When the meal was finished he sat back to contemplate her for long, considering moments. When he leaned forward suddenly, his face just inches from hers, she was so taken aback she jumped with fright. 'Well, Grace, what do you think? I would make a good husband, eh?'

'Ay – ay, Martin – you certainly will,' she whispered, shivering with a combination of nerves and apprehension.

'Forgive me,' he said at once, 'I should have noticed the room's grown cold.' Jumping up, he put a match to the fire. In minutes the flames were leaping up the chimney, shadows prancing all over the darkening room.

'Come, Grace, we'll leave the dishes till later. I want to talk to you very seriously, my dear.'

His big hand was out, waiting, strangely commanding.

Evading it, she sat down on the cheekstone and stared at her hands.

'Grace, my bonny Grace,' he said softly. 'I'm so glad you said just now that you thought I would make a good husband, for it's what I want to be most in the world – to have someone – to love them. You've seen the house, into it I've put half the money I've been saving for years – the other half will pay for a fine wedding. I want you to have the best, Grace, the very best there is. Oh Grace—' He got off his chair and came to kneel beside her. 'I'm asking you to be my wife. You'll make me the happiest man in the world if you say yes. You're so beautiful, all these years I've wanted to touch you, to hold you – but I waited, I never looked at another. It was always you, my darling, only you.'

'No, no, Martin!' she cried, shaking her head as if to clear it. 'You're in love with a ghost – the ghost of your wife! I'll never take her place, never. Please dinna say any more. I – I canna stand it.'

'Wheesht, Grace, wheesht.' He took her hands, speaking once more as if he was addressing a child. 'You must know it's you I love – nay, worship. I would give you everything. What you see here is yours. I want you to have it, you're the only one left I can give it to. My poor mother is old and frail. She hasn't much time left – but you, my darling, you have all your life before you, give me just a little of yourself. Say you'll marry me.'

She continued to shake her head helplessly, the tears of her despair glinting in the firelight as they ran down her face. His manner changed then. He stood up and began to pace, back and forth, back and forth, his shadow leaping on the walls like some dark phantom.

'You can't do this to me, Grace.' He spoke harshly, his breathing heavy and swift as if he had been running. 'I've waited years to ask you this. You were only a child when first I realized I loved you, but I was patient, I waited – Faith! how patiently I've waited. There were times I thought I would go mad with loneliness and wanting, but I kept myself under control—' He spun round on her. 'And now you tell me I'm in love with a ghost. Grace, can't you see? Look around you! I've rid the house and myself of all the reminders of the past. All the ghosts have been laid to rest. It's life I want now. Don't deny me this small chance of happiness, you're all I have left – just for a little while, my darling, just for a little while . . .' His voice had changed once more, it was soft, pleading, half-tearful.

Grace felt weak. The heat from the fire soaked into her, the walls seemed to be closing in, crushing her, expelling all the strength from her body. 'Martin, you're a good man,' she panted out the words. 'I've always admired you and loved you for what you stood for in this community. But I never loved you in the way you mean. I thought you knew that. I had no idea you felt so deeply about me. Oh, I would be a fool if I hadna kent your feelings for me went deeper than just friendship but never – never as deep as you're saying now.' She looked up at him, then quickly away again, unable to face those intense, burning eyes. 'Martin, I should have told you before – I tried to but you seemed no' to want to listen. I – there's a man, a doctor, Gordon Chisholm. I love him, Martin, we love one another—'

'Never mind him, I heard about his visit here last Christmas when I was away visiting my mother. You deceived me that time, Grace, but I forgave you, I'll always forgive you. You ought to have known the gossips would make certain it got to my ears. Forget him, Grace.' He brushed the subject of Gordon aside like a fly from a wall. 'No man but me can guarantee your happiness. You see, Grace,' his voice became soft, sinuous, 'for as long as I've got, I'll be faithful to you. I'm that sort of man. My dear Mary Ann knew the truth of that, God rest her. This doctor friend can only bring you misery. Already he's deserted you, leaving you alone and unhappy. It's quite on the cards he'll become another statistic on a piece of paper. I too could have joined up but I resisted that call to my vanity – for that's all it is, Grace. All this talk about bravery and duty means nothing. They're all trying to prove themselves, reassuring themselves of their manliness. Well, my dear, I don't need to go to war to know I'm a man, and if you consent to be my wife I'll prove it to you with everything I have.'

She could hardly believe her ears. This wasn't the Martin Gregory she knew. All during that evening she had been aware of a cold precision in his manner, an unnatural correctness in his speech. The man she knew had been hesitant, warm, his voice a soft burr that was pleasing to the ears. This man was a stranger to her – as if he was possessed by another self.

She stood up. 'Martin, I'll have to go home now,' she told him nervously. 'Dinna bother getting the trap, I'll walk, it's a lovely night—'

'No, Grace, you can't go! You can't leave without first telling me what I want to hear!' He lurched over to her and threw his arms around her, his breath hot and swift on her face.

'No, oh God, no,' she whimpered. She struggled, fought, kicked. Their merged shadows writhed on the ceiling. Through a red mist she saw them and the thick, black moving mass was for her a culmination of a nightmarish evening. She screamed, a high, clear thread of sound that reverberated round the room and then died, leaving behind a silence that was more opaque than ever.

He blinked at her, his eyes full of hurt bewilderment behind the thick glasses. Temporarily stunned by that extreme expression of her fear of him, his hold on her loosened. She tore herself free, ran to the door and wrenched it open. Never once stopping in her headlong flight, she crossed the dark hallway and ran out of the front door, her feet hardly touching the ground as she darted through the gate and out onto the road. Behind her she heard him blundering about, knocking over furniture, the scrunching of his feet on the stony path.

'Grace! Grace!' he screamed. 'Come back. Don't leave me, please don't leave me! I love you, Grace, I love you-u-u!'

The terrible urgency of his fearful, pleading roar split the night asunder, hammered into the very marrow of her soul. For as long as she lived she was never to forget it, and even as she ran, leaving the schoolhouse far behind her, the echoes of it pounded inside her head, keeping pace with the thundering beat of her heart.

Every second she expected him to pounce on her from behind, but only the silence of the night embraced her and as she neared home her footsteps slowed, faltered. She went up the track, her legs waxen beneath her, and at the little bridge over the Birkie she stopped to lean her arms on the parapet and sink her head into them. The water burbled beneath her, soothing, tranquil. For a long time she listened to it, letting its peace wash over her till at last her heart slowed to its normal beat. She felt drained, exhausted, and very, very cold. In her mad flight she had left her jacket at the schoolhouse and she shivered in her thin clothing. Folding her arms across her breast she made her way slowly up the brae, and as she neared the house her eyes scanned the windows to see if a light still burned anywhere. But, except for the faint candle glow from the room she shared with Evelyn, all was in blackness, and breathing a great sigh of relief she went wearily indoors.

Evelyn jumped out of bed at the sight of her sister's trembling, shaking figure. 'Grace,' she hissed, 'you look terrible – and you're freezing. Come on, into bed quickly.'

She all but undressed the older girl and helped her into her warmest nightdress. Once she was safely in bed, she ordered, 'Wait there and dinna move,' and creeping downstairs, she went to the kitchen where she heated some milk over the fire. It took a little time. The smoored fire sent up more smoke than flames, but she made good use of the waiting time to search in the scullery for the bottle of whisky her mother kept there for special visitors. Once upon a time it had stood boldly on the shelf but now it was kept out of temptation's way, Jamie's thirst for alcohol proving so strong he had once drunk a whole bottle and never remembered a thing about it afterwards. She smiled faintly to herself when finally she unearthed the bottle at the bottom of the meal kist. Her mother

216

could certainly combine initiative with cunning when the need arose, for the dispensing of domestic meal was a woman's prerogative and Jamie was as traditional as any in these parts when it came to such matters.

Adding a good dram to the warmed milk, she cleared everything up after her and then bore the beverage carefully upstairs, evading all the creaking parts of the stairs with an expertise gained through a long experience.

Grace was still awake, wide-eyed and deathly white, though after spluttering down the reviving drink, she became almost incoherent in her desire to relate the night's happenings.

'Take it slowly, Grace,' Evelyn advised patiently.

Grace took several deep breaths and poured out her anguish to her young sister. 'The worst o' it, Evie,' she ended tearfully, was that he knew all about Gordon, all the time he knew and the way he said it made me feel so selfish and deceitful. He was so strange, no' like Martin at all. I'll never forget it, never.'

'Ach, you'll feel better after a good night's sleep,' Evelyn consoled, though she knew only too well that it would be a long time before the incident began to fade from Grace's sensitive mind.

She fetched the hairbrush and began to work it gently over Grace's shining locks. 'Wheesht now, and go to sleep. Tomorrow's Sunday and you can have a good long lie, I'll make sure o' it.'

Like a little girl, Grace allowed herself to be lulled to sleep. When at last she succumbed to her exhaustion, Evelyn sat gazing down on her for a long time. She was not strong, this gentle sister. Nursing wasn't for her, but she loved it and put her all into it, often taxing her strength beyond its limits. She was missing Gordon more than she would ever say, but had come home determined to make the most of a much-needed holiday. And now this. Evelyn sighed and looked towards the window. Beyond the dark panes, not so very far away, Martin Gregory too was nursing his misery. Perhaps at that very moment he sat by his lonely fireside, thinking, thinking of all the empty days and nights that stretched before him. For years he had nurtured his love for Grace, had hoped that one day she would be his. Now he had nothing, nothing to hope for any more. It was over. He wouldn't even have Grace's companionship to look forward to any more, for it was certain that after tonight she wouldn't want to see him again.

Something cold touched Evelyn's heart. Poor Martin Gregory. How awful to be so alone – to have no one. An owl screeched from the barn slates. Far in the distance came an answering call. To Evelyn it was a sound akin to the last agonies of a dying soul. She shuddered and went quickly back to her own bed.

She thought about Gillan. Dear Gillie. How good it was to have him back again. There was something about him that was lasting and true. A life with him would have been secure and happy. A bit turbulent perhaps – there was a lot of passion in Gillie – but she had always understood such feelings, her own heart brimmed with them.

Leaning out of bed, she took her diary from the tin box. The pages fluttered open. From between them she extracted a letter, the only one she had received from David since his return to France. She had sent him dozens, along with several food parcels made up from all the titbits she could scrounge from both Nellie and Martha.

*Darling Evie,*

*Have you ever wanted something so badly it haunts every one of your waking thoughts? Socks, Evie, dry socks. I dream of them, I see them hanging everywhere, but the real thing never materializes. I got your parcel today. Delicious cake, mouth-watering tablet, but not a single solitary sock in sight. If you can, will you send some? A packet or two of Woodbine would also go down well.*

*Sorry to be so single-minded but the war does things to normal thinking. But I'm not entirely lost. When I can't sleep at night I seem to see your eyes laughing at me, and to feel that glorious hair running through my fingers – I daren't let my mind dwell on your body. If you came to me in my dreams the way you came to me in the barn mill I wouldn't be able to do a thing about it – and the waste would injure me more than Jerry ever did.*

*Oh, and soap, Evie. My mother sent some but it's all gone. It's maybe just as well you're as far away from me as you are. I'm not too nice to be near at the moment. I hope you're behaving yourself and missing me enough to save all your love for only me.*

*Till the next time, take care, Bright eyes. Davie.*

Carefully, she put the letter back into her diary. It wasn't a very romantic epistle. Some of Gillan's were far more affectionate. She sighed. Perhaps she was expecting too much. They had only known one another a few short weeks and in that time he had never pretended he was in love with her. She vowed that she wouldn't be so free with her affectionate endearments when next she wrote to him. The socks and cigarettes were already on their way but she might just wait a while before writing. He might see her eagerness as a sign that she was getting serious about him far too quickly . . . But she was serious – she was in love with him. Nothing could be more serious than that. She snuffed the candle and lay on her side. Grace's gentle breathing filtered peacefully through the darkness. She would be all right, Evelyn told herself, maybe a bit upset for a while but Gordon's arrival would soon take her mind off things . . . As for Martin Gregory, he would get over his obsession with a girl young enough to be his daughter. It might take a long time – but in the end he would get over it.

Two days later, Martin Gregory was found hanging from the rafters of his fuel shed. Old Carnallachie and Angus Keith had been passing the school just after ten in the morning, and seeing the children were still playing about outside, waiting for the schoolteacher to come and open up, the two men had gone to look for him.

Together they cut him down and laid him gently on the

floor. He had been dead for some time. Rigor mortis had come and gone, leaving his body slack. A note pinned to his shirt read: *I can't stand the loneliness any longer. Let my mother know how sorry I am it had to be this way. Everything I own is hers, when she dies it will go to Grace Margaret Grant of King's Croft. I bear her no grudges, only my love for her which I take with me beyond the grave. There, in God's keeping, I will find my help and strength and will be alone no longer. Martin John Gregory.*

Carnallachie glanced briefly at the message and drew his hand uneasily across his whiskery chin. 'Faith! I never thought to come across such a thing, Angus. The poor laddie must hae been demented to go and do a terrible thing like that.'

'Ay, indeed he must,' agreed Angus. 'I'd best get along for the minister and the doctor though there's no' much they can do to help Martin now.'

With alacrity he vacated the scene. Doctor McDuff and the Reverend Finlay Sommerville came quickly, the doctor to get down stiffly on one rheumaticky knee to examine the dead man, the minister to mutter a few words of blessing which sounded hollow and lame in the cobwebby silence of the fuel shed.

Despite a steady drizzle of rain, a crowd gathered quickly outside the schoolhouse, to stare with morbid interest towards the shed at one side of the house.

'God rest him! Poor sick cratur,' said George the Forge, his attentions much diverted by a young lassie beside him who seemed about to swoon at his feet at any moment. 'Hold on to me, Lizzie,' he advised with gentle lechery. 'There now, ay, that's right. Old George will look after you.'

'Ay, you can be sure o' it,' Bunty Lovie snorted meaningfully. 'Just watch his hands, lass, they can be all over you at the one time and still seem as if they are innocently folded over his stomach.'

Kirsty panted upon the scene. 'I knew something like this was going to happen. That poor, poor teacher hasna been himself for quite a whilie now. Of course, I ken fine why he took his own life – he was driven to it, oh ay. My Angus was after tellin' me—' here she lowered her voice, and said in a loud whisper '—there was a note pinned to the laddie's sark mentioning Grace Grant, saying how much he loved her and couldna bear his life without her.'

'Never!' intoned Jessie Blair, with huge enjoyment. 'Ach my, that lovely gentle lass. She'll take the news o' this sorely for all her life she's hated hurting anyone—'

'That may be, Jessie,' Kirsty interposed self-right-eously, 'but she's a Grant and it canna be denied they're all tarred wi' the same brush when it comes to men. They just tease and torment them till they canna take any more. Mary was a flirt from the start, Murn chased a married man shamefully and the wee one, Evie, well she canna get enough o' men. Off wi' the old and on wi' the new as brazen as you like – even that Nellie's at it now! Oh ay, wi' none other than Kenneth Mor himself and his wife still warm in her grave. I've seen her wi' my very own een, fleein' up there to Knobblieknowe every chance she gets.'

'Ach, that's just your bad mind, Kirsty Keith!' accused Betsy O'Neil, nostrils aflare with indignation. 'Nellie's just doing her duty as a good Christian woman. All the Grants have been good to Kenneth since Jeannie died. They took in wee Isla and saw to it that Cal and Kenneth never went wi' empty bellies in their time o' need.'

'Ay, and Grace wouldna harm a fly,' Jessie supported stoutly. 'You canna blame her for what happened to Martin when his mind was no' like itself.'

Hinney came over, her lips folded grimly, the little tufts of hairs on her warts glistening with a furring of fine rain. 'Am I hearing Grace Grant's name from this wee corner?' she inquired ominously.

Jessie's treble chins sunk onto her neck, for there was no one in these airts more feared and respected than Hinney when she was in a temper. 'I was just sayin', Hinney, that Grace canna be blamed for what happened to the schoolteacher.'

'Indeed, I hope that's what you are all sayin'.' Hinney

glared round. 'For when gossip o' an unsavoury nature gets goin' in these parts there's no stopping it.'

Kirsty sniffed. 'I'm as fond o' Grace as the next body, but that doesna alter the fact that the very coat from her back is hangin' in Martin Gregory's lobby at this very minute. Angus saw it when he was searching the house for the schoolteacher.'

Whatever else might have been said on the subject was squashed by the arrival of the police, who ordered everybody away from the vicinity of the schoolhouse. Unwillingly, the crowd moved away but only to take shelter under the trees some distance off where, defiantly and doggedly, they waited till police, doctor, and minister emerged from the fuel shed, carrying between them the pitiful bundle that had once been Martin John Gregory, schoolmaster, church elder, and respected member of the community.

Mary poured Doctor McDuff a dram of his favourite sherry, and placing it on a little table beside his chair, she retired to the one opposite to eye him anxiously and say, 'There now, Sandy, drink that up and you'll feel as right as rain in two shakes o' your own coat tails. It must have been terrible for you seeing poor Martin Gregory the way he was.'

As the months had passed, she had gradually gotten over her resentment at having the old man in her home. Grudging tolerance had given way to an amused forbearance, and finally a friendly affection that put them on first-name terms. She had grown into the habit of sympathizing with his little tales of woe and had even come to see him as a father figure in her life. She wrote down all the homely snippets and sent them to Gregor, who wrote back telling her not to spoil old McDuff too much as they might never get rid of him when the time came for him to go.

Sandy McDuff stretched his big, slippered feet to the fire's blaze and took a thoughtful sip of his sherry. 'Ay, lass, it wasna a very pretty sight though of course I've seen

222

few enough of those in the course o' my working life. Mind you,' he continued with a gentle clicking of his teeth, 'it was no surprise to me to hear that the lad did what he did. His mind has been in a bad way for quite a wee whilie now—' He turned to Hinney who was sitting in the ingle nursing a glass of whisky. 'Would you say I was right about that, Hinney?'

'Oh ay, right enough,' Hinney nodded. 'I've watched it coming. He was a poor, unhappy cratur.'

'Ay, and, of course, there were other matters besides love preying on his mind.' The doctor's voice was heavy with meaning. He looked at Hinney. 'It will do no harm to confide in Mary? Martin's gone now and the truth o' his going will come out soon enough after the postmortem.' He turned back to Mary. 'Martin Gregory was a very sick man, Mary, he had a tumour growing in his brain. It altered his personality and made him say and do irrational things. From what I hear he used to be a slow, easy-going sort o' chap, no' like the one I watched going about this last month or so. He had only a short time to live and I suppose he just went mad in himself thinking he would spend that time in his own company, alone as he has been since his wife's passing. He thought maybe to pass his last days with that bonny sister o' yours but it wasna to be, no, and Grace mustna blame herself for what happened. It's been a sad business but it's over with now and Martin Gregory has found his peace at last.'

'Amen to that,' Hinney nodded sadly and wiped a furtive tear away from her eyes.

Mary's face was white with strain, but as the doctor finished speaking she rushed up to hug him so tightly he almost swallowed both his teeth and his glass of sherry. 'Oh, thank you, Sandy, thank you. I was that worried about Grace when I heard the news. I knew she would blame herself for everything but this might make her feel just a wee bittie better.'

'Steady on, lass, steady on,' gasped old McDuff, downing his sherry in one gulp before Mary squeezed the life out of him altogether.

The old doctor's predictions soon proved true enough. The police spoke to various people involved in the case and submitted their statements to the Fiscal, but it was a mere formality and the Sheriff decided there would be no need for an inquiry. The straightforward nature of the suicide and the results of the postmortem quickly closed the case. The death certificate simply showed strangulation as the cause of death and Martin's body was released to his family for burial. His mother requested that he be brought to Dundee, and so he made his last journey back to his old hometown, quietly, with no fuss, only a handful of acquaintances there at the station to pay their last respects to him, for after Mary Ann's death he had kept very much to himself and had no true friends to grieve for him.

Only Grace had been close to him and she grieved for him. The news of his illness had done nothing to soothe her tormented spirit. Again and again his last words whirled in her brain: 'You're all I have left, just for a little while, darling . . . for as long as I've got, I'll be faithful to you . . .'

He had tried to tell her but she hadn't listened. If she had – if she had only known, she might somehow have found the strength and the courage to fall in with his wishes – to comfort him in his last days . . .

She could find no solace in anything or anyone around her. The roup held in the schoolyard, auctioning off those hard-won possessions he had gathered solely for her, was the final, heartbreaking straw. It was as well that Gordon Chisholm came home when he did. He surrounded her with his love, spread his concern and affection to all those who made up Grace's world. The gossips' tongues had been rudely checked when the results of the postmortem became common knowledge, but the whispers and innuendoes had already done their damage.

Grace left Rothiedrum to be with Gordon in Aberdeen. A few weeks later they were married quietly in the city with only family and close friends attending.

Shortly afterwards, Grace told her parents that she was

being posted to a military hospital in London to train for overseas service.

'I have to get right away from here, Mam,' she explained. 'I canna thole it any longer and I need to do this, so dinna try to stop me. Gordon tried to talk me out o' it but I've made up my mind. At least this way I'll get to see him from time to time – try to understand.'

Her great black eyes gazed pleadingly from one to the other. Jamie took her in his arms and held her briefly. 'God go wi' you, my lassie,' he murmured huskily and turned away.

'Mam?' Grace's voice held a note of panic, as just for a moment she thought her mother wasn't going to say anything. Then the loving arms were about her, holding her close, stroking her hair. 'Of all my lassies you're the least strong – and yet in many ways you're stronger than any o' them. God bless you, Grace, I'm proud o' you.'

It seemed that people were coming and going from Rothiedrum all the time these days. Gillan and Alan went back to France, Grace went off to London, Gordon to the casualty clearing station at Corbie. No sooner had they gone than Gregor returned home for a well-earned rest, a much thinner Gregor but still the man that Mary had pined for.

On the evening of his return, after an excited Donald had finally been persuaded to go to bed, he sat contentedly by his own fireside, hardly able to keep his eyes off Mary but managing to look greatly interested in everything that McDuff the Guff had to say. Since his arrival, the old man had taken an utter delight in referring to him as 'Captain McGregor' and now he paced about the floor, waving his coat tails, holding forth about the war and 'what a bloody shambles it had all turned out to be.'

'Still, mustna get carried away, Captain, as long as there's young men like yourself out there patching our lads up we'll be all right, and might even begin to hope we'll win this blood bath before the whole bloody lot drown in it!' In his enthusiasm he was clicking his teeth

225

together like castanets and waving his coat tails so energetically that the cat got up and stalked out of the room, dainty pink nose twitching her disgust of the human animal.

Gregor's eyes were growing heavy with fatigue, and without more ado Mary chased him upstairs to bed. He was waiting for her when finally she came up, having filled McDuff full of cocoa and sherry till he all but fell asleep in his chair.

Mary glanced at Gregor, a strange new shyness in her now that the moment she had longed for was finally here. He looked tousled and boyish, sleepy but aware of every move she made.

To hide her shyness she gave a sudden mischievous giggle and began pacing up and down the bedroom, waving imaginary coat tails and saying, 'Needs must, Captain, needs must. At my age you become just an old gas bag – ay, and smell like one too.' Gripping her lips together she attempted to click her teeth, then stopping smartly at the foot of the bed, she saluted her husband and said sternly, 'Number one wife reporting for duty, sir. Is there anything you desire of me? Name it, sir, and it's yours.'

Laughing, he held out his arms. 'Ay, Mary Rachel, there is one thing you can do. Come over to me this very minute and I'll show you.'

She fell into his arms. 'Oh, Greg, darling Greg, I've missed you so. I've got an awful lot to tell you, so much has happened while you were away—'

His mouth moved over the rosy softness of her cheek. 'All that can wait, I can't. Oh God, I've longed to hold you like this, you smell and taste so good.'

She unbuttoned his nightshirt and laid her head against his chest. 'That's my heart beating in there,' she whispered. 'You took it away wi' you but now it's back and I'm alive again. I could stay here all night just listening to the music o' it.'

His hand moved to her breasts. 'I've got something better planned for tonight – I didn't come all this way just to have you listen to my heart.'

His lips moved over her body, lingering, intimate. She

226

emitted a great sigh and gave herself up to the pleasures that had been denied her so long. Sad and terrible things had happened that summer at Rothiedrum but now they all faded into insignificance. Her husband had returned to her, whole in mind, body and spirit, and for her, in those moments, that was all that mattered.

# PART 3

Autumn/Winter, 1915

# CHAPTER FOURTEEN

The harvest was done. All over Rothiedrum cornyards glowed at the rise of the sun and at the set of it. The well-built ricks were a joy to the eye of every farmer and crofter. They rose up side by side, barley and oat, looking so proud of themselves that an old crofter making his last round of the steadings for the night might pause for a while by his cornyard and imagine his ricks puffing out bloated breasts in an excess of vanity.

A strange peace settled over the countryside at this time of year. In the hollows and the haughs, farmhouse, crofthouse, cottage and biggin sent up dreamy puffs of peaty blue smoke, which drifted into the woods and were wont to hang almost stationary along the course of the river before grudgingly rising to the lower slopes of the hills, there to trail in gossamer ribbons over little hillocks and outcrops whose heather-purpled skin shone through the translucent veils.

It was a time to sit back, take stock, gather breath before the threshing of the grain once more claimed the time of the toil-weary farmfolk.

Over on King's Croft's shorn acres, down by the ley field, the travelling folk had set up their camp, near the Birkie for convenience. Voices echoed over the fields, in the gloaming the fires became orange beacons, sparks rose, crackled, the gypsy fiddles sent plaintive notes far and wide.

It was during this time of quietude that Kenneth Mor and Nellie decided to get married. At first Nellie had protested. It was too soon. What would folks think, say? They would have to wait. It wasn't decent, it wasn't . . .

Kenneth Mor had taken her in his arms, then. 'Wheesht, Nell. Who gives a damn about the gossips anyway?'

'I do, Kenneth, at least I care because my family will get

231

the brunt o' it. We will no' be here to know what's being said.'

Kenneth had to admit the truth of that. His father had recently undergone a serious operation and was unable to do much of the heavy croft work, and so Kenneth had decided to leave Rothiedrum and go back home to his parents and help them run their sizeable piece of land. They were delighted with his decision, and pleased too that he and Nellie were getting married.

'The bairns need a mother, Kenneth,' his mother told him quietly. 'Nell's a good lass, she'll be a great support to you in life.'

But no one was more pleased than Maggie and Jamie. Some of the guilt that had lain over Jamie's life like a dark shadow rolled away. He pulled back his shoulders and hugged Maggie to him. 'At last, Maggie, at last. Our Nell's found her happiness. Och, I'm that pleased I could do a Highland fling here and now.'

And he did, whirling Maggie round so heartily she giggled and fell against him. She kissed him and looked at him with sparkling eyes. 'Ay, Jamie, I never thought I'd see the day but it just goes to show that nothing is impossible. Kenneth will be good for Nellie, he's no' the sort to take her dour ways lying down.'

'But, Maggie,' chided Jamie gently, 'Nell's no' like that now. She's changed into a bonny, even-tempered young woman. She'll never be a ray o'sunshine but then, it wouldna be our Nell if she was just *too* sweet to be true.'

'But what about Murn?' Nellie worried. 'You ken fine how she's aye felt about you, Kenneth. This news is going to ca' the very feet from under her.'

'It's high time Murn grew up,' Kenneth replied. 'You're no' having second thoughts about me, are you, Nell?'

He fixed her with his piercing blue eyes and her love for him washed over her afresh. 'No, Kenneth, never that, and fine you know it. I'll be a good wife to you and a good mother to your children, you need never have any fear o' that.'

He didn't doubt that. He had always known there was

232

more to her than met the eye and in these last months he had discovered a warm, loving woman lying under the brittle shell she showed the world. She was like the women of the Highlands, strong, steadfast. The children loved her, she them. Already little Isla was calling her something that resembled 'Mam,' and Cal readily turned to her with his childish problems.

Kenneth often wondered what he would have done if she hadn't been there in his life. Inwardly he still grieved for his bonny Jeannie and knew a part of him would always remain hers. He had loved her too well to ever love like that again. Nellie knew and understood his feelings. 'As long as I can be with you, to love you and your children, it will be more than enough happiness for me and much more than I ever thought could be mine. Evie was right. The wee besom told me that a life without love in it was like having no life at all – and that's the way mine once was. And – I dinna feel bad about Jeannie any more. I feel welcome in her house wi' her family – as if she was here somehow letting me know it's all right.'

Her words took some of Kenneth's own guilt away. He had been half-ashamed at finding happiness with Nell Grant so swiftly, but now he began to look forward to life instead of dwelling in the past. Both he and Nellie would have liked more time to elapse before deciding on marriage, but the plight of his own family hastened their decision together with the fact that they wanted to be away from Rothiedrum before the onset of winter.

'So it's settled, Nell,' he told her firmly. 'I'll see the minister tomorrow and arrange the wedding for October. That will give us time to settle up here. It should be a good roup. In the years I've been at Knobblieknowe I amassed quite a few bits and pieces so brace yourself, lass, Rothiedrum is about to be set on fire wi' the wagging o' the tongues.'

Murn stared at Nellie, wild-eyed, disbelieving. 'You bitch!' she spat, 'you lying, cheating, cold-eyed bitch! All these years you deceived us into thinking that you hated men, wanted nothing to do with them and all the while you had your eye on Jeannie's husband! And you had the cheek, the brazen cheek to sneer at me for the way I felt about him! My God, Nellie Grant! I've never really liked you but right this very minute I hate the very sight of you! You've made a fool of me, you, him, everyone!

'They must all have known that you were away up there whoring and carrying on but did anyone let on? Oh no! They condoned it and I think I know why. At last! At last, they're going to get rid of you! All the flouncing, the snideness, the prim, old-maidish condemnation of every-thing that was natural and good between a man and a woman. Have you any idea of the fool you made of yourself? How everyone laughed behind your back and wished some poor bastard of a man would take you on so that we could see the back of you once and for all!'

Her voice had risen to a high-pitched, hysterical scream. Nellie had expected anger, tears perhaps, but never, never had she thought to face this stream of vindictive abuse. White to the lips, she clenched her fists and spoke in a voice vibrant with suppressed hurt and rage. 'That's enough, Murn. You have a right to feel disappointment and resent-ment but you have no right to speak to me with such spite and disrespect—'

'You want me to respect you!' Murn raged, malevolence spewing from every embittered pore. 'For your infor-mation, Nellie Grant, I have more respect for a bit cow dung than I ever had or ever will have for you! I despise you – I, I despise you all!' With that she threw out of the house, the door swinging behind her, her steps taking her away from the croft towards the distant fields.

'Will I go after her, Mam?' Evelyn spoke quietly from the bench under the window while Col buried his face in Jamie's shoulder, terrified by the scene that had just taken place in the kitchen.

'No, Evie.' Maggie put aside her knitting and got up to put a comforting hand on Nellie's shaking shoulders. 'Best let her be for a while. She'll take some time to simmer down and the sight of any one o' us right now would just serve to set her off again.' She shook her head. 'In all my years o' living wi' Murn I've never seen her so upset. I knew she had a lot o' anger in her – but until tonight I never knew how much.'

It was a perfect autumn evening, warm, still, the heat of the day lingering like a caress over the tranquil countryside. The sound of the gypsy fiddles rose up from the banks of the Birkie, haunting, evocative. Laughter drifted, the voices of the traveller folk blended with the purling of the brown water rushing over the stones. Murn's steps faltered, stopped, though her heart still ran swift and sore in the breast of her. Crossing her arms over her heaving bosom she pulled herself in tight, as if by so doing she could somehow contain the emotions that seethed within her. Her eyes were staring, dry and painful, as if someone had taken a handful of sand and hurled it into them. 'Oh, God, God,' she whimpered, and fell onto her knees. 'I hurt, I hurt, God, and everyone – everyone's laughing at me behind my back.'

The tears came then, rolling down her face unheeded, swift as the river that ran at her feet. Through a blurred mist she saw the smoke from the campfires spiralling up into a honey-tinted sky. A heron glided past her vision, a great bird with wide wings, soaring, soaring, freedom in every languid, flowing feather.

The strains of the fiddles penetrated Murn's senses. Like one in a trance, she got up from the bank and began to walk slowly towards the source of the sound, her steps taking her over the bridge to the first of the little tents set beside the river. A young man was sitting outside, dark head thrown back so that his eyes were lifted to the vastness of the velvety evening sky. She knew him by sight, her father often came down to join the travellers in their nightly gatherings. He was always welcome among them. He was one of them, part of the brotherhood.

Evelyn often went with him to join the travellers in their infectious revelry but Murn had never deigned to join in. She was a schoolteacher, after all, with her dignity to maintain.

But something had snapped within her that night. She was ready to throw off the flimsy shell of snobbery she had so carefully cast around her. She seethed, burned, pined. For what? For life. For all it had to offer. Now, tomorrow, next week, next year? The young man started at her approach.

'Miss, you gave me a fright creepin' up like that. Here.' He caught a glimpse of her face, its pallor, the hunted expression in her eyes. 'Are ye all right? Wait there, and I'll get ye something to buck ye up.'

He disappeared into the tent, reappeared with a bottle of whisky which he took to her. 'Take just a wee dram o' it, no' too much mind, you look as if you might no' be used to that sort o' thing.'

She held onto the bottle and stared at him. He was no more than twenty, brown-skinned, black-haired and black-eyed, with a mouth that was well formed and slightly cruel. He was thick-set, tightly muscled, big-boned – and he didn't smell all that bad either. He had just bathed in the river, his underclothes were draped over the trees nearby . . . Murn raised the bottle to her lips, all the time keeping her eyes fixed on his. She swallowed, coughed, swallowed again – and kept on swallowing till the young man protested and pulled the bottle forcibly from her grasping fingers.

'What's your name?' she inquired softly.

'Adam, miss, but – here, do I know you? Ye seem familiar somehow—'

'Not nearly as familiar as I'm going to be, Adam – a nice name for a good-looking young man. We'll eat of the fruit, Adam, we'll drink of the wine—'

He had no earthly idea what she was talking about and gaped at her in some trepidation. When she came towards him he began to back off, looking over his shoulder as if afraid someone was going to come up and catch him doing something he shouldn't be.

'Miss, you'd better go home now. My ma will be coming along in a minute—'

'Your ma is too busy enjoying herself to be bothered with you, Adam. There's no one here, only us, so don't worry any more.'

She was right. The bulk of the travellers was gathered

round the communal fire, singing, some dancing to the tunes of fiddle and melodeon.

Murn's fingers were swift and sure as she undressed. In seconds she stood half-naked in front of him, dressed only in her petticoats, the rest of her clothes at her feet. Her lips were parted, her eyes too bright as the whisky throbbed in her blood, burning away the last of her reason. Adam stuttered, stared, became still and transfixed as she pressed herself against him. Laughing, she pushed his jacket down over his shoulders, slid her hand into the open neck of his shirt.

His breath was quickening, his protests growing weaker. She pulled his head down towards her breasts, eased her hand inside the front of his trousers.

After that his arousal was swift. Roughly, he drew her into the tent, threw her down on a pile of bedding and penetrated her body with brutal disregard for her smothered cries of pain. He was sweating, excited, moving inside her with all the finesse of a bull on heat. She lay back, one hand pressed against her mouth, her head turned to one side, seeing nothing, feeling no pleasure as he ripped her tender flesh apart, the great bulk of him filling her, his perspiring face inches from hers, his breath grating in her ear for all the world like a saw rasping through wood. She felt strangely detached, unreal, as if she was floating about in a little world of her own.

While he was busily occupied (in her swimming mind that was how she thought of his contortions), she stretched out her hand for the whisky bottle, uncorked it, and drank down the raw liquid till nothing made sense any more and Adam might have been riding a donkey to market for all she cared about him.

'Enough,' she mumbled, staggering to her feet, throwing him off at a crucial point in his endeavours.

'Here, miss, ye canna do that!' he grated hoarsely. 'I'm no' finished yet! Dyod! Can ye no' see I'm just about bursting?'

She put her head to one side, peered at him through bloodshot eyes and burst into high-pitched, drunken laughter. 'Ach, Adam,' she giggled, 'your name is wasted on you. I've enjoyed myself more riding my old bike. Go and jump in the river – that will soon cool you down.'

With an enraged curse, he threw himself at her and tried to enter her forcibly but the whisky had given her strength. Throwing him off with a contemptuous laugh, she walked outside and straight into the river, petticoat and all, splashing water all over her body, rubbing it into her skin as if trying to erase the feel of Adam's hands on it. From the bank he watched, eyes popping, fumbling to fasten the buttons of his trousers. When she came out he was waiting with a disreputable-looking towel, but she shrugged it off and started walking towards the fire.

'Miss, your clothes!' Adam's voice vibrated with alarm. 'For God's sake put them on.'

But she barely heard him and walked on, straight through a gap in the circle of people and over to the perimeter of the fire. An audible gasp rippled through the gaping throng. One by one the voices ceased, the fingers of the musicians faltered, halted, the last notes of the fiddle tailed off into the silence.

'Mercy on us!' cried one stout woman. 'The lass is demented wi' the drink. Her eyes are staring straight oot her heid.'

'Play!' Murn screamed. 'Get that fiddle going again. I want to dance. I've come to entertain you so the least you can do is co-operate.'

Utterly mesmerized, the young violinist scraped his bow over the fiddle strings. A wild tune leapt from the instrument and Murn began to sway in rhythm to the music. There was something oddly disturbing about the arching of her young body. Her breasts rose and fell, her hair fell about her face, the crackling flames lent her limbs a tawny sheen, with droplets of river water catching the fire's reflection so that each one became an orb of living flame.

The echoes of a primitive past seemed to touch Murn that night, as one moment she spread her arms to the stars as if in supplication, the next to the leaping flames as if in some sort of heathen worship.

The young men and the children were fascinated by the sight, the young women just as hypnotized but hiding it well behind sullen mutterings and criticisms of Murn's lithe body. Older men and women sucked their clay pipes and spat their disgust of the scene onto the ground but not even they could take their eyes off the dancing figure.

Someone threw an armful of wood onto the fire, the sparks crackled, exploded, tongues of flame licked the sky. The melodeon took up the fiddler's tune, the children swayed, youths and boys licked their lips as Murn danced, faster and faster.

Adam lurched into the circle of firelight, eyes wild, mouth twisted, the frustrated heat in his loins churning to fever pitch as he grabbed Murn to him and began to move with her. She was a rag doll in his arms, black-eyed, lips flecked with saliva, damp, matted hair swishing about her naked shoulders.

Murn's abandonment had transferred itself to the young bloods of the camp. They began chanting, softly at first then louder and louder till the fields rang with the primeval sound and the whole scene took on an atmosphere of vieux jeu.

Adam had brought his whisky bottle and was alternating its flow between his own mouth and Murn's. His eyes glazing, his hands wandering over her body, they moved together in a rhythm that was powerfully dissolute and shameless.

The young women had forgotten their resentment of Murn and eagerly followed the young men into the ring of orange-tinted grass. Firelight turned whisky bottles to gold as they were flashed about from one to another, as a recklessness broke through the natural reserve of the travelling people.

'Here, this'll no' do, we canna have this happening here! The police will be down on us in a meenit!' The old men scrambled to their feet, frightened by the turn of events. From along the riverbank came a massive woman, hampered by the basket of washing she was carrying. Throwing it down she hurled herself into the scene. It was big Annie George, the matriarch of the camp, a mountainous mass of fatty arms, legs, and thighs. Magically the young folk scattered, like chaff before the wind, glancing frequently over their shoulders to see if she was after them. But she was busy elsewhere, in amongst the bushes, pulling Adam off Murn.

'Oh no you don't!' she screamed at him. 'This is Jamie's lass and I'm damned if I'll let you harm a hair o' her head. Fetch him, Charlie, he'll have to get her out o' here.'

But some of the men had already gone for Jamie. He and Kenneth Mor came running, the latter plunging into the bushes to grab Murn. He took the poor, besotted girl in his arms where she lay shivering and trembling. Jamie tore the jacket from his back and threw it over his daughter's naked flesh, and then he and Big Annie George rushed off to a nearby tent where between them they soon had a brew of strong hot tea simmering over a little paraffin stove.

Murn spluttered some down; it burned her throat and with a crazed screech she knocked the cup from Big Annie's hand.

'That's enough, Murn.' Kenneth spoke sternly. 'Dinna do this to yourself! You mustna torment yourself for me any longer! You're young, bonny, you must go and live your own life now.'

'I have no life without you,' she sobbed weakly. 'I've always loved you, Kenneth, right from the start – and now that dried-up shrew of a sister has got you! How could you, Kenneth? I would have given you so much more – in me you would have had a real woman—'

He slapped her then and shoved his bristling fiery beard into her face. 'Never you speak of Nell in that way again! She has heart and blood and guts, that woman, and I'm proud o' her and happy that she has consented to wed me. Until you start thinking less o' yourself and more o' other people you'll never be a fit woman for any man – here—' he snatched the bundle of clothing from the sweaty hands of a much subdued Adam '—put these on and never ever in your life again set out to bring shame on your family as you have done this night!'

The blow had spun her face to one side but just for a moment it seemed to bring her to her senses. Slowly, she brought her eyes round to stare at him as if seeing him for the first time, then her head lolled, the pupils of her eyes rolled back, her mouth went slack, her legs buckled beneath her and she collapsed to the ground. Without a word Kenneth picked her up. In a complete stupor she nestled trustingly against him, her arms swinging helplessly as he pushed his way through the little knots of travellers standing about near the fire.

'She just came in about, Jamie,' one man said quietly.

'Ay,' supported another. 'Naked as the day she was born, too. She just seemed to come in to the camp from nowhere.'

'Ach, dinna fash,' Jamie told them, his voice tightly controlled. 'It wasna your fault so just get about your business and think no more of it.'

As he and Kenneth strode over the fields towards King's Croft, he said rather reproachfully, 'You were hard on the lass just now, Kenneth. It's no' like you to be so rough wi' a woman.'

The big Highlander's eyes flashed. 'I'm a man, Jamie, no' some sort o' god to be bowed and scraped to. It was time Murn knew the truth o' that. If this night has done naught else, it's brought her to her senses and made her face facts she never wanted to face.'


For the next two days Murn stayed in bed, too sick to eat or even raise her head from the pillow without the room going round in circles. On the third day she got up, packed, and went downstairs where Maggie was alone in the kitchen making the midday meal.

'I'm leaving, Mam,' Murn stated flatly.

Maggie wiped her hands on her apron. 'Leaving? But lassie, you're in no fit state to go anywhere.'

'I'm sorry, Mam.' Murn sank down on the nearest chair. 'I must go. I – I could never lift my head up here again, not after what I did.'

'But your teaching, Murn! You canna just go off and leave the school in the lurch.'

A faint smile twisted Murn's mouth. 'Don't worry about that, someone will step into my shoes. I've written to the school board telling them I'm sick and have to go away for a long time – they will have heard all about me by now anyway, and wouldn't likely take me back even if I begged them.' The smile crooked her mouth again. 'I'm sick all right – sick in the head, a bit like poor Martin Gregory only I don't have the courage to do as he did.'

'Where will you go, my lassie?'

'I have a good friend who lives in St Andrews. She's told me often enough I can go and stay with her anytime. It might be the making of me. I was growing stale here, it's time I moved on. I've managed to put by a bit of money and might use it to go back to college to try for my MA. I always wanted to do that.'

Maggie sighed heavily. 'It would seem that all my daughters are leaving Rothiedrum for one reason or another, though in Grace's case and your own, running away might be more accurate.'

Murn looked down, her fingers working nervously in old Tab's ruff. 'I know that, Mam, but I'm just not brave enough to stay and listen to all the whispers. It was a terrible thing I did. I just seemed to lose my head altogether. I can hardly bear to think about it, never mind face the folk who watched me making a complete fool of myself.'

'Those of us who are left will have to face them, Murn, and all the snide gossip forbye.'

Murn looked affectionately at her mother's straight, proud figure, the silvered head held high on erect shoulders. 'You've weathered worse, Mam,' she said softly. 'You're strong enough to be able to take it. I'm not and never was.'

'We all have our breaking point, Murn, sooner or later it comes to everyone if they are pushed enough.'

She sounded tired, suddenly defeated. In a great surge of self-reproach, Murn rushed over to her and held her close. 'Oh, Mam, I love you, you and Father, Evie, wee Col. I'll miss you sorely and will never forget how much you and

242

Father sacrificed so that I could have my chances in life. But I won't forget any of you, you can be sure of that – and you mustn't worry about money. I'll send you whatever I can whenever I can.'

'I was not thinking about money.' Maggie's voice was cold. 'I was thinking about Nellie. I ken better than anyone just how difficult she can be at times but she's been a good daughter to me and your father and doesn't deserve the way you've been treating her. She said only this morning that she hoped you and she would make up your differences—' Maggie pushed Murn away to look directly into her eyes '—and I was hoping that you would start behaving like the grown woman you are, Murn, and give your sister your blessing for her future life wi' Kenneth Mor. I knew you would never be persuaded to go to her wedding, but . . .'

Murn sprang away from her mother as if she had been scalded. 'You ask too much of me, Mother.' Gone was the affectionate term of 'Mam', the word 'Mother' came out, cold, solid, unnatural. 'I will never speak to Nellie again, let alone go to her with false wishes for her happiness. I don't want her to be happy, why should I want it when my own state has been reduced to a handful of grey embers? You don't know me, Mother, or you would never have asked such a thing of me.'

'No, Murn, suddenly I find I dinna ken you at all – after all these years of living wi' you, of loving you as one of my dear daughters I feel as if I'm now seeing and hearing a stranger in my home.' Maggie sounded breathless as she went on, 'And until you see reason and allow a bittie compassion into that vain, empty little heart o' yours I would ask that you don't come back here again – much as it grieves and hurts me to have to tell you such a thing.'

Murn went to the door, pale, remote, her sad, sweet young face oddly beautiful in those terrible moments of truth. 'Very well, Mother, I can see very plainly that my welfare means little to you, that your eldest daughter's ill-gotten happiness has a far greater significance in your life. Of course I know why, you've always longed to be rid of her and now you're about to get your wish. And what a clever mother you are—' her laugh was hard, brittle '—you're getting rid of me as well – killing two birds with one stone. There are few mothers in the land who can lay claim to an achievement like that.'

She turned on her heel and walked away, away from King's Croft, down to the gate and along the track with never a backward glance at her childhood home.

Maggie stood stunned, then she ran to the door, made to rush outside, but then stopped. Slowly, she went back into the kitchen, sank into a chair, and wept as she had never wept in all her years as a wife and mother.

The Knobblieknowe roup was over, the cajoling, singsong cries of the auctioneer just another memory in the minds of all those who had come to bid and buy or just listen. The steadings were unnaturally quiet and still without the sounds of the animals, the clip-clop of a Clyde's hoof, the gentle mooing of the cows coming home to be milked, the clucking of the chickens in the yard. The house itself stood dour and silent, its empty rooms hollow and bare, stripped of everything that had made it a home filled with light, love, warmth. Already it held to itself that strange, sad, neglected air peculiar to an empty house no matter how recently vacated. Kenneth Mor stood in the garden, smelling the scent of the last of the summer roses, his keen eyes picking out the absurd little details that ought to have held no more interest for him: the crack in the plasterwork below the parlour window; the missing slate near the chimney stack – the honeysuckle that drooped in the grey aftermath of ebullient summer flowering; the straggling suckers on the roses – Jeannie would have had all that seen to by now. She had loved this garden, had delighted in its sheltered warmth, had lovingly tended the shy primrose, the boisterous hollyhock.

He was a tough, strong man, this fiery-haired High-lander, sure, proud and decisive, but in those pensive moments his heart beat soft and sad within him and he was not ashamed of the silent tear that dimmed his vision as he stood alone in Jeannie's garden. For it had been hers, hers for a little while, and now it would go back once again to nature until other hands looked to it and other eyes found fleeting pleasure in its simple beauty.

'I'm no' leaving you behind, Jeannie lass,' he whispered into the breath of the wind. 'You're coming home wi' me and Nell and the bairns. If only it had been – while you were alive, I wouldna be standing here now, talking to the breezes.'

He pulled back his shoulders, took one last look round and then, with kilt swinging, he turned his back on Knobblieknowe and walked down to where Nellie was waiting for him by the bridge. Taking his proferred hand, she marched with him down the track to King's Croft where they were staying for the next two days till the wedding.

Nellie carried a small bundle in her hand, and as soon as she got home she went in search of Evelyn, finding her in the stable reading a letter she had received the day before from David.

'How is he?' Nellie asked, guessing who the letter was from. It wasn't difficult. Already it was dog-eared from continual reading and rereading.

'Cold, wet, and asking for more socks – delighted with the boots Father sent. He's in Flanders now and will likely be there for quite a while.' She searched in her pocket and withdrew another letter which she handed to her sister. 'This is for us both, but I'll let you open it. Mam got one too, they both came while you were out. I came out the house to let Mam read hers in peace.'

'It's from Grace,' Nellie cried, pleasure lighting her face. Throwing herself down on a nearby hay bale, she tore open the envelope and proceeded to read aloud:

*Dearest Nell and Evie,*
*Was there ever really such a thing as a feather bed in my life? Or does King's Croft only exist in my imagination? No matter which, I'm so bone weary by the time I drop into bed each night, I wouldn't care if I was sleeping on top of Bennachie itself! But don't mind that. I'm truly*

fulfilled working here in France. The hospital is an old château and looks out onto the River Eure. Things are quieter here now and I'm catching up on all my neglected correspondence. Gordon had a few days' leave last week and we travelled to Paris – imagine! Little Grace in Paris! The shops on the Rue St Honoré are almost as good as the ones in Aberdeen and the pavement cafés on the Rue de Vaugirard are as busy as any mart I've ever been to.

I'm showing off here a bit. Evie could probably pronounce all these French street names much easier than I ever could.

Gordon had three days, so we stayed in Paris for that amount of time and enjoyed every minute.

Gillan turned up here the other day, and took me out to dinner in a little inn near the river with lanterns hanging from the trees. He's a bonny young man and a perfect gentleman though my pride was a bit hurt when he started talking about you, Evie, and forgot to stop.

Nellie, I'm absolutely delighted for you and Kenneth Mor. My one regret is that I'll miss your wedding but my love and thoughts will be with you on that day. I've written to Mam and Father so you can read their letter and compare notes.

God Bless you both and take care of one another.

Your loving sister, Grace.


Nellie folded the letter carefully and put it into her pocket. 'How strange it is, Evie,' she said rather sadly. 'Murn gone, never a word as to how she is or where she is – Grace far away in France. I miss her so, she's such a gentle girl, no one could help loving her.'

'I know.' Evelyn shared her pensive mood. 'Everything's changed so much lately and now you're going too – and I'll be the only daughter left here—' The realization of that came home to her fully. 'It will be so strange without you, Nellie. Sometimes I hated the way you bossed me about, but now that you're leaving King's Croft will never be the same again. I'll miss you, Nellie.'

She sounded tearful, and Nellie leaned forward to take

246

her youngest sister's hands and say imploringly, 'Oh, babby, I ken fine how you feel. I'm going to feel gey strange myself for a whilie. This is a big step for me, Evie, marrying Kenneth, going away to live in a place so different from Rothiedrum. I'll feel lost for a time and need all the support I can get before I go. I – well, I feel awful about Murn. I never kent it would end like this between us. Och, I knew it wouldna be plain sailing when she found out about me and Kenneth but – I never dreamt it would turn out quite so drastically.' She squeezed Evelyn's hands, a vulnerable expression making her strong face suddenly defenceless. 'Say you wish me well, babby, I need to have that from you – you were aye that wee bittie special to me even though you might no' have thought so at times.'

'Oh, Nellie, of course I wish you well. I want you and Kenneth and the bairns to be so happy you could burst wi' the joy o' it.'

'We won't be so far away.' Nellie's beautiful amber-green eyes were misty, and all at once she looked like a small girl uncertain of what lay ahead. 'The Clachan of Kenneray is almost in a straight line from here as the crow flies. You can come to visit us. You would love it there, Evie. It looks out over the ocean with the islands of Eigg and Rum in the distance, and Croft Donald stands on the machair wi' a great white beach right in front o' it . . . and of course, I'll be coming back to see you all as often as I can.'

Evelyn shook her bright head, unable to shake off her gloomy mood even for Nellie's sake. 'It won't be the same, and – I've been thinking, Nellie, we have had two roups already in Rothiedrum. Everything comes in threes – and I've been wondering who will be next.'

'Ach, you were aye too imaginative for your own good. Look – this might cheer you up, Jeannie would have wanted you to have them.'

Evelyn unwrapped the knobbly parcel Nellie thrust at her. Inside was Jeannie's collection of small brass ornaments, as carefully polished as they had been when, as a child, Evelyn had made the arduous climb up the brae to

247

Knobblieknowe just to have the privilege of cleaning them and rearranging them on the hearth, where the fire's light had played over them and the window, even the bedroom itself, had been mirrored in them.

They had been such good days and now they were all gone – just as the people who had made up the rich fabric of her life were breaking the ties that had bound them to home and family and were going too. She kept her head lowered, unable to speak for long moments.

Nellie placed a firm, sympathetic hand on her shoulder. 'Thanks, Nellie,' Evelyn murmured at last, 'for thinking to give me these. I shall treasure them always. They meant something special to me but I never knew you even noticed.'

'There's a lot I noticed,' Nellie said softly, 'the little homely things that are aye so important to every one o' us.'

It was a quiet wedding, with only family and a few close friends piling into King's Croft's parlour, though the crowd that gathered outside might have misled a passing stranger into believing that an event of great importance was taking place. But the Grant family and their affairs had been the subject of much interest that year of 1915, and no one with any sense was going to miss the public part of the wedding between Nell Christina Grant and Kenneth Cameron Mor.

Somehow Tandy had contrived to be there, and the two tall Highlanders made a fine sight in their tweed jackets and proudly swinging kilts. For once Tandy had made an effort to tame his head of thick, rusty fair hair though the same couldn't be said of his tawny-yellow eyes which, since he had kittled himself up for the occasion with a good few drams, wore their wild tiger look, which much excited the young maidens in the gathering and incited in them frantic visions of vast feather beds occupied by themselves and the masterful big shepherd.

Kenneth Mor's hair and beard didn't just shine, but glowed with red fire and golden lights, and his piercing eyes sent out blue sparks of nervous exhilaration; buckles and belt gleamed, even the hair of his sporran looked newly groomed while the facets of the big amber Cairngorm stone, which was set into the handle of the Sgian-Dubh sticking out of the rim of his cream wool stockings, shone as ebulliently as the golden October sunshine itself.

Nellie was wearing – or rather had dared to wear after much nervous indecision – a softly flowing mauve tulle blouse tucked into a long, black skirt tightly belted at the waist. On her neat, fair head sat a tiny mauve hat trimmed with purple flowers, and a flimsy lilac veil which barely hid her nervous blushes and the hectic shine of excitement in her beautiful eyes.

'She looks so bonny, Jamie,' said Maggie softly, her mind taking her back to her own wedding day in the sequestered drawing room of her former employer, Miss Beattie, a dragonlike old lady with a soft heart who had chivvied Maggie unmercifully while in her employ, but who had shown her fondness and respect for the young farmtoun lass by providing a wedding and a feast which neither Maggie nor Jamie had ever forgotten.

Jamie squeezed her hand. 'Ay, lass, but never as bonny as you were on your wedding day. I can see you yet, your hair as red as the hill bracken in autumn, face all blushes when Grandmother was brought into Miss Beattie's drawing room in her sedan chair.'

'What a shame she couldna manage to come today—' Maggie glanced over her shoulder '—but at least Mattie is here.'

And Mattie was, as large as life and twice as indomitable, an amazing creation of rose-spattered tulle flowing about her generous frame, her black eyes sparkling under an enormous wide-brimmed straw hat trimmed with pink felt roses.

She had come armed with great parcels of meat and mutton for the wedding tea, and reeked of the slaughterhouse as a result but, not in the least put out, she had sloshed great dollops of Maggie's rose water all over her person. Now the scent of meat, mothballs and rose water vied with one another for precedence, only to come up against the further competition of chrysanthemums arranged in vases on the parlour windowsill.

They all took their places, the Reverend Finlay Sommerville, silvered head shining, pink face glowing, cleared his throat and the ceremony began.

Nellie swallowed anxiously, gave herself a surreptitious pinch to make certain she wasn't dreaming. But no. It was real, all right. She and Kenneth Mor were about to be joined in wedlock. She lifted her head proudly. At last she could do so with good reason, and not just to show her defiance to a world that had criticised her behind her back and told her far too often that she was as good as rotting on the shelf for the rest of her life. Kenneth Mor was warm and solid beside her, his big hand found hers, gripped it reassuringly and her lips lifted in that little sensual smile he had come to know so well.

A short time later, they were man and wife. The news filtered outside. 'Here's to the happy couple.' George the Forge plucked his bottle from inside his sark and tipped whisky into the waiting glasses.

'Hmph, he'll have his sorrows to seek wi' that frozen miss,' said Kirsty spitefully, incensed because she hadn't been asked inside to witness the wedding, and her 'such a good and faithful friend to the Grant family.'

'Not Miss, Mrs,' corrected Betsy. 'As for being frozen, I doubt she could gie you a few lessons on passion, Nellie's a changed lassie these days. I've seen the look in her een whenever she looks into Kenneth's. Hungry's the word and it's maybe just as well she's leaving here or she might have gobbled your man up in one gulp, Kirsty.'

'My Angus would never look at her like!' seethed the enraged Kirsty.

'Ay, maybe you're right.' Betsy looked thoughtful. 'Ogle would be nearer the truth. I've seen him at it too, and growin' that excited wi' his thoughts he's had to wipe his big sweaty hands all over his sark.'

The verbal battle that followed was greatly enjoyed by everyone but as the strains of the piano floated from the parlour window, Kirsty and Betsy were forgotten in the singing and dancing which took place there and then in the field in front of the house.

Mattie gave of her best that day, her vast lungs opening to full throttle as she led the company in song after song. But Nellie and Kenneth couldn't stay long to enjoy the occasion. In the middle of the afternoon, they came hand in hand outside to the waiting trap that was taking them to the station. Kenneth's parents, Iain and Irene Cameron, followed behind, holding onto the small hands of Cal and Isla Nell. The children climbed up, solemn and big-eyed with the excitement of going away to a new place. Yet, through it all Cal remembered Col, the little friend he had always cherished and protected. He held out his hand to the small figure standing lost and bewildered inside the gate. Col's face brightened, he toddled forward and climbed up beside his playmate.

Nellie was making her last farewells, her face tight with the effort of holding back her tears. She held onto Evelyn as if she might never let her go, took Mary and wee Donald to her breast. Tandy strode forward, enclosed her in a bearlike embrace and kissed her so soundly she was left gasping for breath. A cheer went up from the watching crowd.

'Tandy McQueen,' she flared, scarlet to the ears, 'you have no right to take such a liberty.'

He grinned his big, indolent grin. 'Keep a grip o' your breeks, Nell quine. A man has every right to kiss a bride on her wedding day. Anyway, why object now, you aye enjoyed all those secret wee exchanges o' passion we shared in the kitchen and will likely miss them as much as you'll miss me.'

She laughed then, a happy laugh that took away some of her tension. 'I'll miss your cheek – and that's about all I ever had from you.'

She turned to her mother and took her hands. 'Goodbye, Mam, I – I dinna ken what to say . . .'

Maggie's heart grew warm within her. This eldest daughter of hers had for years called her by the formal address of 'Mother'. Now, in these poignant moments it was 'Mam', spoken softly and sweetly like a caress. 'I ken fine what's in your heart, my lassie. Go along now without

251

any regrets. You have your own life to lead now – go and live it well.'

'Ay, and I say amen to that.' Jamie's voice was husky. 'You've been a good, dutiful daughter to your mother and me. Nobody could have asked for better.'

'But no' aye the easiest to live with.' She tried to sound lighthearted but failed. Her father's eyes were on her, dark, gentle, mutely pleading for something which she had never been able to give him.

'Father.' Her voice broke, briefly she put her arms round him. His shoulders were frighteningly frail under the cloth of his best suit. She wanted to tell him that it was all right, that the memory of Whisky Jake no longer terrified her, but not here, with everyone gaping . . .

Abruptly, she stepped away from him. Tandy was lifting wee Col down from the cart. Tears sprang to his big blue eyes. 'Nella.' He walked unsteadily towards her, held up his arms. 'Up, Nella, Col go with you.'

Her hand flew to her mouth. 'Oh, dear God,' she whispered. She daren't allow herself to cuddle him for the last time. Instead she placed her hand on his small, golden-red head. 'My dear wee man,' she breathed huskily, 'Nella has to say goodbye.' She ran to the trap where Kenneth was waiting for her. Tandy flicked the reins, Fyvie moved forward, breaking into a trot on reaching the track.

In minutes the trap was a mere dot on the turnpike, and soon just a cloud of stoor in the distance.

# CHAPTER FIFTEEN

King's Croft was deathly quiet with Nellie's going. Evelyn had never felt so lost, so alone as she did now without any of her sisters around her. The evenings were the worst, with the kitchen so quiet an explosion of sparks in the lum was enough to make them all jump with fright. The clock seemed to tick extra loud, the wind to shriek with extra violence round the steadings and through the trees. As the days passed, wee Col drew more into himself, became withdrawn and unhappy-looking with never a spark of interest to brighten his lacklustre eyes.

Every morning without fail he went to the door and stood there, gazing hopefully to the left and the right of him to see if by chance Nellie's figure was coming down the brae from Knobblieknowe or along the track from the turnpike.

He could pass a whole hour in this way till, finally, dejected, dispirited, he would come back inside and plague Maggie with the oft-repeated question, 'Where Nella? Where Cal?'

When it became obvious that there was no immediate solution to his longings, he would remain silent for the rest of the day, gazing vacantly into space or rocking himself to and fro till Maggie thought she would go mad at the sight of him. Nellie had been the light in the restricted sphere of his confined world. From the beginning she had nursed him, played with him, talked and sung to him and understood his halting, indistinct speech, his huge capacity for giving and receiving love. Of them all, she had always been able to extract the best from his limited intelligence and without the stimulation of her patient persuasion he seemed to wither inside himself, to abandon his frail grasp of the situations and experiences of those around him.

Neither Jamie, Maggie nor Evelyn had much time to spare for him, except in the evenings and by then he had become so introverted after a frustrating day looking out for Nellie that no one could get through to him.

It was only now that those left at King's Croft appreciated how much of the workload Nellie had always shouldered with scant complaint. Now Maggie bore the brunt of the chores herself, though Evelyn helped as much as she could before leaving for Rothiedrum each morning and when she came home at night. For each of them the day began at five in the morning and very often didn't end even when darkness had settled over the countryside. There was always the horses to sort for the night, the peats to fetch, water to be pumped from the well, the preparation of food for the next day, and all the thousand and one small tasks that made up a crofting routine.

There had always been two cows at King's Croft but now, with fewer mouths to feed, one was sold, though that meant less butter and cheese to sell to the travelling merchant or the local market.

Evelyn was glad of the relief from tedium the fringe folk brought to the door of King's Croft. Merchants, pedlars, fishwives, rag-and-bone men, they all came with their colourful store of news of things happening in the far countryside. Coulter and Carnallachie were welcome visitors too and even though they squabbled so much between themselves, it was a delight to listen to their droll, north-east voices recounting the well-worn and much-loved fables that had been passed down through the generations and only gained more colour with the telling. They had the old speak, these venerable worthies, the broad, rich dialect that could only be easily understood by folks whose roots were sunk deep in the loamy soil of the north-east lowlands.

Whenever Coulter's soft, resonant voice filled the kitchen, Evelyn travelled back to the winter nights of childhood when cackling witches had danced in the leaping shadows of lamplight and dreadful spooks waited to catch you by the hair if you dared venture through the dark oblong leading to the scullery. Even yet, she wasn't past such fearful imaginings and wouldn't go outside to the wee hoose or the fuel shed without taking Tab.

It was at this time that Muckle Willie the packman came

back to Rothiedrum. He was one of the most kenspeckle peripatetic figures of that old landscape and was as welcomed by the kitchen maids at the back door of a country mansion as he was at any farmtoun, bringing on his back all the minutiae that induced young lassies to open the strings of their slim purses to purchase a few yards of pretty ribbon, and small bairns to wheedle a halfpenny from a big brother's pocket in order that they might sample the rare treat of a sugar mouse. Thread, needles, collar studs, elastic, combs, bootlaces, all were contained in the large pack Muckle Willie carried. It was a burden that seemed much too cumbersome for such a small creature, already hampered by a hunchback. For he was tiny, was Muckle Willie, no more than four feet high, the complete opposite of his nickname. Muckle meant big in these lowland airts, but it was affection rather than ridicule that had earned him such an unlikely title. He was altogether a quaint, lovable figure. From his chin sprouted a long, pointed white beard with matching beetling brows above deep-set pale blue eyes, and above them again a head of thick, shining silvery hair. His abundant hairiness lent great character to his broad, seamed face which sat well forward on his shoulders, so that his beard perpetually jutted out from his sark and flowed down to the broad leather belt which held together a pair of disreputable white moleskin breeks handed down to him from the ten-year-old son of a mason man. The material of the trousers adhered close to his stick-thin legs and emphasized the generous dimensions of his shoes which, unlike the trousers, were two sizes too big, though that was no deliberate error but a necessity for a man tramping the countryside to earn his living, especially in summer when swollen flesh gratefully filled the empty spaces.

Jamie had often given him a pair of his boots in payment for the small necessities Maggie picked from his sack, and Muckle Willie welcomed the sturdy comfort of the boots as much as he might welcome a lift from a luxurious limousine driven by a sympathetic chauffeur.

Children especially loved Muckle Willie, for he was as

255

agile as a circus acrobat and could throw himself with ease about the floor and furnishings of any kitchen, executing cartwheels and hand stands with the same aplomb as he conducted his sales talk. Some said that he had wasted himself in an occupation that brought scant reward, that he could have made a more lucrative living with his acrobatic performances, but Muckle Willie scoffed at such suggestions and declared that he was 'too much his ain man to make a public spectacle o' himself in front o' sensation-seeking gowks.'

When he presented himself at King's Croft's door Evelyn hailed him with pleasure, and as his arrival coincided with dinnertime, she ushered him inside to sit at the family table where he was plied with broth and potatoes and much questioning about the world outwith Rothiedrum.

It was later, when he was showing Maggie his hand-carved wooden sock dollies, that Evelyn remembered The Loon's claim about his mother and the packman. Evelyn looked at the little man with fresh interest, wondering if there could be any possible truth in the things The Loon had said. Muckle Willie certainly enjoyed a good dram and it wouldn't be so unusual for him to accompany Dottie home from the inn, but as to the rest, she shook her head and pushed it to the back of her mind, too interested in the display of ribbons and bits of lace spread out on the table to wonder further about Muckle Willie's nocturnal habits.

That evening Col laughed as he had not laughed since Nellie's going. With great patience and energy the packman threw himself about the kitchen, all over the furniture and about the floor. Tib the cat and old Tab the sheepdog both rose from the fireplace in alarm and stalked out of the room, but Wee Col clapped his hands, laughed, even attempted to copy Willie as he stood on his head on the clickit rug and from that position sang a bothy ballad.

Later on, when Coulter, Carnallachie and Hinney arrived to ceilidh, Willie entertained them all with his fund of gossip and stories and later still, when he had drunk his small legs to a standstill, Jamie and the other two men carried him to the chaumer above the stables and left him snoring blissfully.

Two nights later, Hinney was seated comfortably in the back of the laird's Rolls-Royce, Coulter having stopped to give her a lift on his way home from taking the laird to an overnight stop with friends. It was a bitterly cold night with a misty haar lying over the fields and a huge orange November moon rising up over Bennachie.

Coulter was humming a catchy little tune under his breath. He had heard it being played on the gramophone by some of the young officers staying at Rothiedrum, and though at the time he had scoffed at such rubbishy trivia it had stuck in his mind, and whether he liked it or no he found himself singing it at every opportunity that presented itself.

Hinney smiled sourly as she watched his snowy head bobbing up and down, his fingers on the steering wheel drumming in time to the tune. She stretched luxuriously on the comfortable seat and settled her weary bones deeper into the thick padding. She had been away for most of the day helping McDuff the Guff with a prolonged confinement, and now she was glad to relax and let Coulter have the responsibility of seeing her home. But her state of repose was short-lived. From the front Coulter let out a sudden yell of fright, the car swerved and almost nose-dived into the ditch at the Boglehowe road end.

'What is it, man! What is it?' Hinney cried testily. 'You near rammed my teeth down my throat stopping the machine like that.'

'Faith, Hinney!' Coulter turned to stare at her in round-eyed dismay. 'I just saw two bodies in the ditch back yonder! Stiff as boards they were and just as dead or my name isna Coulter!'

'Ach, you're haverin', you old fool!' Hinney scoffed. 'I aye said you didna have the een on you for driving one o' these machines. It's stones or the like that you're seein'.'

'It's bodies, I'm tellin' ye,' Coulter responded frenziedly, and so saying he put the gear into reverse and hurtled backwards at such a speed he sent the Rolls zig-zagging all over the road.

'You'll kill us as well as your bodies!' Hinney roared into

257

his hairy ears, but she might just as well not have spoken. He had stopped the engine and was now holding up his hand, his head cocked to the side window. 'Whist, did ye hear that?' he asked in a ghostly whisper. 'A sort o' moanin' sound? I'm thinking maybe we've chanced on a couple o' spooks.'

'Ach, you and your witches and warlocks! Look you, get out this minute and see who it is.'

But Coulter shook his head. 'Na, na, I'm no' goin' out there on my own. I thought you would hae kent about this place, Hinney, you wi' the power and the second sight. This is Boglehowe, wife.' His voice took on a patient note of explanation. 'In the Dark Days all manner o' evil things happened here. Bogles and warlocks gathered up here on moonlight nights.' He glanced fearfully up into the misty face of the moon over which trailed tiny swirls of vapour. 'Nights like this one. They lit big fires up there on Bogle Hill and went cackling and screeching roond it, roond and roond till their minds were that dizzy they didna ken what they were about, and came fleein' doon the brae bearing torches o' fire. Into Lums o' Reekie they went, plundering and killing, and indulging in all manner o' evil things. It was said—' here he lowered his voice to a breathy whisper '—they took living sacrifices back up the Bogle Hill and – and cooked them over the fire—'

'Coulter! you're no' at a ceilidh now and I'll no' stop another minute listening to such havers.' Hinney was out of the Rolls before she could give it a second thought, because when Coulter got going he had the ability to scare the wits out of anybody, no matter how sane or sensible they might like to think themselves. Opening the driver's door, she all but hauled him outside to stand beside her. Then, holding onto one hairy tweed lapel she propelled him forward till they were both standing at the edge of the ditch near the Boglehowe track. Frost-rimmed grasses snapped and crackled under their feet, mingling with frightful snores, grunts and mutterings from the black depths of the ditch.

'I canna look! I canna!' Coulter squeezed his eyes tight shut and crossed the first two gnarled fingers of both his hands.

Hinney glowered at him and then swivelled her head slowly

round to gaze rather fearfully into the dark oblong at her feet. Lying half in, half out of it was Dottie Drummond, beside her, stretched out flat on a bed of frozen water and leaves, was Muckle Willie, his hair and beard shining like beacons in the surrounding darkness. Both he and Dottie were in a drunken stupor, the latter's drab, rank layers of clothing piled up around her like a bundle of rags, her legs sticking out beneath them like two spurtles. Her dirty mutch cap had slipped down over her face to obliterate eyes and nose. Only her mouth showed – and sprouting from one corner of it was the perpetual clay pipe, a tiny spark of red still glowing deep inside the chubby bowl.

Dottie was not completely insensible as she now proved by launching forth into a a garbled version of 'The Ploughman's Laddie'.

> '*Oh, I've been east, and I've been west,*
> *And I've been in St Johnstone;*
> *But the bonniest laddie that e'er I saw—*
> *Was a ploughman laddie dancin'.*

'Is that so,' said Hinney grimly. She poked Coulter in the ribs. 'Open your een. Your ghosts are singin', ay, and if we dinna get them out o' there they *will* be spooks come morning. See you, grab that Dottie under the oxters and I'll go down into the ditch and take her legs.'

But it was impossible to move the hefty woman and just as impossible to move Muckle Willie whose leaden limbs lent weight to his small frame.

Coulter scratched his head. 'I wonder, should I go for Rob Burns? He has an elevator he uses for lifting the hay at hairst. We could just hoist these two up in it and run them home.'

'Ach no, yon wee wheels on it would never see it down the brae. Best go for Carnallachie. He might be a bodach but he's a wiry auld rascal.'

'*Him*!' Coulter spat, but sprachled nevertheless up the brae to Carnallachie's place. The old man came unwillingly, grumbling and muttering at being ousted from the cosy comforts of his fireside, and for all the good he did on arriving at the little scene of drama on the turnpike, he might as well have stayed there. He scratched his head, spat vitriol into the oblivious ears of both Willie and Dottie, and started such a good going argument with Coulter as to how best to deal with the situation that Hinney was moved to bawl at them to be quiet or she would skelp them both round the lugs. And she might have done so too, had not Fyvie came clopping along, Jamie, Maggie, Evelyn and wee Col in the trap, all anxious to be home after an evening spent visiting Mary at Rowanlea.

In no time at all, Dottie and Muckle Willie were sprawled all over the back seat of the laird's Rolls with Dottie drunkenly sucking at her pipe in between singing 'The Ploughman's Laddie', and Willie snoring fit to burst.

Coulter and Carnallachie got into the Rolls and, with the others following in the trap, went bumping up the rough track to Boglehowe. There, the packman was deposited in the old bothy near the stable, whereafter Dottie was man-handled in through the narrow door of Boglehowe's kitchen and along the passageway to her bedroom. At the sight of his mother being half-carried, half-dragged along, The Loon, who had been ensconced cosily by the fire with a child's picture book, whose large letters he had for years attempted to decipher, leapt out of his chair, declared himself to be 'black affronted' and shambled after the procession with eyes agape, the segs on his big clumsy boots ringing hollowly on the bare floorboards.

The menfolk bundled Dottie onto the bed and then quitted the scene with alacrity, leaving the womenfolk to attend to any necessary ablutions.

Maggie lit the messy remains of a candle stuck into the depths of a large chamberpot reposing on a bench under the window. The feeble light flickered over the room to reveal a scene that would have gladdened the heart of any ambitious rag-and-bone man. Heaps of old clothes and piles of ancient books were scattered all over the place. A picture of Dottie's late husband leered from the wall at a crazy angle, the craggy brows on the old bewhiskered face drawn down in seeming disapproval of a small mound of whisky bottles half-hidden under the bed.

The room stank of tobacco smoke and stale whisky and Hinney hastened to the window to try to open the sash. But it was stuck tight with layers of old paint and wads of yellowed newspapers jammed into the cracks to keep out the draughts. 'I'll get the besom for this,' she vowed grimly. 'Last time I was here I made her promise to clean the place up, and she was that sincere about doing it butter wouldna have melted on her whiskified breath. I'm sure if you was to put a match to Dottie's mouth it would go up in flames – dirty old dragon.'

Maggie and Evelyn were attempting to remove some of Dottie's outer layers but it was an impossible task. Every time they got her rolled onto her side she just flipped back again shouting, 'Gie me back my pipe – I canna sleep wi' out it,' and then she started to chant: 'Oh there was a wee baker who lived in Jamaica, he dichted his erse wi' a wee bit o' paper, the paper was thin and his fingers slipped in – and oh what a fix the wee baker was in.' After that she gave vent to great gusts of wheezy laughter which sounded for all the world like Carnallachie's daft cuddy Trudge in one of his mean moods.

'Ach, leave her—' Hinney began, breaking off as her eye caught something hanging out the top of the grubby blanket at Dottie's side. Seizing the chamberpot, she brought it over in order that the feeble light it held might better illuminate the bed. On inspection the object proved to be a thick tuft of sheep's wool, carefully washed, combed and fashioned into the shape of a man's beard, long, flowing and tapered at one end. 'In the name . . .' Hinney muttered.

'Look.' Evelyn was pointing to the foot of the bed where two feet, complete with holey socks, were sticking out the covers.

Tentatively Maggie reached out, gave one of the 'feet' a short sharp tug, and wasn't too surprised when it came away in her hand and soon proved to be no more than a sock dolly complete with worn sock. The three womenfolk

261

looked at one another. 'Are you two thinking what I'm thinking?' Maggie said, with a little spurt of laughter.

Hinney nodded. 'The self-same thing—' She glanced again at the sheep's wool 'beard', then at the remaining 'foot'. 'That besom!' she exploded. 'She's aye thinkin' up ways to torment that poor saft loon o' hers and a gey funny sense o' humour she has too.' Her eyes twinkled suddenly. 'I'm thinkin' the time has maybe come for Pooty to get his own back on her. What do you two say?'

Evelyn giggled, fairly enjoying the evening's unexpected turn of events. 'I say let's go and tell The Loon right now, and see if he agrees to what I think you have in mind, Hinney.'

After initial indignant rantings, The Loon agreed wholeheartedly to Hinney's plan, and after some hummings and hawings Coulter and Carnallachie agreed too, so that the thing was no sooner said than done, the four men departing into the night, returning in a short time with Muckle Willie snoring like a baby in their arms.

Along the dark passageway they transported him, every-one walking on tiptoe, with never a giggle or a murmur though Jamie's shoulders were shaking and Evelyn's hand clamped so hard to her mouth she thought she must surely smother herself before the deed was halfway done.

Dottie was muttering insensibly to herself when the men placed Muckle Willie gently at her side. He was oblivious to everything. Only a few small grunts and groans of protest had so far escaped him on the stealthy journey from bothy to house. Now, as the grubby but soft blankets enclosed his small frame he rolled on his back, emitted a few contented little sighs, opened his mouth and began snoring so loudly the reverberations shook the bed and might have come from the throat of the heavens themselves during a good going thunderstorm.

Every hand there itched to shake Dottie awake, but The Loon wasn't going to be cheated of his big moment. Reaching forward, he placed his big hand on his mother's shoulder, pulled at it insistently and said in her ear, 'Ma, waken up. We've brought your man in to keep ye company

– Muckle Willie. He's cold, Ma, and wants to coorie into ye like the friendly wee man he is.'

Everyone held their breath. Dottie stirred, grunted, slapped her lips together and muttered something about a drink. Her son shook her harder, her eyes opened blearily her nose twitched as Muckle Willie's long pointed beard tickled her nose. At that moment, he threw out one long arm which landed quite unintentionally directly on top of Dottie's large, soft bosom. Slowly her head turned, simultaneously her eyes and her mouth shot wide open and she began to screech at the top of her voice, 'Ye mucky wee trollop! Get out o' my bed this meenit or I'll get the police to ye. Out! Out! Out!'

In her frenzy she reached for the little man, thick, calloused fingers curved ready to pounce, but before she could lay one finger on him the men snatched him away, and still asleep he was borne from the house and taken once more to the comparatively peaceful shelter of the bothy.

The Loon's raucous yells of mirth filled the house. There was no stopping him once he got going, and what with Dottie screeching and him laughing it seemed that all the bogles past, present and future had awakened from their dark slumberings and had gathered en masse to haunt the place.

The three women were weak with laughter by the time The Loon had departed exhausted to his own bed, and Dottie had subsided into a state of hoarse subjugation. Taking pity on her, Hinney filled a whisky pig with hot water and tucked it in at her side, made her drink some tea made with the herbs she always carried in her bag, then tiptoed softly to the door to join the others. Glancing back at the now peacefully sleeping woman, she remarked blandly, 'She'll no' play that trick again, nothing could be surer than that, though mind—' she shook her head laughingly – 'only The Loon could have been taken in by it. Muckle Willie's no more than four feet in length while the beard and the feet were nigh on six feet apart. If The Loon had stopped to take that into account, we wouldna have been here tonight wettin' our breeks laughing when we should all be home and in bed. Coulter will need more than fairy stories to explain away his lateness to her ladyship and I'll need more than a long confinement to explain away mine to my Alistair.'

The humorous little interlude seemed to break the spell of quietude that had settled uneasily about King's Croft. A few days later Evelyn received a short note from Gillan which read: *I'm coming home, Princess. Only for a few days so put on your best bib and tucker. You and I are going places. No excuses. Gillie.*

A strange elation gripped her at the thought of seeing Gillan again. Perhaps she welcomed any diversion that would lift her out of the unsettling depression she had lately sunk into, but she knew it was more than that. She had missed him in her life, more than she could have believed possible, and when he arrived home at the end of November she threw herself into his arms and kissed him so warmly that he drew back somewhat warily and said quietly, 'Steady on. I'm only a friend – remember? If things were different I would carry you off and never let you escape from me again, but I'm only Gillan, Brother Confessor and faithful companion – and if you could, you would wave a magic wand and turn me into David Grainger right here where I stand.'

'There would be no need to do that if regular soldiers got the same amount o' leave as officers seem to get.' She could have bitten her tongue out for her thoughtless words. Gillan looked pale, with a tiredness deep in his brown eyes and a rather dispirited droop about his sensitive mouth. He had none of the ready answers she had come to expect from him and looked hurt at her words. Impulsively, she took his arm. 'Gillie, I'm sorry, I didna mean that. It's just – I really was so pleased to see you and you threw my welcome back in my face. You look – rather weary. Are you all right?'

He shrugged. 'I don't know the answer to that any more. I suppose – the strain gets to you. It's a filthy war, Evie, filthy and bloody. If I could see some reason for all the bloodshed I might feel better, but there's nothing. Only a lot of young lads getting killed and wounded and half the time not knowing what it's all about.' He shuddered and pulled her close to him. 'I want these few days to be good for you and me, Princess. I feel the need – for peace in my life.'

She almost laughed but stopped herself in time. Here was Gillie looking for peace, while she was trying to find some excitement to lend spice to her days. But she said nothing of that. Instead she took his hand – a more delicate hand than ever, she noticed, a tiny tremor in it making her hold it very tightly. 'Dear Gillie,' she said tenderly. 'In your letter you spoke of dressing up and going places. You know I never cared much for that sort o' thing. You need to wind down, Gillie, and there's no finer place than Rothiedrum for that.'

He gave vent to a deep, heartfelt sigh. 'Sounds just what I need.' He smiled at her, a little half-smile that made him seem a small boy again. 'I can't tell you how good it is to see you again, you're the one person who keeps me going out there. Your letters are my lifeline to the real world – this world of clean countryside and bonny girls with green sparks in their eyes.' His voice had grown husky and he seemed very glad to keep a tight hold of her hand as they walked from the little summerhouse back to the kitchens, where Martha had a pot of her tea ready 'so thick you could dance on it' and big doorsteps of bread oozing with homemade black-currant jam. These were the things Gillan liked best and over the next three days, whenever Evelyn could get away, they sat in Martha's warm kitchen or walked together through the winter countryside, hand in hand, not speaking very much but just content to be in one another's company. In the evenings he came over to King's Croft to play cards with Jamie; to listen to Coulter and Carnallachie arguing and telling stories, or to just sit quietly by the fire, talking to Maggie.

In days gone by, she had felt uneasy having the young master of Rothiedrum in her house, never forgetting for a moment that this dark-haired, brown-eyed boy was her cousin. To her he had never fitted into the humble surroundings of her home. She kept remembering about his privileged lifestyle, the luxuries that he had taken for granted from birth. But all that was in her own mind. He had never set himself above anyone, had been natural, frank, and only seemed ill at ease when she was. Now she welcomed him into her home, treated him like a member of her own family – and often surprised herself by thinking how apt it would have been if he and Evelyn had become more than just friends. Then she would sigh and he would smile at her and say, 'A penny for them, Maggie.' And, at that, a warmth would creep into her heart for a lad who called her 'Maggie', and brought the peats in from the shed as if he was a son of the house instead of Gillan the Young Master of Rothiedrum.

His short leave was over too soon, and before he went he held Evelyn tightly and kissed her briefly on the mouth. Then he rushed from her quickly, as if it was too painful for him to linger over the last goodbyes.

The next morning Evelyn received a letter from David. Reading through his neat script she detected an almost jovial acceptance of the terrible conditions in the trenches.

> *There's always something to do to fill in the time. It's freezing cold behind the lines but we keep ourselves warm by going up and down the pleats of our kilts with matches to kill the lice that nest there and drive you dafter with their bites than the Jerries do with their warfare. It's been a wet winter here and the trenches are forever collapsing, so we're kept busy building them up again. The roads are ankle deep in mud and all the socks you ever sent are buried out there in Flanders' fields. One extra long one will do the next time. I'll hang it on the nearest star on Christmas Eve and who knows – maybe Santa will deliver the entire German Army into it so that we can all go home in time for turkey and plum duff. If not, I'll just spend Christmas right here in the mud which is the last word in comfort compared to the billets we go to if we get a few days back from the line. There's nothing there, not even a proper bed, so you just put your waterproof sheet on the ground and pretend you're a Boy Scout.*
> *Dear little Bright Eyes, I won't wish you were here but I*

*wish I was there, in Rothiedrum, your hand in mine, the
sweet smell of you drowning my senses. Last summer is
long gone now yet, if I close my eyes, I can still see it all.
A bit misty and blurred but no matter what, they are the
memories I cling to when all else seems unreal . . .*

Fumbling for her hanky, she blew her nose. Then she
straightened her shoulders briskly and went upstairs to her
room, where David's Christmas box lay open on the
dresser. For weeks she had been putting things away into
it. During the last, quiet month she had sat by the fire in
the evenings knitting and sewing, till her eyes were sore
and Maggie had scolded her for working so late. Socks,
gloves, a warm, woolly scarf had sprouted in rapid suc-
cession from her needles. She had bought three good-
quality linen handkerchiefs and into a corner of each one
had embroidered the intials D. A. G. She had also managed to acquire a small store of cigarettes, tea, sugar, and
chocolate though the shortage of such items hadn't made
it easy. Patiently, she had waited in queues outside
various Aberdeen shops to obtain the precious rations and
even had enough sugar left over to make tablet and
shortbread.

Now she took all the items from the box, as she had
done each time a new thing was added, and gloated over
them as a miser might gloat over a horde of gold. But her
rejoicing came from love not greed, and gleefully she put
everything back into place in the box and closed the flaps
with a small sigh of longing as she wondered when she
would see him again – if she would ever see him again.

Nellie came home for Christmas bringing Cal with her, a
very different Nellie from the one everyone remembered.
Her face and her body had filled out, her hair and eyes
shone with happiness and contentment. The minute she
and Cal stepped through the door, the whole atmosphere
inside King's Croft changed. Col rose up from the
hearthrug and positively screamed with delight, so beside
himself with gladness he didn't know who to welcome

first. Cal made the decision for him by hurtling forward and grabbing his little friend by the arms. Round and round the kitchen they danced, Cal bubbling with laughter, Col's blue eyes sparkling, his red-gold head thrown back in joyous abandonment. When he was finally released, he staggered around for a few dizzy moments and then held out his arms, his cries of 'Nella! Nella!' raising the rafters.

She ran forward and gathered him to her breast, her mouth pressed to his small, warm face, her swift tears wetting the fair tendrils of hair at his ears.

Everyone was speaking at once and a strange kind of wonder filled Nellie's being. She hadn't thought herself so well loved in this house, had believed that she might not be greatly missed, that her going would bring more relief to everyone than it would bring pain. But her mother's face was shining, Jamie's filled with a quiet elation, and Evelyn's eyes were as tearful as her own.

She stood up with Col in her arms. 'It's good to be back. I love Croft Donald and Kenneray but I – I've missed you all and there's so much I want to know. How's Grace? She hasna written this whilie. And Mary? I must go along to see her while I'm here.'

'They're all fine,' Maggie assured her, 'but take off your coat before you start your blethers. You must be ready for a cuppy.'

'And Murn?' Nellie didn't move, her eyes on her mother's face full of an anxious inquiry.

Maggie didn't answer but went instead to put on the kettle, and it was Jamie who said quietly, 'Murn is fine, Nell. She wrote a letter to your mother and me—'

'A note more like,' interposed Maggie abruptly.

'She's working for her MA at St Andrews University,' Jamie continued, 'and doesna think she'll get home for Christmas.'

'The same old Murn.' Nellie's voice held a note of bitterness. 'Thinking o' herself as usual.' She turned away. 'I'm going upstairs wi' my things and then I'll be back down to help wi' the dinner.'

'Nellie, put your things in my room,' said Evelyn. 'I miss having Grace to talk to and you and me could have some nice cosy wee blethers.'

Nellie flushed with pleasure. She was about to say, 'Do you really mean that, Evie?' but a glance at her youngest sister's eager face told her there was no need for words. The two went off upstairs together and Maggie looked at Jamie. 'Marriage to Kenneth has been good for our lass.'

He nodded. 'Ay, Maggie, she's that changed in both manner and appearance I hardly recognized her at first. There was a time when I began to think she would never find real happiness in her life. Strange to think she once hated and feared men so much she wouldna let one put an arm round her without backing away.'

'Ay – strange.' Maggie suddenly remembered last Christmas at the Aulton when Whisky Jake had appeared at Grandmother's house and both Nellie and Jamie had behaved so suspiciously in his presence. She never had gotten to the bottom of that. Whenever she happened to mention it, Jamie had become very evasive and uneasy – the same kind of look he had on him now that he caught the meaningful tone of her voice and saw the questions in her eyes.

Rubbing his hands together, he went to the door. 'I'd best get over to the stable and gie Queenie a rub down. She's been sweating more this whilie back after just a morning in the park, but that's only to be expected wi' a mare seven months in foal.'

Once outside, he stopped to light his pipe with a rather shaky hand. God! would he never be allowed to forget what had happened all these years ago? Nellie was closer to him than she had ever been, but even so she had never spoken her forgiveness in so many words – it was still there, rankling, coming between him and the people who were his world. Damn Whisky Jake! The bugger had cast a shadow over his life for too long, and though it was almost a year since he had last clapped eyes on the man, he was there in his life as effectively as if he stalked every one of his footsteps. As for Maggie – he knew her, she would never let go till the truth of the matter came out – and he was damned if he was ever going to let that happen!

Nellie hurried over her breakfast, anxious to get back to Kenneray before the short December day gave way to dusk. Col sensed that she was leaving. Since rising that morning he had followed her everywhere, plucked out of his introverted world by the sight of her putting things into her suitcase.

He had accepted the fact that she had gone away for a little while but had returned to stay for good. Now the suitcase was out once more – as it had been that other time she had gone from him and he hadn't been able to understand why.

He had refused to eat breakfast and now sat on the hearthrug, rocking himself to and fro, his finger in his mouth, his eyes following every move she made.

When she got up from the table he arose from the fireplace, a lost little whimpering sound coming from his throat, his fingers reaching out to grab at her skirt and clutch the material to his chest. 'No go, Nella, no go.'

'Just upstairs, Col, Nella has to go upstairs.'

And upstairs Col went too, still clinging to her skirt, his whimperings turning to a soft wail of sheer frustration. She came back downstairs with her case and set it on the floor. He looked up at her, the blue of his eyes drowned in a great welling of tears which poured down his face and seemed likely never to stop.

'Father – Mother.' Nellie turned appealingly to her parents. 'Let me take him with me. Just for a few months to see if it will work out. It's a good life for bairns on Kenneray and he'll have Cal there to keep him company – also, well to tell the truth I've missed the wee man and worried about him when you wrote telling me how quiet he'd grown after I left.'

Jamie sat down suddenly and fumbled for his pipe. He had seen this coming, had had a good idea that his eldest daughter might ask to take his son back with her, but now that the moment had arrived he felt as if someone had hit him hard over the heart. He had grown so used to having the wee lad about his feet, and coming home every day from the fields he had looked forward to the smile of welcome lighting up that bonny, innocent little face, yet – it couldn't be denied – the boy had fretted sorely for Nellie – had pined for the company of Kenneth's son. He glanced up at Maggie and saw from her face that the same thoughts were running through her mind. Some of the colour had left her cheeks, there was a sadness in her eyes that matched the feelings in his heart. In the beginning she hadn't wanted to face the reality of giving birth to such a flawed child, but gradually she had come to cherish him, to accept him as he was, to even need his reliance on her when all her daughters were drifting away like snowflakes before the wind.

'What do you think, Maggie lass?' His voice was husky, slightly shaky.

A tension filled the kitchen. Nellie stood poised, waiting, Evelyn and Cal appeared to be holding their breath, even Col had grown silent.

'What would Kenneth have to say about it?' Maggie spoke at last, her hands still and seemingly peaceful in her lap.

Nellie moistened her lips. 'He – ach – to tell the truth it was Kenneth who suggested I ask you. He knew how much I was missing the bairn and both him and Jeannie aye did have a soft spot for Col. Kenneth's a big man wi' a heart to match and both Iain and Irene Cameron enjoy having wee ones about the place. I was thinking too, it's high time Col had a bit o' learning dinned into him. There's a lot o' brightness lurking inside that wee head o' his that just needs bringing out. Irene was an infant teacher before she married and has the patience o' Job when it comes to teaching. When she saw Col that time she was here for the wedding, she felt he had more brains than met the eye and is just itching to get her hands on him to see what he's made of—'

She came to a full stop suddenly, realizing that she had been carried away by her enthusiasm, that it might be hurtful to her parents to impress upon them all the things

that might be done for their son when they had given so much
of themselves in the rearing of him.

But neither her father nor her mother took
offence.'You're right to feel that way, Nellie,' said the latter.
'I have often thought a bit o' learning wouldna do the bairn
any harm. There was a time when I thought maybe Murn—'
she paused, and went on – 'he's been a lost, lonely wee soul
without you, lass. Take him away before I change my mind –
and you had better hurry if you want to catch the ten o'clock
train from Aberdeen.'

Cal let go of his breath in a soft, triumphant whoosh, Col
sensed the lightening of the atmosphere and gave everyone a
watery smile.

Evelyn stood up. 'I'll go and get his things.' She ran
upstairs, crying a little as she packed her small brother's
possessions into the one suitcase left in the house. Fifteen
minutes later she was back upstairs in her own room, waving
rather forlornly from the window as Jamie drove Nellie and
the boys away to Lums o' Reekie station in the trap.

Withdrawing to her bed, she sat down on it and wrote into
her diary: *I'm the only one of the family left now at King's
Croft. It's so quiet I come upstairs on tiptoe, when before I used
to clatter my feet on the stairs and no one heard me for all the
bustle round about. I wonder when we'll all be together again
as it was in the old days. The way things are now, I shouldn't
doubt for a moment that things can ever be like that again but
somehow I can see it happening. I'm all mixed up. I should
want it to happen, yet I don't. It won't be a happy time and I'm
afraid of what lies ahead.*

Trembling a little, she rolled onto her back and gazed up at
the ceiling. The silence of the house embraced her. She would
have to enjoy this quiet time while she could – if the niggling
sense of foreboding in her heart would allow her to enjoy any
sort of peace in the days and nights that stretched ahead . . .

Jamie came into the kitchen, slowly, rather unwillingly.
Maggie was standing by the fire, one hand resting on the
mantelpiece as she gazed into the glowing embers.

'So, that's that,' she said, without looking up. 'Another o' our bairns gone. In the space of just a year they have all left home for one reason or another.'

'We still have our Evie,' he reminded her softly.

'Ay, but for how long? One o' these fine days she'll get up and go just like the others, and where will we be?'

He went over to stand near her. 'We'll still have each other, lass, we'll aye have each other. That's how we began our lives together and that's how we will end up.'

She turned her head to look at him. He was smiling at her, his brown eyes reflecting many of the uncertainties she was putting into words.

'Oh yes, my dear, dear Jamie, we'll still have each other.' She put her hand out to him. He took it, kissed it, a spark of the old chivalrous gypsy Jamie shining out of his face. Gently he pulled her to him and held her close, and just for a moment she was a young girl again with all her life stretching before her on a smooth, unblemished path. But it had proved to be a rough road, full of unexpected twists and turns that no inexperienced girl could ever have foreseen. But always there had been this man, sometimes faltering at her side but never straying from it.

She held on to him and forgot for a while the faces of her daughters, whose youthful smiles had once gladdened her heart in almost every room she entered.

# PART 4

Winter/Spring, 1916

# CHAPTER SIXTEEN

It was warm in Grandmother's kitchen. The old lady was asleep, tired out from a night of feeble coughing and difficult breathing. A kettle on the fire sent busy little puffs of steam into the atmosphere and Evelyn made sure it was topped up with water before settling herself wearily into a chair by the old lady's bedside. The house seemed very quiet without the cheerful presence of Aunt Mattie. She had had to go into hospital for a small operation, and Maggie had asked her youngest daughter to go over to the Aulton for a few nights to take care of things. Evelyn had been due some time off from Rothiedrum House so she had acquiesced willingly to Maggie's request, only too anxious to do anything she could for people who had always been kind to herself and her family. This was her second day at the house in College Bounds.

Grandmother was no worse than she had been the previous day, but was no better either. She was suffering from a bout of bronchitis coupled with severe laryngitis and could barely croak, let alone speak. Her condition wasn't dangerous, only very uncomfortable and painful, but because of her great age and frailty the doctor was keeping a strict eye on her, and had only just left a few minutes ago with instructions to Evelyn to keep the old lady warm. 'Also, keep that steam kettle going and see she has steam inhalations every two hours or so. She's a stubborn old besom and won't do a thing she's told so, if you have to, tie her hands behind her back!'

Evelyn had nodded soberly, but soon erupted into giggles at the gumsy old face Grandmother pulled at the doctor's departing back. She might not be able to speak, but she still had her sense of humour and her young companion felt greatly cheered to see such a typical display of acerbity.

Now she was fast asleep, little puffing snores issuing from her sunken mouth. Evelyn pulled the curtains across the bed to keep the lamplight from shining in the old lady's eyes and then she sat for a while, weighed down by fatigue, for she hadn't been sleeping well lately. The unease that had haunted her for weeks had in no way diminished. If anything it had grown more intense with the passing of time, so that even in daytime she found herself unable to settle.

With a sigh, she got up to go to the window and pull back the curtains. The January darkness had fallen over the countryside more than an hour ago, and because it was teatime the street was very quiet with soft lights from cottage windows throwing out pools of warmth. One or two people were standing by their gates talking, but otherwise there was no sign of life. She was glad that her father had promised to look in on his way back from seeing Aunt Mattie at the hospital. She had undergone her operation yesterday morning and, according to a neighbour's report, was rallying round quickly.

Evelyn let the curtain fall back. She stood looking into the room, wondering if she should go and make herself a cup of tea. Earlier, she had fed Grandmother some thin soup and had even fed Ging the cat, so there didn't seem to be anything else to keep her occupied till Jamie came by.

Rather disconsolately she wandered round the room, then, with sudden decision she fetched writing materials from the bureau and settled herself at the fire in order to write to David. Often she wondered why she bothered. His letters to her were few and far between. A brief note had come at Christmas to thank her for the parcel she had sent, but since then there had been nothing. Nevertheless, she refused to believe that his feelings for her had died completely, and she spent her reflective moments making all sorts of excuses for him. She told herself it was quite one thing to sit at a cosy fireside with pen poised, but another matter entirely if you were stuck in a grim trench with water at your feet and bursts of gunfire rattling every nerve in your body. With her vivid imagination, Evelyn could picture something of what it must be like for David and all

278

the thousands like him. What could he write about anyway? How many of his mates had been killed? How many wounded? The kind of food they had to eat, the kind of places they slept in? With all that in mind she always tried to keep her letters as lighthearted and cheerful as possible though she was finding it more difficult as time went on and there seemed little likelihood of him getting home on leave. The few days he did get now and then were taken behind the line, and with no proper billets to go to he had told her he would rather stay where he was in the trenches.

With another long sigh, she bent her bright head and applied herself to the task in hand. Ging got up from his place on the rug and leapt onto her knee, scattering the empty pages. The big cat was warm and soft as he settled himself comfortably on the girl's lap. The heat from the fire soon had his slanty eyes blinking sleepily. Evelyn lay back, her fingers curling into the cat's silken marmalade fur. Her pen slipped from her grasp and rolled down into the space between the cushions. She didn't retrieve it. She was soon as fast asleep as both the cat and Grandmother, her nights of broken sleep at last taking their toll.

Something warm and oozy was clinging to her neck. At first she thought it was Ging displaying his affections by licking her skin and kneading her breasts with his paws. She smiled drowsily and put out her hand to caress him. Then she froze. A sickening smell washed into her senses: whisky fumes mixed with tobacco. Her heart gave a lurch, and very slowly she opened her eyes. A great black hairy blob was blotting out the lamplight. She could see nothing of the room, for she was enclosed in a sweating, fumbling mass of brutal bone and muscle. Whisky Jake's mouth was clamped against her face, slimy, wet, a great slack blubber of a thing, crawling like a slug all over her face, her neck – down to the bare flesh of her breasts which he had exposed with a sly, furtive loosening of her blouse buttons. His breath was already heavy and hoarse, grating into her ears, his huge rough hands travelling all over her body, one pummelling at her breasts as if they were made of rubber, the other sliding up her leg to her thigh. He had undone his fly buttons. His arousal was apparent as he pressed his hardness against the soft flesh of her belly, his grunts growing in volume as he began to insinuate his vile state of nakedness into her hands which had been folded peacefully in her lap.

Her slumbering senses came forcibly and horrifyingly alive. Terror leapt into her throat, her heartbeat thundered, gushed in her ears. She was about to open her mouth to scream when she remembered Grandmother. The old lady had a weak heart. That, coupled with her present illness was a dangerous combination. If she was roused suddenly from sleep by the sound of screams filling her kitchen, there was no knowing what might happen.

Evelyn's slight young body came alive then. She struggled and fought, tried to push the man's perspiring bulk away from her but she might just as well have tried to move a brick wall for all the good it did her.

Jake's sneering laugh blew in her ears. 'So, you've come alive, my beauty. And here was me thinkin' I was going to have you without any fuss. Lie back and enjoy it – it willna be the first time for you, you're as hot-arsed as the rest o' yer sisters and dinna try to deny it. I've seen you flaunting the goods wi' my own een. First wi' a farm laddie, then wi' a sojer and as if that wasna enough, you tramp the countryside wi' a young gentleman who gowps at ye as if he could eat ye. Oh ay, old Jake's seen it all and now it's my turn. Like a gift ye were, lying back sleepin' like a baby when I came in about to see the old lady. Jist askin' for it you were so dinna say another word or I'll knock ye both silly and senseless.'

Evelyn barely heard him. Panic was turning her limbs to jelly. His salivating lips had opened, his teeth were biting into her neck, his weight pinning her hard against the chair back. His mouth came round, closed in a loose, slobbering mess over hers. She was seized with a feeling of suffocation. She could hardly breathe let alone give vent to the cries for help which rose in her throat, for in her terror she had forgotten Grandmother, had forgotten everything in her fight against the drunken beast lying on top of her.

Twisting down in the chair, she tried to bring up her knees to get him where it would hurt most but the move was to her loss, his gain. The bones of his legs ground into hers, forcing them down. With a savage spurt of slurred laughter he wrenched up her skirt, forced his hand against the small of her back and tried to thrust himself into her. His mouth slackened and she tore her own away, gasping for air, a gurgling scream rising from her painful lungs. With a muttered curse he grabbed the long mane of her hair, forced her face brutally against a cushion, so that for a few sick moments she could get no air at all into her lungs though her breasts were heaving with the effort. Blackness threatened to engulf her – she awaited the deliverance it would bring as the first waves of faintness washed over her.

Through a chink in the curtain round her bed, Grandmother saw everything. The sound of voices and crashing furniture had awakened her from a deep sleep. One of the voices belonged to Whisky Jake and her first reaction was one of annoyance. She had never liked the man. Wherever he went he caused trouble, and had been banned from several of the travellers' encampments. He also had a police record for drunken and disorderly behaviour and attempted ravishment of young girls. Besides all that, he was possessed of a most unpleasant personality and both Mattie and Grandmother had discouraged him from coming to their house. But still he came, pretending friendship when all the time he was only out to get what he could. Twice he had stolen money from Grandmother's purse, and the last time she had threatened him with the police and a warning never to come back.

Now here he was again, drunk by the sound of him – and making a nuisance of himself. But it was worse, much worse than that. What Grandmother saw through the curtain made her struggle up and attempt to pull it back. But it was too far out of reach of her trembling hand and she lay back on the pillows, gasping for breath, her heart fluttering weakly in her thin old breast. She tried to shout but only a hoarse, rasping sound came out. Weak tears of exhaustion and helplessness squeezed themselves between her wrinkled lids. Making a great effort, she tried once more to cry but the wheezy croaks which issued forth were completely lost on the great black hairy beast who was in her house, attempting to ravish a young girl whom Grandmother loved with all the passion of her fierce old heart . . .

Jamie came into the house in the Aulton quietly, mindful of Grandmother's illness and the fact that she might be asleep. When he opened the door of the kitchen, he stood for a few moments hardly able to believe the evidence of his own eyes. Rage boiled up in him, a rage such as he had never experienced before. That pig! That drunken, lecherous pig was at it again – this time with his youngest daughter, the child he adored.

Something happened to Jamie King Grant that evening in Grandmother's house. For the first time in his life he temporarily lost his sanity, let go of the quiet reasoning that had stood him in good stead all the days of his life. His staring eyes fastened onto a pair of kitchen scissors lying on the table and without a second thought he darted forward, picked them up, and plunged them hard into Whisky Jake's side.

The big man screamed, staggered back, blood gushing from the wound. With a roar of disbelieving fury he spun round, arms outstretched, and made to go for Jamie. Instead he faltered, teetered where he stood, a monstrous sight with his lips drawn back in a snarl, eyes wild and gaping, and then he fell back towards the fireplace, his clutching fingers knocking over the steaming kettle from the hob. Its scalding contents gushed out, all over his trouser legs and feet. His agonized screams filled the kitchen and he collapsed where he stood, writhing in pain.

The door flew open. Several people rushed in from the street. One man muttered, 'In the name o' God!' and ran outside again to make for the Town House.

Evelyn gazed at her father with dazed eyes. Then she was up, running towards him to collapse against him and bury her face in his chest. Shakily, he put his arms round her. 'There, there, my babby,' he soothed, stroking her hair, 'you're fine now. You're safe. I'm here.'

Within minutes the police arrived and were quick to size up the situation. A barely conscious Jake was taken off to hospital with a policeman in attendance. Evelyn, white, trembling, almost incoherent, had to give her version of what had taken place. 'Please, let my mother know what happened,' she sobbed, as Jamie was arrested and led away. 'She'll worry if my father doesna come home in time.'

The constable was a young man with a kindly face. He assured her that everything would be taken care of, then, rather embarrassed, he told her that she would have to undergo a medical examination, and would she mind coming along with him.

Before very long, the house in the Aulton was quiet again. The doctor had been called to attend to Grandmother who was in a state of near-collapse. Her wheezing breaths rasped in her throat alarmingly, and the two neighbours who had pledged themselves to remain with her till medical help came eyed one another in some trepidation as they held a steaming bowl of water under her nose and made her take deep breaths.

Nevertheless, they were able to whisper excitedly to one another about the night's happenings as they bustled about, making tea and laying out clean towels, the hot beverage to soothe Grandmother's nerves and their own, the towels for the doctor who arrived in time to avert a fainting turn, not in Grandmother – she was far too tough for that – but in one of the neighbours, who had talked herself into a state of such excitement that she was as short of breath as the sick old lady, who glowered at her darkly from the bed and growled in disgust at not being able to give vent to her opinions on the matter.

Maggie lay wakeful in bed, alone for almost the first time since her marriage. Her mind was whirling as it tried to sort out all the momentous happenings of the past two days.

The morning after his arrest, Jamie had been taken before the Sheriff in Chambers, represented by a solicitor obtained for him by the police. He had been remanded in custody and bail refused – as if they could have afforded bail anyway, Maggie thought bitterly as she tossed and turned. His case was to be set out before Lord Kirknaben in a few weeks time. Mr John Barclay, the solicitor, had told Maggie that her husband would need proper representation in court – either a private counsel or a defence supplied by the Poor Law.

Maggie's head had lifted at that. She would have to get the best legal help there was for Jamie – but how on earth was she to pay for it?

She moved restlessly, making impossible plans, rejecting them. She even half-thought of selling the one valuable asset they had at the croft – the Clydesdale mare, Queenie, complete with unborn foal. But she pushed that idea away almost before it was formed. Queenie was their bread and butter. Jamie would pine away altogether if she were to take such a drastic step.

Yet she would have to get money to pay for a good lawyer – the very best money could provide . . . Outside her window the rain pittered dismally, adding to her sense of desolation. How quiet the house was, with only herself and Evelyn in it. Her darling lass! She had been so pale and silent since her return home. Maggie's fingers curled at her sides. That Whisky Jake! He had been in a critical condition when taken to hospital, and it was only the skill of the surgeons which had saved him. He deserved everything that had happened to him. If she had witnessed him trying to ravish her youngest daughter, she wouldn't just have wounded him – she would have killed him!

Lady Marjorie could hardly contain her apprehension as Maggie was ushered into the sitting room. This tall, white-haired woman in shabby clothes looked so incongruous in the elegant surroundings, so completely out of her depth as she stood hesitantly in the middle of the room. With an inward shudder of distaste, her ladyship noted the drooping hemline of the visitor's dark green tweed coat, the old-fashioned hat sitting on top of that cloud of silvery hair. Yet, it was such beautiful hair – despite its colour – though even that was attractive enough, so finely did the natural waves frame the rather noble face. But those boots! Black, buttoned up the side, so highly polished one could see the subtle tints of the Persian rug reflected in them – but no amount of polish on earth could disguise their obvious vintage.

Almost before Lady Marjorie had issued the invitation for her visitor to sit Maggie had seated herself, placing her black woollen gloves neatly on a marble-topped table at her side, arranging herself neatly in the confines of the deep leather armchair so that she looked for all the world as if she had been used to such comforts all her days.

Like mother like daughter, her ladyship thought with a slight sniff. Utterly devoid of manners but possessed of an almost insolent knack of managing to look quite the lady despite the awful garb.

Lady Marjorie rang the bell and a maid came in bearing a tea tray, which she placed on a trolley beside the couch. With a few quick words her ladyship indicated her desire to remain undisturbed for the next half-hour and the maid politely withdrew, though not without a swift glance of appraisal in Maggie's direction.

Maggie sipped at her tea but refused to take anything from the plateful of dainty morsels held out to her. She had no appetite. She needed all her strength to drink the tea without choking on it. It had taken days of indecision before she had finally made up her mind to ask for this meeting with the lady of the manor, so to speak, and she had had to swallow a lifetime of pride in the process.

She had taken time with her appearance before venturing out, dressing in her best Sunday clothes and doing and redoing her hair before it was arranged to her satisfaction. She had spent much of the previous evening ironing, polishing boots and handbag, and finally bathing in the zinc tub which she had dragged to the fireside and labouriously filled with kettle after kettle of boiling water.

Yet, despite all her care she felt stiff and out of place in these grand surroundings, though never for one moment would she give this superior-looking cousin of hers any reason to think she was feeling anything but calm and self-possessed in her company.

A pregnant silence had fallen over the room. She cleared her throat and spoke, her voice ringing out, clear and precise. 'You know who I am, of course,' she began, and Lady Marjorie's mouth gave a small, imperceptible twitch. She knew perfectly well what the other woman meant, but the words sounded so imperiously regal they might have come from some grand old duchess impressing her position on some insignificant minion.

A faint, unwilling stab of admiration pierced her ladyship's stiff façade. Uncle Lindsay had been right about this woman – she was everything he had said she was, and on her mettle she was even more. That haughty way she carried herself, that arrogant lift of her handsome head – she was an Ogilvie all right, no doubt about that.

'Indeed I do, Mrs Grant,' she intoned politely. 'We have met before, you know.'

Maggie's lips tightened. 'You ken fine what I mean. We're cousins you and I, and if you feign surprise at that then you're wasting your time and my own, and that is a precious commodity of which I have little to spare.'

Her ladyship gasped. This condescending crofter's wife was blatantly implying that she was the one granting the favour of this meeting, when . . . 'Yes, of course I know,' she snapped, then composed herself – she mustn't allow this woman to get under her skin – 'My uncle told me the whole story of his – his unsavoury past, but how he chose to spend his misguided youth has got nothing whatsoever to do with me.'

'As you like.' Maggie twitched her frock into place about her knees and looked her hostess straight in the eye. 'I will not waste time with further preamble. The fact is, you and I are cousins whether we like it or no. I have never asked anything o' this family and never thought I would, but something has happened to change all that and I wish you to hear me out.'

In a few sparse sentences she told her cousin about Jamie's predicament. When she had finished speaking, there was a silence in the room except for the rapid drumming of Lady Marjorie's fingers on the arm of her chair. Her dark eyes were veiled, hiding her small surge of triumph. She held the trump card now – and she would play it well, make this haughty woman squirm just a little bit before she deigned to offer help.

'Really, Mrs Grant,' she said sweetly, 'I don't see what I can do. There are people much better placed than I to help cases like yours. I can give you some addresses—'

'I wonder what the folks hereabouts would have to say if they knew you and I were blood kin.' Maggie spoke musingly, absently. 'A story like that would fairly set the gossips' tongues a-wagging – and, of course, it would eventually reach the ears o' people in high places. Your friends would be amused, they would certainly laugh among themselves behind your back – and of course your husband has a reputation for fair dealings with all and sundry, no matter if they be cottar or farmer. I wonder if I did the wrong thing coming to you. It might be best if I go directly to him—'

'Enough!' Lady Marjorie brought the palms of her hands down on the chair arms and jumped up as if she had been scalded. She began to pace, the nostrils of her rather thin nose pinched in agitation. What a fool she was to think she could outsmart someone like Margaret Grant! People of her breeding would stoop to anything. She had all the trump cards up her shapeless sleeves and her words had very subtly implied – blackmail.

She stopped pacing and faced her cousin. 'How much?'

'Just enough to see that my Jamie gets the best help there is,' Maggie said softly, surprised to find she was enjoying herself. 'I dinna want money mind, oh no, I couldna bear the actual exchanging o' hard siller, it would be far too undignified. A gift perhaps, a piece o' jewellery that would fetch a reasonable price. After all, we are cousins – and what could be more natural than a rich relative presenting a nice gift to a less well-off member of the family?'

'I'll be back in a moment.' Lady Marjorie swept out, to return some little time later bearing an oblong leather box which she opened to reveal a somewhat ugly gold necklace set with blood-red garnets. 'I never liked it,' she said shortly. 'My uncle gave it to me some years ago. It seems fitting that it should be given to his daughter in her time of need. It should fetch a good price – enough for what you want.'

'How kind.' Maggie accepted the necklace graciously, lifting it out of its velvet bed to hold it up to the light. 'Ay, I think Father would like me to have this – yet, in a way it seems a pity to sell it. Each of these stones is like a small drop o' frozen blood, as if they had been preserved for a time like this to give life where it was most needed.' She beamed her radiant smile on her cousin. 'If it had been money I would have felt obliged to pay it back somehow – but as this is a gift, there will be no need of that.'

Lady Marjorie cleared her throat. 'I'm – truly sorry this terrible thing has happened to Evelyn. I've had my ups and downs with her during her time of working here, but – oh, what's the use of denying it? I like the girl, she's as pert and frank as yourself, Maggie Grant, but she has a way with her that's utterly charming. I thought she was looking rather pale and quiet, now I know why – and I'll try my best to see that none of the other servants worry her too much with their questions.'

Maggie's face softened. 'Thank you for that, you're no' as hard as you would have folk think. 'Tis a pity you and me never crossed paths sooner, we might have learned to like one another – despite everything.'

Picking up her gloves from the table, she waited while her cousin rang for the maid before making her gracious and unhurried departure, looking neither to the left nor the right as she went downstairs, and failing to see Evelyn gaping at her in astonishment from the kitchen regions.

The little parlour maid's tongue had been busy, and Evelyn had been the first to hear that her mother was upstairs taking tea with her ladyship.

The very next day Maggie took the train into Aberdeen. Selling the necklace didn't prove as easy a matter as she had imagined. Four of the jewellers she went to weren't interested. Times were hard, they told her. It was wartime after all and people had more important matters on their minds these days. Only the rich had money to spare for frivolous things like jewellery, but it was doubtful if even they would look twice at the somewhat unattractive necklace.

Maggie's first enthusiasm was wearing off with depressing rapidity by the time she approached a seedy-looking shop in a back street. The man behind the counter had a narrow rat-like face, beady eyes, and a habit of licking his lips whenever the word 'money' was mentioned. At sight of the necklace he hummed and hawed for fully five minutes, though his tongue was hanging out as he took the item to the window to examine the stones better.

When he came back he eyed Maggie from head to foot in silent, furtive assessment. Up went her head, out went her hand to take the piece of jewellery from his somewhat grubby fingers. He snatched his own hand away as if it had been burnt, and in an oily voice made her an offer for the necklace. She hesitated. It wasn't nearly as much as she had hoped for, and she was about to refuse when her aching feet reminded her that she hadn't been off them most of the day, and she might have to tramp many more weary miles before getting another offer – if she got one.

With great dignity she accepted the man's offer, though her eyes flashed when his own gleamed with greedy delight.

But she was pleased enough to get the money in her hand, and there was quite a spring in her step as she made her way to the office of Mr John Barclay.

'A good KC will cost quite a lot of money, Mrs Grant,' he told her when he had heard her out.

'You needna worry your head about that,' she said briskly. 'I am quite able to meet any costs involved.'

'Then I will endeavour to get in touch with Mr Ian Peddie, KC. He is one of the best defence counsels to be had in these parts, and you can be assured that he will prepare a good case in your husband's favour.'

Outside in the street, Maggie straightened her hat and took a deep breath. The fingers of dread which had clutched round her heart over the past terrible days and nights relinquished their hold – just a little.

In the quiet of the kitchen that evening, Evelyn questioned her mother as to her reasons for visiting Lady Marjorie at Rothiedrum House. 'You've never gone there before, Mam,' she said in some bemusement, her face in the lamplight pale and strained from her recent ordeal.

'Well, Evie, there's a—'

'First time for everything,' finished Evelyn triumphantly.

'Ay, that there is,' Maggie agreed, and went on to tell her daughter almost flippantly that she had had some business matters to discuss with her ladyship; that as these had been of a private and personal nature she wasn't at liberty to discuss them with anyone, and that it would be wise if Evelyn held her tongue and said no more on the subject.

'Just know this, my lassie,' she said quietly. 'There's help to hand for your father, ay, and I don't mean from the Poor Law either. In the weeks to come you will likely ask yourself many times how I came to manage it all but dinna pester me about it for I will have more than enough on my mind as it is. Maybe one o' these days I will tell you about it, but right now there's work to be done and only you and me left to do it so save your strength for what lies ahead.'

In the dark days that followed, Evelyn was to observe the emergence of a new and totally ruthless Maggie. She had always known that her mother had a great store of different kinds of strength, but now she was to witness a blossoming of power and determination that soared far beyond the sort that had always dealt so efficiently with all the daily domestic crises in and around the croft. Maggie Innes Grant was a woman with a fight on her hands and she would use any weapon she could to help the man to whom she had pledged her devotion all those years ago.

Jamie was disbelieving when Maggie came to visit him and tell him about Mr Ian Peddie, KC. 'But Maggie lass, we could never afford the likes o' him! We could never raise the money for a private defence counsel.'

Maggie looked down at her hands, for she didn't want her husband looking into her eyes as she voiced the lies she had to tell. 'Jamie, there are one or two wee secrets I've kept from you over the years. You know of course the story o' my poor mother, I told it to you often enough way back in the beginning, but I never mentioned that she received the gift of a precious piece o' jewellery from the gentleman who got her into trouble. She never wore it but kept it by her until I reached the age o' sixteen years, when she gave it to me along wi' plenty o' fine words about keeping it till a day dawned when I might need to sell it. Well – that day has come, Jamie my man, and you are going to get the services o' Mr Ian Peddie, the best lawyer there is in these parts.'

Jamie took her hand and held it tightly. 'Maggie, there's a wee touch o' romance somewhere in that story but, whatever, you're a genius. What would I ever have done without you?'

'I suppose,' she said thoughtfully, 'we really ought to feel grateful to my father – whoever he was.'

Once outside, a little fillip of joy seized her. She felt almost lighthearted. If she didn't watch out, this business of lying could get to be a habit – yet she forgave herself quite easily and readily. She hadn't really lied, just twisted the truth a bit and in a burst of expansiveness she sent up a silent prayer of gratitude to her father, Lord Lindsay Ogilvie who, if he had done nothing else for her, had helped her during this difficult time, however indirectly. With her head held high she marched along the street – and when she thought no one was looking, gave a frisky skip of satisfaction.

The voice of Miss Beattie came to her across the years. 'Really Margaret, how indecorous.'

A small boy was eyeing her solemnly. Clapping her hand to her mouth she hurried along, her shoulders shaking in a very indecorous fit of the giggles.

# CHAPTER SEVENTEEN

It was as Evelyn had foreseen. All the family was gathered round the kitchen fire as it had been in days not so long gone. Only Jamie was missing and his name was not mentioned very often. It would have brought to the surface all the unspoken fears, the suppressed tears. Tomorrow morning he was to go up before Lord Kirknaben in the High Court on a charge of attempted murder, and tension ran high that evening at King's Croft.

Murn had come home the previous week, nervy, irritable, hardly casting a glance in Nellie's direction since she had arrived some days ago. But Nellie was far too preoccupied with her own thoughts to be bothered much by Murn's pettiness. This terrible business with her father and Whisky Jake had brought back to her all the horrors of the past. Old wounds had been opened, scraped raw as the sordid details of Jake's attempted rape of her little sister had unfolded in letters from her mother.

She had curled up inside herself visualizing what Evelyn must have suffered, but at the end of the day it was her father who had captured the greater part of her sympathies.

In her torment she had walked for miles along great tracts of white beaches, the boom of the Atlantic in her ears, the wonderful soothing solace of wide empty spaces all around her, thinking of her father shut up in a claustraphobic prison cell. He that had been used to fresh air and freedom all the days of his life. Her heart had cried then for that kindly, gentle man, and had become filled with a swelling tide of love such as she had never felt for him before.

His life had revolved round his home, his family. For them he had worked his fingers to the bone, and for his youngest daughter he had almost killed a man in an uncharacteristic burst of blinding fury.

Since childhood she had harboured grudges against her father, had viewed him through the eyes of one blinded by mistrust, but that day on the lonely beaches of Kenneray the mists of bitterness and contempt rolled away and at last she was able to face the truth about her father. He was a good, honest, loving man, a bit weak about some things but utterly strong in his loves and loyalties. She knew that if he hadn't been drunk on the night Whisky Jake had raped her, he would have defended her as fiercely as he had defended Evelyn.

Admiration and gratitude flooded her being for Jamie King Grant, washing away the anger that had lurked inside her for so long. All she wanted to do now was to help him – and, if that meant exposing herself in the process – well, so be it. It was a crucial time in her life. She thought of her husband, what he would have to say about a wife with such a dark past. But she needn't have worried. That night, when her halting revelations had come to an end, he put his arms around her and held her tight. 'I aye knew you had courage, Nell, I never knew how much till now. It took a lot o' guts for you to bare your soul to me, and it will take even more if you go ahead wi' what's on your mind. I'll no' try and stop you—' he laughed '—as if I could, anyway. You're a thrawn besom once your mind is made up but you'll no' stop me coming wi' you to give you all the support I can. The bairns will be fine here wi' Mother.'

And so they had arrived in Rothiedrum, Nellie going almost at once to visit her father. For a few fraught moments they had regarded one another, then she had put her arms around him and said huskily, 'It's all right, Father. What was between you and me is done with. I've never told you how – how much you mean to me, but I'm telling you now. I canna bide long – I have to go right away and see someone.'

But he had clung to her arm. 'No, lass, no,' he had pleaded, 'I'll no' let you do anything that will hurt you. Besides – at the end o' the day it will do no good.'

He was gaunt-eyed, old-looking. Nellie had kissed him on the cheek, told him not to worry, and had then gone to seek an interview with Mr John Barclay. He had listened intently as she spoke and clasped his hand warmly over hers. 'I'll certainly let Mr Peddie know about this, Mrs Cameron. I hope and pray it may do some good but I warn you now – don't raise your hopes too high.'

Mr Ian Peddie was doubtful about Nellie's evidence being used in court. It could, he told the lawyer, prejudice the case against Jake McPhee the plaintiff. Nevertheless, he had made haste to speak to Lord Kirknaben about the latest findings. The judge, however, had sternly decreed that they could not be used by the defence at Jamie's trial and this decision had been relayed forthwith to Nellie.

Seething with indignation, she had marched straightaway to tell her story to the local newspaper. When she had finished speaking, the editor regarded her with frank admiration. He knew all the Grants by sight, was personally acquainted with Jamie and had been as shocked as everyone else in those parts when the news of his arrest had broken. Standing up, he placed a firm hand on Nellie's shoulder. 'Both cases will have to be heard before we can do anything, lass, but you just wait till it's over and we'll splash what you've just told me so far and wide they'll be knowing about it in Timbuctoo and beyond.'

And with that Nellie had to be content, though she was far from satisfied and could only relieve her anxieties by pitching so headlong at all the tasks in and around the croft that it was like having the old Nellie back again – much to the chagrin of the cats, who skulked about in the yard after being ousted from the comforts of the fireside by the business end of a broom.

That was one thing about Nellie, Evelyn thought as she watched her eldest sister scuttling to the door with the mats, there was no aura of the visitor as there was with Murn, who had lounged about since her arrival with the air of one who was there as a guest and expected to be treated like one.

Now that it was the night before the trial everyone was far too keyed up to do much more than sit at the fire talking in

294

low voices, even Nellie who, having exhausted her energies, sat quietly with Kenneth and Grace on the bench under the window. The latter had travelled with her husband from France to arrive only yesterday, both of them taking some well-earned leave from their respective hospitals. Maggie hadn't been able to believe her eyes when the pair of them appeared unexpectedly at the door. Grace had dropped the small case she was carrying and simply walked into her mother's arms, Major Gordon Chisholm coming behind to enclose the two of them in such a reassuringly strong embrace that Maggie had released some of her pent-up tears into the rough khaki of his jacket before rushing to put on the kettle.

Grace looked incredibly well and bright. Maggie had expected her health to have suffered during her hectic time in France, but though thinner than ever, she had never been bonnier with her gentle face upturned to the solidly bearded one of her husband, and her great dark eyes filled with compassion when she found a sparrow with a broken wing fluttering about in the byre.

'Evie, get a box for the poor wee beggar.' Gordon had laughed when his young wife came in bearing the injured bird. 'I'll get no peace till it's splinted and bedded. Do you know, she keeps a menagerie full of these things in the tent she shares with another lass, who is as daft about animals as herself. I dread to think what life will be like for me when we eventually set up house together. I'll be knee deep in cages and boxes and the Lord alone knows what I'll find in my bed besides herself.'

'Tent?' Maggie had said faintly.

'Ay, Mam, didn't I tell you that in my letters?' Grace sounded too innocent to be true. 'The main hospital is crowded with injured soldiers so the nursing staff have to sleep in tents. Ach, dinna look like that,' she had laughed, 'it's no' as bad as it sounds – except when it rains and we have to walk on duckboards because the ground gets so soggy.'

The chatter of both Grace and Gordon had done much to relieve the heavy atmosphere in the house, touching as they did only on the lighter aspects of their work, though, in Gordon's case in particular, that was no easy matter with his mind reeling from the terrible injuries he had to deal with every day and often into the night as well. Big, generous, warm-hearted as ever, no one would have guessed by looking at him that he was so bone-weary all he wanted was to be quiet and alone with his wife.

But she sensed his hidden exhaustion, his need for solitude and had made him get out of the house. Together they walked quietly by the Birkie, lovers still, so enraptured at being together again that they spoke little but clung to one another in the little pine woods above King's Croft. As always her capacity for passion had taken his breath away. She was so gentle, this young wife of his, so languorously graceful in her movements that, at the start of their married life together, he had been pleasantly taken aback to discover a Grace so filled with fire that she had seemed something of a stranger to him in those first breathless days.

It was a part of her known only to him, and he cherished the knowledge of it to himself as much as he cherished her devotion to him and her absolute commitment to all living creatures, animal and human.

She had sent him out that evening to escort Mary from Rowanlea, and now they both came in, a mildly drunk Tandy at their heels, fire in his tawny eyes as he caught sight of Nellie and Kenneth.

Pandemonium reigned in the kitchen as the two big Highlanders greeted and slapped one another, Tandy so overcome with emotion that he forgot to order his dogs outside. Into the scene they came, along with the cats who slunk close to the dogs till they were safely inside and able to disperse to the most comfortable areas in the room. Red-faced, Murn turned away, as embarrassed by Tandy's appearance as she had been by Kenneth's, so certain that everyone must be talking about her that she had gone to bed early every night since her arrival lest she come face to face with visiting neighbours. But she worried needlessly. The travelling folk were a discreet lot and had been as tight-lipped about the affair as any member of the family. Jamie was still one of them, and it would take more than a wayward daughter to make them relinquish their loyalties. They had rallied round Maggie in her time of need. If one or another of them happened to be passing, they came in about the croft, even going so far as to take the horses out to plough the winter fields, asking in payment only a bed in the barn and a supper of brose.

The neighbours, too, had been ready with their support. Hard though their tongues had wagged over Jamie's arrest, every last man of them had stoutly declared that he would have reacted just the same in like circumstances. They had shown their sympathies in practical ways, so that Maggie found much of the heavier croft work taken off her hands. Coulter, who had 'only been playin' himself at Rothiedrum', to quote himself, moved into the chaumer above the stables so that he would be at hand to help with the horses and pigs, asking nothing more in return than his simple bed and board.

Carnallachie, 'the best pigman in a' the airts', as he frequently described himself, hastened round every day to give Coulter the benefit of his knowledge. In the ensuing arguments the pair fairly flew at one another's throats though theirs was an old battle, tinged with friendly malice, spiced with all the verbal abuse of two rather lonely old men only too glad of a good going disagreement to brighten their day.

So King's Croft was never without a neighbour or passing traveller popping in to see what help was needed, and if Murn hadn't been so wrapped up in her own mental agonies she would have seen that not one of them gave her a second glance. But worry she did, to the extend that she had given less thought to her father's plight than to her own, and could hardly bear to look at Kenneth Mor without all the old humiliations and frustrations crowding back.

But with Tandy's enthusiastic arrival she had no chance to scuttle away up to her room, for after the first rapturous greetings the shepherd produced a bottle from the folds of his plaid and proceeded to pour drinks for everyone, passing her a glass with a friendly kiss on the cheek and never an indication that she was only to be tolerated because she was a Grant, albeit a visiting one.

She began to relax, to look even a trifle shamefaced as she glanced around at all her sisters gathered there in support of their mother. She had not uttered one word of apology to that beautiful, strong woman who looked so lonely without Jamie at her side. For the first time remorse swamped Murn's being. Going over, she placed a hand on Maggie's arm. 'I'm – sorry, Mam.' She forced the words to come out. 'I was a bitch and I – I hate myself for it.'

'Stop hating yourself, lass,' Maggie advised quietly. 'No one else does. They're all far too busy thinking o' your father to worry about anything else.'

Murn's colour deepened. Raising her eyes, she met those of her eldest sister on the other side of the room. Hesitantly she smiled, fearful of rejection, but Nellie's generous mouth widened and her fair head moved in a slight nod. Relief washed over Murn. It was all right. They were sisters again. Not two cats who had fought tooth and claw over the same man – at least, she had fought, Nellie had always been far too dignified and level-headed for that. They were qualities she had always admired and envied in her elder sister. They had won her the man she wanted – *that* man, so tall and straight, so wonderfully Highland. But no more of that! He was Nellie's now and she would have to accept it – however unwillingly.

Major Gordon Chisholm – everyone delighted in stressing his rank as they had done with Gregor when he had last been home on leave – moved to Maggie's other side. Placing his arm round her shoulders, he raised his glass. 'To Jamie,' his voice rang out, clear and precise, 'and a prayer that God will be right there with him in the dock tomorrow.'

'To Jamie!' The cry rang out. Evelyn gazed at all the well-loved faces around her and her heart wept for the absence of the most beloved one of all.

She was pale with apprehension of what the morrow

would bring, and could hardly bear to sit still. She longed to rush out to the quietness of the stable and read again the letter she had received from David that morning. In it he had been warm and loving, telling her how much he missed her and longed for the day he would see her again. She hadn't told him about her ordeal. It was too starkly alive in her mind for her to be able to bring herself to write about it, and if she couldn't bear to see it in black and white how would he feel reading about it? He might see it all in a warped light. She herself felt degraded and soiled beyond measure – and she couldn't bear it if he thought that way too, so though his letter brought her a certain measure of comfort the biggest part of her remained afraid. She had to force herself to join in company that only recently she had pined for. Now she ached for them all to go away, yet when the time came for everyone to depart she panicked at the thought of the uneasy quiet that must soon fill the room.

Both married couples were staying with Mary at Rowanlea and they all went off into the night, accompanied by Tandy, though he was returning later to share the chaumer with Coulter.

At the last minute Nellie came rushing back to draw Evelyn to her. 'Evie, Evie,' she murmured, stroking the bright hair and holding close the slender young body. 'Try no' to worry your wee head about tomorrow. When the time comes for you to have your speak, just try to remember – we'll all be there praying for you.'

She went away quickly and then just Maggie and Evelyn were left, Murn having gone up to bed some time ago.

Mother and daughter sat, one on either side of the fire, the clock ticking loudly in the sudden quiet of the room. The lamplight poured over Maggie's white hair. She was straight-backed and composed, her hands folded peacefully in her lap, her mouth softly relaxed as she gazed pensively into the flames.

Amongst themselves her daughters marvelled at the quiet dignity which had carried her through to this night. They wondered too how she had managed to cope with the expenses involved in Jamie's trial, which included a complete new rig-out for herself and Evelyn to be worn for the first time the following morning. She had told her daughters the same story she had told Jamie. They all knew about her beginnings, she had never hidden the facts from them and none of them questioned what she now told them, though Nellie said later to Grace, 'There's a puzzle somewhere about our mother's life. I've always felt it but now I feel it even more, though knowing how canny she is wondering is as far as we'll ever get.'

'Mam.' Evelyn broke the silence. 'Let me do your hair.'

Maggie assented at once. 'All right, Evie. It's a long whilie since you did that for me.'

Evelyn went to fetch her mother's hairbrush, and standing at her back undid the two thick plaits of hair which she wore coiled round her head. The heavy tresses cascaded in a shimmering silvery curtain down over Maggie's back to her waist. In a few short minutes a real peace descended over the room, brought about by the homely ritual. The brush whispered through the rippling strands, Maggie's eyes grew heavy, Evelyn felt lulled into a state bordering on tranquillity. Outside in the yard Coulter clattered about with buckets of water for the horses, a frisky wind moaned through the trees and rattled the lum cowlings. But inside King's Croft all was warm and peaceful and safe – just for a little while.

The courtroom was crowded. The folk of Rothiedrum were easily distinguishable amongst the rows of faces. The O'Neils of Cragbogie took up at least a dozen places; beside them, Hinney and Alistair of Hill o'Binney cringed in their seats as the youngest O'Neils made unnecessarily loud comments to one another.

Behind them were the Keiths of Dippiedoon, Kirsty sniffing her disapproval of Betsy's unruly family, though even she had to smile sourly when one of the boys stood up to remove his coat and accidentally knocked awry a staid lum hat one row down. Kirsty was dressed completely in black, the same kind of garb she wore to kirk and to funeral gatherings. She sat ramrod-straight in her seat, her keen eyes darting restlessly about but coming to rest again and again on the Grants sitting quietly together at the front. Her curious glances were not lacking in sympathy. In common with everyone else, she had been shocked by recent events and for once made no comment about the blow Jamie's arrest must have been to Maggie's pride, a quality which had always been a sore point with Kirsty and one which had hitherto provided much fuel for her busy tongue.

'Though mind,' she whispered to her husband, Angus. 'There doesna seem any shortage o' siller in that family, though there's little enough of it in the normal way o' things. Just look at that coat she's wearing. It must have cost a pretty penny, and that hat – a bittie too pretentious to my way o' thinking and hardly fitting for a crofter's wife. But then, Maggie aye did fancy herself head and shoulders above the rest o' us. You dinna think, Angus, she's been to one o' these moneylenders? If so, she'll never be able to pay it back unless she sells the horses – ay, and maybe her soul forbye.'

'Wheesht, woman,' urged a discomfited Angus, wondering what his wife was going to say next, but her attention had wandered to the colourful knot of travelling people. For once she was silent as she mused about the possibility of any of them being called as a witness. She settled herself back in her seat, eyes glinting with unconcealed curiosity regarding the identity of those faces vaguely familiar to her, pondering on where she had seen them before and from which part of the country they hailed.

The folk of the farmtouns were well represented that day. People who knew Jamie and his family well, others who were only slightly acquainted but knew enough about the Grants to hold them in respect. All in all, it was a gathering of homely country people brought there by sympathy, curiosity, and in some a downright thirst for scandal and its damnatory associations.

Maggie sat very still and upright, conscious of the people around her and their varying odours. The smell of stale tobacco was prevalent, all mixed up with foot leather, naphthalene, newly ironed silk. Her outwardly calm exterior gave no indication of the fears that had beset her through the lonely hours of the previous night, fears that had only receded slightly with the arrival of dawn. She thanked God for the comfort of having her family around her but how sorry she felt for Evelyn. She who had once greeted each new day with delight had been too sick with worry to eat anything that morning.

Both Maggie and Nellie had sat with her for as long as possible in the corridor outside the courtroom where she had to wait with the other witnesses, but she had told them she would rather be alone, and they had left her looking delusively tranquil but for two spots of colour high on her cheekbones and her soft young mouth trembling.

It was good to have Nellie present at such a time, Maggie decided. Often she had cursed the young woman's stubbornness, the strength of character that had in the past so often manifested itself in silent disapproval. She wasn't saying anything now, but her vitality of spirit reached out to those closest to her and Maggie, whose own vigour had reached a low ebb, basked in her eldest daughter's stamina and unconsciously squared her shoulders.

A subtle change in the atmosphere surged around the room. The rippling of sound which had previously filled it gradually died away except for a few murmurings and throat-clearings. Another sound took over, electrified the crowd with its heraldic significance, blasted the eardrums of those sitting near enough to bear the full magnitude of the fanfare of trumpets which preceded the entry of the Lord Justice.

In the cells beneath the courtroom, the echoes of the metallic cacophony seemed to the waiting Jamie like some hellish prelude to the arrival of Satan himself. He held tight to his frayed nerves. Soon the waiting would be over with, and he would be taken up there to face the unknown fate that awaited him. He wondered which was worst. The long weeks of dread anticipation of this day – or the trial itself.

Soon he would know the answer – and the hand that held his stubby Stonehaven pipe to his mouth shook a little. They had allowed him the comfort of the homely pipe. The familiar feel of the warm bowl reassured him slightly and he took a deep breath and sat back to wait.

The figure who entered the courtroom might indeed have sprung from the black, ungodly soil of some dread, unknown land. Lord Kirknaben, renowned for his severe and unbending nature, had been called many things in his time. 'The Black Judge', 'The Dark De'il', 'Old Nab 'Em', to mention just a few. His curly grey wig framed a dark, satanic face; enormous, winged black eyebrows shaded a pair of deep-set, glittering black eyes. His aristocratic nose dominated a small, thin mouth. He had the uncanny appearance of a hawk ready to pounce on its victim. Dressed in white robes emblazoned with scarlet crosses, he was a tall, spare, commanding presence, and as the last notes of the trumpets died away the court arose as one to its feet, several of the crowd averting their eyes from the keen penetration of Kirknaben's lordly stare as if they were the ones about to be brought to trial.

Maggie studied him and her stomach flipped over with dismay. She prayed silently and swiftly, 'Oh God, help my Jamie, help him to say the right things. Help us all to be strong.'

Majestically, the judge took his place. Amidst much discomfited feet shuffling the court took theirs and a short, fearful silence filled the room.

Then Jamie appeared from below, brought up by two constables wearing white gloves and carrying batons. His once brown face was deathly pale. He looked thin and ill and it was all he could do to straighten his sagging shoulders. The mass of faces turned towards him instilled in him more terror than the worst nightmares he had experienced since his arrest. Panic constricted his throat, filled his bladder. He felt like some helpless animal trapped by a multitude of hunters. Dear God, he thought, please allow me to keep my dignity, whatever happens.

As he reached the dock, he stumbled and would have

fallen but for the swift support of one of the policemen. He took his place. The mists of fear before his vision allowed him to see only a vast sea of white blobs dotted with black. He took a deep breath. The mist cleared a little. He saw his daughters, their husbands, their dear, familiar faces reflecting the agony he was feeling. He saw Maggie – his Maggie – her unwavering gaze on him, her eyes telling him of her unswerving love and loyalty. A numbness seemed to grip him then, banishing his panic. He threw her a crooked little smile of reassurance – where it came from he didn't know but it was there, hovering on the brink of his consciousness.

Mr Ian Peddie was sitting at the front, rustling his papers a trifle impatiently – as if he couldn't wait to get started. He had made out Jamie's case as 'Defence of Self – Defence of Another'. It looked good on paper. He felt confident it would read equally well. Clearing his throat he stole a sidelong glance at his colleague, Mr Hugh Dalrymple the Advocate Depute, as cool a customer as one could hope to meet and a great dramatist in the courtroom. There would be a lot of show, a good deal of sardonic strutting and pontificating for the benefit of the jury. Mr Ian Peddie, on the other hand, used different tactics. He neither played to the balcony nor to the judge but stated his defence in plain, almost simple terms. He had never let go of that homely, confiding touch. Men and women understood what he had to say and he prided himself on how successfully his courtroom procedure had worked. He rubbed the edge of his aquiline nose and his lazy, warm smile radiated across to Jamie whose identity was now being established, after which the charge of attempted murder with a dangerous weapon was put before him. He was asked how he pleaded. Guilty or not guilty?

'Not guilty.' Jamie's voice wasn't quite steady. His words sounded unreal in his own ears yet their very utterance brought home to him the reality of this most dreadful day in his life.

Mr Hugh Dalrymple gathered up his papers and rose to his feet. Mr Ian Peddie glanced up at the thin, clever face and thought, No show without Punch. The curtain opens, the audience awaits.

Mr Hugh Dalrymple started to speak. The trial had begun.


Evelyn was in the witness box. The first part of her ordeal was over. Mr Ian Peddie had been gentle with her as he had taken her back over the events of the night in the Aulton. At first her mind had been confused, certain aspects of the events leading up to Whisky Jake's attack on her a complete blank, but Mr Peddie was the epitome of patience and gradually it all fitted together, the pieces slotting into place like some intricate jigsaw puzzle. She could feel the sympathy of the courtroom, was aware of the strength of her family reaching out to her.

Now it was Mr Hugh Dalrymple's turn to cross-examine. Looking into his dark, sallow face, his black mocking eyes, she knew there would be no pity there. And he was merciless, starting off his questions quite innocently and slowly, pacing about with his hands folded behind his back, nodding his head thoughtfully as she spoke. Quite suddenly his whole attitude changed, he began to shoot questions at her, barely giving her time to answer, tripping her up, twisting everything till she started to falter, to stumble over what she was saying. He brought back all her previous feelings of degradation, made her feel soiled beyond measure, all the while casting Whisky Jake in a benign light till her head began to reel and her heart to pound so fast she thought she would faint there and then in the witness box.

Quite suddenly his tactics changed again. 'How old are you, Miss Grant?' His tone was pleasant, conversational.

'Seventeen.'

'Ah, seventeen, such a tender, innocent age, and if I may say so, you are a very attractive young lady. No doubt there is a young man – or would it be more apt to say, young men, in your life?'

At that Ian Peddie was on his feet, appealing to the judge that such a question was entirely irrelevant to the case.

'M'Lord, I was merely trying to establish if Miss Grant

has had some experience of the opposite sex,' Mr Hugh Dalrymple drawled suavely. 'It would be helpful for me to find out if I am dealing with a completely inexperienced girl or otherwise.'

The judge overruled Mr Peddie's objection, and it was a triumphant face that Hugh Dalrymple turned back to Evelyn as he repeated his question.

'Ay, there have been young men.' Her voice was barely audible, and she was asked almost coldly to speak up for the benefit of the jury. Haltingly she told him about Johnny, and as she spoke all the old pain came squeezing in on her, crushing her till she felt her heart would burst with grief. When she finished speaking a murmur of sympathy ran through the courtroom. Through a mist she saw her mother's sad face, her father's white, strained one.

Hugh Dalrymple offered words of sympathy but he hardly gave her time to draw breath before he continued his relentless line of questioning and in a dull, flat voice she told him about David, proudly throwing up her head as she finished and saying in a strong voice, 'He's in France now, fighting for his country, I dinna ken when I'll see him again, or if I'll ever see him again. But I tell you this, I'm glad to have known him for the wee while we had together.'

'Quite so, quite so.' He went on to question her further, mainly about Whisky Jake and how long she had known him. 'And that night in your aunt's house, when the alleged assault took place, did you by any chance give Mr McPhee any indication that his attentions would be welcomed by you?'

Up until that moment Evelyn had been afraid of the cold-eyed Advocate Depute. Now all her fears left her to be replaced by a rage so powerful that she trembled with the force of it. Clenching her fists she faced Hugh Dalrymple squarely, her green eyes glittering dangerously as she cried passionately, 'Where I come from people wi' filthy thoughts like yours would be shunned for the rest o' their days. I was brought up in a decent home and was taught good manners from the cradle! I ken fine what is right and what is wrong, but your sort are more to be pitied

306

than laughed at for you havena even the manners or the decency to ken how to address a lady properly!'

The courtroom erupted in uproar with everyone laughing and clapping and the judge crying vainly for order. Evelyn subsided, shocked and horrified at herself. What had she done to her father? The judge would see her outburst as an indication that unruly behaviour ran in the family. Trembling, she glanced at him. To her astonishment she saw a ghost of a smile hovering at his mouth, and his admonishment of her was severe but surprisingly brief.

Hugh Dalrymple was visibly shaken. After a few more questions she was dismissed and walked gladly from the witness box, her head high, a glow in her heart. Nellie followed her out to the corridor. 'Evie, you wee de'il, you should have held your tongue but I would have done exactly the same in your shoes for I suffered along with you back there.'

'Oh Nellie,' Evelyn spoke miserably. 'I've done nothing to help Father and I had planned out so carefully what I was going to say.'

Nellie squeezed Evelyn's small hand, her eyes bleak with the knowledge that her youngest sister had conducted herself with far more decorum than she could ever have done if it had been her in the witness box. Perhaps it was as well that circumstances had prevented her from giving evidence. She wouldn't just have shouted at Hugh Dalrymple, she would have slapped his face for him!

One of the neighbours, who had rushed into the house in the Aulton on hearing Whisky Jake's screams, was now in the witness stand. It was while the prosecuting counsel was on his feet that the door opened and a minor commotion was heard outside. A court official came in, and went straight to Ian Peddie to murmur something in his ear. A strange light appeared in his eyes. Standing up, he begged Hugh Dalrymple's pardon and then walked over to speak quietly to the judge.

Lord Kirknaben listened sourly to what he had to say.

With a slight nod of his be-wigged head he rapped imperiously for order, then announced there would be an adjournment for lunch.

Without further ado Mr Ian Peddie left the courtroom, the light in his eyes more pronounced than ever as he went to meet a key witness in the case.

The court had reassembled. An expectant murmur ran round the room as everyone wondered to each other what was happening. They didn't have to wait long for an answer. The door was thrown wide and into that hallowed room came a procession the like of which had never before penetrated its oaken walls. Grandmother was borne in, a frail but grand old lady, dignity in every wrinkled limb, her head held high, her shrunken frame adorned from head to foot in black silk. Aunt Mattie had been over-zealous with the flat iron, and a scorch mark on the collar of the dress was disguised by an enormous fantail of ancient black lace; the full, voluminous skirt was pulled well down over the stick-thin legs, but even so the black woollen stockings showed plainly against a pair of bunion-embracing pink bedsocks. It had been a supreme effort for the old lady to leave her sickbed, but she had not been known as the matriarch of the travelling people for nothing and she was determined to appear in court that day. The question of mobility had been a difficult one. She was too old and weak to sit in any kind of wheelchair, and so those travellers who had settled down in Aberdeen for the winter were called into service. Now she reclined amongst her cushions in the mode of transport she had used in her latter travelling days, a sort of sedan chair made of cowhide and wood and as elegant in its way as any fashionable carriage in the land. She had been brought along from the Aulton in the doctor's trap, and hadn't stopped complaining till she was safely settled amongst her cushions on the sedan chair.

The four policemen who carried her in were red-faced with self-consciousness, and their various moods were not improved by Grandmother's barked orders warming their ears when they inadvertently jolted her in setting her down beside the witness box.

The travelling people in the room looked at one another in delight. None of them had forgotten Grandmother. Not a few had had their ears cuffed whilst under her administration, but they all remembered her with affection and forgot the scoldings in warm recollections of childhood days when she had mothered them all in their turn and given them puffs of her clay pipe when no one else was looking.

Aunt Mattie had come in at Grandmother's back and now settled herself beside her erstwhile friends. She was received with pleasure amongst them, and had to place a warning finger against her lips as a buzz of whispered questions arose from all sides.

Grandmother was sworn in. She was pert, confident, imperious and absolutely lucid in her description of the things she had witnessed in her kitchen on the evening of Whisky Jake's attempted ravishment of Evelyn.

Clearly and concisely she answered all the questions put to her by Mr Hugh Dalrymple, and when he suggested that she had been too ill on the evening in question to be able to make much sense of anything she almost snapped his head off with her assertions to the contrary, and turning to Lord Kirknaben she told him, 'I might be auld but I'm no' blind and in the Lord's sight I'm tellin' the truth o' the matter and that's that.'

The judge had not batted one bushy eyebrow during the old lady's entry, but now one hairy appendage arose in a somewhat admonitory gesture, though the dry, tight smile he bestowed on her was brought about by admiration of her undoubted command of both the situation to hand and of Mr Hugh Dalrymple, who was visibly wilting under the pressure of her asperity. Several times in the next half-hour order had to be called in court, as the old lady's droll wit sent wave after wave of amused titters through the gathering. She was also able to throw in a damning indict-ment of Whisky Jake's character despite Lord Kirknaben's admonishments, and when the time came for her to be freed from the witness stand she was smiling triumphantly and waving an encouraging hand at Jamie as

309

the policemen manhandled her chair into a carrying position.

'I'm no' leaving,' she told them sternly as they were about to take her out of the room. 'Put me doon beside Mattie here and be canny aboot it. I'm no made o' rubber in case ye havena noticed.'

The judge was talking to the jury, summing up the case. They retired to deliberate, their sedate demeanour giving no indication of the shouting and debating that was to follow in the jury room.

The jury seemed to the waiting crowd to be gone forever, but eventually they returned and the Clerk of Court asked who spoke for them. The foreman stood up. 'I do.'

'And what is your verdict?'

The foreman cleared his throat almost apologetically as he replied, 'Guilty with a recommendation for leniency.'

Lord Kirknaben took heed of the jury's recommendation for mitigation of sentence and pronounced a sentence of four years' imprisonment on Jamie. No amount of rapping for order could stem the flow of utter astonishment that ran through the crowd, for everyone had expected a much harsher sentence, twelve years at least for such a serious crime as attempted murder. Grandmother's evidence had undoubtedly swayed the judge's thinking, and he gave her an almost conspiratorial nod of his elegantly adorned head as he got up to make his gracious way out. But to Maggie and her family the sentence was almost too much to bear. During the passing of it Jamie had stood quite straight and proud, but as he was led away to the cells below he sagged as if weighed down by a great burden.

Maggie had to brace herself before going to see him. The tears that she had fought so long to contain threatened to spill over but she knew that for his sake she had to summon every last ounce of her self-control. When finally she faced him she was silent, unable suddenly to find any words of comfort for the man she had loved for the greater part of her life. This tired, beaten soul was her Jamie, the gypsy king who once strode tall and proud through life and whose dark eyes had flashed with the love and delight of it.

'Jamie.' She held out her hand. He took it and held it tight. 'Jamie,' her eyes filled with tears, 'after all these years o' living with you I – I dinna ken what to say.'

'Maggie, Maggie lass.' He took her to him and held her close. 'It could have been worse. The judge was lenient. Four years may sound a lot but it will pass, dinna worry about me. It's you I'm thinking about. How will you manage the croft on your own?'

'The neighbours have been good, Jamie, things will go on, but I wonder if I can – without you.' The days and nights stretched before her – empty, meaningless.

'You and Evelyn will have each other – look after her well, Maggie, it will take her a long time to get over this.'

The skin of his hands was rough and calloused with a little dent on the inside of each thumb where he had held the plough. 'I'll do that, Jamie.' The tears could not be held back any longer. Her hands slid out of his, and she went hurriedly away from him before the pride that had held her together all her days crumbled into ruins and became just so much chaff in the wind.


Three weeks later Whisky Jake came before Lord Benelvie, a mild little man with faded blue eyes and a habit of seeming half-asleep when serving in court. Whisky Jake, looking little the worse for his experiences, fairly bristled with contempt as he beheld the judge's benign, puckered, elf-like face under the heavy wig. 'You could sweep the gutters with the poor wee bastard and still he wouldn't waken enough to protest,' he thought, with a self-satisfied curl of his cruel lips.

Mr Duncan Sneddon made out a good case on his client's behalf. Jake had applied to the Poor Law for aid and this strutting young peacock had been the result. Still he was good, Whisky Jake had to admit that. Take away all the acting and he was as hard as any man Jake had ever encountered. But his voice was too soft, about as effective as spreading dung on Tarmacadam – still, what he had to

311

say made up for the lack of forcefulness. Hugh Dalrymple, on the other hand, boomed, pontificated, and expostulated like some bloody prima donna on stage. He gave Jake a hard time of it, but even so he was feeling smug as the judge gave a discreet, stuttering cough before pronouncing sentence. Whisky Jake puffed out his chest and threw Mr Duncan Sneddon a sly, almost triumphant smile. The doddery old gnome in the judge's chair had a reputation for doling out lenient sentences, he looked as if he was about to fall asleep as he opened his mouth – to yawn or to speak? Whisky Jake gave a mental snigger and set his shoulders well back.

Twelve years' penal servitude! The effect of Lord Benelvie's words on the packed courtroom was as devastating as Lord Kirknaben's had been. Jake just about choked on his rising gorge, and had to be thumped on the back by one of the be-gloved policemen who looked as if he was enjoying the experience. The prisoner recovered and was led away, a stream of vitriol issuing from lips that were twisted with fury.

Despite herself, Maggie smiled. Good riddance to bad rubbish! It would be a long while before that filthy beast was set free to mix with decent folk.

Nellie sat quiet, though she seethed inside. It had been a dreadful experience. All the time she had been aware of Jake's glittering black eyes, and though the courtroom was well-lit she remembered the darkness, the evil phantoms of the nightmarish world, a wild beast who stalked the night and had taken as its victim an innocent young girl whose future life would be warped by the premature exposure to such ungodly lusts.

Now it was her turn to demonstrate her power. It would mean another kind of exposure, that of laying bare her soul to the world – but for her father's sake she was prepared to do it, and the sooner the better!

The very next day a reporter from the local newspaper appeared at the kitchen door. Maggie opened the door to him, hesitating when he announced who he was and why he had come.

312

'Let him in, Mother.' Nellie's voice floated through. 'I've been expecting him.'

As the young man was ushered inside Nellie remained where she was at the fireside, quite calm-looking except for those external signs which had always betrayed her inner agitation, twin spots of colour burning high on her cheeks, a flush on her neck rapidly rising to stain her ears. Only she, Maggie and Evelyn were present in the house, the others having departed to their respective homes and tasks – even Kenneth had had to go back to Kenneray to help with the winter ploughing.

George Robertson might be young but he was highly efficient at his job. In a few short minutes he had extracted enough relevant information from Nellie to make both Evelyn and her mother sit back in their seats as if a heavy hand had pushed them. But neither of them uttered a word – they were too dumbfounded even to think properly and so George Robertson made notes, drank tea, even seemed to thoroughly enjoy himself in the homely atmosphere of the kitchen. Mentally he was rubbing his hands together. This would make a nice change from war news – ay, he could hardly wait to get back to the office to set it all out as dramatically as he knew how. He adjusted his spectacles and smiled encouragingly at Nellie – a good-looking young woman, a bit skinny maybe but eyes that said it all and a mouth that was made for more than just talking.

'Keep going, Mrs Cameron,' he urged pleasantly. Nellie did, as if she was glad to get it all out of her system at last, as if she couldn't stop once she had started. When George Robertson finally departed Evelyn got up, squeezed her sister's hand in the passing, and went up to her room leaving the other two in the kitchen together.

Nellie moved restlessly under her mother's keen scrutiny as she wondered what was coming. The secrets of her heart had been held there for so long now that she felt strangely lightheaded, as if something dark and heavy had been lifted from her. But – how must it have sounded to those who had hitherto accepted her strange ways as a part of her personality?

313

'That was a brave thing for you to do.' Maggie shook her head as if still trying to assimilate everything she had just heard. 'I can understand you so much better now – I only wish I had known all those years ago. I never could fathom why you mistrusted men so much – even your very own father.'

'You mustna blame him for what happened,' Nellie urged. 'He was drunk at the time and as witless as the next man. For too many years I hated him for it, but it's over wi' now and I just hope that what I had to tell will do him some good. Now—' she jumped to her feet – 'I hardly tasted my tea for all that talking and I'm that drouthy I could drink a pot to myself. Would you like another cup?'

'Do you think—' Maggie spoke firmly '—I might have a dram instead? I never expected any o' this today and the shock o' it is telling on me now.'

'Ay, why not?' Nellie marched to the scullery and returned with the whisky bottle and two glasses, saying with a droll little smile, 'And I might as well join you – after all – it's no' every day I get to tell my life story to the newspapers – is it?'

The following day the story broke. The whole of the north-east fairly vibrated with the wagging of tongues. Rothiedrum, hardly recovered from the last series of sensational happenings to beset the Grants, rose from its knees to fly to one another's houses, clutching newspapers and paper bags filled with precious savings of tea, for it was considered impolite in those days of shortage to visit a neighbour and expect them to dole out their tea ration. Before the next few days were over, Bunty Lovie was so hard put to supplying her customers with the scarce commodity that they were forced to resort to buttermilk and anything else their farm animals could provide in the way of liquid, though in the case of the menfolk there was little problem as they could always fall back on George the Forge's homemade beer with never the need for any excuses to their womenfolk as regards alcoholic excesses.

Such was the public outcry over the whole affair that

Jamie's counsel sought to appeal over his sentence, which was eventually halved to two years.

Maggie was out in the stable when this news came to her. Queenie's breath blew soft over her cheek as she stroked the velvety nose and murmured comforting sounds. A week before the new foal had dropped warm and steamy from its mother's body. Everyone had rejoiced, but none more than Jamie when he heard the glad tidings. 'We'll get a good price for it, Maggie,' he had told her with conviction. 'It will see you by for a whilie anyway.'

Five days later the foal was dead, its intestine ruptured through colic.

'These things happen, Maggie lass,' Tandy had comforted awkwardly.

'Ay, they happen, Tandy,' Maggie agreed dully and walked out of the stable and over the yard to Jamie's shoppe. There she sat for a long time. All around her the cobwebs were already gathering. They hung from the rafters, wafted in gossamer trails over the bench and the lasts and the pairs of boots standing on the shelves waiting for the final touches.

'You'll wait long to be finished now,' she whispered into the silence, and putting her head in her hands wept bitter tears of loneliness and frustration.

Now this news. Brought to her by Nellie who had stayed with her since Jamie's trial in February. It was March now, and the scouring dry winds of early spring swept over the countryside. Around this time Jamie would be striding out to assess his 'bit ground', letting his optimistic imagination have full rein as his eyes swept over his few acres, picturing the waist-high corn, the fields of golden hay. In the normal way of things it was a good time for them all, an awakening, an anticipation of summer suns and soft rains that would give to them what every crofter and farmer needed to keep their lives in balance – an abundant 'hairst' and a contented stock of animals.

But as Nellie came over the yard to the stable, Maggie wasn't looking forward to anything. She was looking back, back at a past that seemed all at once rosy and desirable despite its ups and downs and disquieting uncertainties. But all along there had been Jamie, and now that he was no longer by her side she felt all her old strength slipping away leaving her vulnerable and afraid. As if on the breath of the wind, his voice kept coming to her: '*We'll still have each other, lass, we'll aye have each other.*'

The eyes she turned on her eldest daughter were dull and uninterested, but for the sake of conversation she said, 'The old lass is missing her foal, Nellie, she canna understand why it's been taken from her.'

'She'll get over it,' Nellie said gently. 'We all have to carry on no matter how hard it seems at the time.'

She put her arm round her mother and led her over to the corn kist where she made her sit down. Her voice was soft when she broke the news to her mother, very un-Nellie-ish and sympathetic.

A small stab of hope pierced Maggie's heart when her daughter had finished speaking. She glanced through the door of the stable to the bare parks lying beyond. A shaft of sunlight was breaking through the clouds. Upon it rode a flock of gulls, their wings flashing pure white as they swooped down into a golden pool of light that seemed to swallow up the winter grey of the earth leaving it rich and fertile and ready for the first scatterings of spring seeds.

Coulter was clattering about in the yard, taking swill to the pigs. Queenie gave a quiet little snicker and nuzzled Maggie's arm gently with her nose. Bella, the cow, was lowing a trifle impatiently from the byre, as if she couldn't wait to be released from her long winter of confinement.

Maggie stood up and smiled at her daughter. 'There's work to be done, Nellie, and when next I see your father I want to be able to tell him his acres have been planted.'

# PART 5

# Summer/Autumn 1917

# CHAPTER EIGHTEEN

Evelyn ran swiftly through the long grasses on the end rigs of the cornfield, her limbs flashing golden against the bright bitter green of the sprouting corn. Beneath her feet a myriad of wild flowers danced in the June breezes, above her the sun blazed in a brilliant blue sky; on the hedgerows masses of perfumed pink and white hawthorn flowers hung over the heads of meadow-sweet, and the butter-coloured blossoms of the broom splashed themselves daringly over the sombre dark green of their foliage; in the little pinewoods above King's Croft carpets of bluebells flourished under the cool shadows of the trees. Evelyn paused atop a hillock and spread her arms as if to embrace the glories of the summer's day to her heart. Yet she couldn't contain the joys of that day inside herself. A peewit scuttled hurriedly by, ushering her fluffy round babies away from any hint of danger, and Evelyn tossed back her red head and gave a chuckle of pure delight. She didn't want to look back, back at King's Croft lying down there in the hollow, looking so peaceful with a thin curl of smoke rising from the chimney and the washing flapping lazily on the drying green. It was difficult to believe that Grace lay ill in bed behind one of those attic windows, recovering from an operation for stomach ulcers but more from the grief that had made the long climb back from her illness one she'd had neither the will nor the strength to face. Her beloved Gordon lay dead in a grave in France, killed by a shell that had hit the field hospital in which he had been working. Many of the patients and medical staff had been buried in the rubble of the building, most of them killed outright, including Major Gordon Chisholm. He had been in the operating room at the time. Working to the last.

Evelyn shuddered and turned her eyes away from her home. It was too painful to visualize a Grace so drastically changed in mind, body, and heart that she hadn't wanted to share her old room with her youngest sister but had asked instead to sleep in the one once shared by Nellie and Murn.

Evelyn walked on, forcing her mind onto happier things. In two months time her father would be coming home, his sentence having been reduced to eighteen months. It would be so wonderful to have him back again – yet nothing would ever be the same as it had been. Everyone had been good, helpful, kind. Neighbours and friends had rallied round to help all they could but it hadn't been enough. King's Croft had gone downhill, signs of neglect were evident everywhere. Evander Forbes had told Maggie that she need only pay half-rent for the croft, but typically she had told him she could manage and in the process had used every last penny from the money she had made out of selling her cousin's necklace. Lady Marjorie herself had come to visit Maggie. She had arrived looking very much on the defensive, but went away again with a humble expression on her face and did not even complain when the hem of her elegant dress got covered in dung as she was crossing the yard to the waiting trap.

Evelyn never knew what transpired between her mother and the mistress of Rothiedrum, but afterwards, neither Evelyn nor Maggie were ever without work of some sort from the Big House, be it cushion covers to embroider or loose covers to hem. Evelyn was glad enough of the opportunity to make a little money, for she had been needed so badly at home that she had had to leave her job at Rothiedrum, but she knew it galled her mother to apply herself to such menial tasks for the gentry.

'Why do you do it, Mam?' Evelyn had once asked.

'A cat may look at a Queen,' her mother answered with a wry little smile.

'But Mam, never in all your life before have you implied that any member of Rothiedrum House is better than your-self!' Evelyn cried, feeling that if her mother lost her pride in herself, she would lose everything.

'You mistake my meaning, lassie,' Maggie replied with a conscious lifting of her chin. 'Try putting the boot on the other foot and you will know who licks which.'

Evelyn stared at her mother for a long, breathless moment. Then, as one, they burst into such infectious laughter that old Coulter stepped in from the yard to take advantage of their lighthearted mood and help himself to tea from the ever-brewing pot on the hob, and to new baked soda scones from the plateful cooling on the table.

Evelyn thought of these things as she came out onto the turnpike, which she crossed to take the short cut along to Rothiedrum House. Gillan was sitting with his mother on the wide lawn in front of the house. Mother and son made an elegant picture in such an attractive setting, with a magnificent copper beech tree spreading its dappled shade over them and two golden spaniels reclining beside the little white garden table in front of them. Lady Marjorie looked cool and sophisticated in a pale green silk dress with a huge picture hat casting its shadow over her smooth-skinned, attractive face. Gillan was wearing only a light shirt and flannel slacks and from a distance he looked handsome, fit and suntanned. But he had been badly wounded in the first phase of the Battle of Arras, suffering a broken hip and multiple fractures. He had spent some time in a French hospital recovering from his wounds before being shipped home to a hospital in England, and from there to Rothiedrum. He had been home for almost a month now, trying to reconcile himself to the wonderful peace of the north-east countryside after the din and upheaval of the front. He was one of thousands who had been wounded at the Battle of Arras, thousands more were dead or missing. The north-east alone had lost the cream of its youth – skimmed off, and the blood of it washed away in the mud and rainwater of the front lines.

Whole families had been devastated by the losses of fathers, sons, brothers, uncles. Arras had been a time of pride and of mourning for Scotland. Many sons of Rothiedrum would never come back. Alan Keith had been killed at the Battle of the Somme in November 1916.

Evelyn had been helping Coulter clean out the pig pens when she knew Alan was no longer of this life. It had been a cold, frosty winter day, mist lay dank in the haughs, the

Birkie chuckled secretively beneath wraiths of haar, the dour-grey shoulders of Bennachie loomed sullenly through blankets of slow-moving white cloud, all over the parks the breath of every living creature emerged to hang in condensed little puffs, Coulter's own mingled with his pipe smoke, a plump drip suspended from the end of one dilated nostril as he humped forkfuls of pig dirt over to the dung pile.

Evelyn giggled at sight of the drip, and was about to offer Coulter her hanky when her eye was caught by a movement in the fields beyond King's Croft. A figure was striding over the braes from the direction of Dippiedoon, a solid enough figure it seemed from this distance, yet the mists surrounding it lent an insubstantial aura to the briskly swinging limbs, the proud kilt frisking about legs that plunged down into the clinging haar. The figure came nearer and she saw the tall form, the dark hair, the thin, clever face of Alan Keith.

Pushing back her hair, she was about to exclaim, 'Alan's come home!' but something beyond the realms of reason stayed her.

'Alan.' Her lips formed the name as the figure came nearer, clear, clean, and whole, a little smile quirking the sensitive mouth she knew so well. His long legs carried him swiftly, soon he had reached the gate to come out onto the track, then he was coming over the cobbles, straight towards her. She put out her hand as if to touch him, but shivered instead when he looked into her eyes and the voice of him spoke inside her head.

'Florrie's well, Evie, Johnny too, they both send their love.'

That was all, no more, no less, just an echo of Alan's voice, a mere sensing of thoughts reaching her from him. A feeling of such cold gripped her that she felt numb with it. Her hand went to her mouth, the hand that only a moment ago had reached out – to touch someone that was without substance.

'Alan, I'm so sorry, I wanted so much for you to live.'

She hadn't uttered a single word but the spirit that was

Alan received the message from her mind. 'Dinna grieve for me, Evie.' The pale mouth was smiling a little. 'You of all people ought to know this was the way I wanted it to be. After Florrie, there was nothing – now there is everything and I'm content.'

Then he was gone from her, as if he had never been, leaving her strangely calm as she said to Coulter, 'Alan's dead, Coulter, I saw him and he spoke to me.'

The old man stopped dead in his tracks, his grizzled face blanching under its weathered tan. 'Havers, lassie,' he spoke forcibily, 'there's no one here but you and me and yon pigs grunting in the pen.'

'He came to me, Coulter, over the brae from Dippiedoon. He said he was happy, that he wanted it to be the way it was.'

Coulter rasped a horny hand across his nose and glanced uneasily over his shoulder. Of all the people in Rothiedrum he knew best about witches, fairies and bad wee elves who did awful things to folk if they were out of temper, but ghosts – that was another matter entirely – yet who was he to discount the mysteries that lay beyond the grave? Evie was a bright, healthy, happy lass, but there had been talk. It was said that, like Hinney, she had the sixth sense and sometimes knew when something was about to happen or sensed it had happened before anybody else kent a thing about it . . .

Reaching out, he put one big strong old hand on her shoulder. 'Come on, quine, there's work to be done. We'll ken soon enough if anything has happened to the Keith lad so dinna dwell on it any longer.'

'Alan's dead, Coulter,' she repeated, weak suddenly, glad of Coulter's strong arm about her as he led her into the house for 'a wee tate o' the de'il's spirit.'

The report of Alan's death reached the Keiths soon afterwards. 'He died bravely and selflessly,' it read. 'You have every reason to be proud of having such a brave young man for a son.' Kirsty Keith immediately went into mourning and hadn't come out of it. She grew quiet, introverted, talking in a strange, distant voice of the past, of Alan in his childhoold, of Alan in young manhood living for the day when his talents would take him on to art college. The future had shone brightly then, now there was nothing, only empty dreams of what might have been.

Remembering that time, Evelyn shivered despite the sun's heat beating off the lawns of Rothiedrum. Gillan saw her approaching and came forward to meet her, still limping, a defect that might never leave him though in every other aspect he was well and vigorous with the smile back in the deep brown of his eyes.

'Princess.' He took her hands and stood back to admire her. At nineteen she had grown into a beautiful young woman, slender and shapely in her light summer dress, the bodice of it moulding to the soft curves of her breasts. Her thick curtain of red hair was now piled up on top of her head and pinned in place, but on her flight over the fields a few shining strands had come loose to fall about her small ears in attractive disarray.

'You'll never grow up, will you?' he laughed. 'Still the untidy little girl I first met in George the Forge's smiddy one summer day such as this one.'

'Ach, I would hate ever to be all stiff and perfect,' she told him with a touch of annoyance, because Lady Marjorie was looking her way and she could almost picture the elegant eyebrows raised in disapproval. Gillan led her back to the table where his mother greeted the new arrival with a slight nod. 'Pour yourself some tea, Evelyn,' she invited, 'we have just had ours. You can't stay long, I'm afraid. We have a guest staying, and as he's rather old we like to give him all the peace and quiet a person of his age needs.'

At that, Gillan threw back his head and burst out laughing. 'Uncle Lindsay – old! He'll still be young when he's a hundred and that's eons away, so he's got plenty of living to do. What's gotten into you, Mother? You know he loves having young people around, and enjoyed meeting Evie last time he was here.'

Evelyn laid the flat package she had been carrying on the table. 'Dinna worry about it, Gillie,' she said with a haughty toss of her head that was not lost on her ladyship. 'There are some o' us who canna spare the time to be idle—' here she looked so directly at Gillan's mother that the good lady gave a small, audible gasp and flushed crimson with ill-concealed annoyance. 'I won't stop to drink tea,' Evelyn continued, secretly enjoying the woman's discomfiture and Gillan's obvious amusement. 'George the Forge promised me a brew of his ale if I went along to help him wi' the horses, so if you'll pardon—'

'Evelyn Grant!' Lady Marjorie's cry of outrage couldn't be contained. 'You don't mean to tell me you actually drink ale with the village blacksmith? From what I hear, the man is a positive ogre where young women are concerned. Such are the disgraceful happenings in his premises that I have had occasion to ask my husband to speak to him about his behaviour.'

'Did Father do it?' Gillan inquired with interest.

Her ladyship's lips snapped tightly together. Not only had Evander refused to speak to the blacksmith, he had actually laughed his head off at the recounting of some of George's adventures, so that Lady Marjorie had eventually taken herself off, huffed, insulted – and secretly fascinated by the tales of the big-bellied man who had for years kept the Rothiedrum horses in good fettle, and who had once dared to pinch her bottom when she ventured into the smiddy to find out when her son's horse would be ready.

More might have been said on the subject, but a tall, distinguished-looking gentleman was just then coming out of the French windows and making his way towards them. He was dressed in frock tails and a pair of such ancient plus-fours that the knee of one leg was faintly discernible through the worn threads. Wings of white hair escaped a scuffed lum hat, his smooth face was lavishly covered in white whiskers threaded through with streaks of auburn, his eyes under a set of enormously bushy eyebrows were keen and piercing and utterly void of deception of any kind. He was twirling a walking cane as he approached, throwing it up in the air, trying to catch it though missing four times out of five.

'Saw a chap do this in the Boer War,' he chuckled as he drew nearer, 'he was a drum major and nearly had us all killed we were so busy watching him twirling and throwing. I've practised the same bloody moves for years but never could master much of it.'

He pulled up abruptly at the sight of Evelyn who was standing watching him, pleasure lighting her face. 'Child,' he beamed, throwing out the palm of one hand in a delighted gesture, 'how wonderful to see you again – and how you've grown since that last time. You were just a scimp of a lass then, now . . .'

He took her hand and pumped it up and down heartily while she beamed at him with pleasure equal to his. 'Sir,' she acknowledged, 'I never kent you were here. How truly good it is to see you again.'

'Just arrived a few days ago, Evelyn. I thought it was time I popped over to see the old landscape.'

'I had no idea you two had met before,' commented Lady Marjorie dryly.

Lord Lindsay Ogilvie turned to his niece. 'Of course you did, Marjorie, no doubt old Chamberpot set the jungle drums a-humming in order that my meeting with Evelyn would reach your ears in good time. You never made a convincing liar, my dear, and your abilities on that score have not improved with time.' He swung his attention back to Evelyn. 'It must be, let me see—'

'Four years,' supplied Evelyn, sucking in her breath with delight at his use of her favourite nickname for Mrs Chalmers. 'Gillie had the house to himself and invited me over to meet you. I was about fifteen then.'

'Uncle.' Her ladyship had stood up in some agitation. 'I really think you should go back to the house and lie down for a while. You said yourself the journey took a lot out of you and Miss Grant is just leaving anyway.'

'Nonsense, Marjorie,' Lord Lindsay answered skittishly, 'I am quite recovered from my travels and I'm sure Evelyn can spare some time for an old man.' Graciously, he crooked his arm. She took it, giggling a little, both at the surprise of the occasion and at the look of outrage on Lady Marjorie's face.

'You don't mind, do you, Gillan old man?' Lord Lindsay winked at his grand-nephew who had been observing the exchanges with a great deal of unconcealed enjoyment.

'Of course not, Uncle.' He nodded with a complying wink. 'You two young people go along and enjoy yourselves.'

The old man threw back his head and roared with gratified mirth before sweeping Evelyn away towards the house. He led her upstairs and along a corridor to his bedroom, saying at the door, 'I know it isn't the done thing for a gentleman to invite a lady into his bedroom—' he paused, remembering. It was exactly what he had done with Evelyn's grandmother, a red-haired young maidservant who had bowled him over completely with her chaste beauty. He had been nineteen, she a year younger. It had been a brief, passionate affair, filled with vain promises, vows of undying love. Margaret Innes Grant, as she now was, had been the result of it – and now Evelyn, his grandchild . . . totally ignorant of who he was yet as drawn to him as he was to her.

'Sir?' She was looking at him in puzzlement and he shook himself out of his reverie to lead her into the room and make her sit down on the padded window seat.

'I was hoping you would come, my dear child,' he said, going towards a bureau and unlocking one of the drawers. 'I have something I want to give you.'

Coming back to sit beside her, he placed in her hands an oblong leather box. 'Open it, Evelyn,' he urged, 'it isn't a very pretty thing but it caught my eye when I was in Aberdeen yesterday visiting some old friends and I felt somehow – drawn to it.'

Rather unwillingly, Evelyn opened the box to reveal an unattractive gold necklace set with blood-red garnets. Lifting it out of its box, she held it up. The sunlight thrust spears of light into the stones, setting the hearts of them on fire. For a long time she stared at the glinting stones; then she put the necklace back in its box and shut the lid with a snap before looking wordlessly into his face.

'Of course I knew you wouldn't accept it, Evelyn,' he

327

told her softly, 'but listen to me just for a few minutes. Have you ever seen something and felt somehow it belonged – in the family—'

He paused once more, his thoughts carrying him back to the previous day and the shock of seeing his niece's necklace reposing in the grubby window of a back-street jeweller's shop. On going in to inquire about it, he had learned from the proprietor that the necklace had been sold to him almost two years before. But what with the war and all – no one had seen fit to buy such a fine piece of jewellery.

The little man – he had been little, seedy, and with a sly look about him of an opportunist mentally rubbing his hands together – had managed to get a few grumbles out of his system before Lord Lindsay probed deeper. The man had been quite eager to talk. Hadn't the gentleman heard of the scandal that had shaken the north-east back in early 1916? It had been in all the papers. Everyone had known of it.

'Never mind that,' Lord Lindsay had interrupted. 'The necklace? Can you describe the person who brought it to you?'

The little old man could. Very precisely he had drawn a perfect word picture of Margaret Innes Grant right down to her shabby clothes, her air of having bestowed a favour upon him with the transaction.

'Proud she was, sir, despite her clothes. A way of holding herself, straight up and down, and a kind o' haughty way of lookin' down her nose as if the like o' her was better than the like o' me. Ay, and she had a nerve too for it was only later that I found out she was the wife o' the man stood up for attempted murder. Mind you, no one ever blamed Jamie Grant for what he did to that bloody auld tink. Might have done the same myself if it had been my daughter. But forbye, I darena like to think where the wife got the necklace. She didna look the thieving sort, but then, one can never tell what goes on under a body's skin.'

Lord Ogilvie had put two and two together. His daughter had eaten humble pie in her endeavours to get her husband the best defence counsel she could, and his niece had handed over something that was scant loss to her one way or another. In a way it was poetic justice, but he had been too preoccupied at the time to fully appreciate that fact. He had bought back the neckace and paid far too much for it despite a bout of haggling, which only resulted in a pittance off the display price. The fly little beggar had probably only paid Maggie half of what he was now gloating over, but Lord Ogilvie was feeling far too buoyant to give it a second thought. He was a very rich man. His daughter would never deign to take a farthing off him, but through his granddaughter he might successfully decant the necklace back into the Grant family – and if Maggie found out about it so much the better. It would be too late for her to do anything as she couldn't very well make her daughter give it back . . .

Evelyn was regarding him in some bemusement. 'I'm not family, Lord Ogilvie, and you ken well enough I cannot accept this from you so please – dinna embarrass me by going on about it.'

'Evelyn.' He took her hand and smiled beguilingly into her eyes. 'My dear child, you are every bit as proud and as stubborn as I am myself. We're a couple of mules you and I, kicking against one another, but believe me I – I feel that you have as much right to be in this house with this family as I have myself and forbye all that, I happen to know that you have been through troubled times recently.' She started a little at that and made to pull away from him, but he held tight to her hands. 'Child, I know all about it, the servants have a way of broadcasting such things—' He hadn't been long enough at Rothiedrum House to have heard anything much in the way of gossip, but it was the first thing that came into his head. 'Take this necklace and make an old man happy. I bought it with you in mind and if you can't bring yourself to make use of it now, then think of the future. Your father is coming home soon, I believe – home to what? A once prosperous little croft falling in ruins about him? The realization that his wife and daughter have suffered badly in his absence and have had to go without in order to keep a roof over their heads? Oh, I know Evander is a good landlord and probably offered your mother all sorts of help, but if she is anything like her daughter she will have refused all such offers – and for what? Pride is a fine thing in its place, but too much of it can be as ruinous as too little.'

Evelyn fought a short, bitter battle with herself. She couldn't accept this gift from a man she barely knew. It was against everything she had ever been taught, against all her own principles – but then she thought of her father, how frail he had become in prison, how much he was looking forward to coming back to a place that only existed in his memories . . .

'All right,' she found herself saying, 'I shouldn't but – I will and och – to hell with it! I dinna ken right what I'm saying but thank you. It will come in fine for—'

'A rainy day?' he suggested with a twinkle.

'Ay, if you like – and while you're in the mood for giving there's something else I would like, that bonny red rose in your buttonhole. I'll press it into my diary and think o' you whenever I open the pages.'

Solemnly, he removed the dusky blossom and fixed it to the collar of her dress. It nestled against her skin, fragrant, flawless, as smooth as the bloom on her own young face. Taking out a grubby linen square, he blew his nose loudly. 'A very satisfactory afternoon of transactions – I've never known such a happy time—' His voice was husky. He turned away, shoulders stooped, suddenly looking old. 'Excuse me, child, something in my eye, I think—'

A pain, raw, unexplained, gripped her heart. Gently, she placed her hand on his arm. 'Please, sir . . .'

Abruptly, he turned back to her. 'Enough of the "sir", just call me plain old Oggie – it's what my devilish friends call me and I like it far better. A title can be irksome to someone like me – far too stuffy for words.'

'Oggie.' She giggled at the feel of the name on her tongue. 'Right, Oggie it is, but only when we're alone together, Lady Marjorie would think me both mad and bad if I took such liberties in front of her.'

He stood up and saluted her, his hand knocking the lum hat into a rakish angle. 'Evie and Oggie will walk together in the rose gardens before dinner and I will tell you about an Irish batman I had in the Boer War.'

'What was his name?'

He paused only momentarily. 'Foggie!'

Giggling like a couple of children, the old man and the young girl walked arm in arm down the back stairs and out into the sun-drenched gardens.

When she got home she went up to her room and put the leather box containing the necklace into the lockable tin box that housed her diary and a few other personal items. The hand that turned the key in the lock shook a little as guilt, shame and a touch of defiance accelerated her heartbeat. Straightening, she stood back to stare at the box sitting innocently under her bed. The ugly bit of jewellery would stay there, she decided. She would never look at it again, never even dream of using it for the things suggested by Lord Ogilvie. She had only accepted it to please him. He didn't understand how people like herself lived – didn't know what it was like to be poor but proud. Her father would come home. Things would get better. In time King's Croft would be as it once had been and the only way to achieve that was by hard work and unstinting effort . . .

A sound at her door made her turn her head sharply. Grace stood there, thin, gaunt, a shadow of the beauty she had once been. 'Evie, I thought I heard you coming up.' Her voice was weak, barely audible. 'Would you come in and read to me for a whilie? It's so quiet in the room by myself.'

Evelyn's heart lifted. For the first time since coming home Grace had admitted to a rebellion against her own company – and she also wanted her sister to read to her. At long last she was sitting up and taking an interest in life.

Evelyn took her sister's frail hand. 'Ay, of course I'll read to you – and Grace, I was wondering what to do about a hedgehog I found yesterday in a ditch. It had been hit by something and its leg was twisted a bittie. It's in a box in the byre – and I got rid of all its fleas by bathing it in a mild solution of carbolic. Will I bring it up so that you can have a look at it?'

Grace smiled. 'Ay, you fly wee whittrock, bring it up – and you needn't have bothered your head about the fleas. They don't go on humans though it's maybe just as well you got rid o' them. Mam would have a fit if she saw an army o' fleas marching about on my bedcovers – all following a poor wee hedgehog who canna run fast enough to get away from them!'

It was very pleasant to be walking in the Aulton with Gillan, Evelyn thought. His hand was clasped companionably over hers, his walk slow and easy as they strolled past the Town House towards the Brig of Balgownie. The Cathedral bell was chiming out the hour of noon and the Chanonry gentlemen were making their leisurely way home to lunch. It was all very peaceful with the fronds of summer greenery overhead and the June sun hot on their bare arms. Gillan had rolled his shirt sleeves to the elbows, his limbs were healthily sunburned and his face wore a relaxed look as he talked about the small pleasantries of life. She had felt very close to him these last few weeks. He had stopped trying to impress his feelings on her and as a result there was an air of ease between them, a harmony such as had never existed between them before.

It was as she had always wanted it. They were just good friends – yet, contrarily, she had on several occasions found herself hankering after something more, though what it was she could never quite be certain for she had no desire to reawaken his old passions nor the feeling of guilt inside herself at not being able to respond to him as he had wanted. She loved him as a brother – that was all, and all there ever would be between them, and she was glad that she had been able to make his time at Rothiedrum a happy one for soon he must return again to lead his men in a war that seemed to go on and on. He was Captain Forbes now. Strange to think of him like that, she mused, looking at him quickly. He was only twenty-one after all, yet he was a

332

leader of men and a bit of a war veteran in his own way with a few decorations for gallantry.

He caught her look and smiled, his teeth white in his tanned face. Swinging his hand high, she said exuberantly, 'Oh, Gillie, it's so good to be with you like this. I've loved my time with you this summer. I hope when the war finishes we'll walk again in the Aulton – it never changes and some summer's day in the future we'll come here again and walk hand in hand along the Chanonry with the college gentlemen strolling by and maybe the urban cows skittering along to do awful things all over the professors' polished boots.'

She was still suddenly. How silly to say the Aulton hadn't changed! Of course, it would never be the same again without Grandmother and Aunt Mattie in the cottage in College Bounds. The old lady had passed away peacefully in her sleep one winter's night last year, and come the spring Aunt Mattie had returned to her nomadic way of life, and was probably at this very moment encamped in some green spot beside a Highland loch or a tumbling river. A mood of poignancy seized Evelyn as she remembered Grandmother and Aunt Mattie and all the lovely times of fun they had shared in the house in the Aulton – except for that last traumatic time . . . It had changed everything, altered the lives of people she loved most.

'I'll look forward to that day, Princess,' Gillan was saying, looking at her with a tender light in his eyes. She shook herself free of her gloom and, giggling, pointed along the road to where the cows were making their determined way towards the professors, whose footsteps noticeably quickened and whose benign expressions had altered to scowling annoyance.

She was struck suddenly by the similarity of this moment with that other time in the Aulton when she had met Grace and Gordon and they had all laughed together at the antics of the mischievous cows – only now she was with Gillan, and that other beloved face which she saw only in her dreams was missing from the scene . . . But he *wasn't* – he was standing before her, blotting out the sun – a tall, dark commanding figure staring at her as if she wasn't really there. Only she had got it all wrong. She was there, all right. He was just a figment of her imagination – an oddly substantial visitation born of all her wishful thinking, her longing.

'Evie, are you all right?' Gillan was shaking her arm, anxiously scanning her face. She closed her eyes and opened them again, thinking to find the vision of David Grainger gone from her sight, but he was still there and he wasn't a dream but a very real man eyeing her and Gillan speculatively.

'Davie,' she whispered, 'I – I thought I was imagining things.'

She could barely get the words out. She felt unreal, apprehensive of this stranger who was watching her with brooding dark and critical on his face. Two years had passed since last she had looked into those velvet brown orbs – almost a year had gone by since his last letter to her. She had gone on writing for some months, but when no reply came back she had given up hope that he had any feelings left for her. Now here he was, the very sight of him doing uncomfortable things to her senses, robbing her of all the anger she had built up against him, tearing down the barriers she had thought firmly erected round her vulnerable heart.

'Are you – home on leave?' she heard herself say, politely, distantly, as if she was speaking to a stranger whom she'd never known, never loved. Yet he *was* a stranger now, one who looked very thin and ill and whose hand trembled quite badly when he reached into his pocket for a packet of Woodbine.

'In a manner of speaking.' He sounded equally polite. 'I took it in the chest this time. I've just spent six weeks lying in a French hospital and got back here a week ago. This is my first day out – the lure of all this bonny sun was too much for me to bear.'

Gillan had entangled his hand from hers. 'Look, I'll get along and leave you two to talk.'

He sounded embarrassed and began to walk away but

Evelyn caught his sleeve and made him stop, feeling very much in need of his presence in these awkward moments. 'No, Gillie, stay here . . .'

'Let him go, Evie.' David's voice was soft, slightly dictatorial. 'He's right. You and I need to talk.'

But something in her rebelled against him. Why should she give in that easily? She had suffered too much by his silence. Her heart was sore with the hurt of her love for him but it had grown a little harder, a little less susceptible to persuasion.

'Come with us, Davie,' she invited him pleasantly. 'We're just going along yonder to the bridge. We can talk there where it's fine and quiet.'

'Dammit, Evelyn!' He ground out the words, the muscle in his jaw tightening to steel. 'I need to talk to you alone – now!'

'I can meet you – tomorrow perhaps.' Her face was flushed, her eyes sparking defiantly.

He looked at her for a long, suspenseful moment; then, turning abruptly on his heel, he walked away – not quickly, she realized he was too ill for that, but steadily and surely till he was lost from sight round a bend in the road.

'Hell, Evie!' cursed Gillan. 'What's got into you? I know fine you've deliberately avoided speaking of him but I'm well enough acquainted with you to know he's been there in your mind all along, yet first chance you get you send him packing with his back well and truly up. He doesn't look the sort to suffer feminine wiles gladly, so don't blame me if you never see him again.'

'That's right, stick up for him! You men are all alike when it comes down to it. And dinna you dare make out I'm just a stupid girl. It's the wiles of you men that make folk like me act the way we do, so stop passing judgement on things you ken nothing about!'

'Oh, Evie.' He pulled her to him and put his arm round her waist. Shamefaced, he went on, 'I didn't mean what I said – it's just, well, I always seem to come between you and your loves. I've never forgotten that time at the old mill with you and me and Johnny, and I never will. It's been a heavy burden on my conscience and I won't come between you and any other man again. Come on, we'd better get back to the station. I promised Maggie I'd look in on the way home, so stop sulking and move that lovely little bum of yours.'

She had to smile. Only Gillie could talk to her like that and get away with it, and she didn't look back once as he took her hand and marched her firmly along – though every fibre in her longed to break away and run after the young soldier who had captured her heart so easily from the first moment of their meeting in the sun-dappled shadows of Cobbly Wynd.

# CHAPTER NINETEEN

Two weeks later Evelyn was walking over the fields swinging a milking pail, on her way to milk Bella who was ambling towards her, slavers of anticipation running from her muzzle as if she was already savouring the titbit of oatcake nestling in the girl's pocket. Evelyn had just come from mucking out the byre. Her boots were caked with dung, her sacking apron streaked with dust and cobwebs. Bits of hay adhered to the tresses of hair escaping the scarf she had tied so carefully round her head that morning but which had loosened during the day's labours.

It was a dull, warm afternoon. The scent of wild thyme blew down from the hills, the green stalks of corn and barley glistened after a shower of heavy rain. The earth was already drying in the heat of the afternoon, the rich smell of it mingling with a hundred others just as tangy and heady.

In the distance a figure was coming over the field towards her. She could make out neither form nor feature but something about the measured, purposeful stride awakened her heart so that it seemed to stop for a long, frightening moment before galloping on at a pace which left her breathless.

The figure came nearer, slowly it seemed to the waiting girl, yet it was almost upon her before she had time to collect her senses into any semblance of order.

David Grainger was looking better than that last time she had seen him in the Aulton with Gillan. His smooth dark skin had caught the sun, the look of strain had disappeared from his face, the weariness caused by pain had departed from his eyes. They were filled with that half-amused, half-mocking expression she remembered so well. He was master of himself again. When he paused to take out the familiar packet of Woodbine his manly hand was rock steady, the match never wavered as he held it to the tip of his cigarette.

Blowing out a cloud of smoke, he gazed at her through the

haze. A quirk of laughter twisted his mouth. 'Where are you going to, my pretty maid?' His voice was deep velvet with a nuance of challenge in it.

She caught her breath as she answered in a low voice, 'I'm going a-milking, sir, she said.'

'What is your fortune, my pretty maid?'

'My face is my fortune, sir, she said.'

'Then I can't marry you, my pretty maid.'

'Nobody asked you, sir, she said.'

There were a few moments of silence. The breezes blew over the fields, Bella stopped in her tracks as if sensing that some obstacle had just come between her and the mouthwatering oatcake. David tossed away his half-smoked cigarette, Evelyn dropped the milking pail. It landed on its side and rolled in a semi-circle before coming to rest in a clump of broom. Without another word the girl and the young man walked into each other's arms. Their lips met hungrily, passionately. The scarf fell from her hair, and the thick, red curtain tumbled down her back to her waist. They kissed as if they would never stop, again and again, deeper and deeper. No other world existed for them but the one created by their encircling arms and seeking mouths. Two years of separation were wiped out as if they had never been. Her endless days and nights of loneliness were forgotten, her anger melted away like barbs of ice in a hot sun. 'Davie, I've missed you so badly,' she murmured against his mouth, 'I thought I would never see you again.'

The tears were running down her face. He was tender and loving as he kissed them away. She laid her face on his shoulder, delighting in the feel of rough cloth against her skin, in the smell of him: shaving soap, warm skin, tobacco.

He was obviously thinking the same things about her. Laughing into her hair he told her, 'I love my girls to smell of the farmyard. Dung has always been a particular favourite of mine.'

She reddened, covering her confusion by saying lightly, 'How many girls have you got?'

'Oh, dozens! Here, there, and everywhere. I even keep a few in the trenches to do all my washing and ironing.

You're my favourite though, aye was from the moment I saw you.'

Something warm and wet was pushing itself between them. They sprang apart, shouting with laughter as Bella's exploratory nose wormed its way under Evelyn's arm and sniffed impatiently at her pocket. Evelyn took out the oatcake and pushed it into the waiting jaws, and while the cow was busily occupied the pail was recovered from the bushes along with the tiny three-legged stool that had been nestling inside it. Setting one under Bella's udder, the other under herself, Evelyn set about milking the cow, but David intervened. 'Let me do that,' he offered, 'it will make a change from squeezing rainwater from my socks. I got quite good at this sort o' thing last time I was here helping your father with odd jobs around the croft. I like him. He's a good farmer and very patient with city-born folk like myself who couldn't tell a bull from a cow till he showed me the difference. Is he still making his boots? That pair you sent me lasted so well they seemed indestructible.'

'Father isna here any more.' She spoke slowly, unwilling to bring out all the sordid details about Whisky Jake, the trial, her father's subsequent imprisonment, but once she began to speak of it she found it quite easy to tell. The words flowed from her, she felt as if poison was gradually being washed from her system.

He was frowning. 'You never mentioned any o' this in your letters.'

She shook her head. 'I couldn't, I thought in some way you – might blame me for the things that happened. I hated Whisky Jake for what he tried to do to me but more, I despised what it did to me afterwards. I had no respect for myself, I felt dirty and degraded. I couldn't believe any of it had happened and the truth only really sunk in when Father's trial came up and he was sent to prison.'

David stood up, and setting the milk pail on level ground he sent Bella off with a slap on her rump before turning to Evelyn to say in an offhand voice, 'You should have told me about all this. I would have understood. As it is I wonder – you didn't encourage the bastard tink by any chance, did you?'

339

She backed away from him, her eyes wild. 'That's why I never told you! I remembered how jealous you were. I kent inside myself that you *wouldna* understand no matter what you say now.'

'For God's sake, calm down,' he threw at her harshly. 'I don't believe you would get mixed up with filth like that but you are fond of the men, Evie. Take the other week for instance, when I came upon you in the Aulton. You were hanging onto that chap's arm as if you would seduce him given half the chance—'

'Gillie is my friend!' she tossed back at him. 'We've been friends since we were just bairns and nothing that you imply has ever happened between us.' She raised her head, unaware of how attractive she looked with her flowing hair shining in the sunlight breaking through the clouds and her green eyes glittering in her suntanned face. 'But even if it had,' she continued with spirit, 'it would hardly be any business o' yours. What did you think I was going to do wi' myself after you left? Sit at the fire like a grannie, twiddling my thumbs or knitting all those endless pairs o' socks you kept asking for? Did you maybe picture me in mourning clothes, all black and weeping and tearing my hair for a selfish bugger of a soldier who hadna even the decency or the manners to thank me or my family half the time for the things we scrimped and saved to send—?'

'By Christ! You're a buggering wildcat and no mistake!' His fists were bunched, his jaw clenched so tight the skin over the muscles shone tautly. 'They should have girls like you at the front fighting Jerry. You wouldn't need weapons, the sparks in your eyes would be enough to fry the whole German Army, not to mention the power o' your tongue! You would just have to stand at the wire, open your mouth and let the red-hot bullets spew out. A few o' your sort and the British Army could scrap all the machine guns and rifles ever invented, for you very nearly killed me just now with just a few choice words.'

His eyes were blazing; a wild beast lurked in their depths for a few seconds then departed back into the darkest recesses of his heart. Taking a deep breath, he looked at her standing just a few yards from him. Her small fists were clenched over her dirty apron, her breasts rising and falling as if she had been running, her sunkissed limbs were the shade of honey-gold, one leg marred by a long, ragged scratch where it had caught the bramble thorns; strands of rich hair were blowing over her face, a face that registered anger, hurt and bewilderment all at the same time. He was struck by the untamed quality of her beauty in those fury-laden moments. 'You've got freckles on your nose – no' to mention a ton o' dirt.' Picking up the stool he tucked it under one arm, seized the brimming milk pail, and holding out his free hand said persuasively, 'Come on, we'll talk as we go. Get some o' that rage out o' your system.'

As they walked over the fields the inevitable questions came out. Why had he stopped writing? What had he been doing with himself this past fortnight? Why was he so hurtful to her one minute and so loving the next?

'After a while I could find nothing to write about,' he explained somewhat impatiently. 'I suppose I was de-pressed. I thought I was never going to see you again anyway and didn't see much point in going on with it. Since I got back here I've just been marking time till I felt fit enough to come and see you. As for that last bit – well, if you must know, you're the only girl I know who can instill such feelings of jealousy in me that I have to lash out. I just can't bide the thought of any other man's hands on you – be they friend or foe.'

She felt slightly cold despite the warmth of the day. He was talking about the David she didn't understand or like very much, a possessive David who could be so warm and friendly one minute, so dark and dour the next – and he had said it again, 'the only girl I know'. Was it just an innocent figure of speech, or did he really have many girlfriends? She had thought as much the first time she had met him – and the young waitress in Bert's tearoom had certainly confirmed that women liked him – but 'like' was too mild a word, 'desire' would be much more accurate.

She said nothing, but made a silent vow that she would never give in to him as easily as she had done two summers

341

ago. She had cheapened herself by her willingness to capitulate to that warm, persuasive charm of his, and it wouldn't happen again.

Unconsciously, she threw back her head. His eyes lingered on her mouth, the arch of her throat and he wondered how soon she would be his again. However, the mild expression on his face when they reached King's Croft and crossed the yard into the kitchen, leaving the milk pail at the door, belied any such thoughts.

Maggie and Grace looked up in surprise as the young soldier came over the threshold. But Maggie hid her feelings well as she chased her youngest daughter back out of the house to remove her dung-clogged boots. She extended a polite hand to the visitor. He took it warmly and then turned his attention on Grace, his eyes giving no indication of the shock he felt at seeing such a travesty of a once lovely young woman. Going to her, he held her slender hand in his and bending his head, kissed her full on the mouth. She backed away from him, shock lying across the pale transparency of her face. Evelyn, coming in at that moment, reddened and looked quickly at her mother, but Maggie had turned away to put on the kettle and seemed not to have noticed anything amiss. A commotion at the door diverted everyone's attention. Two sheepdogs and a cat were squabbling over the contents of the milk pail. Before anyone could move the pail toppled over and a stream of milk went worming through the cobbles, eagerly followed by the cat who lapped at the trickles, though the dogs weren't so lucky. Skelping and yelping they raced across to the fields, Evelyn close on their tails with a broom.

'I'm sorry, Mam,' she said anxiously the minute she got back indoors. 'I forgot all about it – I, I should never have left it out there.'

'No, you shouldn't,' Maggie scolded. 'Your head's been on upside down ever since you came home. Go and fetch some from the milk shed for there's none in the scullery for the tea.'

She turned back to the fire to pour boiling water into the

342

teapot, her face crimson with rage. But it wasn't the spilt milk that had upset her. There was no use crying over that, she thought wryly. It was the arrival of David Grainger that had triggered off her anger. He was so different from Johnny and Gillan in every respect. Both these young men had made no secret of their affections for her daughter. Johnny was gone now but Gillan was still there with that open, frank love for her youngest daughter. Whenever he came to the croft he showed, both by word and deed, the feelings that were in his heart, and by his very honesty Maggie had never felt any need for alarm. David Grainger was different. He was a young man with plenty of experience of the opposite sex. She knew fine well he'd had experience of Evelyn, though how far it had gone she had no idea. Yet when he was in the company of her family he never indicated that she was in any way special to him – almost as if he was trying to impress upon everyone his powers of self-control.

These last two years Evelyn had lived in hope of seeing him again, and even when he had stopped writing Maggie knew that her daughter had never given up that hope. Now here he was, large as life and twice as charming – oh, he had charm all right – and an ease of manner which was utterly likeable and acceptable. Young women could very easily be bowled over by that deep, smooth voice, those velvety eyes that had so much depth they could drown the resistance of any susceptible girl and leave her gasping for air in the process.

A rather subdued Evelyn was setting out cups, glancing frequently in her mother's direction to see if she was still angry. Maggie caught the veiled looks and gave a small sigh. That girl! Jamie was right about her. With just one appealing look, she could charm the petticoats from her grannie and come back later for the drawers!

'Ach, dinna worry your wee head about the milk,' she told Evelyn when they were alone in the scullery for a minute. 'It was an accident and could have happened to anybody.'

'It wasna the milk – was it, Mam?' Evelyn's words were

direct and true. 'You dinna like Davie very much – I felt it from the very first time he ever came here.'

'I dinna like what he's doing to you – what he's done to you.' Maggie was equally direct. 'You havena heard from him for nearly a year. Now he's back and already you've forgiven and forgotten everything. Just you be careful, that's all I'm saying. You're no dealing wi' Gillan now. This one won't take no for an answer.'

She went out of the small room leaving Evelyn to stare after her, aghast at her words and more determined than ever that she wouldn't give anybody cause for concern in her behaviour with David Grainger.

When she returned to the kitchen he was talking about Jamie, telling Maggie that he would help in any way he could until her husband's return. 'Not that I'll be here for that long, Mrs Grant,' he went on, absently ruffling the ears of old Tab who was leaning against his knees. 'I'll maybe have six weeks at the most before I have to go back, but a lot can be done in that time, even if I have to do the light jobs to begin with.'

'That's very kind o' you, I'm sure,' Maggie said in acknowledgement, 'but we have auld Coulter here and aye the odd traveller or neighbour looking in. Besides, you should be taking life easy and I won't have you racking yourself on my account. Now, if you will be excusing me, I have the hens to see to.'

Later, when Evelyn was walking him to the station to catch the train back to Aberdeen he said with a faint trace of annoyance, 'Your mother doesn't like me very much. Your father did; I got on well with him but never felt really at ease with her.'

'Ach, Mam always takes a bit of getting to know. Father likes everybody and gets on well with them.' She spoke as airily as she could, still smarting from all the upsets of the day and the cold realization that not everybody loved David as she did. 'You didna help matters by grabbing and kissing Grace the way you did,' she went on firmly. 'She's been very ill. Since last you saw her she married a fine man

344

called Gordon Chisholm. He was a surgeon and got killed in a field hospital in France. I would have told you about it but you had stopped writing long before that, and when it happened I had given up writing to you.'

He seemed not to hear the reproach in her voice. '*That* Gordon Chisholm? The one I met in the Aulton? Major Chisholm? His name was well-known among the chaps who got wounded and came back to tell the tale. Everyone respected and liked him.'

'My family loved him,' Evelyn said sadly, 'it was so brief for him and Grace. She is still trying to get over the shock o' it. We all are, but she was his wife and I cry for her knowing how much she misses him.'

He was quiet for the rest of the way to Lums o' Reekie. She had never seen him so subdued, and to break the silence she began telling him about the rest of the family.

'They've all gone away to different places.' She sighed wistfully. 'Nothing's as it was at King's Croft, though thank heaven Mary's still living near enough to call in often – whenever she can get away from McDuff the Guff that is,' she giggled suddenly, 'he's the old locum in Greg's place. To begin with, Mary couldna stand his farting and all his other eccentric habits. But she's gotten over that now and fusses over him as if she was his daughter, while he dotes on her and brings her wce gifts of sweeties and flowers. Peggy the maid has it that the pair of them are sweet on one another, and Mary just skirls with laughter at such utter nonsense and can hardly wait for Greg's leaves so that she can imitate both Peggy and McDuff.'

He was laughing now, the tiny creases at the corners of his eyes crinkling up, his teeth white in the brown of his face. The station was quiet when they reached it with Saft Sam nowhere in sight. Without warning David pulled her into the waiting room and encircled her with his arms. 'I can hardly believe I'm with you again,' he whispered into her hair. 'You feel and smell so good – now that you've washed the muck from your lovely body.'

'Davie,' she said warningly, 'it won't be like the last time. I canna risk . . .'

For answer he smothered her words with his mouth, the kiss deepening till his tongue was touching hers, melting away her resistance. Her own responsive mouth merged into his even while she hated herself for being so weak as not even having the will to try to struggle or break away.

'No, Davie, no,' she gasped at last. 'I won't let myself give in to you this time – we'll be friends—'

'Friends!' He spoke the word derisively. 'Evie, I thought you'd grown up in my absence. How can we be friends feeling as we do? You want me as much as I want you, and before I go back to give another piece of myself to Jerry I'll prove to you just how daft and meaningless your words are. I ache for you, Evie. I've hardly had a wink of sleep since I came home for thinking about you. Can't you see I'm crazy about you?'

He was saying all the things she had ever dreamed of hearing. A half-sob escaped her, tears of frustration pricked her lids. 'Bugger you, Davie Grainger,' she said weakly, 'I was just starting to get over you – now you're back and I hate myself for loving you all over again!'

He held her gently and stroked her hair. They stood for a long time, lost, not speaking, content to be close to one another, to be at peace for a while before passion of one sort or another robbed them of their serenity.

'Ay, ay, a fine night for it.' Saft Sam was at the door, an earth-caked trowel in his hands, smiling down at it as if he was addressing its dirt-encrusted metal.

The two young people jumped apart, David to straighten his tie, Evelyn to wipe away the tearstains on her cheeks.

'Sam!' she cried angrily. 'You're like an old tom cat the way you prowl about!'

Sam remained unperturbed. 'I just thought I'd better tell you the train is coming in. I saw the pair o' you sneaking in here earlier and kent fine what you'd be up to.'

'The train?' David spoke rather dazedly. He and Evelyn stood listening. Sure enough there was a rumbling, a busy huffing and puffing of steam and pistons. Neither of them had heard a thing, though the engine was shunting into the station and must have made its usual important sounds as it came along the line.

346

'I thought as much.' Saft Sam nodded with satisfaction at his own powers of observation. 'You never so much as kent you were standing here in my waiting room – let alone heard a bloody great steam engine charging ower the points.' He shook his head sadly. 'Ay, that's what love does to you – addles the mind and dulls the hearing.'

'You've had experience o' it then, Sam?' David asked.

The booking clerk hurled his spit onto the platform, ground it in with the heel of his boot, and looked thoughtful. 'Oh ay, I have that. No' my own, mind you, oh no, I was aye too wise to get caught in that trap but I've had plenty experience o' other folk's. You'd be amazed at the sort o' things that goes on in these country waiting rooms – ay – amazed. Many's the eyeful I've had and if I hadna aye been a gentleman I could have seen more, for I was never heard either comin' or going – now, you had better come along and get your tickets – ay, ay – amazed . . .'

He drifted away still muttering to himself. The two left behind looked at each other, and as one burst into skirls of merriment.

'Ay, ay – amazed,' David repeated as he took Evelyn's hand and led her along to the booking office to get his ticket.

'"Now the last days of many days, All beautiful and bright as thou. The loveliest and the last is dead, Rise, Memory, and write its praise!"' Gillan smiled at Evelyn. 'Shelley wrote these lines for us, Princess, the last day, the last minute has come and I must say goodbye.'

It was peaceful in the shaded woods skirting Rothiedrum House. The July morning was sunless but hot, and the small groups of wounded officers sitting about on the lawns or walking in the gardens were dressed only in light shirts and slacks. Laughter drifted from the terrace where two young VADs were walking with several of their patients; Matron's meaty voice boomed from the open French windows, rising a few octaves as her discussion with Lady Marjorie about a forthcoming garden party dissolved into an argument.

347

Gillan inclined his head in the direction of the house. 'Good job I said my goodbyes to Mother before *that* started, or I might have tried to come between them only to get injured all over again.'

'I wish you had.' Evelyn tried to sound lighthearted but failed. 'I hate having to say goodbye to you.'

For answer he took her hand and led her deeper into the woods till eventually they came to the deep-shaded green water of the Kelpie Pool. It was very quiet and serene there with a lone blackbird trilling its heart out from some hidden bough, but the young man and the girl standing side by side in the little glade heard in their minds the echoes of childish laughter, imagined the gleam of brown bodies tumbling and splashing.

'I come here often and think of those days.' Gillan spoke at last, his face pensive, his dark eyes filled with a poignancy for times gone never to return. 'I'll never forget that day I came out of the woods and surprised you all in the pool – Johnny and Florrie – Alan, you – a little girl yet but growing up before my very eyes.'

'And now they're all gone.' Her voice was husky. 'Only you and me are left, Gillie.' She turned to him suddenly. 'I dinna ken why, but I feel – frightened – you've gone away many times before but this is different. I can hardly bear to let you go.' Impulsively she put her arms round him and buried her face in his neck. 'Oh, Gillie, I canna explain. I feel somehow that everything is about to change. I've known you so long, maybe I've taken you a bittie for granted. I want you to know how much you've always meant to me, how much I'll miss you – wherever I go.'

'Princess, oh my beautiful Princess. I wish I'd known all this sooner. Now you tell me, when Father is waiting to take me to the station, and I must walk away from you in just a little while. But I'm the one who's going, not you, I hope you'll still be waiting for me when I get back.'

'No, Gillie.' She sounded breathless, the tears were pouring unheeded down her face. 'I feel – I feel as if you'll never come back, that the leaves will fall again and again from these trees and neither o' us will be here to see them.

This is goodbye for the last time, Gillie, and my heart is bursting with sadness.'

'Evie, please don't say things like that.' He crushed her to him. The fragrance of her hair was in his nostrils, her slender body was warm and soft under his hands. In those precious moments he fought a thousand emotions, wished a thousand wishes that he knew might never come true. 'Wish me luck, Princess,' he whispered into her hair. '"And wilt thou leave me thus, That hath loved thee so long, In wealth and woe among? And is thy heart so strong – As for to leave me thus?"'

'No, my heart isna strong,' she said shakily. 'It never was and it never will be. I love Davie and I ken fine I shouldna be saying the things to you that I am, but there are different ways o' loving someone and I have a lot o' love in my heart for you, Gillie.' She drew away and held him at arm's length. 'You ken only too well that I wish you all the luck in the world. I'll pray for God to keep you safe.' Unclasping her gold locket from her neck, she fixed it round his. 'This belonged to my grandmoher, think o' it as a kind o' good luck charm.'

He opened the locket and looked at the two pictures side by side, one of Megsie Cameron as a young and lovely girl, the other of Evelyn at sixteen, vibrant, her eyes filled with sparkling life. 'Two beautiful girls,' he mused, 'one so gloriously alive – the other—' he looked up, 'Uncle Lindsay seemed very interested in this picture of your grandmother that time you came to the house and showed it to him.'

She gave a watery smile. 'Oggie just likes women – especially women with red hair. What a pity he had to go away to Edinburgh. I could have been doing wi' his company while you were away.'

'Dear old Oggie, he's great company isn't he? Everyone thinks so, that's why he had to go and look up all his old friends. They would never forgive him if he went back to Africa and never a glimpse of his whiskery old face.' He stepped back from her, his eyes very tender as he murmured, 'Goodbye, my darling Evie. "By absence this good means I gain, That I can catch her, Where none can

watch her, In some close corner of my brain: There I
embrace and kiss her; And so I both enjoy and miss her."'

And he was gone from her, striding away through the
trees, never looking back though over and over his hand
was raised to his eyes – as if he was wiping away the tears
that his manliness hadn't allowed him to spill in front of her.

In the long summer days that followed she pushed Gillan to
the back of her mind, guilty that she was able to do so but
well aware that she owed the companionship of David
Grainger to that success. Every other week he travelled to
Glasgow to visit his parents, but the rest of the time he
spent with her and another kind of guilt beset her then in
knowing that they were both behaving selfishly towards
their families. He should have spent much more time with
his, she with hers. As it was she hurried through her daily
chores, skimping over each one, cutting corners where she
could, all so that she could run to him and feel his arms
about her, hear him talking, see his eyes lighting at sight of
her. Maggie scolded, berated and argued with her but to no
avail, her youngest daughter was in love and was blind and
deaf to all reasoning, oblivious to all pleading. She lived
and breathed for David Grainger and was determined to
spend every minute with him that she could. Together they
rode the country lanes, cycled to the sea, walked hand in
hand through rain, heat, wind into soft, summer gloamings
where all the cool shadows were made for them alone and
the secret places of hidden haughs were their special dis-
coveries.

She learned that he was a keen golfer and didn't mind
when he wanted to go off to the wide, windy links above
Aberdeen. She simply went along with him and though
once or twice he seemed irritated by her presence, she put
his moodiness down to the terrible wounds he had suffered
in the Battle of Arras.

Last time he had been reluctant to talk of his experiences
on the battlefield, this time he didn't mind telling her and
even seemed relieved to get some of it out of his system.

'During the First Phase we were lodged in chalk caves

below Arras,' he told her, 'quarried for the rebuilding of the city years ago. Imagine, Evie, twenty-five thousand troops all living together underground – in sewers and ditches of the ancient fortifications. Poor sods! We were well enough fed and watered yet even so I often felt like a stinking rat, but at least it was shelter. Out in the assembly trenches we were knee deep in mud with sleet and snow blowing in our faces – and that was in April! Worse than the north-east lowlands any day. I got it at Feuchy Chapel—' He grinned wryly. 'Didn't even have time to cross myself before I went out like a light. Next thing I knew I was lying in a field hospital wrapped up like an Egyptian mummy. That was one Blighty I didn't welcome. I still feel as if half my inside is missing though the doctors insist everything is still there – with maybe just a few o' the corners knocked off.'

But the longer he was home the less he talked of war, and more about what he wanted to do when it was over. 'I want to travel, Evie,' he told her, his brown eyes glowing. 'There's so much of the world to see and I intend to explore it all while I'm young. I never want to settle down – no' for a long whilie anyway.' He took her hands and smiled at her. 'You understand that, don't you, lass?'

He was telling her much the same things she had once told Johnny, only her views had altered since those early days. She would have liked nothing better than to be able to look forward to a future as the wife of David Grainger, only she didn't tell him that. She sensed his restlessness, his need for freedom, and it was because of this more than anything that she didn't give in to his pleas when passion gripped him.

'No, Davie,' she would tell him with difficulty, for her own desires were at a high pitch during those halcyon days and it took every shred of her willpower to turn away from him.

It was over too soon. The pain, the passion, the anger, the laughter. Towards the end of August he walked with her for the last time over the heather braes and up towards The Devil's Door, a great gap in the crags opening out onto a yawning chasm with a treacherous drop to the river far below. It was a hot day with a burning sun beating down from a cloudless blue sky, and a haze of heat lying over purpled, faraway hills. The skylarks were trilling, endlessly, ecstatically; the hill burns were frothing after a spate of rain and the brown water tumbled down, sweetly, interminably. She knew the dangers lying in wait for her in such a place, dangers that were not external but lay within herself, those of poignancy, of loneliness to come, of love which had given her no peace since meeting him and had grown to such greatness she could hardly endure its powerful possession of her senses.

His hand in hers was warm, strong, his voice was velvet-soft, hushed as the breezes blowing over the hill, intimate as the harebells that touched the spring waters with their fluted petals.

Somewhere in the distance the stalkers' guns reverberated off the bens, a remote sound, lost, lost in that other world where men took pleasure in killing innocent creatures. She was minded of another time, another man's hand in hers on such a day as this, her father's hand, brown, workworn, the big sturdy boots of him thrashing the heather stalks as he walked, his fine mouth twisting as the sound of the hunter's gun reached his ears, as if the cries of some dying animal had somehow penetrated a vulnerable part of his soul to cause him distress. That was the day she had known there was no stopping her encroaching womanhood. Her father had reassured her, had told her she was 'just a wee lass yet' but they had both known it was just talk, that her childhood was more behind than in front of her. She hadn't known how painful growing up would be, how readily her heart would hurt, first with Johnny and now with this man, so tall and warm by her side, so readily charmed by the attractions of high places, by the small creatures they encountered as they walked. Sometimes she wished she had never met him, that fate had placed her far away from Cobbly Wynd that day he had come silently behind her as she gazed into the window of Bert's Tea Shoppe. But they had met, had loved, had parted only to meet again and all the pain she had experienced through loving him was cancelled out on this day, so close to parting with him again yet so precious in its intensity she wanted to hold each second of it to her heart so that she would never forget one look, one touch.

On reaching The Devil's Door they paused to catch their breath and to gaze in awe at the brown tumble of the river, so far beneath the sound of it came only as a muffled continuous sigh.

He turned to her, his smile warm upon his lips. 'It's only you and me and the river, Evie, the rest o' the world is far away.'

'Too far – for safety.' She said the words quickly for fear her breathless heart wouldn't allow her to get them out.

'Evie, you've always been safe with me,' he chided gently, 'you know I would never do anything to hurt you—'

'Ach, I know nothing o' the sort,' she countered swiftly, 'you *have* hurt me, Davie, in a hundred different ways. You say things . . .'

'Love never hurt anyone.' His fingers were on her hair, unpinning it, letting the heavy fiery coils fall down about her shoulders. He ran his hands through it, held it up so that the sun shone through it. 'Look at it,' he breathed, 'it's beautiful—' his eyes fastened on her mouth '—as you are, Evie, so beautiful I wonder that I've managed to control myself all this time. If I hadn't been ill – you would never have gotten away with it . . .' His mouth came down over hers, bruising in its possessive power. She couldn't fight him any longer and her first instinctive protests were born of mere feminine caution, a token that she felt she owed herself, nothing more. It would have been useless to struggle anyway, he was crushing her against him, forcing her to respond to his demands. She stopped fighting him, allowed herself to enjoy the warm, moist hardness of his mouth. His exploring hands touched her breasts; she shivered and gave a little cry, so feeble she was ashamed of her own weaknesses, 'Davie, I canna let you do this . . .'

'Wheesht, babby.' He sounded tender, soothing, yet all the while his expert hands were doing things to her that neither soothed nor reassured. Passion swept through her like a tidal wave, her legs felt so weak beneath her she made no murmur when he pushed her down onto the cool grass that grew inside The Devil's Door. He undressed her quickly before removing his own clothing – and then it was only burning skin, touching, pressing, naked flesh, quickening, hardening. They were wild in their desire for one another, lost in a world that was theirs alone up on the top of the hill with the shadow of The Devil's Door cool above them.

He went into her with an untamed ardour that swept her to the crests of rapture. Yet even as she went with him to the top of the world, a small uneasiness plucked at the depths of her inner consciousness. But it was too late to pay heed to that faint, warning voice and it grew still, became forgotten as rapture engulfed her, claimed every one of her senses. Far below the river hushed, the wind ruffled the delicately hued heather tips, in the valley a dog barked in the ripening fields.

The afternoon shadows had lengthened and darkened when the young man and the girl at last aroused themselves from their bed of crushed grasses. With dazed eyes they saw gloaming stealing over the countryside, looked in disbelief at the long, dour shadow of The Devil's Door blackening the hillside.

The sun's heat had diminished. She was cold and the feel of her cotton dress against her skin did nothing to warm her. '"But sorrow returned with the dawning of morn, And the voice in my dreaming ear melted away."'

She wasn't aware that she had spoken her thoughts aloud. David glanced at her questioningly. 'What was that about sorrow?'

'Och, just a poem by T. Campbell – it's called "The Soldier's Dream."'

A smile of amusement touched his mouth. He glanced at her hair, dishevelled, falling about her face, lending her that untamed quality that never failed to excite him. 'You are a soldier's dream – and the dream of every rich-blooded man in or out o' uniform. That hair o' yours. A lad in our platoon kept a lock the same colour. He was a dreamer if

354

ever there was one but a bloody brave soldier when it came
to the bit. He took a Blighty to eternity last winter at the
Somme. A thin bit o' a lad he was, used to draw things that
made us laugh when there was precious little to laugh
about. He came from these parts—'

'You canna mean – Alan Keith?'

'Ay, that was his name. Don't tell me he was another one
o' your conquests?'

She shuddered. Not that again! The darkening of the
eyes, the thinning of that wonderful mouth . . .

'Alan and I grew up together—'

'Not another o' your childhood sweethearts! Wasn't
Johnny Burns enough? No' to mention that smooth-talking
public schoolboy – Gillan Forbes I think you called him.'

'I told you about Gillie.' She spoke as evenly as she
could. 'As for Alan – he was in love wi' Florrie O'Neil and
probably died loving her. Why do you always have to twist
innocent things? You make things up in your mind and
keep worrying at them, the way a dog worries a rat . . .'

'Evie, don't, don't be angry. I'm sorry I spoke like that
but – you're such a bonny girl and I know fine other eyes
have looked at you and wanted you. Try to understand,
Evie, I'm going away, back to a war that never seems to
end. You'll be alone again – and you might forget me – start
looking around.'

'I won't forget you, Davie, and I won't start looking
around. All that is in your own mind. I'll miss you, every
minute of every day, but that doesna mean I'll throw myself
at the first man who comes along—'

He pulled her to him and whispered, 'Och, Evie, I
believe you. Don't say another word about it, just let me
hold you – who knows when we'll meet again? Let's make
the most of these last few minutes together.'

His mouth was warm against her own, the heat of his
body burned into hers – yet even so a coldness gripped her
once more as the cruel fingers of a dreadful uncertainty
squeezed themselves round her heart till it hurt with the
pain.

# CHAPTER TWENTY

Jamie was home. He sat by the fire in the chair that had once been Andra McKenzie's and which had passed on to Jamie as his natural successor. Evelyn looked at her father. 1917 had seen the men in her life come and go – and now this man who had given her the most undemanding love of all, a man with haunted black eyes, uneasy-looking as he sat in the chair that was his, in the house that was his, yet he was so much a stranger that Evelyn's eyes filled with tears. His homecoming fulfilled the dream she had cherished in her heart since the day he went from King's Croft, destined not to return for nearly two long years. He was home, everything was as it had been before he went away but the reality of Jamie King Grant was a pitiful travesty.

From the moment he stepped over the threshold he was too humble, too grateful for everything. The smallest services were received in the manner of a polite visitor who must soon get up and go with suitable words of thanks on his lips.

His appearance had changed drastically from the Jamie of old. His clothes sat ill on him. His best Sunday suit settled uneasily about his thin, stooped shoulders. His hair was now completely white with not the slightest trace of black in it; his once brown skin was jaded and tired; the hand that held the familiar Stonehaven pipe to his mouth was mottled with purple stains and looked too frail to have once been strong enough to guide the plough.

Yet somewhere in those beautiful black eyes there lurked a small spark that might have been hope. Nellie had arrived from the west to welcome him home. Grace sat on one arm of his chair, her hand resting lightly on his shoulders. Gregor was home on leave from France and he, Mary and wee Donald had gone to Craiginches Prison in Torry to fetch Jamie home.

Murn was the only daughter who wasn't present. She had travelled far since leaving home, and had written from Australia to send her father her best wishes and a hope that he would have a happy future now that the worst was behind him.

Yet even without Murn and wee Col it was a sizeable family gathered in the kitchen to welcome home the head of the house, and Jamie had been overwhelmed by it all. Hardly had he recovered from all the rapturous welcomes than a few of the neighbours dropped by to wish him well, not least Tandy who took charge of the bottles and passed round the drams with his usual flambuoyant flair. Jamie drank too much too quickly, perhaps hoping to anaethsetize himself into a state of calm, but it didn't work for him. His nerves were raw, his eyes darting about the room as if wishing he could escape the well-meaning sympathies, the kind words of encouragement.

Tandy drew Maggie aside and told her, 'I'll get rid o' them. Jamie looks as if he could be doing wi' a bittie quiet.'

'If you would, Tandy, I canna bear the noise myself so God alone knows how my poor man must be feeling.'

So saying she rushed to quieten Donald who was marching round the kitchen banging a wooden spoon off a tin lid.

After that it was just the family, Nellic bustling about in her purposeful fashion getting a meal ready, Maggie helping her, Grace and Evelyn perched silently one on either side of their father's chair for suddenly there was nothing to say to the man around whom their lives had once revolved. Gregor and Mary, with their son in tow, took an early departure. At the door Gregor turned back. 'Bed early tonight, Jamie, doctor's orders.'

'Anything you say, lad,' Jamie nodded, lying back in his chair as if he could have carried out Gregor's advice there and then.

Peace began to settle over the kitchen. Jamie stretched his feet to the fire with a contented sigh, though his eyes roved to the distant fields beyond the window. Haymaking was in progress presided over by Coulter, Jacob Scott from

Knobblieknowe, The Loon, and one or two travellers who were encamped by the river. The scent of new-mown hay wafted sweetly into the kitchen. Jamie sniffed the well-remembered smell of it but he made no comment; instead he began to talk in a quiet, thoughtful voice about his life in prison. 'It wasna too bad a place. At least you could see the Dee from up there and the Wellington Bridge, and away beyond the city o' Aberdeen. The governor was a good man. He found out I was a shoemaker by trade and got me into the shoe repairs shop – ay, Major Forbes was all right and in fact they were all kind to me. I canna complain about my treatment and made a wheen o' friends during my time there.'

Maggie and her daughters looked at one another. At that moment Craiginches Prison was far more real to Jamie than anything else, and they all knew suddenly that life would never be the same for him again – or for any of his family.

That evening he fell asleep by the fire long before it was time to go up to bed. It could have been Maggie's stepfather, Andra McKenzie, sitting there in the straight-backed chair known to the family as 'The Throne'. Like Andra, Jamie had aged too soon, too quickly. At barely sixty-three his face had the parched, taut skin of a much older man, the flesh had fallen away from his throat leaving it furrowed and dry, his lids were purpled with tiny veins, faint dark smudges showed under his eyes, the muscles of his arms had softened, his shoulders narrowed. Maggie looked at him with a mist of tears in her eyes – and knew he would never work King's Croft again.

Lady Marjorie settled herself in the ingle and raised her teacup to her lips. Taking a few quick sips she replaced the cup in its saucer, sat back and looked at her cousin. 'Well, Margaret, I'm not going to beat about the bush. I heard that Jamie was home but long before that Evander and I discussed your position here at the croft.' She paused and glanced up at the peeling plaster on the ceiling, the patches of damp on the gable wall. 'It's in a bad way, Margaret, but if you feel you can carry on here Evander will see to it that all the necessary repairs are carried out.'

Maggie folded her hands in her lap and gazed steadily at her visitor. During Jamie's imprisonment an oddly understanding relationship had sprung up between the two women. They weren't exactly friends but quite a lot of the enmity they had felt for each other had long departed. Each was fascinated and curious about the other's lifestyle; Lady Marjorie was frankly open about wishing to keep their relationship strictly to themselves, but as Maggie was of a like mind she had ceased to regard the other as some kind of ogre to be avoided at all costs. The anger had gone out of her concerning the Forbes family, and as a result she was more natural in her cousin's company and had even discovered some of the warmth lying under her ladyship's cool exterior.

Since the meeting between the two in Lady Marjorie's elegant sitting room, that lady had come to admire her cousin's pride and her great strength of character and had set out to do everything she could to help the Grant family in Jamie's absence, though perforce her charity had to be of a strictly practical nature. Maggie would not take anything for nothing and hard siller only exchanged hands when it had been earned and not before.

When her cousin had finished speaking, Maggie shook her head slowly. 'No, Marjorie, I dinna feel I can carry on here – in fact, we'll be leaving as soon as we've found somewhere else to go. Jamie is no' a well man – it will be some time before he gains some o' his old strength so you can tell your husband no' to bother his head about the croft on our account.'

The other woman nodded rather pensively. She knew her cousin's succinct words hid a world of doubts, fears, and heartache. 'I'm truly sorry to hear that, Margaret. I had hoped – well, never mind what I was hoping. I may be able to help you find a new life for you and your family. We have friends staying just now. Colonel Richard Baird is a trusted business acquaintance of my husband's as well as a close family friend. He and his wife, Lady Elizabeth, live at Dunmarnock, a large country estate in Renfrewshire on the fringes of Glasgow—' she hesitated and smiled at her cousin – 'I apologize for taking so long to get to the point, I just wanted you to hear some of the facts about the Bairds. The truth is they are looking for a gardener and a house-keeper. Things have been so difficult since the start of the war with all the servants leaving to do their bit one way or another—' Be careful, you silly woman, she told herself ruefully, this is Margaret Grant you're speaking to, don't mention the word 'servant' so lightly or she might take offence – 'A cottage in the grounds goes with the job. There might be a place for Evelyn, too – it's a big house and a fair number of the girls have left. If you like, I can arrange for you and Jamie to have an interview with Lady Elizabeth whenever it suits – though it will have to be sometime this week as they leave on Friday.'

Maggie stood up and extended her hand. 'Thank you, Marjorie – tomorrow morning, if that's all right. If your friends find that we are suitable it means Jamie will still be close to the land, and I can go from Rothiedrum wi' an easy heart and a good bit o' dignity.'

Lady Marjorie smiled sourly. 'That was something you always had plenty of, Margaret. There were times you held your head so high you appeared to be looking at the top of the hills.'

'Better that than aye gazing at the ground though, mind, Pooty Drummond has a habit o' doing that and aye seems to come across the odd bob or two. In his own way he's maybe wiser than any o' us.' She threw her cousin a sidelong glance. 'Your mind will be easier when the Grants finally uplift their roots from these parts.'

'No, Margaret, that is where you are quite wrong. Uncle Lindsay was right about you, if you had had anything to say about the Forbes family you would have said it long ago. I've come to know you rather well these past years and in some strange way I'll miss the challenge and the spice of your company.'

It was Maggie's turn to lift her lips dourly. 'Never mind, you'll have Matron to keep you going for as long as the war lasts – and my father wasn't entirely right. I've had plenty to say about the Forbes family but nothing that either he or you would have cared to hear – so put that in your pipe and smoke it, then drink up your tea so that I can refill your cup. All this blethering has made me drouthy, but then all you gentry folks are the same – you would talk the hind legs off a donkey and then wonder why your backside has suddenly hit the dust.'

Lady Marjorie threw back her head and skirled with laughter while Maggie went to fetch the teapot from the hob to fill the empty cups.

Lady Elizabeth Baird was small, pleasant, and inclined to plumpness. She had a rather disconcerting habit of putting her head on one side and staring into space for minutes on end, so that one was lulled into a sense of thinking she was lost in a world of her own till she leapt up from her chair and began fluttering about the room, straightening an ornament here, pumelling a cushion into shape there.

Maggie decided she had either been without servants for so long she had grown used to doing things by herself, or else she was one of those eccentric members of the gentry who had always done things her own way no matter how many servants were at her beck and call.

She also had one of these rare, unexpectedly radiant smiles that completely charmed whoever she happened to be with, and both Maggie and Jamie warmed to her after the first few nervous minutes. Jamie had willingly acceded to this interview, confirming Maggie's suspicions that he had been worrying and wondering how he was going to be fit enough to carry on with the croft. Nothing was said about his spell in prison. 'Better not mention it,' Lady Marjorie had advised as she was taking her leave the day before. 'It might only jeopardize your chances, though knowing the Bairds they aren't the sort to judge a man by the cut of his cloth – and don't take that the wrong way, for heaven's sake,' she had added hastily, 'you know very well what I mean so don't start looking down your nose at me!'

The interview lasted for a brief half-hour at the end of which Lady Elizabeth beamed her approval on the pair and told them she was quite satisfied with them, and how soon could they fill the positions offered?

'It will have to be around the end of October,' Maggie decided. 'We have a lot to see to here and—' she stole a look at Jamie standing quietly at her side '—my husband has always been a thorough man. He'll want to see in his last hairst before leaving the croft.'

'Hairst?' questioned Lady Elizabeth, with her head on one side.

'Harvest,' Maggie explained patiently.

'Ah yes, of course.' The little woman smiled sympathetically at Jamie. 'You'll find life a lot easier working with us. There are fine conservatories and greenhouses at Dunmarnock and much of the winter work is carried out indoors. Mr Kerr, our head gardener, is an easy man to get on with and I'm sure you and he will work together well. As for you, Mrs Grant, you'll be in charge of household affairs – I'm sure you'll manage well. You're a capable woman and Lady Marjorie tells me you're something of a diplomat when it comes to handling people, so no doubt you'll get on well with the rest of the staff . . .'

The door opened and a tall, military-looking gentleman with fierce blue eyes and a clipped grey mosutache popped his head round it.

'Richard dear, we've had the most successful morning. Mr and Mrs Grant are ideal for what we have in mind and I've just heard that there's a younger daughter who could well take Maisie's place.'

'Good, excellent.' The Colonel sounded vague. 'Have you seen my pipe, Beth? I left the damned thing somewhere and can't for the life of me remember where.'

'Top inside pocket, Richard,' twinkled his wife.

'Oh, ah – of course, knew I'd put it somewhere safe.'

The door closed and Lady Elizabeth laughed. 'Appearances are deceptive where my husband is concerned. He *looks* so alert and growlish but he would forget to wear his own teeth if I didn't remind him.'

A strangled sound escaped Maggie. The little woman grinned at her. 'Go ahead and laugh, my dear, we are all human after all and I never could stand snobbery. I tell Marjorie so all the time, and though she peers down her nose at me sometimes, there are other times when she simply bursts out laughing in my face.'

Maggie and Jamie took their leave. Once outside, the latter took his wife's hand and squeezed it. 'I'm thinking we'll be all right wi' the Bairds, Maggie. They're as human as the next body and can stand a bit o' a joke.'

'Ay, Jamie, we'll be fine – except I ken fine your heart is breaking at the thought o' leaving Rothiedrum behind.'

'Ach well, it had to happen sometime, lass.' His voice was husky and he took out his hanky on the pretext of blowing his nose. 'Sooner or later it had to happen. The crofting life is for a young man and I'm no' that any longer. The years have stolen up on me without me noticing and I'll no' be sorry to take on an easier way o' living. It's you I'm thinking of, lass, you've aye been your own boss and you might no' take kindly to your new position in some other body's house.'

'Jamie, Jamie,' she chided gently, 'what you're really saying is I might be too proud to take kindly to servants' work. In my own way I'm a snob, but you heard Lady Elizabeth just now. If she canna stand snobbery, far be it for me to start coming the uppity miss now, so stop your blethers and let's get home – Evie will be wondering what's keeping us.'

The family took the news with varying degrees of regret and shock. Evelyn ran up to her room and cried her heart out into her pillow; Grace put on her jacket and went to the stable to sit on the corn kist and think everything out quietly; Mary agreed with her parents that they were doing the best thing for everyone concerned; Nellie wrote suggesting that they all come to live in Kenneray and take up the crofting life there; Maggie wrote back saying that the reason they were leaving King's Croft was to get away from that sort of existence, and that Nellie wasn't thinking straight to suggest such a thing.

Whatever anybody thought, the animals were sold as

soon as the harvest was safely gathered. Coulter stood with
Evelyn watching Queenie and Nickum being led away, and
blew his nose hard. Next came Swack and Fyvie, their
hooves ringing on the cobbles for the last time. The Clydes
plodded away obediently enough, but at the last moment
Fyvie, the little sheltie, tossed his mane and dug in his
hooves, the glance he threw back at Evelyn so filled with
reproach it was as if he knew full well he was leaving the
croft forever. He had been more than just a carthorse, he
had been a faithful and trusted family friend. For more
years than any of them cared to remember, he had taken
them to markets, cattle shows, anywhere they had wanted
to go. He knew every inch of the turnpike and many's the
night he had brought his weary travellers home without so
much as a flick of the reins to guide him.

Jamie hadn't been able to bring himself to witness the
departure of his beloved horses, and so Evelyn got the full
brunt of Fyvie's knowing, sad gaze.

'I canna bear it, Coulter,' she cried, turning away.

'Lassie, lassie!' Coulter said huskily. 'I canna right take
it myself. I've kent you since you were just a wee babe in
arms and now you're leaving. Rothiedrum will no' be the
same place without the Grants.'

Tearfully, she put her arms round his old shoulders and
kissed the tip of his nose. 'The Grants will no' be the same
without Rothiedrum, Coulter. I'll never forget you, never,
and someday I'll come back here and live among you all
again.'

'Ach, I'll be dead and buried when that day dawns,' he
said bleakly. 'And by then you'll have forgotten that the
likes o' auld Coulter ever existed.'

'Never, never,' she vowed brokenly, 'and even if you are
dead, I'll come and visit your grave and lay heather and
harebells on it and speak to you the way I'm standing
speaking to you now.'

The old man and the young girl were suddenly overwhelmed by tears. Unashamedly they clung to one
another, silently remembering the nights of winter ceilidhs
when his resonant voice had spun one fable after another,

and the cheeky wee dwarves of his imaginings had seemed to beckon from the kitchen door with their smiles of mischief and fun.

The croft was silent without the snickering of horses from the stables, the soft moos from the byre, the clucking of the chickens, the boastful crows of the cockerels, the squeals and grunts from the pigsty.

Evelyn and Grace moped so badly Maggie came up to their room one night and said firmly, 'I have written to Nellie. You have both to go there for a holiday before we leave here – and no "buts" from either of you. I havena had Jamie to myself since he came home and we want a time o' quiet to ourselves, just a wee whilie to take stock and look back on all our years together at King's Croft. It's no' often a husband and wife have one another to themselves, and with the animals away we'll have plenty o' time to look around us and remember.'

Next morning Evelyn sought out her mother, and showed her the necklace given to her by Lord Lindsay Ogilvie.

'I didna want to take it, Mam,' she explained anxiously. 'But he insisted and so I took it and hid it and almost forgot about it till last night. We could sell it and keep on the croft. With the money we got for it we could afford to hire all the help we wanted, and Father would never need to lift a finger if he didna want to.'

Maggie was staring at the necklace. To Evelyn's complete astonishment she suddenly threw back her head and roared with mirth. 'The old rascal!' she panted, wiping her eyes with a corner of her apron. 'He did this deliberately, knowing I would find out about it eventually. Ay, he's a cunning old fox is Lord Lindsay Ogilvie and someday I'll tell you about him and me, Evie, but right now you put that necklace back in its box and hide it. There might come a day when you'll have sore need o' the siller it will fetch. One way or another it will prove its worth, so dinna say another thing about it. The crofting life is over for your father and me. No amount o' jewels will bring back our youth and enthusiasm, so just you get used to the idea o' leaving here and go upstairs this minute and get packed. Grace badly needs a holiday and you could be doing wi' one yourself. You've been looking peekit this whilie back and a good dose o' sea air will do you naught but good.'

Kenneray was a delight. Croft Donald was sturdy and weatherbeaten, surrounded by tracts of emerald green machair cropped short by the sheep which perpetually roamed the hills and the beaches of that wild, rugged coastline. Nellie and Kenneth welcomed the visitors with open arms, both Cal and Col danced with joy at sight of them and from all quarters the animals mewed and barked a welcome. Col had grown into a fine, handsome boy with a light in his blue eyes when he brought out the picture books he had learned to read, and the small collection of wooden toys he had fashioned under Iain Cameron's patient guidance. At almost nine the little boy was still small and backward for his age and always would be, but he was so happy in his life in Kenneray his eyes glowed with the love of it and his eager, bubbling laugh was never far from his lips.

Both Grace and Evelyn settled into the homely routine of the croft as if they had known it all their life. 'If Mother and Father won't come and live here there's no reason why you two shouldn't,' urged Nellie, her own fulfilment showing in her beautiful eyes, in the soft burgeoning of her hitherto gaunt frame.

Grace hesitated over the offer but eventually shook her head, her black eyes wistful as she told her elder sister, 'I would be as much use here as a candle in the heavens. You said yourself, Nell, that the crofting life was never for me and you were right. If I go with Mam and Father, at least I might be able to get back to the nursing again. Renfrewshire isn't so far from Glasgow and they always need nurses in the cities.'

Evelyn too declined, but for very different reasons to those of her sister. She would have liked nothing better than to live and work on Kenneray's beautiful shores, but something had happened to make that an impossible dream. At first it had only been the merest suspicion but as the weeks passed, grew into months, her fears had grown into a terrifying certainty. It was on Kenneray that she finally faced up to the truth – she was carrying a child – the child of David Grainger, a young soldier who had only written twice since his return to France and who now seemed to have forgotten her completely. She felt numb with the shock of her discovery and could no more plan a life for herself on Kenneray than cope with the fears that each day held for her.

She and Grace spent a lot of time together walking along the wide, windswept beaches, the Atlantic booming in their ears, the call of the seabirds all around, lacy scallops of surf surging to their feet as they passed.

One day Grace stopped to lean against a rock and gaze pensively far out to sea. 'Oh, Evie,' she whispered, 'it's so hard to forget someone you have loved as I loved Gordon. I think o' him all the time. He was such a good man, he had so much to offer the world and now he's gone. I miss his wonderful, gentle love, I miss the caring that he gave me so willingly. I feel so alone, so unloved – no one else will ever love me as Gordon did.' She turned to her young sister, whose eyes had grown big and afraid as they looked unseeingly towards far horizons. 'I ken fine Davie hasna written you, Evie,' Grace continued. 'I can sense your terrible sadness. We mourn together, you and I, only there's hope for you yet, Davie is still o' this earth, Gordon is gone from it forever.'

Evelyn shook her head. 'No, Grace, no hope. I think I always knew it might end like this. Davie needs his freedom, he told me so often enough. He's afraid to get too involved with anyone, far less a lass o' the farmtouns who could only offer him her love. Maybe I smothered him a bit, showed him my love too freely.'

'Ay, and gave it too freely to be wise about it.' Grace sounded strange and Evelyn looked at her quickly. The lovely, troubled face was averted from her for a moment, and then the great dark eyes were on her, full of a wisdom that had always been there but which had grown deeper

367

with her experiences of love, of war, of death and grief. 'I ken about you, Evie,' she said softly, 'you're carrying Davie's baby, aren't you?'

Evelyn was so taken aback she could only stare at her sister. 'You – know? But how? And if you do then so must Nellie, Mam – everyone!'

But Grace shook her head calmly. 'I'm a nurse, re-member? You're still a skinny wee thing, yet but I share a room wi' you and I've noticed things. Your white face in the morning, all the colour gone from it, the untouched breakfasts, the need to rush out to the wee hoose the minute you get up and the look o' death on you when you get back.'

'Oh, Grace,' Evelyn breathed, so filled with shame she couldn't look her sister in the eye. 'I canna believe it myself yet, and here you are – knowing more about me than I do myself.' She began to cry softly, helplessly. Grace's own eyes filled with tears and the sisters clung together, weeping over their separate heartaches, while all around the sigh of the wild sea washed into their senses and eventually brought them a kind of peace.

'I blame it all on war.' Grace's voice was unusually bitter. 'War took Gordon, keeps taking Davie out o' your life till neither o' you ken if you're coming or going. It does wicked things to the mind and the body. I've seen young boys, torn apart, worrying because they were afraid in the battlefield, tears in their eyes when they were awarded some decor-ation for bravery. I ask you, Evie, what good is a bit coloured ribbon to a sightless, armless young man who can neither see nor feel it?'

'He just knows it's there.'

'Ay, he knows it's there – just as he knows his arms and eyes aren't. None o' it makes any sense and we'd better get back before I say too much.'

They turned their footsteps homewards. 'What will you do, Evie?' Grace asked gently. 'Have you thought about it at all?'

'Things keep darting into my head then out again. I know one thing, though, I won't burden our parents wi' this, no'

368

at this time o' upheaval in their lives. I'll go with them to Glasgow – after that I'll find somewhere of my own to live, I'll get a job – dinna worry about me, I'll manage somehow.'

Almost as soon as they got back to Rothiedrum, Evelyn went into Aberdeen with a wild plan in her head to go up to the barracks at Castle Hill and find out if anyone there knew anything of David. She hadn't told him about the baby, hadn't told anyone. Only Grace knew and she would never say anything. Gillan still wrote his warm little letters to her, but she had stopped writing back. She was so consumed by guilt and shame she could find nothing to say to him. If he ever found out about her she felt she would die. She could picture his face. First the shock, then the hurt, after that the gradual acceptance, the willingness to help a girl he loved devotedly and unselfishly even though she had brought him nothing but pain.

Her wandering footsteps took her past Grandmother's house in the Aulton. How wise that dear old woman had been, how excellent a judge of character. She had sized up David Alexander Grainger well enough: 'a brave soldier doesna necessarily make a good husband.' The querulous voice spoke inside her head, and she could almost see the bright old eyes scrutinizing her face.

'I never got the chance to find out what kind o' husband he would have made, Grandmother.' She whispered the words as she passed by the gate, remembering as she did so all those people who had tried to warn her about David. Even old Coulter had poured his advice into her ears and she hadn't taken heed – hadn't listened to any of it.

Leaving the Aulton behind, she walked into Aberdeen and suddenly she was *there*, in Cobbly Wynd, her steps stumbling a little on the cobbles. It was October, the bright leaves of autumn were skirling and dancing in the wind, a row of old men were sitting on the bench under the trees, smoking their clay pipes, talking eagerly amongst themselves. It was as it had been that other day, three years ago almost to the day – *three years*! It seemed so long ago, yet in many ways it was as if it had all happened yesterday – but so much had changed since then. Love had come to her like a dream in the night – and like a dream it had slipped away from her, transient, unreal – except for the life growing inside her at that very moment. *That* was real enough, real and terrifying . . . She was pulled abruptly out of her reverie by the sight of a young girl leaning against the railings under the trees. Something about the face was familiar. A memory came back to her, a young soldier leaning from a carriage window, a girl running up to talk to him . . .

Evelyn's heart beat a little faster. Maybe this girl might know something of David. He had said she was the sister of a mate of his . . . Before she could change her mind, she went over to the railings. 'Please excuse me,' she began, 'you dinna ken me, but I saw you once at the station saying goodbye to a soldier and I felt I would like to speak to you.'

The girl looked at her dully. She was a ghastly yellow colour, her blue eyes were dazed, her lips devoid of colour. 'I'm sorry, what did you say?' She shook her head as if to clear it and straightened, only to stagger back and resume her hold on the railings. 'I feel – funny,' she panted, 'sick – dizzy.'

Without another word, Evelyn took her arm and led her across the road into Bert's Tea Shoppe. It was crowded, no one noticed the two girls slipping into seats at a table in the corner . . . Memories crowded in on Evelyn. It was at this self-same table that she and David . . The waitress was waiting to take their order. A different girl from the last time, big, buxom, dour. Evelyn ordered tea. When it came, the girl drank it thankfully. Her name was Anna Miller. She began to talk in a low voice, rapidly, as if she was desperate to unburden herself to somebody.

'In case you havena guessed already I'm pregnant – four and a half months gone. My father was all for throwing me out but my mother stopped him. I suppose I should be grateful to have somewhere to stay, for I dinna ken if the bairn's faither is alive or dead. It might be better for him if he was, if no', my brother will do Jerry's job for them.'

'He'll come back – when the war's over.' Evelyn felt slightly uncomfortable. She hadn't expected so many revelations in such a short time, but the girl was determined to talk.

'He'll no' come back!' she said scornfully. 'The minute the war's over wi' he'll be away to other lands. He's the wandering sort, yet – at the time I thought he cared enough about me to maybe write once in a while but Alex Grainger is no' the loving kind. I was a fool to be taken in by him but he's the type women fall for. Good-looking, sweet-talking. He took me in good and proper, made me feel sorry for him, said he had come home on sick leave only to find his girl carrying on wi' another.'

'You – you said Alex Grainger?'

'Ay, David Alexander Grainger, but I liked Alex best, it suited him somehow. I liked him ever since my brother brought him home once for tea, but he never gave me a second look till June past. I could hardly believe it when he came looking for me. Upset he was, ay, and ill too – but no' too ill to do this.' She placed her hands on her stomach, her mouth twisted into bitter lines.

Evelyn stood up. 'I must go, Anna. I – I hope Alex Grainger comes back to you . . .' She had no recollection of walking out of the tearoom into the street, but suddenly she was there, the autumn leaves swirling at her feet, her mind in such a turmoil she could make no sense of anything for the next hour but just kept on walking, anywhere, everywhere, eventually ending up sitting on the harbour wall gazing at the oily waters of the North Sea slapping beneath her. It all made sense now. David's rage that day he had come upon herself and Gillan in the Aulton, the two weeks' absence before he had calmed down enough to seek her again. He had certainly amused himself well in those weeks – had gone straight into the arms of another, blindly, selfishly, without thought for anyone but himself . . . Her fingers crept to her neck. The hard band of his gold signet ring cut into her flesh as she gripped it viciously. '*Some day you might need it to fool the world.*'

'Ay, Davie,' she whispered, 'how right you were . . .' She blinked the tears away from her eyes. But that was only one way out – there were others, plenty of them.

# CHAPTER TWENTY-ONE

It was cold on the hill. An autumn mist blurred the outlines of the crags, the tinkling burns were more heard than seen, the mournful bark of a stag in rut sounded from some other ben. Yet still the bracken glowed, like fire amid smoke; rich, red, and damp. Evelyn climbed slowly, her mind quite calm, taking each step carefully, not looking back. She knew the way by heart. Below her, the lums of Rothiedrum smoked peacefully, the crofts and farmhouses sat sturdy in the haughs, the bulk of each one looking rather ghostly in the pearly white haar.

The Devil's Door loomed suddenly, a grey spectre that rose up in front of her to startle yet reassure her by its presence. Without faltering, she walked into the great gloomy opening and stood gazing down to the mist-swathed river far below. She stood there for a long time, thinking of many things but mostly of her parents. They would be hurt and shocked for a while but they would get over it – in time people got over anything. Whichever way you looked at it they would be hurt – whether she lived or died. It was better this way. At least her mother could still keep her pride, her father his cherished illusions about his youngest daughter.

She shuddered as she gazed around her. What a dreadful place for a child to be conceived – dreadful and shameful. Satan himself seemed to lurk among the grey stones, waiting to lure the weak into acts of sin. It had been sinful to start a new life here, just as sinful to take that life away deliberately – but such a child would be tainted from the start. This way it would always keep its innocence – even though its mother had lost hers a long time ago.

The raw cold seeped into her bones, she put frozen fingers to her lips as a stab of fear pierced her to the marrow. No! She wouldn't turn back now. There was

373

nothing to go back to. Rothiedrum and all it meant was about to slip out of her reach – the hurt of going would be too much for her to bear. She was leaving it all right, but not in the way either her mother or father intended.

She took a deep shuddering breath. Her hands went to her belly. The flatness was going, Davie's child was growing, bigger and bigger with every passing minute. His voice seemed to come to her from the mists at her back. She looked behind her shoulder. There was nothing, only the ghosts of the hillside, floating and swaying. Giddiness swept over her, her foot slipped on a wet stone, her stomach lurched and then she was falling, falling – into nothingness.

'Lassie! Lassie! Are ye all right? Open yer een, Evelyn Grant. I hope yer no' playin' games wi' me for I have no time nor inclination to be bothered wi' ye.'

She did as she was bid, slowly, painfully. Her head throbbed where she had knocked it, she ached all over – but she was alive, miraculously alive! It wasn't mist which blurred her vision now, it was tears, welling spilling. Blinking and shaking her head she saw Carnallachie's grizzled face swimming in front of her eyes.

'Carnallachie – I fell,' she whimpered.

'Ay, ye did that,' he said with vicious assurance. 'Right into a bog! You shouldna hae been wandering aboot in this haar. Here—' he peered at her more closely – 'you've hurt yourself, quine. Let me tak' a look at ye.'

Without further ado he laid his poached sack of salmon behind a rock, and kneeling in the mud beside her he began to work her limbs gently up and down. 'Dinna worry noo,' he assured her as gently as his gravelly voice would allow, 'I'm the best man in these airts wi' this sort o' thing. I'm good wi' pigs as ye ken fine yourself, and the leg o' a bit quine is no' that different from an old sow's trotter.'

Good wi' pigs! Evelyn lay back in the sucking mud that had saved her life and gave vent to weak, slightly hysterical laughter while the old man examined her to make sure there were no bones broken.

'That's guid ye can laugh,' he told her sourly, 'for yer whole body will be as sore as a hangover come mornin'. Nothing broken though, no' even yer spirit, so if ye can sit up and put an arm aboot my shoulders I'll trundle ye along to my cart over yonder. Trudge will see ye get home in no time.'

'Trudge see me home,' she smiled faintly, 'he canna see himself home at the best o' times.'

'Ye've no' lost yer cheek either,' Carnallachie told her grimly as he straightened his back, supporting her weight on his strong old shoulders. Her eyes travelled up the face of the hillside. Only the uppermost buttresses of The Devil's Door were apparent from this angle, but it was enough for her to shiver at the remembrance of the strange oppressiveness she had felt. But the dark thoughts had been there long before she reached that satanic pile, yet even so she cursed inwardly and thought, You let me down – you, you devil you.

'Ay, let me down right enough,' she muttered under her breath.

'Eh, what was that?' Carnallachie cocked a hairy lug. 'Ye'll no' be tellin on me, Evie, will ye now?'

'Telling on you?'

'The salmon, you daft lassie! The laird has more than enough for his own table and will no' miss a few wee minnows.'

'No, I'll no' tell, you ken that fine.' Her natural sense of humour quite suddenly and firmly asserted itself. 'Just so long as you see that one o' your wee minnows finds its way to the Grant table.'

Carnallachie was almost speechless with indignation – almost but not quite. 'That's gratitude for ye! Here's the very mannie who saved your life and all you can do in return is take the very meat frae my mouth. It's well seeing ye're Jamie's lass! He never passed me wi' my sack but he was lookin' for a share in it – ay, even though his was burstin' wi' his own ill-gotten gains!'

Everyone made a fuss of her. She lay in bed for three days, bruised in mind, body and spirit. McDuff the Guff came to look her over, pronounced that she would live, left a bunch of michaelmas daisies on the bed, and departed with such a hearty flourish of his coat tails that she was forced to rise from her bed and throw wide the window to allow the fresh air to swoop in and dispel the product of his needs.

Grace came to sit with her for an hour or two every day, saying nothing about the accident till the colour was starting to come back into her sister's smooth cheeks. 'I know what you tried to do, Evie,' she said at last, 'and I'm no' going to lecture you – just make you promise never to try the like again.'

'I promise, Grace, I didna seem to ken right what I was doing. I'm fine now though, so stop looking at me as if I was going to jump out the window at any minute.'

Her eagerness for life was returning, each morning she opened her eyes just a little bit earlier, sat up and looked at the world beyond the window that little bit sooner.

As soon as she felt strong enough, she walked to the little kirkyard beside Loch Bree to say her goodbyes to those loved ones who had played such an important part in her life. Not that she had ever felt that they were there under the mossy old stones. It was just a focal point to come to and remember for a while all the things they had done together when they were alive. She moved among the granite slabs, a small, slight figure, grace in every line, the bright light of day shining on her serene features, glinting on the richness of her lovely hair. Under each stone she placed a small spray of wild hill flowers, then she stood back, looking at each name: Florrie O'Neil, Johnny, wee Janet Burns. 'I love you all,' she said simply, 'and I hope you have forgiven me for trying to join you before my time was come. I'm leaving this place soon but I'm no' leaving you. You'll come wi' me, wherever I go, whatever I do. Johnny – I, I went wild after you left me – but it's over now. I'm myself again and I'll try never to let go of me again. Now I'm going home for my tea – you know how Mam hates to be kept waiting.'

Then came the farewell ceilidh at Hinney's house: Tandy striding about playing the pipes; Bunty Lovie listening avidly to all the gossip; Betsy O'Neil and Kirsty engaged in one of their much-loved, mildly malicious verbal battles; Lilly Lammas exchanging recipes with Jessie Blair, though keeping a safe distance for Jessie's personal hygiene had not improved with time; Coulter and Carnallachie vying with one another as to who could tell the best tale, sing the most popular bothy ballad; The Loon and his mother pinching some of Alistair's bogy roll tobacco, then arguing as to who should have the first draw of the clay pipe.

When it was over, the Grants walked home together in silence, each lost in his or her own personal memories, Tab padding softly at their heels, his breath wheezy in the tired old lungs of him. He was the only one left of all the animals that had ever graced King's Croft. The cats had been dispersed to various new homes, Hinney taking two to keep her own three in ferocious fights for supremacy in a household bursting at the seams with four-legged creatures. Coulter was taking old Tab to live out his last days in the old bothy over yonder by the Mains, but the Grants could hardly bear to part with him and were hanging on to him till the very last moment.

But he took the matter out of their hands. He had been uneasy for a long time, his senses telling him that everything around him was changing, that the easy days and the peaceful nights spent at King's Croft's fireside were about to be done with – and he too old and weary to be bothered with the changes to come.

The October nights were chill now, and when they returned from the ceilidh he crept to his usual place at Jamie's side, his white muzzle resting on that comforting knee, the misted opacity of his half-blind eyes gazing unblinkingly into the orange glow of the well-kent fireplace.

'You're just about done, Tab lad,' Jamie whispered softly into the still-alert ears, 'just about done.'

Ay, old Tab was done all right. That night he passed away peacefully in his sleep, his muzzle lying soft on the hearthrug, his eyes gazing sightlessly up the empty lum, his body stiff and weary no more but arched easily like a puppy at rest; the tail that had wagged a thousand welcomes fanned out behind him – as if he had died waving it in one last, triumphant flourish.

He had been with Evelyn for sixteen of her nineteen years. She had known him from the time he had slipped tiny and wet from his mother's body and it was she who carried him now, out to the gnarled apple tree at the edge of the drying green. He had watered it well during his lifetime, it seemed fitting that he should lie under its twisted roots, giving it nourishment in days to come, perhaps coaxing a blossom or two from branches that had borne little enough fruit in all the time it had stood on that spot.

When Jamie had thrown the last spade of earth over the fresh mound Evelyn walked silently away to the empty stable, took her diary from her pocket and wrote: *Old Tab died last night. The only life left now at King's Croft is human life – and no man nor woman ever gave such love as an animal gives – and all without saying a single word.*

The day of the King's Croft roup came only too soon and was, for all the Grants, the saddest part of all. The event had been well advertised in the slender columns of the local newspapers and quite a crowd gathered in the cornyard to await the arrival of the auctioneer. It was a chill, windy day for late October but not so unusual in those parts when the start of the long north-east winter could arrive any day now, heralded by dustings of snow on the hilltops together with bitter winds howling low over the plains.

The auctioneer was a small, wiry man with a ferret-like face and a gift for the blarney passed on to him by his Irish grandmother – and so well had she taught him that he could have talked her out of her stays and maybe her bloomers as well and left her feeling grateful at receiving twopence for the lot.

His rostrum, an upturned farm cart, was soon the focus for all eyes. Most of the neighbours had come to lend a bit of support to the Grants. They waited with Maggie and Jamie in the barn, out of the blast of the wind, murmuring comforting homilies about the weather and how well the roup was being supported, but Kirsty's quick eye was alert to the odd bargain that might be picked up, and Betsy O'Neil was most interested in the condition of the beds since her own had taken such a pounding over the years of use that anything with a spring or two still intact looked like the last word in comfort.

Everything that could be was sold as quickly as it took the auctioneer's smooth tongue to set up the bidding. The farmyard implements went like magic; household effects just as quickly, everything that had taken Maggie and Jamie a lifetime of sweated labour to acquire, even down to the clickit rugs, Jamie's chipped shaving mug, Maggie's handmade knitting bag. The very cart on which the auctioneer stood was bought from under him with its new owner retiring to the shelter of the byre to await the end of the roup. The dung from the midden went to Carnallachie who looked mighty pleased with himself for having acquired the precious stuff from under the nose, so to speak, of Danny the Fist who had begrudged bidding one penny higher than necd be. Everything from that year's harvest went, the hayricks, the cornstacks, sacks of potatoes, the very turnips fattening in the drill.

When it came to Jamie's lasts, hammers, nails, and bags of leather pieces, it was too much for both him and Maggie to bear. They turned away, tears in their eyes.

'Grace will have a cup o' tea ready.' Maggie's hand was under her man's elbow, leading him over the yard to the kitchen.

Up in her room Evelyn too turned away, unable to watch the proceedings a moment longer. She had packed all her own personal possessions away into the trunks waiting downstairs to be sent on to Dunmarnock House. There remained only a few items, things that she had left to the last minute before removing them from their familiar surroundings. They lay on her bed in neat, chronological order: the sampler made for her by Florrie for her fifteenth birthday, on it the words: *Evelyn and Florrie – Best Friends. 1913 and beyond*; the silk stockings and the little corn dolly

Johnny had given her to mark that same birthday; the little velvet box containing the pearldrop presented to her by Gillan at Christmas 1914; the simple but beautifully carved jewel box David had given her for her seventeenth birthday.

Carefully she gathered them all up, wrapped them in tissue paper and packed them into her case. Only the tin box containing the garnet necklace and her diaries was left. The necklace she hardly looked at, the diaires she tossed half-scornfully onto her coverlet. It was silly to keep them. They were full of childish nonsense, immature dreams that had never come true. Picking them up, she was about to take them downstairs to the bonfire smouldering at the edge of the green when something in her romantic heart stayed her. She would keep them, she decided. One day she would bring them out and read them, perhaps laugh at the small events of an Aberdeenshire childhood she had once thought would last forever . . .

Impatiently she wiped the tears from her cheeks. That was that, over with, finished. She gazed around the little room she had slept in all her life. How bare it looked without all the little familiar things! Only her bed was left and that because Maggie had deemed it fit only for the bonfire – in a little while Jamie would take it to bits, carry it away downstairs to the waiting fire . . .

'I loved the nights I spent here,' she said aloud to the echoing walls, 'even when candle shadows danced all over you, they were spooks I kent well and liked to imagine I was afraid of. Strange walls await me now and God alone knows what ghosts and bogles lie in wait for me . . .'

With a shaky finger she traced the fragile outlines of a petrified spider's web on the corner of her window, then gently rubbed it away. It would never do to leave that on the pane – whoever came here next might not like spiders.

They spent their last night at Mary's house. When everyone arose next morning Jamie was nowhere to be seen, but Evelyn knew where she would find him. King's Croft was already deserted and neglected-looking in the early morning light when she made her way up the track. No smoke from the chimneys, the curtainless windows like empty eyes gazing broodingly over the fields. She walked on quickly and soon saw the figure of her father leaning over the dyke looking quietly towards the stubble field. There he had stood each wakening spring, when the widening skies had wrought in his imaginative soul visions of good corn ripening on the stalk and the glad song of the peesies had found its echoes in his heart.

'It wasna much, Evie,' he said as she came up. 'Just a few acres that often robbed me o' more than they gave – but they were my life, lassie, my life.'

His voice was husky, broken. Wordlessly she put her arms round him, and they stood together for a long time gazing over the fields before turning and making their way down the track for the last time.

It all happened quickly after that, Mary's tearful farewells, her repeated invitations for them all to come and stay with her whenever they could. 'I'll be waving as the train passes,' she told them at the last moment.

'We'll never see you,' Grace said in a funny, choked voice.

'You will, you will, I promise.'

The walk to the station was short and unreal. Saft Sam for once was at a loss for words, and turned away to blow his nose as the train moved out of the station taking the Grants away from Rothiedrum.

'I can see Mary,' Evelyn pointed. A white banner was fluttering in the garden of Rowanlea. Mary had tied a pillowslip to the end of a broom handle and was waving it backwards and forwards with all her might.

'Trust Mary.' Maggie shook her head. 'She aye could think up some way of letting her presence be known.'

Evelyn watched the dear green fields of her childhood slipping away, the crofts and farmhouses that were as familiar to her as her own home: Cragbogie where Florrie had lived and died; Carnallachie's place; Boglehowe wherein the Loon and his mother fought their harmless battles; Birkiebrae in whose fields Johnny had walked;

Knobblieknowe that had once rung with the sound of the pipes and with the laughter of Kenneth Mor and his bonny Jeannie. The Manse, the kirkyard, and opposite – King's Croft – sad, empty, nothing left but the bare bones and the echoes . . .

Evelyn's eyes misted, she wanted to cry and never stop crying. The blue of the hills wavered against the sky. Her heart seemed to grow still in her breast for she sensed that she would never see her bonny hills again, never walk in the heather or see the blood-red blobs of the rowan berries splashed against the branches . . .

Dippiedoon flashed by, Hill o' Binney – Rothiedrum House. She hadn't written to say goodbye to Gillan. Somehow she couldn't tell him she was going, or about the thing she had done. She could well picture his reaction to that, the hurt surprise in his eyes. He had never stopped hoping that she might fall in love with him, that they could be happy together despite the difference in their respective backgrounds . . .

A tiny pulse beat deep in her belly, just a small quiver but enough to make her draw in her breath. Through all her lonely hours of uncertainty she hadn't spared much thought for the baby in her womb. Now it came home to her fully. This was Davie's child. His blood flowed in its veins – it might have his eyes, his mouth. She straightened in her seat and glanced at her father sitting silently in his. His brown eyes were glazed with unshed tears, his fingers working restlessly on the thick tweed of his best jacket. Beside him Maggie was as upright as ever but her mouth was sad, and her face had gathered new lines during the last traumatic weeks.

Grace was looking from the window, her great dark eyes dry yet burning with grief held tight in her heart.

A ballad came unbidden into Evelyn's mind: 'It's Mormond Braes where heather grows, Where aft times I've been cheery, O Mormond Braes where heather grows, It's there I lost my dearie.'

She turned her eyes away from the rain-speckled window, took a deep breath and began to sing:

382

'There's as guid fish intae the sea,
As ever yet was taken;
I'll cast my line and try again,
I'm only ance forsaken.'


Maggie hesitated, looked once at the Lands of Rothiedrum sitting snug amongst the couthy hills, then she pulled her gaze away and rested it on Jamie. She smiled at him, took hold of his hand, squeezed it, then took up the song, her voice growing stronger, sweeter by the minute.

A smile stole into Jamie's black eyes. He set his shoulders back against his seat. 'Mustna let the crown slip off my proud old head,' he chuckled.

For the first time in days Grace smiled, a slow, sweet smile that gave her face something of its former serenity. 'Ay, the Grants are coming,' she said softly, 'Glasgow had better unfurl its banners.'

Evelyn kept on singing, a determined spark in the green of her eyes. The child within her stirred again. At least she had something left to live for – Davie's child, Davie's child. The wheels seemed to chant out the words that were in her heart as the train sped on to pastures new.